BY EMILY GIFFIN

Something Borrowed
Something Blue
Baby Proof
Love the One You're With
Heart of the Matter
Where We Belong
The One & Only
First Comes Love
All We Ever Wanted

ALL WE
EVER
WANTED

ALL WE
EVER
WANTED

A NOVEL

—

Emily Giffin

BALLANTINE BOOKS

NEW YORK

Published in the United States by Ballantine Books, an imprint of Random House, a division of Penguin Random House LLC, New York.

BALLANTINE and the HOUSE colophon are registered trademarks of Penguin Random House LLC.

LIBRARY OF CONGRESS CATALOGING-IN-PUBLICATION DATA
Names: Giffin, Emily, author.
Title: All we ever wanted : a novel / Emily Giffin.
Description: New York : Ballantine Books, 2018.
Identifiers: LCCN 2018005082 | ISBN 9780399178924 (hardcover) |
ISBN 9780399178931 (ebook)
Subjects: LCSH: Married women—Fiction. | Single fathers—Fiction. | Teenagers—Fiction. |
Domestic fiction. | BISAC: FICTION / Contemporary Women. |
FICTION / Romance / Contemporary. | FICTION / Literary.
Classification: LCC PS3607.I28 A79 2018 | DDC 813/.6—dc23
LC record available at https://lccn.loc.gov/2018005082

Target edition ISBN 978-1-9848-0055-8

Printed in the United States of America on acid-free paper

randomhousebooks.com

2 4 6 8 9 7 5 3 1

Target Exclusive Edition

Title-page and chapter-opener images: copyright © iStock.com/Bannosuke

Book design by Victoria Wong

For Edward and George,
with love and pride

ALL WE
EVER
WANTED

chapter one

NINA

It started out as a typical Saturday night. And by typical, I don't mean normal in any mainstream American way. There was no grilling out with the neighbors or going to the movies or doing any of the things I did as a kid. It was simply typical for what we'd become since Kirk sold his software company, and we went from comfortable to wealthy. *Very* wealthy.

Obscene was the description my childhood best friend Julie once used—not about us, but about Melanie, another friend—after Melanie bought herself a diamond Rolex for Mother's Day and then offhandedly remarked at one of our dinner parties that homemade pottery from her kids "wasn't going to cut it."

"She could feed a Syrian refugee camp for an entire *year* with that watch," Julie had groused in my kitchen after the other guests had departed. "It's *obscene*."

I'd nodded noncommittally, hiding my own Cartier under the edge of our marble island, as I silently reassured myself with all the ways my watch, and therefore my life, were different from Melanie's. For one, I didn't buy the watch for myself on a whim; Kirk gave it to me for our fifteenth anniversary. For another, I had always *loved* when our son, Finch, made me presents and cards in his younger years, and was sad that those had become relics of the past.

Most important, I don't think I ever flaunted our wealth. If anything, it embarrassed me. As a result, Julie didn't hold our money against me. She didn't know our exact worth but had a general sense of it, especially after she'd gone house hunting with me when Kirk was too busy, helping me find our home on Belle Meade Boulevard, where we now lived. She and her husband and girls were regular guests at our lake house and our home on Nantucket, just as she happily inherited my gently used designer hand-me-downs.

Occasionally Julie *would* call Kirk out, though, not for being showy like Melanie but for having elitist tendencies. A fourth-generation silver-spoon Nashvillian, my husband grew up en-sconced in a private-school, country-club world, so he'd had some practice at being a snob, even back when his money was merely old, and not yet obscene. In other words, Kirk came from a "good family"—that elusive term that nobody ever came out and defined, yet we all knew was code for having old money and a certain well-bred, refined taste. As in: he's a *Browning*.

My maiden name, Silver, held no such status, not even by the standards of Bristol, the town on the Tennessee-Virginia border where I grew up and Julie still lived. We were no slouches—my dad wrote for the *Bristol Herald Courier* and my mom was a fourth-grade teacher—but we were squarely middle class, and our idea of living large was everyone ordering dessert at a nonchain restaurant. Looking back, I wonder if that may have explained my mom's preoccupation with money. It wasn't that she was impressed with it, but she could always tell you who had it and who did not, who was cheap and who was living beyond their means. Then again, my mom could pretty much tell you anything about anyone in

Bristol. She wasn't a gossip—at least not a mean-spirited one—she was simply fascinated by other people's business, from their wealth and health to their politics and religion.

Incidentally, my dad is Jewish and my mother Methodist. *Live and let live* is their mantra, an outlook that was passed on to both my brother, Max, and me, the two of us embracing the more attractive elements of each religion, like Santa Claus and Seders, while punting Jewish guilt and Christian judgment. This was a good thing, especially for Max, who came out during college. My parents didn't miss a beat. If anything, they seemed more uncomfortable with Kirk's money than with my brother's sexuality, at least when we first began to date. My mother had insisted that she was just sad I wouldn't be getting back together with Teddy, my high school boyfriend, whom she adored, but I sometimes sensed a slight inferiority complex, and her worry that the Brownings were somehow looking down on me and my family.

To be fair, a half-Jewish girl from Bristol with a gay brother and no trust fund probably wasn't their first choice for their only child. Hell, I probably wasn't Kirk's first choice on paper, either. But what can I say? He picked me anyway. I'd always told myself that he fell in love with my personality—with *me*—the same way I fell in love with *him*. But in the past couple of years I had begun to wonder about both of us, and what had brought us together in college.

I had to admit that when discussing our relationship, Kirk often referenced my looks. He always had. So I'd be naïve to think that my appearance had nothing to do with why we were together— just as I knew, deep down, that the patina and security of a "good family" had, in part, attracted me to him.

I hated everything about that admission, but it was definitely on my mind that Saturday night as Kirk and I took an Uber to the

Hermitage Hotel for about our fifth gala of the year. We had become *that* couple, I remember thinking in the back of that black Lincoln Town Car—the husband and wife in an Armani tux and a Dior gown who were barely speaking. Something was off in our relationship. Was it the money? Had Kirk become too obsessed with it? Had I somehow lost myself as Finch grew older and I spent less time mothering him and more time in the role of full-time philanthropist?

I thought about one of my dad's recent remarks, asking why my friends and I didn't just skip the galas—and give *all* the money to charity. My mom had chimed in that we might be able to accomplish "more meaningful work in blue jeans than black tie." I had gotten defensive, reminding them that I did that sort of hands-on work, too, such as the hours I spent every month answering calls on Nashville's suicide helpline. Of course I hadn't admitted to my parents that Kirk sometimes minimized that kind of volunteering, insisting that I was better off "just writing the check." In his mind, a donation of dollars always trumped time; the fact that it came with more splash and credit was beside the point.

Kirk was a good man, I told myself now, as I watched him take a swallow of the bourbon roadie that he'd poured into a red Solo cup. I was being too hard on him. On *both* of us.

"You look fabulous," he suddenly said, looking over at me, softening me further. "That dress is *incredible*."

"Thanks, honey," I said in a low voice.

"I can't wait to take it off you," he whispered, so the driver wouldn't hear him. He gave me a seductive look, then took another drink.

I smiled, thinking that it had been a while, and resisted the urge to tell him that he might want to slow down on the booze. Kirk didn't have a drinking problem, but it was a rare night that he didn't at least catch a red-wine buzz. Maybe *that* was it, I thought. We definitely both needed to ease up on our social calendars. Be less distracted. More present. Maybe that would come when Finch went to college in the fall.

"So. Who have you told? About Princeton?" he asked, clearly thinking about Finch, too, and the acceptance letter he'd just received the day before.

"Other than family, only Julie and Melanie," I said. "What about you?"

"Just the guys in my foursome today," he said, rattling off the names of his usual golf buddies. "I didn't want to brag . . . but I couldn't help myself."

His expression mirrored the way I felt—a mix of pride and disbelief. Finch was a good student, and had gotten into Vanderbilt and Virginia earlier that winter. But Princeton had been a long shot, and his admittance felt like a culmination and validation of so many parenting decisions, beginning with applying Finch to Windsor Academy, the most rigorous and prestigious private school in Nashville, when he was only five years old. Since then, we had always prioritized our son's education, hiring private tutors when needed, exposing him to the arts, and taking him to virtually every corner of the globe. Over the past three summers, we had sent him on a service trip to Ecuador, to a cycling camp in France, and on a marine biology course in the Galápagos Islands. I recognized, of course, that we were at a distinct financial advantage over so many other applicants, and something about that (especially the check we'd written to Princeton's endowment) made me feel a little guilty. But I told myself that money alone couldn't gain a kid admission to the Ivy League. Finch had worked hard, and I was so proud of him.

Focus on that, I told myself. Focus on the positive.

Kirk was looking at his phone again, so I pulled mine out, too, checking Instagram. Finch's girlfriend, Polly, had just posted a photo of the two of them, the caption reading: We're both Tigers, y'all! Clemson and Princeton, here we come! I showed the picture to Kirk, then read aloud some of the congratulatory comments from children of our friends who would be in attendance tonight.

"Poor Polly," Kirk said. "They won't last a semester."

I wasn't sure if he meant the distance between South Carolina and New Jersey or the mere reality of young love, but I murmured my agreement, trying not to think of the condom wrapper that I'd recently found under Finch's bed. The discovery was far from a surprise, but it still made me sad, thinking of how much he had grown up and changed. He used to be such a little chatterbox, a precocious only child regaling me with every detail of his day. There was nothing I hadn't known about him, nothing he wouldn't have shared. But with puberty came an onset of remoteness that never really cleared, and in recent months, we'd talked very little, no matter how hard I tried to break down his barriers. Kirk insisted it was normal, all part of a boy's preparation to leave the nest. *You worry too much*, he always told me.

I put my phone back in my bag, sighed, and said, "Are you ready for tonight?"

"Ready for what?" he asked, draining his bourbon as we turned onto Sixth Avenue.

"Our speech?" I said, meaning *his* speech, though I would be standing beside him, offering him moral support.

Kirk gave me a blank stare. "Speech? Remind me? Which gala is this, again?"

"I hope you're kidding?"

"It's hard to keep them all straight—"

I sighed and said, "The *Hope* Gala, honey."

"And we are hoping for *what,* exactly?" he asked with a smirk.

"Suicide awareness and prevention," I said. "We're being honored, remember?"

"For what?" he asked, now starting to annoy me.

"The work we did bringing mental health experts to Nashville," I said, even though we both knew it had much more to do with the fifty-thousand-dollar donation we'd given after a freshman at Windsor took her life last summer. It was too horrible for me to process, even all these months later.

"I'm kidding," Kirk said, as he reached out to pat my leg. "I'm ready."

I nodded, thinking that Kirk was *always* ready. Always on. The most confident, competent man I'd ever known.

A moment later, we pulled up to the hotel. A handsome young valet swung open my door, issuing a brisk welcome. "Will you be checking in tonight, madame?" he asked.

I told him no, we were here for the gala. He nodded, offering me his hand, as I gathered the folds of my black lace gown and stepped onto the sidewalk. Ahead of me, I saw Melanie chatting amid a cluster of friends and acquaintances. The usual crowd. She rushed toward me, giving me air kisses and compliments.

"You look amazing, too. Are those new?" I reached up to her face, my fingertips grazing the most gorgeous chandelier diamond earrings.

"Newly acquired but vintage," she said. "Latest apology from you know who."

I smiled and glanced around for her husband. "Where is Todd, anyway?"

"Scotland. Boys' golf trip. Remember?" she said, rolling her eyes.

"That's right," I said, thinking that it was hard to keep up with Todd's boondoggles. He was worse than Kirk.

"Will you share this fella with me tonight?" Melanie asked with a shimmy of her shoulders as Kirk rounded the car and joined us.

"I'm sure he has no objections," I said, smiling.

An accomplished flirt, Kirk nodded, giving Melanie a double-cheek kiss. "You look *stunning,*" he told her.

She smiled and thanked him, then shouted, "Omigod! I heard the *fabulous* news! Princeton! You must be so over-the-moon proud!"

"We are. Thanks, Mel. . . . Has Beau made a final decision?" Kirk asked, shifting the attention to Melanie's son. His friendship with Finch, going all the way back to the first grade, was really the reason Mel and I had become so close.

"It's looking like Kentucky," Melanie said.

"Full ride?" Kirk asked.

"Half," Melanie said, beaming. Beau was an average student but an amazing baseball player, and had similar offers from a handful of schools.

"That's still *really* impressive. Good for him," Kirk said.

For years I'd had the uncomfortable feeling that Kirk had been jealous of Beau's baseball career. He often accused Melanie and Todd of being obnoxious, bragging too much about all-star this and that. But now it was easy for Kirk to be gracious; Finch had won, after all. Princeton trumped baseball. At least that's how I knew my husband saw it.

As Melanie flitted off to greet another friend, Kirk announced that he was going to find the bar. "Do you want a drink?" he asked, usually quite chivalrous at the start of the evening. It was the end of the night that sometimes got iffy.

"Yes. But I'll go with you," I said, determined to spend quality time together, even in a crowd. "Can we please not make it a late night?"

"Sure. That's fine," Kirk said, slipping his arm around my waist as we walked into the glittering hotel lobby.

THE REST OF the night followed the usual gala script, beginning with cocktails and a silent auction. There was nothing I really wanted, but reminding myself that all the money was going to a good cause, I bid on a sapphire cocktail ring. Meanwhile, I nursed a glass of sauvignon blanc, made small talk, and reminded Kirk not to drink too much.

At some point, the dinner chimes sounded, the lobby bar stopped serving, and we were herded into an expansive ballroom to find our assigned tables. Kirk and I were at a ten-top, front and center, seated with three other couples we knew reasonably well, plus Melanie, who kept me more than entertained with a running critique of the décor (the floral arrangements were too high), the cuisine (chicken, *again*?), and the egregiously clashing red and maroon attire of the gala co-chairs (how could they not have thought to coordinate?).

Then, as an army of waiters trotted out our standard chocolate mousse desserts, the gala chairs introduced Kirk and me, heaping praise on us for our commitment to this charity and so many others. I sat up as straight as I could, feeling a bit nervous as I heard *So, without further ado . . . Nina and Kirk Browning.*

As the crowd applauded, Kirk and I rose and made our way to the short staircase leading up to the stage. With my hand in his, we ascended the steps, my heart pounding with a rush of adrenaline that came from being in the spotlight. When we reached the podium, Kirk stepped forward to take the microphone while I stood at his side, pressing my shoulder blades together, a smile plastered across my face. When the applause died down, Kirk began to speak, first thanking the co-chairs, their various committees, our fellow

11

patrons, and all the donors. He then got to the reason we were here tonight, his voice growing somber. I stared at his strong profile, thinking how handsome he was.

"My wife, Nina, and I have a son named Finch," he said. "Finch, like some of your children, will be graduating from high school in just a couple of months. In the fall, he will be headed off to college."

I looked past the bright lights into a sea of faces as Kirk continued. "For the last eighteen years, our life has revolved around him. He is the most precious thing in the world to us," he said, then halted, looked down, and took a few seconds to continue. "And I just can't imagine the horror of losing him."

I lowered my gaze, nodding in agreement, feeling a stab of overwhelming grief and compassion for every family devastated by suicide. But as Kirk went on to talk about the organization, my mind guiltily wandered back to *our* life, *our* son. All the opportunity that stretched ahead for him.

I tuned back in to hear my husband say, "So, in closing, Nina and I are so honored to join with you in this important cause. . . . This is a fight for *all* of our children. Thank you so much. And good night."

As the crowd applauded once again, and a few of our closest friends actually stood for an ovation, Kirk turned and gave me a wink. He knew he'd nailed it.

"Perfect," I whispered.

Only things were actually far from perfect.

Because at virtually that very moment, our son was across town, making the worst decision of his life.

chapter two

TOM

Call it father's intuition, but I knew something bad was happening to Lyla before I actually *knew*. Then again, maybe my gut feeling had absolutely nothing to do with intuition, or our close bond, or the fact that I'd been a single parent since she was four years old. Maybe it was simply the skimpy outfit she'd tried to leave the house in just hours before.

I'd been cleaning the kitchen when she slinked past me wearing a dress so short that you could see the bottom of her ass—a part of her anatomy that her eight hundred Instagram followers had come to know well, thanks to countless "artsy" (according to Lyla) bikini shots she'd posted before I instituted my bright-line social-media bathing-suit ban.

"See ya, Dad," she said with practiced nonchalance.

"Whoa, whoa," I said, blocking her path to the door. "Where do you think you're going?"

"To Grace's. She just pulled up." Lyla pointed out the front window of our house. "See?"

"What I see," I said, glancing out the window at Grace's white Jeep, "is that you're missing the bottom half of your dress."

She rolled her eyes and hitched an enormous tote bag over one shoulder. I noticed that she wasn't wearing any makeup. *Yet.* I wasn't a gambling man, but I'd bet a hundred bucks that by the time Grace's car was at Five Points, the black shit Lyla put around her eyes would emerge, along with boots to replace her untied sneakers. "It's called fashion, Dad."

"Did you borrow that *fashion* from Sophie?" I asked, referring to the little girl she regularly babysat. "Although it might even be too short for her."

"You're hilarious," Lyla deadpanned, staring at me with one eye, the other covered with a mane of curly dark hair. "You should do, like, stand-up."

"Okay. Look, Lyla. You're not going out of the house in that." I tried to keep my voice low and calm, the way a psychologist had advised we speak to our teenagers at a recent lecture at Lyla's school. *They tune us out when we yell,* the lady had said in her own monotone. I'd glanced around the auditorium, amazed to see so many parents taking notes. Did these people really have time to consult a notebook in the heat of the moment?

"Da-*ad*," Lyla whined. "I'm just trying to go study with Grace and a couple other people . . ."

"Studying on a Saturday night? Seriously? What do you take me for, anyway?"

"Our exams are coming up . . . and we have this big group project." She unzipped her backpack and pulled out a biology text-book, holding it up as proof. "See?"

"And just how many boys are in your study group?"

She fought a smirk and lost.

"Change. Now," I said, pointing down the hall toward her bed-room, my mind filled with the horrifying possibilities of the real-life biology lesson she could get in that outfit.

"Okay, but every minute I waste debating this with you is, like, a percentage point off my grade."

"I'll settle for a C and a longer dress," I said, then resumed my cleaning to indicate the conversation was over.

I could feel her staring at me and, out of the corner of my eye, saw her turn and stomp down the hall. A few minutes later, she returned in a potato sack of a dress that only worried me more, as it confirmed that she'd be changing clothes—right after she spackled on the makeup.

"Remember. Be home by eleven," I said, even though I had no real way of enforcing her curfew when I wouldn't be back until much later than that. I was a carpenter by trade, but to make a little extra cash, I also drove a few nights a week for Uber and Lyft, and Saturday was my best night.

"I'm sleeping over at Grace's. Remember?"

I sighed, because I vaguely recalled giving her permission, though I had forgotten to call Grace's mother to verify the plans. I told myself that I had no reason to distrust Lyla. She could be rebellious on the margins, testing the boundaries the way teenagers do. But for the most part, she was a good kid. She was smart and studied hard, which was why she'd ended up at Windsor Academy after attending public school through the eighth grade. The transition had been difficult for us both. My challenge was around logistics (she could no longer take a bus to school) and economics (tuition was over thirty grand a year, though fortunately, more than eighty percent of that was covered by financial aid). Her stress had more to do with the intense academics and an even more intense social scene. In short, Lyla had never before been around so many rich kids, and it had been a bit of a struggle to keep pace in their polished, privileged world. But now, nearing the end of her sophomore year, she had made a few friends and seemed happy overall. Her closest friend was Grace, a little spark plug of a girl whose dad worked in the music industry. "Are her parents home?" I asked.

"Yeah. Well, her mom is, anyway. Her dad might be out of town."

"And Grace has a curfew?" I asked, feeling sure she did. I'd met her mother only a few times, but she seemed to have a good head on her shoulders, though her decision to give her sixteen-year-old a brand-new Jeep was, in my book, suspect.

"Yes. And it's eleven-*thirty,*" she said, looking smug.

"Eleven-thirty? For a sophomore?"

"Yes, Dad. That's everyone's curfew but mine. Or later."

I didn't believe this but gave in with a sigh, having long since learned to pick my battles. "Fine. But you have to be back at Grace's by eleven-thirty *sharp.*"

"Thanks, Dad," she said, blowing me a kiss on her way out the door, just the way she used to do when she was little.

I caught it in the air and pressed it to my cheek, the second part of our old routine. But she didn't see me. She was too busy looking down at her phone.

FOR SOME REASON, it was that air kiss that I thought about as I returned home around one-thirty in the morning, poured a Miller Lite into the frosted mug I kept in the freezer, and heated up a plate of two-day-old chicken tetrazzini. It was the last communication I'd had with Lyla—not a single text or call since. That wasn't all that unusual, especially on nights I worked late, but it still nagged at me, along with a weird feeling of unease. Nothing catastrophic or doomsday, just fear-of-her-having-sex kind of worry.

A few minutes later, my phone rang. It was Lyla. I felt simultaneous relief and worry as I answered and said, "Are you okay?"

There was a pause before I heard another girl's voice in my ear. "Um, Mr. Volpe? This is Grace."

"Grace? Where's Lyla? Is she okay?" I asked, panicking as I suddenly pictured my daughter in the back of an ambulance.

"Yeah, yeah. She's right here. With me. At my house."

"Is she hurt?" I asked, unable to think of another reason Lyla wouldn't be calling me herself.

"No. Um. Not like . . . *that*."

"Like *what* then, Grace? Put Lyla on the phone. *Now*."

"Um. I can't do that, Mr. Volpe. . . . She can't really . . . talk. . . ."

"Why can't she talk?" I said, growing increasingly frantic as I paced around our small kitchen.

"Um, well," Grace began. "She's kind of out of it. . . ."

I stopped pacing long enough to put my shoes back on. "What's going on? Did she take something?"

"No. Lyla doesn't do drugs, Mr. Volpe," Grace said in a steady, firm tone that calmed me just a little.

"Is your mom there?"

"Um, no, Mr. Volpe. She's out, at a benefit thing . . . but should be back soon." She continued to babble an explanation of her mother's social itinerary, but I cut her off.

"Dammit, Grace! Could you please tell me what the *hell* is going on?"

"Um, well . . . Lyla just drank too much. . . . Well, actually, she didn't drink *that* much. She only had a little bit of wine and, like, one drink . . . at this party we went to . . . after we studied. . . . But she didn't really eat dinner. I think that was the problem."

"Is she . . . conscious?" I asked. My heart raced as I wondered if Grace should hang up with me and call 911.

"Oh, yeah. She's not passed out. . . . She's just really out of it, and I'm a little worried, and just thought you should know. But honestly, she didn't do any drugs or even drink that much . . . as far as I know. . . . But we were apart for a little while. Not that long—"

"Okay. I'm on my way over," I said, grabbing my keys as I tried to remember the exact location of Grace's house. It was somewhere in Belle Meade, where most of the Windsor kids lived, but I'd dropped Lyla off there only a few times. "Text me your address. Okay, Grace?"

"Okay, Mr. Volpe. I will," she said, then resumed her disjointed mix of confessing and downplaying.

Somewhere between the door and my car, I hung up on her and started to run.

AFTER RETRIEVING A semiconscious Lyla from Grace's, Googling "alcohol poisoning," and talking with Lyla's on-call pediatrician, I concluded that my daughter wasn't in any immediate danger. She was just run-of-the-mill-dumb-teenager drunk. So there was nothing for me to do but sit with her on the tile floor of her bathroom while she moaned and cried and repeatedly slurred, "Dad, I'm so, *so* sorry." Occasionally she even referred to me as Daddy—my former name, which, sadly, she'd dropped a few years back.

Of *course* she was wearing the dress I'd told her not to wear and her eyes looked like a panda's, ringed in black. I didn't bother to lecture, knowing she likely wouldn't remember anything anyway. I did ask her some questions, though, hoping that the booze would act as truth serum, and that I could get enough of the story to be able to effectively cross-examine her in the morning.

The conversation was fairly predictable, going something like this:

Did you do drugs? No.

Did you drink? Yes.

How much? Not that much.

Where were you? At a party.

Whose party? A boy named Beau.

Does he go to Windsor? Yes.

What happened? I don't remember.

And that was all I got. Either she *really* didn't remember—or she was just telling me she didn't remember. Regardless, I was left to fill in the blanks with less than pleasant imagery. Every so often, she'd crawl back to the toilet and puke while I held her tangled hair out of the way. When I felt sure nothing was left in her stomach, I fed her sips of water with a couple Tylenol, helped her brush her teeth and wash her face, then got her into bed, still wearing that dress.

As I sat in the armchair in her room and watched her sleep, I felt waves of all the predictable anger, worry, and disappointment that come with being the father of a teenage girl who has just fucked up. But there was something else nagging at me, too. And as hard as I tried, I couldn't stop myself from thinking of Beatriz, the only other person I'd ever taken care of like this.

chapter three

NINA

Of all people, it had to be Kathie Parker to tell me what Finch had done.

In my younger years, I had the occasional frenemy—a girl who found a way to ruffle my feathers and bring out the worst in me. But in my adult life, Kathie was the closest—really the *only* thing— I'd ever had to a nemesis. On the surface, we were friendly, sharing a social circle, frequenting the same country club, and attending the same parties and girls' trips. But secretly, I couldn't stand her, and I got more than occasional clues that she felt the same way about me.

Kathie, who came from old Nashville money like Kirk, always seemed to be looking for ways to take me down a notch. One tactic she enjoyed was to subtly reference my background, asking random questions about Bristol or my family, particularly in front of other people. This was, I believe, her way of insinuating that notwithstanding my in-laws, I, personally, would always be "new Nashville." (I'd actually heard her use the ridiculous term before.) She was also the master of the backhanded compliment in the "bless your heart" vein. She would say things to me such as "I *love* your dress—I have a wonderful seamstress who could raise that hem a touch for you." Or, after peering into the backseat of my car in the parking lot following a spin class, "Goodness, I wish I were as laid-back as you when it comes to clutter!" which could be directly followed by "You're so lucky you sweat the way you do. It gets out all the toxins!"

Melanie told me to take it as a compliment. Her theory was that with the sale of Kirk's company, I had usurped Kathie's status as Queen Bee of Nashville's social elite.

"I have no desire to be Queen Bee of anything. Besides, you can't be the Queen Bee if you're from Bristol," I said.

"You can if you marry Kirk Browning," Melanie said. "He's got it *all*. Compared to Hunter, for sure."

I shrugged, thinking of Kathie's husband. Like Kirk, Hunter was from the landed gentry of Nashville, but he was rumored to have burned through a lot of their family money on bad deals.

"She also resents your looks," Melanie said in her usual blunt way. "You're richer *and* prettier. Younger, too."

I laughed her comment off but couldn't help thinking that the "richer" part really did correlate with an increase in Kathie's jabs. More than that, though, I think Kathie knew that I saw through her two-faced Bible-beating bullshit. To be clear, I have no problem with religion or people who are religious, even those who are outspoken about their faith. What I can't stand are the judgmental hypocrites—people who talk a big Christian game yet don't even make a cursory *attempt* to follow the Golden Rule, let alone some of those pesky commandments. In a Schadenfreude nutshell, Kathie not only thrived on the misfortune of others but used tragedies as opportunities to showcase her devoutness. Something bad would happen, and she'd be first on the scene, offering prayers on Facebook, dropping off a casserole, or calling a special session of her Bible study group (which was as exclusive an invite as one to a garden party at Buckingham Palace—perhaps that's part of why she viewed it as an affront that I always declined to join). To be fair, I'm sure that *some* of Kathie's prayers were sincere, certainly in matters of life or death. But I truly believed she relished the smaller emotional setbacks of others and even occasionally rooted for someone's marriage to fail or kid to screw up.

So she really hit the jackpot the night of the Hope Gala when she found me in the ladies' room. "Oh, hello there, Nina," she said in her high, fake voice, joining me sink-side. We made eye contact in the mirror and smiled at each other as I continued to touch up my makeup. "You look so *lovely* tonight."

Lovely was her favorite word, and one I had actually excised from my vocabulary as a result. "You, too! Congrats on the Italy trip," I said—because she had just outbid Melanie during the live auction to win two first-class airline tickets to Rome and a week's stay at a Tuscan villa.

"Thank you, hon! Melanie wasn't too upset, was she?" she asked, her voice revealing her insincerity.

"Oh, no, not at all," I lied out of loyalty to Melanie, who had been infuriated by Kathie's smug paddle-raising. "I think she was secretly relieved *not* to win it. Todd *hates* when she bids on trips."

"Yes," she said, nodding. "I've heard he's rather . . . tight. . . ."

"Oh. It's not *that*. It's just those annoying blackout dates," I said, walking the line between being an outright bitch and simply raining on her parade. Feeling transparent and maybe a little guilty for stooping to her level, I added a chipper footnote. "Of course, Tuscany's lovely *any* time of year."

"Yes, it is," she said breezily. "Besides, I was bidding more for charity than the trip itself."

"Certainly," I said, noticing, not for the first time, how seldom she blinked. It made her big, wide-spaced eyes even more irritating.

Meanwhile she gave me a look so grave that I had no real choice but to ask what was wrong.

She inhaled deeply, pressing her palms together while she glanced up at the ceiling, as if gathering strength. "Oh, dear. Do you *not* know? . . ." Her voice trailed off.

I knew her pretense to compassion well—and that the charade was simply a precursor to gossip. Perhaps someone had passed out at the dinner table. Or was dancing inappropriately with someone else's spouse. Or had debuted a bad boob job. There was plenty of fodder to work with at any gala.

"Don't know *what*?" I asked, against my better judgment.

She winced, pursed her lips, then drew another amazingly slow breath. "Finch's Snapchat," she whispered on the exhale with a fleeting but unmistakable expression of glee.

My heart sank, but I told myself to remain strong, resist her entrapment, say nothing. So that's what I did, simply staring at my own reflection, brushing an additional layer of gloss over my lipstick.

It was clear that my silence both confused and frustrated her, and it took her a few seconds to find her footing. "You obviously haven't seen . . . ?"

"No. I don't have Snapchat," I said, seizing a slice of the moral high ground that comes with opting out of any form of social media.

She let out a little laugh. "Well, good heavens, I don't *either*. And even if I did, it wasn't on his 'story.' . . . Apparently he sent the photo to his friends."

"Then how did *you* see it?" I asked, putting my gloss back in my bag.

"Someone took a screenshot and it spread. Like wildfire . . .

Lucinda sent it to me a few minutes ago. During Kirk's speech, actually. But don't worry. She won't share it further. She's very discreet when it comes to these sorts of things, and we've been strict with her about appropriate usage of social media."

"That's so *kind* of her," I said, thinking of Kathie's daughter Lucinda, and how she shared her mother's meddling tendencies. My mind raced with the possibilities. What could Finch possibly have texted that could warrant all of this drama? Perhaps he'd bragged a bit too much about Princeton? Or maybe he was drinking a beer in celebration? I reminded myself to consider the source—that this was vintage Kathie, stirring the pot so she could look superior, then play savior. But I still caved, turning away from the mirror and staring directly into her bug eyes. "So what was in the photo, Kathie?"

"It was a photo of a girl," she quickly replied, lowering her voice to a loud whisper, likely hoping that people were eavesdropping.

"And? So?" I said, trying to remain unflappable.

"So," she began. "So . . . the girl was basically . . . *naked*."

"What? *Naked?*" I said, crossing my arms in disbelief. There was *no* way, no *chance* Finch would ever do something so stupid. Everyone knew that that was 101 on how to get thrown out of Windsor, right up there with stealing.

"Well . . . *half* naked, anyway . . ."

I bit my lower lip, now envisioning a lingerie-clad model—or perhaps a risqué photo of Polly, who could be known to dress a bit provocatively, but no worse than many of the other girls. "Well," I said, turning again toward the door. "Kids will do that—"

Kathie cut me off. "Nina. She was passed out. On a *bed*."

"Who is this *she*?" I snapped.

"Her name is Lyla. I guess she's a sophomore at Windsor? Hispanic girl. Maybe you should see it. . . ." She whipped her phone out of her Chanel bag and pulled up her text messages, an image filling her screen. She held it out for me to see.

I took a deep breath and looked down. At first glance, all I saw was a girl lying on her back on a bed, mostly dressed or at least far from naked, and I felt a small wave of relief. But as I peered more closely, I saw the details. Her little black dress hitched both up and down, as if someone had tried unsuccessfully to yank it off—or haphazardly put it back on. Her thighs slightly apart. Her calves dangling over the foot of the bed, her bare feet not quite touching the floor. And her left breast spilling out of a bra, nipple and all.

There were other details, too, less jarring than the girl herself, though somehow still disturbing. The dingy clutter of a teen boy's bedroom. A tan comforter. A nightstand covered with beer bottles and crumpled tissues. A poster of a band I didn't recognize, its members grungy, menacing, tattooed. And very strangely, a green Uno card in the girl's left hand, her fingers curled around it, her nails painted crimson.

I took a few breaths, trying to remain calm, hoping that there was some explanation. That, at the very least, this image had nothing to do with Finch.

"Did you read the caption?" Kathie asked, still holding the phone in front of my face.

I looked down again, squinting at the photo, this time seeing Finch's name, as well as the words that were typed onto the image, blending in with the comforter. I read them, hearing Finch's voice: Looks like she got her green card.

My heart sank as any defense of my child melted away.

"I'm sorry," Kathie said, slowly pulling her phone away from me, then stowing it in her bag. "I especially hate that this happened on a night when you and Kirk are being honored. . . . I just thought you should know."

"Thank you," I said, and as much as I wanted to shoot the messenger (or slap her across the face), I knew that Kathie was no longer the point. "I have to go now. . . . I need to get back to Kirk."

"Of course you do," she whispered somberly, giving me a pat on the arm. "Bless your heart, Nina. I'll be praying for y'all."

WITHIN THIRTY MINUTES, Kirk and I were home, and I'd received the image from two other friends, including a hysterical Melanie, who recognized her son's bedroom and was racing home herself.

"What in the *world* was he thinking?" I asked as Kirk and I stood on either side of the island in our kitchen.

"I can't imagine," Kirk said, shaking his head. "Maybe it was a dumb inside joke?"

"An inside *racist* joke?" I said, a fresh wave of despair washing over me.

"Well, it's not really racist per *se*. . . ." Kirk said.

"Seriously? *Green* card? It's *totally* racist. Kathie said she's Hispanic," I said.

"Well, she really doesn't look Hispanic. . . . She just looks . . . like a brunette. Italian, maybe."

I stared at him a beat, then shook my head, unsure how to even respond to this.

"Kathie doesn't know everything," Kirk said, reaching for the bottle of whiskey he'd left on the counter. I pushed it away from him.

"Okay. Look, Kirk. Even if she's not Hispanic, his comment is *still* offensive and racist *toward* Hispanics," I said, my voice steadily rising. "And regardless of this girl's race or ethnicity, her *nipple* is showing! So if he did this, joke or not—"

"Then he's in trouble," Kirk said. "Obviously. But maybe there's more to the story. . . ."

"Such as?" I said.

"I don't know. Maybe someone took his phone. Maybe it's a doctored screenshot. I have no idea, Nina. But try to calm down. We'll get to the bottom of it soon enough."

I nodded and took a deep breath, but before I could reply, we heard the front door open, followed by Finch's footsteps in the foyer.

"We're in the kitchen!" I called out. "Can you come here, please?"

A second later, our son appeared wearing a light-blue T-shirt and khaki shorts. His wavy blond hair looked messier than usual, and his whole appearance suddenly seemed to be cultivated, preppy sloppy.

"Hey," he said, heading straight for the refrigerator with only a glance our way. He opened it and stared inside for several seconds before pulling out a bag of sliced roast beef. He peeled off a few pieces, then tossed the bag back in and pushed the door shut with his elbow.

"Aren't you going to make a sandwich?" I asked.

"Too much trouble," Finch said.

"How about a plate?" I said, anger bubbling inside of me. "Can you at least put that on a plate?"

He shook his head, grabbed a paper towel from the roll, then headed for the family room, stuffing roast beef in his mouth as he went.

"Where're you going?" I called out after him.

"To watch TV," he replied without looking back.

"Come back here, please," I said, circling the counter to stand alongside Kirk. "Dad and I need to talk to you."

I glanced at Kirk, who wore a casual expression as he drummed his fingers on the edge of the counter. I nudged him with my elbow and made a mean face.

"Listen to your mother, Finch," he said. "We want to talk. . . ."

Finch turned around, looking more confused than worried, as I wondered how much he'd had to drink. "What's going on?" he said, putting the last of the roast beef in his mouth and talking as he chewed.

"Will you please come here and sit down?" I said, pointing to one of the barstools.

Finch did as I asked but wore an expression of defiance.

"How was your night?" I said.

He shrugged and replied that it was fine.

"What did you do?"

"Went over to Beau's."

"Did he have a party?" I asked.

"No. Not a party. He just had some people over. Why? What's with the third degree?"

I elbowed Kirk again, and he issued a perfunctory "Don't talk to your mother like that."

Finch mumbled "Sorry" as he ran his hand through his hair.

I waited for him to look back at me before I asked my next question. "Were you drinking?" I said, uncertain of what I wanted the answer to be. Would that make it better or worse?

"Yeah," Finch said. "I had a few beers."

"How many?" I asked, wishing that Kirk and I had been stricter about drinking. We'd never come out and given him our permission to consume alcohol, but we had looked the other way on a beer here and there. It was, after all, why we allowed him unlimited spending on Uber.

"I didn't really count," he said. "Maybe three or four?"

"That's too many," I said.

"I didn't *drive*."

"Well. Isn't that *great,*" I said. "You deserve a medal."

Finch heaved a sigh and said, "Why're you so pissed off, Mom? You *know* I drink."

"We're both very, very upset, Finch. But it's not just about the drinking," I said, then took a deep breath, pulled my phone out of my purse, and found the image saved to my camera roll. I slid it across the counter and watched him look down at it.

"Where did you get that?" he asked.

My heart sank.

"Mrs. Parker showed it to Mom. At our event tonight," Kirk replied.

Finch glanced at me as I nodded. "Yeah. So let that one sink in. . . . But, honestly, is that really what you're worried about here? *Where* I got it?"

"I was just *wondering,*" Finch said.

I took a breath and said, "Did you take it?"

"Mom, it's a long story . . . and it's not as bad as it looks. . . . I bet she wouldn't even be that mad. . . ."

"Who is she?"

"Just some girl," he said.

I turned the words over in my head, feeling absolutely sickened. "Does this girl have a name?" I asked him.

"Yeah. It's Lyla Volpe. . . . Why?"

"*Why?* Because you posted a photo of her half naked, Finch. That's *why,*" I said, feeling myself become hysterical.

29

"It wasn't posted. It just got sent to a few people. And she wasn't half naked, Mom."

"I saw her nipple, Finch," I said. "That counts as naked to me."

"Well, it's not like *I* took her clothes off. . . ."

"Well, that's a relief," I said, my voice dripping with sarcasm. "Because that would make it assault."

"*Assault?* C'mon, Mom. You're overreacting," he said with a weary sigh. "Nobody assaulted her. She drank too much and passed out. That's not *my* problem."

"On the contrary, son, this *is* your problem," Kirk said, as if the gravity of the situation was finally setting in for him. "Many people have seen this photo. It's out there."

"And . . . *green* card, Finch? *Really?*" I said.

"It was just a joke, Mom."

"It's *racist,*" I said. "You took a photo of a half-naked girl who was passed out, and then made a *racist* joke about her."

"I'm sorry," he said, lowering his eyes and voice.

"That you *did* it? Or that you got *caught?*" I asked.

"C'mon, Mom. Please. Stop. I'm *really* sorry."

"What were you thinking? I mean, actually what was going through your mind?" I said.

Finch shrugged. "Nothing."

"Nothing? *Nothing?*" I said, floored by his answer, though maybe it was better than if he had set out to hurt someone. Still, the result was the same. The injury wasn't any less.

When he didn't reply, I got *more* upset. "How could you do this, Finch? I just don't get it. It's so . . . *cruel*! This is not the way your father and I have raised you!"

"And beyond that, do you realize what you've risked here?" Kirk asked, finally raising his voice, too. "How stupid and irresponsible this was? You could be *expelled*!"

"C'mon, Dad, that's crazy," Finch said.

"No, it's not," I said. "It's not far-fetched at all, actually. Hell, forget Windsor. You could be sued in *court*."

"On what grounds?" Kirk asked me, as if I were a legal expert.

"I don't know—I'm not a lawyer," I said, my voice rising. "Defamation? Child pornography?"

"Pornography? Come *on*, Mom," Finch said.

"Yeah. This is hardly a porno," Kirk chimed in.

"*Porn,* Kirk," I said. "They dropped the *o* two decades ago."

"Yes. Because that's the important point here," Kirk said under his breath.

"Look. There is enough here to bring a lawsuit," I said. "I am certain of that. Bottom line, this girl and her parents could always claim emotional distress—"

"Mom, there's no emotional distress," Finch said.

"There's not?" I asked, incredulous. "How would you know? Did you ask her? Do you care about her feelings at *all*?"

"She'll be fine, Mom. This kind of thing happens all the time."

"Happens? It doesn't just 'happen.' You *did* it!" I started to rant again.

Kirk held up his hand and said, "Look. It's not about the girl."

"It's *not*?" I said. "What's it about, then, Kirk? Enlighten me?"

Kirk cleared his throat. "This is about his shitty judgment." He turned his gaze to Finch and said, "Son, you showed terrible judgment tonight that could jeopardize your future. You really have to think—"

"Not just *think*. You have to *feel,* too," I said, cutting Kirk off. "You can't treat people like this."

"I don't, Mom. It was just—"

"A lapse of judgment," Kirk finished for him.

"Well, unfortunately, it's not that simple," I said.

Because deep down, I knew that even if every person out there deleted the picture from their phones, and Lyla and her parents and the administration of Windsor never caught wind of it, and Finch truly *was* sorry, everything had *still* changed. At least for *one* of us it had.

chapter four

TOM

I'll never forget the first moment I laid eyes on Beatriz. I was sitting in a dive bar in Five Points, back when East Nashville had not yet become a hipster hangout and had *all* been a dive. *My* dive. It wasn't the kind of spot you'd expect to see a beautiful girl, especially all alone, but she walked in solo, which was kind of alluring in and of itself. She happened to also be my type, with dark hair and eyes, bronzed skin, plenty of curves. The tight red dress didn't hurt her cause, either.

"Don't even think about it," I said to my buddy John without averting my gaze.

John laughed. "Who? The J.Lo lookin' one?"

I said yeah, her.

"Why? Did ya fuck her?" John asked, chewing on a straw, watching her as she approached us. He was the kind of loud, good-looking guy that hot girls gravitated toward, especially in bars late at night.

"No. But I'm gonna try," I said with a laugh. "And then I might marry her."

John laughed. "Yeah. Ooookay," he said, hopping off his stool. He slapped me on the back, and when she was within earshot, he added, "Good luck with that, buddy."

She glanced at him, then smiled at me, clearly aware of why he thought luck was needed.

"May I?" she asked, gesturing to the now free stool.

"Yes," I said, catching a whiff of her hair. It smelled like that suntan oil girls slathered on themselves. Coconut, I guess. I tried to think of something clever to say but came up blank, so I just said the truth. "I don't do pickup lines, but . . . you're the most beautiful girl I've ever seen." Then, realizing how cheesy that sounded, I stupidly added, "In this bar."

"In this bar?" she asked with a low, sexy laugh as I noticed that her left front tooth was adorably crooked. She looked around, glancing purposefully at a group of not very pretty girls sitting on the other side of me.

"Okay, fine. *Anywhere,*" I clarified, no longer caring if I sounded cheesy. She was *that* pretty.

"And that's not a pickup line?" she said, as I noticed a trace of an accent. Even better.

I shook my head and stammered, "No. . . . Well, maybe it is. . . . But I don't want to *just* pick you up. I want to *know* you . . . everything about you. . . ."

She laughed that laugh again. "*Every*thing?"

"Everything," I said, then rattled off questions. "What's your name? How old are you? Where are you from?"

"Beatriz. Twenty-five. Rio," she said, the last word rolling from her full lips, stained the exact shade of her dress.

"In Brazil?"

She smiled and asked if I knew of another Rio as the bartender approached her. Without hesitating like most girls do, she ordered a drink I'd never heard of, rolling more *r*'s. She did the reach for her oversize woven bag that looked like it should smell of pot, or at least incense, as I put my hand on hers. "I have a tab," I said.

She smiled, staring into my eyes. "Do you also have a name?"

"Tommy . . . Tom . . . Thomas," I said—because people called me all three.

"Which do you prefer?" she asked.

"Whichever *you* prefer," I said.

"I want to dance, Thomas," she said, throwing her shoulders and hair back.

I was pretty stoked that she picked my full name, but I shook my head on the dancing. "Anything but that," I said with a laugh.

She gave me a fake pout, and I said a prayer that someday soon we'd be close enough for *real* pouting, explosive fights, and passionate making up. "Please?" she said with a tilt of her head.

"I can't dance," I confessed as the bartender finished making her drink and placed it in front of her.

"Everyone can dance," she said, swaying her shoulders to "Free Bird." "It's just moving to music." She squeezed the lime into her drink, then stirred it with her skinny straw before taking her first sip. As I watched her lips curve around the glass and her hair fall forward around her face, I had a little trouble breathing. I glanced away, contemplating another drink for myself. I already had a decent buzz but could've used a little more liquid courage. I decided against it, though, wanting to remember everything about our conversation, and asked what she was doing in Nashville. She told me she was an au pair for twin toddlers in Brentwood but had the weekend off. She said she'd chosen Nashville because of the music scene.

"Are you a musician?" I asked, intrigued, though musicians were a dime a dozen around here.

She nodded. "I'm a singer. Trying to be anyway."

"What kind of music?"

"Sertanejo. It's like Brazilian country. . . . Music about partying and love . . . and heartbreak . . ."

I nodded, entranced. "Maybe you'll sing for me sometime?"

"Maybe," she said with a slow smile. "And what about you, Thomas? Are you from Nashville?"

"Yep. Born and raised."

"What part?" she said.

"You're looking at it," I said.

She laughed, putting her thumb just inside her lower lip. "You were born in a bar?"

"No," I said, smiling. "I mean East Nashville. This side of the river."

She nodded, as if she knew what I meant—that the Cumberland River separated the glitzy downtown from my gritty neighborhood.

"Why aren't you out on Lower Broad?" I said, silently adding *with all the other pretty girls*.

"Because I can't meet boys like you over there." She smiled, and I smiled back at her. We sat in silence for a few seconds before she said, "And what do you do, Thomas? What's your job?"

"I'm a carpenter," I said, staring down at my thumbs as I tapped them on the bar. I braced myself for *that* look. The one some girls will give you when you tell them you don't have an office job and went to college for only a year and a half before running out of money, dropping out, and falling into a woodworking gig.

But if she felt at all disappointed, she didn't show it. She even looked a little intrigued, though maybe that was wishful thinking on my part. I'd been fooled before by girls who insisted they loved a man who worked with his hands. I'm glad she didn't say this but simply asked, "So you make furniture?"

"Yeah."

"What kind?"

"All kinds," I said. "Tables, shelves, dressers, desks. I love drawers."

She laughed. "Drawers?"

"Yeah. Drawers," I said. "Not the cheap kind that rattle along metal tracks . . . but smooth, polished wood on wood . . . drawers with hand-cut dovetail joints that whisper when you glide 'em open." I gave her a low, breathy whistle.

She leaned toward me, nodding as if she understood I was talking about craftsmanship. Artistry. Furniture that might become a family heirloom—though I wasn't that good. *Yet.* I had finished my apprenticeship but was still learning so much.

"Like antiques? Before they become antiques?" She leaned closer, her breath warm on my cheek.

"Yeah," I said. She was a magnet, an absolute force field, and I couldn't stop myself from kissing her. I brushed my lips against hers, tasting lime and liquor. Her lips were perfect, and my heart exploded in my chest. After several dizzying seconds, she pulled away, just far enough to tell me that I might not know how to dance, but I sure could kiss.

I caught my breath and managed to say back, "So can you."

"May I ask you a question, Thomas?" she whispered into my ear.

I nodded, my vision blurry.

"Do you make love the way you dance? . . . Or how you kiss?"

My skin on fire, I looked into her eyes and told her she could find that one out for herself.

A FEW HOURS and drinks and even some dancing later, we were back in my crappy studio apartment having ridiculously good sex. I was twenty-nine and single, so it wasn't the first time I'd slept with a girl I'd just met, but this was different. This was making love. Before I met Beatriz, I would've said that instantaneous love was impossible. But all rules and logic went out the window with her. She was that amazing. She was magic.

BARELY THREE MONTHS later, we were married and she was pregnant, though it actually happened in the reverse order. It didn't matter; I would have asked her to marry me anyway, though her pregnancy expedited things and also threw a few curves (no pun intended) our way. For one, my mother was wary of Beatriz, questioning her motives for "getting pregnant," clearly suggesting that she was using me to stay in the country. I made the mistake of sharing this with Beatriz, who was understandably hurt, and I found out the hard way that forgiveness wasn't her strong suit. It was a trait she'd apparently inherited from her father, an orthopedist for the Brazilian national soccer team, who was already pissed at Beatriz for moving to the States to pursue a singing career. Her getting knocked up by a carpenter didn't help their relationship any, though her stepmother—the only mother Beatriz had ever known—was mostly to blame for that turbulence. It was classic Cinderella shit.

So, anyway, things were strained with both of our families, and we blew off most of our friends, spending every minute together. It was probably unhealthy but felt like us against the world. We were insatiable and invincible—or so we thought. Even after Lyla burst onto the scene in all her colicky glory, and Beatriz fought the baby blues and gave up her singing dreams, and I had to work odd menial jobs to make ends meet, we *still* kept the passion going.

But at some point, around Lyla's second birthday, things began to change with us. Love began to feel more like lust—and it stopped conquering all. Although we'd always had something of a turbulent dynamic, both of us prone to jealousy, the fighting got worse. Or maybe we were just having less sex, which made the fighting *seem* worse. In any event, Beatriz blamed me, saying that I was always stressed out and never wanted to go out or "do anything." For a while, I believed her theory and felt guilty and neglectful. I kept promising her that I'd work a little less and try to be more fun. But I slowly began to see that Beatriz's sole version of fun had become partying. *Hard.* It wasn't that I didn't see the merits of unwinding with a few beers. But more and more, Beatriz was *always* tying one on, her hangovers making her more depressed and totally useless the next day. Sometimes she was so out of it that I had to stay home from work and take care of Lyla. Which meant we were more broke than ever.

Even worse, she started to hide things from me. Not big things, just random shady shit with her phone and laptop. But it was enough to make me stop trusting her, then begin to dislike her. I still loved her, though, because she was Beatriz, and also the mother of our child.

Then, one summer night, just after we'd moved into our Craftsman bungalow on Avondale Drive (where Lyla and I still live), everything exploded. Our argument started that morning when I suggested we do something as a family, just the three of us. Maybe go to the zoo or have a picnic in Cumberland Park or visit my mother (whom Beatriz still couldn't stand but had learned to tolerate because of free childcare).

I was trying hard to salvage things between us, but Beatriz quickly shot me down, saying she'd already committed to a cook-out with friends. Which friends, I asked. She told me. I said I didn't like those people—or the person she became around them. She more or less fired back, tough shit, she was going, and she would be taking Lyla with her.

"Am I even invited?" I asked, which, crazily enough, didn't seem to be a given.

She shrugged, then said sure, I could come if I wanted, but she understood if I didn't. I took it as my cue to head to the workshop, where increasingly I'd been finding peace. But later that afternoon, as I put my tools away, I got a funny feeling in my gut that something was wrong. So I tracked down her friends' Inglewood address and drove over to the party.

The second I pulled up, I could see Beatriz on the front porch, dancing with some loser I recognized from her MySpace page. Both of his hands were on her ass, and it didn't look like it was the first time they'd been there. Lyla was nowhere to be seen. Enraged, I jumped out of my car and walked over to the house, climbing the porch steps. "Where's Lyla?" I said, doing my best not to knock the guy out. He dropped his hands right away, looking guilty as hell. I waited for the same expression to cross my wife's face, but she was shameless and glazed, clearly drunk or high, probably both.

"Where's Lyla?" I shouted this time.

Everyone got quiet, staring at me, except for Beatriz, who said, "God, Thomas. Chill out. She was right here. Just a few seconds ago."

I looked at her, and it suddenly hit me that she was wearing a bikini under her tank top—and her hair was wrapped into a wet bun. So she'd been swimming. Which meant that these fucking idiots had a swimming pool. I panicked, pushing past everyone, tearing through the house, then onto the back porch. It was one of those elevated decks with a long flight of stairs down to the lawn. I did a quick scan of the yard and, sure enough, there was the pool. Beyond a group of older kids playing Marco Polo was Lyla, all alone, perched on the edge of it. A black 3 FEET was painted on the side—shallow but still way too deep for a four-year-old who had only taken a couple of swim lessons in her life.

I sprinted down the stairs and over to her, calling her name. Logically I could see that she was safe, but I had the irrational feeling that something bad might still happen while I watched. My voice scared her—probably because she thought she was in trouble—and she tipped forward, nearly falling into the water. I scooped her up and covered her face with kisses. I knew I was traumatizing her, but I couldn't stop. I held her in my arms and ran back to my car, this time going the long way around the house. I didn't know if Beatriz was still on the porch, or whether she saw us, but if she did, she didn't follow me. I strapped Lyla into her car seat, drove her home, gave her a bath and a snack, reliving the fear over and over. I finally put her in bed with me, both of us falling asleep. Beatriz never called to check in.

I don't know what time it was when she finally stumbled home, only that it felt like the middle of the night. "Get *out*," I told her. "You're not sleeping here."

"This is my bed, too."

"Not tonight it's not."

"Where do you want me to sleep?" she said.

"I don't care. Sleep on the couch. Anywhere but here."

We began to fight. There were no apologies, only accusations and sorry-ass excuses. *I'd* embarrassed *her*. I'd overreacted. I was a paranoid, jealous dick. She'd left Lyla alone for only a few minutes.

"It takes three minutes to drown!" I shouted back at her. "One hundred and eighty seconds to lose her. Forever."

We went round in circles, making the same points again and again. At some point, I called her a drunk. She asked me what had

I expected? I'd fallen in love with a girl at a bar. Like it was something to be proud of.

"Yeah. Well, you're a *fucking* mother now," I shouted.

"It doesn't change who I am," she said, raising her chin defiantly.

"And who *are* you?" I asked. "Other than a party girl who fucks on the first night?"

She couldn't have looked more stunned if I had slapped her across the face. "Is that how you really feel about me?" she asked, her accent thick, the way I once adored and now couldn't stand.

I said yes, wanting to punish her for the image I couldn't shake of Lyla sitting on the edge of the pool. I told her I had no respect for her, that she was a terrible mother, and that Lyla would be better off without her. That it was better to have *no* mother than to have a mother like her. I braced myself for more fighting, but she only bit her lip and said, "Well. I'm glad I finally know what you really think of me. *Tom.*"

As I watched her turn and walk out of the bedroom, closing the door behind her, I panicked a little, knowing I'd gone too far. That I'd been both cruel and hypocritical—after all, I'd fucked on the first night, too. I knew that part of me still loved her and would always love her, but I also knew that we were heading down a road to divorce. A lifetime of shuffling our child around between two places we couldn't afford. I pictured stepparents and half siblings, fighting and bitterness. I pictured hate.

But in my wildest, worst imagination, I didn't expect what I found the next morning: a sloppy note on the kitchen table telling me she was leaving us. I told myself that she didn't actually mean it. That surely she would come home.

But days turned to weeks turned to months. I called and emailed and left her messages—some concerned, most angry—but there was no word back from her. It was infuriating and confounding and humiliating, but mostly it was just sad. I was sad for myself—and devastated for Lyla.

The fact that I had no answers for my daughter made it even harder. I tried to convince myself that Beatriz *was* dead, remembering my words the night she left, thinking that it actually might *be* better. Besides, it was the only explanation I could really wrap my head around. I mean, I got the *leaving* part. Hell, there were times I almost beat her to the punch—or at least fantasized about taking off. It was the *not coming back* that didn't make sense, especially for a mother. Dads picked up and left all the time, whether to start a new family or just to be alone. But mothers always seemed to stay in the picture, somehow.

She's gone was the simple explanation I always gave Lyla.

"Gone *where*?" Lyla would ask, sometimes through tears, though usually she would be crying about something else first.

At which point, I would answer vaguely, referencing a beautiful place (heaven? a beach in Brazil?), always careful not to lie. She was going to need enough therapy as it was without adding her father's deceit to the equation.

Over time, Lyla's memories of her mother became diluted, and the subject of "Mommy" arose less and less. My own mother stepped in to fill the void, helping with Lyla's haircuts and clothing, the nuts and bolts of being a girl. That helped. But at the end of the day, I was a single parent, raising a child alone. I cooked and cleaned, drove her to the bus stop in the morning, met the bus in the afternoon, and put her to bed at night. I arranged my work schedule around her activities and virtually eliminated my own social life. I eventually dated a bit here and there—my mother was always willing to babysit so I could go out—but nothing ever got serious. In part because I never met anyone that great, but also because I didn't have the time, energy, or extra cash for anything other than Lyla. If that sounds like I'm complaining, it's because I am. Parenting can be a real drain, even when sharing the misery with a spouse. Alone it was hard as fuck.

But we got by just fine, and I took great pride in the fact that I was raising such a good kid. Lyla was beautiful, smart, and kind, and my world revolved around her. We both got over Beatriz and moved on with our lives.

Then, five years later, with no warning at all, she came back. It was Lyla's ninth birthday. The timing was so messed up that it made me want to issue a memo to deadbeat parents everywhere, advising them to please make contact *before* or *after* their child's birthday. To reappear *on* the actual day, or any other day of significance, was both narcissistic and wildly disruptive, particularly when there had been no expectations of your coming back whatsoever. When you'd been gone so long there wasn't even a *thought* of you in the kid's head.

Such was the case that year. I was hit or miss with the party thing, mostly because I had trouble planning in advance, but also because venue parties were too expensive. But I'd gotten it together and allowed Lyla to invite three friends for a sleepover. With a June birthday, she usually had nice weather, but this evening was especially idyllic. The girls ran around in the backyard and played in the sprinkler while I grilled hot dogs and hamburgers. Afterward, we had a chocolate cake, compliments of my mom, and Lyla opened her presents. The girls then hunkered down in their sleeping bags to watch a movie that looked a little bit scary for their age. I remember checking the rating and asking if all their parents were okay with a PG-13 movie (they said they were), and feeling pretty damn good about my competence as a single dad before I turned in for the night.

The next thing I knew, Lyla was shaking me awake. She looked stricken.

"What time is it?" I said.

"I don't know," she said. Because kids never do.

"What's wrong?" I asked, noticing on my alarm clock that it was close to midnight. "Did something happen?"

That's when Lyla sat on the edge of my bed and dropped the second biggest shock of my life. "Mom's at the door," she informed me. "She wants to talk to you."

THAT'S ABOUT WHERE I left off on memory lane when I fell asleep in Lyla's chair after her puke fest. I awoke in the early morning to the sound of her phone vibrating. I got up and walked to her bedside, checked to make sure she was still asleep, then picked up her phone and entered 1919—the pass code I'd glimpsed over her shoulder a few days ago. A not so small part of me hoped she'd changed it since then, but the digits worked, and I found myself with complete access to my daughter's personal life. Short of reading her journal, which I knew she kept in her top-left desk drawer, this was the ultimate invasion. I felt conflicted—*guilty*—but I told myself that her safety and well-being trumped her privacy, and both were at stake here. So I clicked on the text message icon and stared down at her in-box.

Most of the names that filled the screen I recognized, and all were girls. A wave of relief washed over me, though the fact that boys hadn't texted her didn't preclude the possibility that something had happened with one of them. I tapped on Grace's name. Her most recent message, the one that had just come in, read: Are u okay? Sorry I called ur dad but you scared me!! I hope ur not in too much trouble??

My thumb hovered over the screen for a few seconds before I

really crossed the line. Trying to think and talk like Lyla, I typed:
Ugh. So hungover. What happened?

The moving ellipses appeared, then Grace's reply came back
with lightning speed: Um u don't remember?

My heart raced as I typed as fast as I could: No. Tell me.

I held my breath, waiting longer this time.

U passed out. I'm sooo sorry I left u for so long. I didn't know u were
so wasted. What did u drink???? Did you hook up w Finch?

I don't know, I typed.

Grace sent a sad-face emoji, and then, in a separate text: Something I need to tell you . . . There's a pic of u being sent around. IDK who
took it. But I think Finch.

My stomach dropped as I wrote: A picture of what? Do you
have it?

Yeah.

Send it to me.

I steeled myself as an image appeared in the thread, too small
to really make out. I tapped to enlarge it, then zoomed in to see my
little girl, lying on her back on a bed, her breast completely exposed. I wanted to throw up, just as Lyla had last night, but my
nausea turned to rage when I read the caption on it: Looks like she
got her green card.

Fuck, I typed, forgetting I was supposed to be Lyla for a second,
although I was sure she swore to her friends. What the hell does that
mean?

IDK. He's calling you an illegal or something. I guess because ur half
Brazilian?

I'm a fucking American. . . . And even if I weren't . . . I typed, too
infuriated to finish the sentence.

Grace replied: I know. I'm sorry. But at least you look hot!

I shook my head, marveling at the shallowness of the comment, and nearly outed myself—they'd both find out eventually, anyway—but decided against it. My heart simply couldn't take any more.

Gotta go, I typed.

K. TTYL, she wrote back.

I deleted the thread, my head filled with awful images, some of them imagined and one of them very real.

"YOU READY TO tell me what happened?" I asked Lyla a few hours later, when she finally emerged from her bedroom, looking some combination of queasy and embarrassed. I was sitting in our living room, where I'd been waiting for her.

"You already know what happened," she said softly, likely because she and Grace had pieced things together. Her phone was in her hand now. She put it on the coffee table, screen down, then sat next to me, probably to avoid my gaze. "I had too much to drink."

"*One* drink is too many. You're underage," I said.

She slid down on the sofa closer to me, then dropped her head to my shoulder. "I know, Dad," she said with a sigh.

It felt like a ploy, a bid for sympathy. I stayed strong. "So. How much *did* you drink?" I asked.

"Not that much, I swear." Her voice shook a little, though I couldn't tell if it was from emotion or from her hangover.

"Is that typical for you?"

"No, Dad. . . . It's not *typical* for me."

"So is this the first time you've gotten drunk?"

She hesitated, which of course meant that it wasn't, but also that she was considering lying about it. Sure enough, she gave me a straight, unwavering yes.

I stood, circled the sofa, and sat in the chair right across from her. "Okay, so here's the deal," I said, clasping my hands together, my voice firm but not loud. "I need you to be straight with me. I won't punish you if you are, but you have to be one hundred percent honest. Otherwise, your life as you know it is over for a very long time. Got it?"

Lyla nodded but did not meet my gaze.

"When did you have your first drink?" I asked.

"Last summer," she said, her eyes still glued to her lap.

"So you've been drinking since last summer?"

She hesitated for several seconds before nodding. "Yeah. Not all the time or anything. But yeah. Sometimes. Every now and then."

I took a deep breath and said, "Well, let's start right there. With drinking, generally."

"Dad—" she said with a weary sigh. "I know—"

"You know *what*?"

"I know what you're going to say. . . ."

I stood up, calling her bluff. "Okay. Fine, Lyla. Your choice. We'll just go the punishment route here."

As I walked past her, she reached up and tugged on the back of my shirt. "I'm sorry, Dad. Sit down. I'll listen."

I stared at her a beat, then sat back down next to her, thinking once again of the birthday night Beatriz came back. She'd been drunk, of *course*. I made her leave, but she came back the next morning and stayed in town for about a week, promising Lyla she'd move back to Nashville—which I took as more of a threat than a promise. One night things got ugly, and Beatriz told Lyla that her dad had too big a temper problem for her to stay. Then she took off again.

That was seven years ago, and since then, I hadn't been able to keep up with all the places Lyla said her mother had been living (Los Angeles, Atlanta, San Antonio, and back in Rio, to name a few) or the number of times she'd passed through town, graced us with her intoxicated presence, made Lyla a few empty promises, then disappeared again. With the help of a school guidance counselor I talked to following one of Beatriz's more egregious interruptions, I'd vowed to stop denigrating her in front of Lyla, and I had kept my word up until now. This was too important. Besides, I told myself, alcoholism isn't a character flaw—it's a *disease*.

"It's safe to say that your mom's an alcoholic," I began.

Lyla made a clicking sound and rolled her eyes. "Um, yeah. I know that, Dad."

I nodded, choosing my words carefully. "Okay. Well, then, do you also know that alcoholism runs in families?"

"Dad, *please*! I'm not an *alcoholic*," she whined. "I don't drink like *that*. And besides, Mom is way better now. She's been going to meetings."

"Well, she's *still* an alcoholic," I said. "That doesn't go away with meetings. And it will always be in your genes. It will *always* be a danger for you."

"I don't drink too much."

"Well, the 'too much' happens gradually, Lyla. It's a slippery slope. It was for your mother."

"I *know* all of this, Dad—"

I cut her off. "Let me finish. . . . Beyond that, we have more practical concerns . . . meaning all the bad decisions people make when they've been drinking. Take last night, for example. . . . Do you even remember what happened?"

She shrugged and said yes, then added, "Sort of."

"Sort of? So that means there are things you *don't* remember?"

She shrugged again. "I guess."

"Were you . . . with . . . a boy?"

"Da-*ad*," she said, looking appalled.

"Answer me, Lyla."

"There were boys *there,*" she replied. "If that's what you mean."

"No. That's not what I mean. You know what I mean. . . . Did you have sex?" I forced myself to ask. "Could you be pregnant?"

"Dad!" she shouted, putting her hands over face. "Stop! No!"

"So no, you couldn't be pregnant because you didn't have sex? Or no, you couldn't be pregnant because you used birth control?"

She stood up and shouted, "Oh my *God,* Dad. Just go ahead and ground me! I'm not having this conversation with you!"

"Sit down, Lyla," I said as sternly as I could without actually yelling. "And don't you *dare* talk to me like that."

She bit her lip and sank back into the sofa.

"Did you have sex last night?" I asked.

"No, Dad," she said. "I didn't."

"How can you be sure if you don't remember?"

"Dad. I'm sure. Okay? Just stop."

I took a deep breath, then cut to the chase. "Okay, then. Who is *Finch*?" I asked.

She stared down at her fingernails, her lower lip quivering. "I *know* what you did, Dad. I know you talked to Grace on my phone. She sent me screenshots. I read the whole thing. Just admit it."

I confessed with a nod, bracing myself for a self-righteous tirade about her right to privacy. But she somehow exercised a modicum of restraint.

"Who is he?" I said.

"He's a senior," she said.

"Does he go to your school?"

She nodded.

"Well, then," I said. "I'm going to be letting the Windsor administration know about this."

"Oh my *God,* Dad," she gasped, jumping up, her eyes wide and frantic. "Don't do that. *Please!*"

"I have to—"

"You can't! Please . . . I won't drink ever again! And I'll forgive you for snooping through my phone! And you can ground me, whatever. . . . Just please, *please* don't turn him in." She was now shouting, leaning over the coffee table, her hands in prayer position.

I was accustomed to her melodrama (she was, after all, a teenaged girl) and knew I'd get pushback. But something about her reaction seemed irrationally over the top. I ran through the mental calculations, wondering whether there was more to the story than I knew. I asked if she was telling me everything; she promised that she was. "It's just not that big of a deal," she added.

"It *is* a big deal. It's a *huge* deal," I said, as calmly as I could. "And something needs to be done about . . ."

She shook her head, now in tears. *Real* tears—I could always tell when she was fake crying. "No. It doesn't, Dad. It really doesn't. . . . Can't we just drop it?"

"No, Lyla. We can't just drop it."

"Why, Dad? Why not? God! I just want this to go away. Please. Can't we just let it go away and not make it a bigger deal than it needs to be?" she begged.

I looked into her eyes, wanting to stop her tears, give in. After all, I told myself, she had enough challenges in her life. They weren't insurmountable, of course, nor were they holding her back in any major way. But they were *there*, and they were *real*. For one, she was a carpenter's daughter at a rich-ass school filled with entitled kids. For another, her mother sucked. So of *course* I was tempted to take the path of least resistance and give her what she wanted now. But was that best for Lyla in the long run? Didn't I owe my daughter more? Didn't I need to show her how important it was to stand up for herself and for what's *right*? And besides, even if I caved, would anything really "go away"? Or would the problem just resurface, sometime later when we least expected it, the way her mother always did?

I suddenly thought of Beatriz again—her face on the night I told her it was better for Lyla to have *no* mother than *her* as a mother. It wasn't true; I shouldn't have said it; and I wished so deeply that we had her around now. That we weren't so alone.

"We'll see, Lyla," I said, often my go-to answer. Then I stood and told her I'd be back later, pushing down all my terrible, guilty emotions and focusing on what needed to be done. For my daughter's sake.

"Where are you going?" she asked, her voice high and sad.

"To the workshop," I said, pretending to be matter-of-fact. "You might want to drink a lot of water."

chapter five

NINA

First thing Monday morning, I got the call I'd been both expecting and praying I wouldn't receive. Although I had rare occasion to talk to him, Walter Quarterman's name was programmed into my phone. I saw it appear on the screen, but I was too scared to answer. Instead, I waited, then listened to the voicemail he left, asking if Kirk and I could please come in and speak with him that afternoon about a "serious issue that has arisen."

Walter, or Mr. Q as the kids called him, was the long-tenured and enigmatic headmaster of Windsor Academy. On the surface, he was a stereotypically serious academic with white hair, a bookish beard, and wire-rimmed glasses. But at some point, we'd all discovered that he'd been quite the hippie activist in his former life, the kids unearthing (and publishing in the student newspaper) a photo of Mr. Q protesting the Vietnam War at Yale, his beard darker and longer, his fist in the air as he carried a sign that read: HEY, HEY LBJ! HOW MANY KIDS DID YOU KILL TODAY? It made him something of a cult figure with the students, though many of the parents appreciated his politics less. In fact, Walter took some heat during the 2016 presidential campaign, when he made a few not-so-subtle anti–Donald Trump references about wanting to build bridges at Windsor, not walls, irritating many in our conservative, predominantly Republican enclave of Nashville.

Kirk was among that miffed contingent, and he was even more riled when the subject of transgender bathrooms was raised later that year. I understood where he was coming from, at least as a practical matter, as there was only one transgender student at Windsor that we knew of. But mostly I was all about taking the path of least resistance, whether at Windsor or in our community, and especially with my husband. Only occasionally did I take a real stand with Kirk, at least on anything smacking of political correctness, such as my insistence that we make our holiday cards as inclusive as possible.

"But 'Happy Holidays' sounds so cold and corporate," Kirk had said when the debate first arose several years back. I resisted the urge to tell him outright that he needed to stay in his lane. He did our finances, and I handled cards and gifting, holidays and decorating, and really anything related to celebrations or making our lives feel more special. It was a nineteen-fifties sort of split, but it had always worked for us.

"Okay. What about 'Merry and bright' or 'Comfort and joy' or 'Peace on earth'?" I had thrown out to appease him.

"I hate all of those things." He'd smirked, obviously trying to be funny.

I'd smiled—because he *was* pretty funny—but pointed out that we had Jewish friends. My own *dad* was Jewish.

"Not really," Kirk had said.

"He's as Jewish as you are Christian," I'd said.

"Yes, but *we're* sending the card. And *we're* Christian. Get how that works?" Kirk had asked with a trace of condescension.

I'd dug in. "But we're wishing *them* a happy holiday. You

wouldn't think it bizarre if the Kaplans sent us a card wishing us a 'Happy Hanukkah'?"

"I wouldn't care," Kirk had said with a shrug. "I don't care if someone sends me a Kwanzaa card if that's what they want to do. But I don't want anyone to tell *me* what to do, either."

Maybe that was it in a nutshell, I remember thinking. Kirk *really* didn't like to be told what to do, a trait that had become more extreme over the years. It was probably a function of getting older— I think we all become exaggerated versions of ourselves, and Kirk had always been independent and strong-willed. But sometimes I worried that it had more to do with his love of power—power that seemed to increase along with financial wealth. I'd recently called him out on this, accusing him of having the "old-rich-white-guy mentality," pointing out that it was often *that* guy who was cutting a line at the airport, or blathering away on his cellphone after the flight attendant asked for devices to be put away, or pretending not to see you when you were anxiously trying to merge in traffic (all of which I'd observed Kirk do on a fairly regular basis). His response was simply that at forty-six, he wasn't yet "old."

All of this is to say that I wasn't completely surprised at his reaction when I called him at work to tell him about Walter's voicemail.

"Does it have to be *today*?" he said.

"Um, yes. I think it does," I said. "Our child is in trouble."

"I know that," he said, tapping on his keyboard. "We're the ones who spent the entire day yesterday crafting his punishment. Does Walt know how hard we're coming down on Finch?"

"No. Of course not," I said with a loud sigh, thinking that it was *Walter,* not *Walt.* "Because as I told you, he left a voicemail—I haven't spoken to him yet."

"Well, we need to tell him that—"

"Kirk," I said. "Banning Finch from all social interaction—"

"And driving, except to school," Kirk said.

"And yes, driving his *Mercedes SUV* anywhere but school—"

"Why do you say it like that, Nina? You agreed on buying that car for him."

It was an ancient battle. It had been nearly two years since I had argued it was outrageously excessive to buy a sixteen-year-old a G-wagon, and Kirk had replied that it was excessive only if we couldn't afford it—and we could. I remember how he had deftly compared it to our furniture—and my wardrobe, saying some might consider those things "excessive," too. At the time, I was flustered—because he was right, at least on the surface. Only later did I distinguish the difference. Namely, that I wasn't a teenager. I was an *adult*. For Finch, a car like his was a windfall, an indulgence, a tacit seal of entitlement. Moreover, I often had the feeling, with both Kirk and Finch, that they wanted things for the status of owning them, and I can honestly say that I'd never, not once, purchased *anything* with the goal of impressing *anyone*. I just *loved* design and fashion. For *myself*.

"I know I agreed to get him the car," I said. "And I regret it. . . . Don't you see that it might have contributed to this?"

"No," Kirk said. "I don't."

"Not at *all*? Don't you think spoiling him has had a cumulative effect?"

I heard more clicking as he mumbled, "What happened Saturday night has nothing to do with being spoiled. It was just stupid. . . ." His voice trailed off, and I could tell he was only half focused on our conversation.

"Kirk. What are you *doing*?"

He launched into a technical explanation of his current con-sulting gig—something about a CRM implementation.

"Well, I'm sorry this is interfering with your work, but do you think you could stop doing it for a few minutes and focus on Finch?"

"Yeah, Nina. That's fine," he said with a sigh. "But we've been over this a hundred times. All day yesterday. What he did was wrong. And he needs to be punished. He *is* being punished. But he's a good kid. He just made a mistake. And the car and our life-style choices have nothing to do with the poor judgment he exer-cised on Saturday night. He's a typical high school boy. Boys do dumb things sometimes."

"Regardless," I said. "We still have to deal with it. . . . I still need to return Walter's call."

"Okay. So then go call him," he said, as if *I* were the one trying *his* patience.

"I'm about to," I said. "But I wanted to check with you first. What time is your flight?" I couldn't remember the details of his trip, whether it was for business or pleasure or, most likely, plea-sure disguised as business.

"Three-thirty," he replied.

"Great. So you have time."

"Not really. I have a meeting and a couple calls before then."

I took a deep breath. "So should I just go ahead and tell Walter that you're unavailable because you have more important things to do today?"

"Jesus, Nina," he said, now on speakerphone. "No, you shouldn't tell him *that*. You should tell him that we are aware of the situation. We are handling it at home. But of course we would be happy to discuss it with him. However, nothing works for our schedule today. I could come in later in the week. . . . Or we could do a conference call on my way to the airport?"

"I don't think Walter wants to do a *conference call,*" I said. "He asked us to come *in* and *see* him. Today."

"Well. As I said. I cannot. So maybe you could just go alone."

"Are you serious?"

"I trust you to handle this one and represent us both."

I shook my head in disbelief. Was he being passive-aggressive? Or was he burying his head in the sand? Or did he actually think that what Finch had done was not *that* big a deal?

"Don't you realize what's happening here?" I finally asked. "Finch is in *trouble.* With Walter Quarterman. With Windsor Academy. He's in trouble for posting a sexually explicit photo with a *racist* caption. This is real." ·

"C'mon, Nina. Stop exaggerating. The picture was not sexually explicit. Or racist."

"Well, I disagree. And more important, I think Walter disagrees. Clearly he thinks there should be consequences to this post—"

"Would you please stop saying that? He didn't *post* anything. He sent it to a few friends," Kirk said.

"What difference does *that* make?" I shouted. "He might as well have posted it! Everyone forwarded it around. You know a kid got thrown out of Windsor for sending a picture of his penis—"

"C'mon, Nina. This wasn't a *dick* pic. It was a little side boob."

"Kirk! First of all, this was no *side* boob. Everyone and their grandmother knows that it comes down to whether or not the nipple is showing. But let's put that aside. How about the *racist* caption?"

"It wasn't *that* racist."

"Like not being *that* pregnant?"

"There are degrees of racism. There are no degrees of pregnancy. You either are or you aren't," he said. "And this is a classic example of political correctness run amok."

"'Looks like she got her green card'?" I said slowly. "You think that's okay, Kirk?"

"No. I don't think it's *okay*. I think it's extremely rude, and yes, it's a *little* racist. . . . And I'm very disappointed in him. Very. You know that. Finch knows that. But I don't think it rises to the level of me changing my flight so that *both* of his parents can sit through being chastised by the raging liberal headmaster of Windsor Academy."

"This isn't about politics, Kirk," I said, wondering how I seemed to be losing ground since yesterday. It was as if work was more important to him than Finch.

"I know that. But Walt will do his best to turn it into something political. Just wait and see—"

"You know Windsor has an honor code—"

"But Finch didn't *break* the honor code, Nina," he said. "You and I read it together. There was no lying. No cheating. No stealing. It was an off-color remark, but he sent it *privately*—and he wasn't on school property. He wasn't using a school device, and he wasn't on their network. I really think that this is being blown out of proportion—and everyone is overreacting."

"Okay," I snapped. "So what you're telling me is that I won't be seeing you at the meeting?"

"Not if it's today," he said. "Because I'm not changing my flight."

"Well, it's good to be clear about what, exactly, your priorities are. I'll tell Walter you were otherwise engaged, and I'll try to remember to send you an update on our son's future," I said, slamming down the phone.

* * *

I DIDN'T KNOW if it was the hang up that did the trick, or whether I'd gotten through to him about the stakes involved, or whether he simply didn't trust me to handle the meeting *his* way. But after I'd CCed him on an exchange with Walter's assistant in which we'd scheduled a two o'clock meeting, Kirk pulled into the Windsor guest parking lot about five seconds after I did. We made eye contact through our car windows, and he gave me a conciliatory wave. I forced a smile back, still pissed, but also intensely relieved that I wasn't going into that school alone.

"Hi, honey," he said a little sheepishly after we both got out of our cars and stepped onto the sidewalk. He leaned in to kiss my cheek, resting his hand on my back. "I'm sorry I upset you."

"Thanks," I said, softening slightly. It wasn't often that Kirk actually apologized—so it always meant something to me. "So you got a later flight?"

"Yeah, but I'm in coach. Business class was fully booked," he said.

Oh, cry me a river, I thought, as we walked toward the entrance of the building, its stone Gothic architecture seeming more foreboding than it ever had, including when I brought Finch here a dozen years ago for his admissions interview.

Kirk opened the door for me, and we entered the quiet, overly air-conditioned lobby, which was more like a foyer, decorated with antiques, oil paintings, and Oriental rugs. The longtime receptionist, Sharon, looked up from a file folder to say hello. She had to know who we were by now, but she pretended that she didn't.

"Hello. We're here to see Mr. Quarterman," I said, my stomach in knots.

Sharon nodded briskly, then pointed to the clipboard on the counter in front of her. "If you'd sign in, please?"

I carefully printed our names, just as Walter entered behind us, carrying an old-school leather briefcase with a hue that verged toward orange.

"Kirk. Nina. Hello. Perfect timing," he said, his expression as inscrutable as Sharon's.

We said hello back, and he quickly thanked us for coming in on such short notice.

"No problem," Kirk said lightly.

"Of course," I said, nodding.

"Let's head to my office?" Walter said, gesturing down the hall.

I nodded again as he led us down a long corridor. Along the way, he made measured small talk, first remarking on the speed of the passing school year, then apologizing for the construction noise coming from the renovation of the athletic facilities across the courtyard.

"It's looking good," Kirk said.

"Yes. Still in Phase One, though. We have a ways to go," Walter said.

"How's the capital campaign coming along? Have we reached our goal yet?" Kirk asked. I knew his question was purposeful, and I had the feeling Walter knew it, too.

"We have," he replied. "Thank you again for your very generous contribution to the campaign."

"Of course," Kirk said, as I thought of the form letter we'd received thanking us for our pledge, along with the hand-scrawled note from Walter at the bottom: *We appreciate you! Go Wildcats!*

A few seconds of silence later, we rounded the corner into Walter's office. I realized it was the first time in all these years that I'd actually been inside it, and for a few seconds, I just took in the details—the dark wood ceiling beams. The wall of books. The large desk covered with stacks of papers and more books. Then, as we walked the whole way in, I spotted Finch, sitting forlornly on a wingback chair, wearing his school uniform of khakis, a white button-down, and a navy blazer. His hands were folded in his lap, his head lowered.

"Hello, Finch," Walter said.

"Hello, Mr. Quarterman," Finch said, finally looking up. "Mrs. Peters said I should just wait here for you. That's why I'm here. . . ." His voice trailed off.

Before Walter could answer, Kirk chimed in with "We didn't know Finch would be joining us." It was clear that he didn't approve of the decision—or at least resented that we hadn't been warned ahead of time.

"Yes," Walter said. "I thought I mentioned that to Nina in my message."

"No. I don't believe you did," Kirk answered for us. "But that's okay."

Walter's secretary appeared in the doorway, interrupting the awkwardness to offer us a beverage. "Coffee? Tea? Water?" she asked.

We all declined the offer, and Walter gestured to the empty chairs flanking Finch's. As we sat, he pulled up a fourth chair, completing our circle. He then crossed his legs at the knee, cleared his throat, and said, "So. Is it safe to assume we all know why we're here?" His voice rose in a question.

Kirk responded with a loud *yes* that made me cringe.

Walter looked at Finch, who said, "Yes, sir."

"So I don't need to show anyone the photo that Finch took— and sent—of another Windsor student? You've both seen it?" he said, glancing at me, then Kirk.

I nodded, my throat too tight and dry to speak, wishing I had asked for that water, as Kirk said, "Yes. We're unfortunately familiar with the image. Finch came home Saturday night and shared it with us. He was very contrite."

I glanced at him, taken aback by his mischaracterization and more so that he would lie in front of Finch. Then again, I wasn't that shocked. He'd told plenty of white lies before. Come to think of it, I had, too, although I think in circumstances much more innocuous than this.

"So you're familiar with the caption he penned as well?" Walter said.

"Yes. Though obviously he didn't *pen* anything *per se*!" Kirk chuckled.

Walter flashed a tight-lipped smile. "Figure of speech. But you did see it?"

"Yes," I echoed quietly, shame now overpowering my nervousness.

Walter's hands came together prayer-style and he raised his fingertips to his lips, looking reflective. A thick silence filled the office. I shifted in my seat and took a deep breath, waiting.

"Well. I think, unfortunately, Finch's words speak for themselves. But I wanted to give him a chance to explain here, to all of us, any context. Perhaps we are missing something? A piece to the story?"

We all looked at Finch. I felt the simultaneous instinct to both protect and strangle him. Seconds passed before he shrugged and said, "No, sir. Not really."

"Is there anything at all you want to tell us about what happened?"

I prayed that he wouldn't lie, that he'd instead launch into a heartfelt apology for mocking a defenseless female peer, hurling a racist insult at her, insinuating that she was beneath him or somehow did not belong.

But when he finally opened his mouth, he simply said, "Um. No, sir. I really don't have an explanation. It was just a joke. . . . I wasn't thinking. . . ."

Kirk cut in, saying Finch's name, his brows sharply raised.

"Yes?" Finch said, looking at his dad.

"I'm sure you have *something* more to say about this?" It was the ultimate in leading questions.

Finch cleared his throat and tried again. "Well, I don't really have anything else to explain . . . except that I didn't mean for it to get around the way it did. . . . And I really didn't mean it as an insult to Lyla. . . . I was just trying . . . to be funny. It was just a joke. . . . But I see now that it wasn't funny. I actually realized it wasn't funny that night. When I told my parents about it."

My insides clenched as I listened to my son follow his father's lead and skew the truth—no, flat-out *lie*—and noted that he'd yet to utter the word *sorry*. Kirk must have noticed it, too, because he said, "And you're very, *very* sorry. Right, son?"

"Oh, God—gosh—yes. I'm so sorry I did that. And wrote that. I didn't mean anything by it." Finch inhaled, as if he had something more to add, but Kirk cut in again.

"So, as you said, Walt, the photo speaks for itself. It was in poor taste. It was wrong. But I think what Finch is trying to tell us is that there wasn't further malicious intent. Right, Finch?"

"Definitely," Finch said, nodding. "Absolutely not."

Kirk continued, "And we want you to know that Finch is being severely punished at home for his lapse of judgment. I can assure you of that, Walt."

"I understand," Walter said. "But unfortunately, the situation is a little more complicated and requires more than simply doling out a private punishment."

"Oh?" Kirk said, adjusting himself in his chair, literally shifting into what I knew to be his offensive mode. "And why is *that*?"

Walter inhaled audibly through his nose, then exhaled through his mouth. "Well. For one thing, Lyla Volpe's father called about the photo. He's understandably quite upset."

His use of the word *understandably* was not lost on me, but Kirk pressed on. "And for another?"

"Well," Walter said calmly. "For another, Finch's actions were in contravention of our core values as expressed in Windsor's Code of Conduct."

"But this didn't happen at Windsor," Kirk argued. "It happened at a friend's home. On private property . . . And . . . and is this girl even a minority?"

I stared at him, mouth agape, stunned by the question.

"The Code of Conduct does not have geographical restrictions. It applies to all students enrolled at Windsor, wherever they may be," Walter said calmly. "And yes, Lyla is part Latina, actually."

Finch looked appalled by his father's question, too, but then I wondered if it was actually just panic. Maybe the direness of the situation was beginning to sink in for him. He turned to Walter and said, "Mr. Quarterman . . . am I getting suspended?"

"I don't know, Finch. But if these charges go forward to the Honor Council, and I see no reason why they wouldn't, the issue of suspension will ultimately be decided by that group."

"Who's on this Honor Council?" Kirk asked.

"Eight students. And eight faculty members."

"And? How does this work?" Kirk pressed. "Would Finch have representation? I assume we can bring in our lawyer?"

Walter shook his head. "No. That's not the procedure we use for these matters. . . ."

"So he doesn't get a *fair* trial?"

"It's not a trial. And we like to think that it's very fair, actually."

Kirk sighed, looking extremely put out. "And if he's ultimately suspended? What's involved with that? What are we talking, exactly?"

"That varies. But if Finch were to be suspended, he would not be allowed to walk at the graduation ceremony. And we would be required to notify the colleges to which he's been accepted of his suspension."

"He just got into Princeton," Kirk said.

Walter nodded and said yes, he was aware. He then added his congratulations.

"Thank you," Kirk and Finch said in unison. Kirk added, "So then what?"

"I'm not sure what you mean."

"I mean, regarding Princeton?" Kirk asked.

Mr. Quarterman raised his palms and shrugged, looking conspicuously indifferent. "How Princeton handles the news of Finch's suspension would be entirely up to them."

Finch's eyes widened. "Could they un-accept me?"

"Revoke your acceptance?" Walter said. "Of course they could. They're a private institution, just as we are. They can do as they see fit under the circumstances."

"Wow," Finch said under his breath.

"Yes," Walter said. "So as you see . . . there could be very serious ramifications."

"Oh, for God's sake!" Kirk shouted. "For a thirty-second lapse of judgment he could lose eighteen *years* of hard work?"

"Kirk," Walter said, his voice and posture growing subtly more imposing. "We don't know the outcome of this yet. And we also don't know what Princeton would do if Finch were suspended.

However, I'm sure you understand the seriousness of that picture, as well as the racist nature of your son's words."

There it was. The R word. I'd said it myself—and aloud to Kirk and Finch—but it was so much worse hearing it from another. My eyes welled up.

Kirk took a deep breath, as if regrouping. "Okay. Well, is there any way to handle this privately? Our son's *entire* future is at stake here, Walt."

"The Honor Council *is* private. All proceedings would remain completely confidential."

"Right. But I mean . . . *privately* privately?"

"You mean avoid the Honor Council altogether?" Walter said, raising his brow.

"Yes. I mean . . . what if we talked to the girl's parents?"

Walter began to answer, then stopped, then started again. "Calling Lyla's father is up to you," he said. "I'm not sure that would change anything. . . . But in my experience, sincere apologies never hurt in these kinds of situations . . . in life, *generally*."

In that moment, I could tell that Kirk had just detected a path to getting his way. I knew the expression well—the glimmer in his eyes, the way his face sort of relaxed. "Okay, then," he said, rubbing his palms together. "We'll call her parents—and take it from here."

Walter nodded, looking apprehensive at best. "She lives with her father," he said.

"Okay. I assume his number's in the directory?" Kirk asked, shifting in his seat, glancing at his watch.

"It is," Walter replied.

I struggled to think of something meaningful to say, something to offset Kirk's sudden cavalier tone, but he seemed to be on a roll I couldn't curtail.

"Okay, great," he said, standing abruptly. "Well, I hate to dash like this, but I have a flight to catch. I've already pushed it back once today for this."

"I'm sorry you had to change your travel plans," Walter said, not sounding the slightest bit sorry.

The two of us stood as Kirk said, "No worries. Not a problem at all."

"Good. Well, then. Thank you all for coming," Walter said, shaking my hand, then Kirk's. Finally, he turned to Finch and said, "Okay, young man. You may return to class."

"Yes, sir," Finch said, getting to his feet. He glanced at his father, then stood up a little straighter.

"Anything else you want to say here, son?" Kirk prodded him.

Finch nodded, took a deep breath, then shifted his gaze from his father to Walter. "I just want to say . . . that I'm very sorry, again, for all the trouble I've caused, and I'm ready to take the consequences, whatever they may be."

His words sounded sincere, and I had to believe that he *was* genuinely remorseful. After all, he was my son. He just *had* to be sorry.

But as Walter nodded and patted him once on the back, I caught a glint of determination in Finch's eyes. Something that channeled his father and made me shiver a little inside.

chapter six

LYLA

It was official. I hated my life. Like literally everything about it. I mean, I knew it could be way worse. I could be homeless or have a terminal disease or live in a country where militants throw acid on girls when they try to go to school. But beyond those kinds of true tragedies, it was really hard to find anything to be grateful for lately.

For starters, my dad had busted me for drinking and was really upset and angry and disappointed in me (the disappointed part hurt the worst). Second, there was a photo of my boob, nipple and all, being passed all around school. But I probably could have gotten over those two things. Because I knew Dad would eventually forgive me, and the photo, while humiliating, at least wasn't *ugly*. It was actually sort of artsy and cool, even though I'd never have admitted that to anyone. Even my best friend, Grace, said I looked good in it. My hair was arranged perfectly on the bed. And my black slip dress was super cute, worth every dollar of my babysitting money. Honestly, the shot almost looked like I posed for it, minus the nipple. The nipple was what made it so horrible. And the caption about the green card, which was so rude to immigrants. It made me think of the Sayed family, whose backyard abutted ours

69

and who were just about the nicest people you could ever imagine. They'd actually become American citizens a couple years back (I babysat their toddler during their ceremony), but I knew they still got anti-Muslim you-don't-belong-here type comments from a few losers in our neighborhood. Mostly, though, we lived near really cool people—lots of artists and musicians—people who would never say something so offensive and bigoted.

So yeah, I got why Dad was upset about the nipple and caption. I did. But the part that really crushed my heart was that *Finch Browning* was responsible for it all. The boy I'd been obsessed with for going on *two years*. Finch was a popular senior—way out of my league—and had a beautiful girlfriend named Polly, who was as perfect as he was. In other words, it was a waste of time for me to like him, even before this happened. But you can't help the way you feel—and my feelings were real. Grace, who is very protective of me, sometimes annoyingly so, tried to tell me that it was just a stupid crush. After all, she said, I didn't really know him. But I felt like I *did* know him, that's how closely I observed him, day in and day out. I knew, for example, that Finch was on the quiet, serious side compared to the other loud boys in his friend group, but he could be really funny in a sarcastic, low-key way. I knew that he was very smart and in all honors classes. His locker was insanely organized, and the inside of his car was clean and neat (I may have peeked in it a time or two), and he was never late or rushing to class at second bell. He had his shit together. Of course his executive functioning, as our guidance counselors called it, wasn't the main attraction. As is often the case with a crush, there was just something about him that drew me to him. Something I couldn't put my finger on.

Finch was just so, *so* cute. I loved his wavy blond hair and his deep blue eyes and the confident way he walked and how hot he looked in his basketball uniform (although he managed to look really good in his school uniform, too). Mostly, though, I loved the way he looked at me. I remembered the first time he ever gave me that look. It was last year, on about the third day of school, back when I was brand new. We were in the dining hall, both of us putting up our trays after lunch, and he gave me a double take, followed by a slight smile. It melted me, and it wasn't the last time it happened. There was something undeniable between us—something that wasn't one-sided. A little charge of electricity.

About three months ago, when I'd finally admitted my feelings to Grace, and told her about Finch's ongoing eye contact with me, she tried to say that he was just flirty that way, and that I shouldn't get my hopes up. He would never break up with Polly. But even she had to admit that it meant *something* when he started following me on Instagram, going back and liking several of my older selfies. At the very least, we agreed, he thought I was pretty.

Then, last Friday, we got the invite to Beau's party. Once again, we were in the dining hall, only this time Finch came up to me and Grace as we stood in the salad-bar line.

"Hey," he said, looking right at me.

"Hey," I said back, dying inside.

"What're you girls doing tomorrow night?" he asked.

I started to tell him the truth, which was absolutely nothing, but Grace gave him some other answer about various options we had.

"Well, Beau's having a few people over. If you want to stop by, that'd be cool."

"Yeah, we'll try to swing by," Grace said, as if we'd scored plenty of invites to senior parties.

I followed her lead and said, "Yeah. We'll try, for sure."

* * *

71

THE NEXT DAY, we continued to play it cool as we got ready for the party over FaceTime, holding up various outfits while we strategized what I would tell my dad. I certainly didn't tell him about the party. Dad is stricter than her parents, and I couldn't risk that he might tell me I couldn't go, or God forbid, call Beau's parents, who I felt fairly confident did not know about their son's gathering. I'd heard plenty of rumors about how much Beau got away with.

Predictably, I had some trouble getting out of the house, and I almost overplayed my hand by telling Dad I was going to be studying. He totally called bullshit on that but ultimately let me go, just giving his usual overprotective spiel about being careful.

And I *was* careful. At first. So was Grace. We only had one drink while we got dressed at her house—Chardonnay that we drank from stemmed glasses. It was all very grown-up and civilized, and we vowed that we wouldn't get drunk or make asses out of ourselves.

But then we got to Beau's, and I felt so nervous and giddy in Finch's company outside of school that I sort of forgot my promise to myself and started downing Jack and Cokes.

At one point, Grace and I stood in the kitchen, covertly watching Finch and his friends across the room, cracking up and ripping on each other while they played a variation of Uno as a drinking game. Every few minutes, Polly would come over and sit on the arm of his chair, leaning down to whisper something in his ear or rub his neck. She was wearing a light denim miniskirt, a white tank top, and gladiator sandals, the straps winding halfway up her long, thin calves. Her strawberry-blond hair was in a loose French braid, and she wore turquoise earrings and a leather choker. I was so jealous of her that it hurt—literally gave me chest pains—and I told Grace I wanted to leave. Then I caught Finch looking over at me.

He smiled, and I smiled back. Grace saw it, too, and actually got excited for me. "Oh my God," she said. "He's flirting with you right in front of Polly!"

"I know," I said, still making eye contact with him, my heart racing.

A few minutes later, after Polly had sucked Finch into some kind of side drama, Grace and I went upstairs and joined a few random people who were chilling in Beau's bedroom, vaping and listening to stoner music. We took a couple of hits, and also drank a beer from the stash in Beau's bathtub, but Grace eventually declared the mood "way too mellow" and went back downstairs. Feeling a little dizzy and tired, I told her I was going to stay put for a bit, then curled up on Beau's bed so that I could close my eyes for a few seconds. Grace said okay and promised to be right back. And that's the last thing I really remember before I dozed off.

The next thing I knew I was on my bathroom floor, puking and crying next to my dad.

chapter seven

TOM

All the following night, Lyla continued to beg me not to, in her words, "narc on Finch." She threw out every rationale imaginable. That I was blowing things out of proportion. That Finch was usually a nice guy and did we really want to ruin his future? (Um, yes, I did.) That if I "made a big deal out of it," it would only mean more eyes on the photo, and she might even end up getting in trouble for drinking at the party. (Her most solid points, but risks I was willing to take in exchange for simple justice.)

I pretended to give it some thought, vacillating for a second or two here and there, but on Monday morning, when we pulled into the circular driveway in front of her school filled with all those entitled rich kids, I knew there was no way in hell I could just drop it. What kind of message about her self-worth would that send to her?

"Have a great day, Dad," Lyla said, getting out of the car, pleading with her eyes.

"You, too, honey," I said, looking away.

She continued to stare at me, then said under her breath, "Please don't call the school today, Dad."

"I love you," I said in response.

"Love you, too, Dad," she said, closing the door. I watched her walk a few steps before I drove away, feeling nauseated.

After her drop-off, I drove to my workshop, but I remained in my car as I looked up the number for Windsor's headmaster. Lyla referred to him as Mr. Q and seemed to indicate that she liked him, but the few times I'd met him, I'd gotten an intellectual, elitist vibe. So I braced myself for the worst-case scenario as I entered his number on my phone. I couldn't imagine him outright siding with Finch, but I know the way the world works. For one, birds of a feather. For another, guys like Finch always get away with things—and a lifetime accumulation of no consequences was how we probably got to this point.

My jaw clenched as I listened to the sound of his phone ringing. A woman answered. "Mr. Quarterman's office," she said.

"Is he there, please?" I said.

She informed me that Mr. Quarterman was in a meeting, then asked if she could take a message.

"Yes. You can," I said tersely. "This is Tom Volpe. I'm Lyla Volpe's father. She's a sophomore."

"Okaaay. And this is . . . regarding . . . ?" she said.

I bristled. To be fair, this woman had no way of knowing that I was calling about a serious matter. But her blasé tone still annoyed me. I took a breath, then said, "This is regarding an offensive photo of my daughter taken by another Windsor student."

"I beg your pardon?" she said, as if *I'd* just offended *her*.

My blood pressure starting to soar, I talked with exaggerated slowness. "One of Windsor's students . . . a boy by the name of *Finch Browning*, took a photo of my daughter, Lyla, at a party over the weekend. . . . She was asleep, and her breast was exposed," I said. "He then proceeded to give the photo a *racist* caption before sending it along to his buddies. I am beyond livid and would like to discuss this matter with Walter Quarterman. *Today.*"

"Yes. Yes, of *course,* Mr. Volpe," she said, her whole tone changing into one of grave concern. "Let me track him down right away. What number is best for you?"

I gave her my cell, then hung up without saying goodbye.

Within moments, my phone rang.

"Hello. This is Tom," I said.

"Mr. Volpe?"

"Yes."

"This is Walter Quarterman. Returning your call." His voice was softer than I remembered from his school persona, almost in the category of gentle. It disarmed me but not enough to offer any niceties. Instead, I got right down to business, telling the whole story and sparing no details, including the fact that Lyla had been consuming alcohol. He did not interrupt once and waited until I was completely finished before he told me he had actually already seen the photograph, that another parent had sent it to him over the weekend.

I felt a strange mix of relief and rage. I was glad he had seen it—it was very difficult to capture the essence of the offensive image with mere words. But I was incrementally more pissed that he, and others, had seen my little girl in such a state. And why hadn't *he* called me *first*?

"And you saw his caption, too?" I asked.

"Yes," he said. "It was appalling. I'm so sorry."

I eased up just a bit as he went on to tell me he'd already made a call to Finch's parents. "I can assure you that we will get to the bottom of this, and address it appropriately." He spoke calmly but not condescendingly.

"Thank you," I said.

"I do need to inform you of one thing, Mr. Volpe," he said. "I hesitate to even bring this up, because it's so ancillary to the issue at hand, but are you aware that drinking, even off campus, is against Windsor's Code of Conduct?"

"Yes," I said, although I'd done a little research last night and knew from reading the online Windsor handbook that there was no formal punishment for the first documented use of drugs or alcohol, simply a warning that went into a student's file. This was Lyla's first offense and, in my mind, would only reinforce our discussion about drinking and serve as a deterrent for the future. I said as much to Quarterman, then added, "I want you to know I take drinking very seriously."

"Thank you," he said. "You'd be surprised, Tom, that many parents really do not. . . . It makes things much more difficult when students are getting mixed signals from the adults in their lives."

"Yes," I said. I hesitated, then added, "Lyla's mother is an alcoholic."

"I'm sorry," he said, actually *sounding* sorry.

"It's fine," I said. "She's not in our lives. . . . It's just . . . part of my daughter's medical history. . . . That's why I mention it."

"Of course."

"And as a result of her drinking, you should be aware that my daughter was *passed out* when that photo was taken of her. It wasn't as if she posed for it. . . . She was unconscious . . . completely vulnerable."

"I know, Tom."

"In some ways, the caption actually upsets me more than the photo," I said, because if I was being painfully honest with myself, I could imagine taking a similar shot when I was a dipshit teenager—if I'd grown up in a cellphone generation, had a buzz, and seen a girl with her boob hanging out of her dress. The caption, though, was a different story altogether. It was not only ignorant—Lyla was as American as the boy was—but also offensive. "It was way out of line."

"I agree one hundred percent."

"He needs to be punished."

"Yes. And it is very likely that he will be."

It was the first red flag in the conversation, and I could feel my usual cynicism kicking in along with a dose of self-loathing for letting him manipulate me this far into our conversation. *"Likely?"* I said. "I'm sorry. Why is there *any* question? We both saw the photo. We both read the caption. There seem to be almost no facts in dispute here."

"Yes, yes. I understand, Tom," he said. "But we have a process. . . . We need to hear his side of the story, whatever that is. We need to trust the process and allow him a defense."

"There's *no* defense for what that boy did to Lyla."

"I agree. But we still have to get all the facts. . . . And putting Finch aside for a moment, I just . . ." He paused. "I just want you to understand there could be some unpleasant implications for Lyla as all of this unfolds over the next few days and weeks."

"You mean the warning about drinking that'll go in her file?" I asked, wondering if I'd read the handbook incorrectly. I told myself that it didn't matter. I had to do this.

"No. . . . Well, I mean *yes*, there is that. But I'm referring to the greater, unavoidable *practical* repercussions. For Lyla. Unfortunately and very unfairly, there sometimes are some of those."

"Repercussions? Such as *what*?" I said. "Are we talking *social* ramifications?"

"Yes. From the other students. Her classmates," Quarterman said, clearing his throat. "It isn't right—but there could be some backlash. It has happened before."

"Are you saying Finch is some big man on campus? And it might damage Lyla's popularity?" I said, my voice rising as I got worked up again.

"Well, I'm not sure I'd phrase it like that. But yes, it could create some tricky terrain for Lyla. And it will certainly add fuel to the fire with respect to the photo. Is that something that you and your daughter are prepared to deal with?"

"Yes," I said. "For one thing, the photo is already out there. You know how quickly these things spread. I'm sure the whole school has seen it already. For another, Lyla made a mistake by drinking, but she has *nothing* to be ashamed of. This boy is the one who should be ashamed. This image says way more about *him* than *her*. That's the message that I hope Windsor will send to the students and parents at the school should they choose to insert themselves."

"I hear you, Tom. I really do," Mr. Quarterman said. "And believe me, I am most certainly not trying to talk you out of anything. Not at all. I want you to know that we are here to support Lyla. . . . I just want to make sure you're ready for what may lie ahead."

For one beat, I pictured my daughter's pleading eyes and tone this morning and found myself hesitating. Then I envisioned that photo again, coupled with those casual, cruel words, and reassured myself that I was doing the right thing.

"Yes," I said. "I'm ready."

THAT AFTERNOON, WHEN I picked Lyla up from school, she would not look at me. Before I could confess, she stared out the window and said, "Please tell me that you weren't the reason Finch's parents were at school today."

I pulled away from the curb and took a deep breath before

answering her. "I *did* call Mr. Quarterman, Lyla. But he had already seen the photo."

"Wow," she said, one of her favorite, and my least favorite, declarations. "Just *wow*."

"Lyla. I had to—"

"Whatever, Dad," she said. "Just forget it. You don't get it. It's not even worth trying to explain it to you."

"I'm not sure what that means," I said. "But I'll tell you this— *you* are worth it. And if you can't see that, I've done something wrong."

As we pulled up to a red light, I turned to stare at her profile, but she refused to look back at me. I could tell in that moment that she had completely shut down, and that she wouldn't be talking to me anytime soon. I had grown accustomed to the silent treatment over the past year or so, and I actually didn't hate her tactic. It was better than fighting, and I found that after a little time, tensions eased and things generally resolved themselves.

So I left her alone that night, letting her skip dinner, knowing she'd eventually come out of her room if she got hungry enough. The next morning, too, I didn't press her, listening to the news on the way to school rather than attempting any sort of conversation.

But by the following night, when she *still* wasn't talking to me during our dinner of Chinese takeout, I lost it. I told her I'd had enough of her sulking, and she was lucky I hadn't punished her for the drinking.

"Okay, Dad," she said, looking defiant. "You want me to talk to you?"

"Yes," I said. "I *do*."

"Okay. Well, how about this? I *hate* you."

The words hit me in the gut, but I pretended not to be fazed. "You don't hate me," I said, through a bite of shrimp fried rice.

She placed her chopsticks down on her plate and glared at me. "I actually *do* hate you right now, Dad."

I was comforted by her qualifier—*right now*—and told her she'd get over it.

"No, I won't. I can totally forgive you for what you did on my phone—even though it was total *bullshit*." She paused, clearly expecting me to object to her language. When I didn't, she continued, "But I will *never* forgive you for this. This is something that happened to *me*, not *you*. I asked you—I begged you—not to get involved. Not to tell the school—"

"Mr. Quarterman already knew, Lyla," I said.

"That's not the point. I asked you not to make a bigger deal out of everything . . . but you did anyway. . . . And now you've totally ruined my life."

I told her to stop being melodramatic.

"I'm *not* being melodramatic. Do you have any idea how much worse you've made everything?" she said. "Stuff like this just happens in high school. . . . People take stupid pictures . . . and then it just . . . goes away."

"A picture never goes away."

"You know what I mean, Dad! People move on. You just guaranteed that they don't move on. And that *everyone* sees it. *Everyone*. And Finch Browning might get suspended!"

"Good. I'm glad to hear that. He deserves it."

"What? No, Dad. If he's suspended, he might not be able to go to Princeton."

"Princeton?" I said, disgusted. "That asshole got into Princeton?"

"Oh my *God*, Dad!" she shouted. "You're missing the point—"

"No. *You* are," I said, thinking she looked exactly like her mother right now. Her eyes always reminded me of Beatriz, but when she got this angry, the rest of her face did, too. I blurted out the observation, instantly regretting it. There was already enough going on without throwing that into the mix.

"Funny you should mention Mom," she said, crossing her arms, her expression becoming defiant.

"And why's that?" I said.

"Because I've been talking to her about this . . ."

"Oh?" I said. "And how is your ol' momma doing these days? Recording any albums? Landing any plum acting roles? Getting married for the third time?"

"Yes. Two of those three, actually," she said. "She's doing great. Really great."

"Terrific," I said. "Just super."

"Yes. And she said I could come visit her."

"And where is she now?" I asked, though I knew she was back in Rio, according to the return address scrawled on the Easter card still displayed in Lyla's room.

"Brazil," Lyla confirmed.

"Well. You don't have a passport. And I'm not funding your trip to Brazil."

"I'm working on the passport. And Mom said she'd buy my ticket."

I let out a bitter laugh. "Oh yeah? How nice of her. Tell her while she's at it, she's only about a decade behind in any kind of financial support." I stood and carried my dishes to the sink.

Lyla said nothing, and I got more upset.

"Hey, I've got a great idea!" I said, returning to the table. "Why don't you go live with your mother this summer? Since your life is so ruined here and you'll never stop hating me?"

I didn't mean it—not even a little—and regretted the words as soon as they were out of my mouth, even before I saw the hurt in Lyla's eyes.

"Great suggestion, Dad," she said, nodding. "Thanks so much for your permission. I'll tell Mom that's what I want to do."

"Fantastic," I said, storming out of the kitchen. "Just do the dishes first. I'm sick and tired of doing everything around here."

chapter eight

NINA

"How'd you think that went?" Kirk asked under his breath as we walked toward the parking lot following our meeting with Walter.

"Awful," I said, though that word wasn't nearly strong enough to describe my profound disappointment verging on devastation.

"Yeah. He's pompous as hell. Condescending and superior . . . typical liberal," Kirk muttered, walking more briskly.

"*What?*" I said, though after that performance, nothing should have surprised me anymore.

"Walt," he said. "He's brutal."

I quickened my pace to keep up with Kirk's long, angry stride. "It's *Walter*. Not *Walt*."

"Whatever."

"And Walter's not on trial here. *Finch* is."

"Not yet he's not," Kirk said as we reached our cars.

"But he *will* be on trial. . . . I think that's pretty clear," I said, opening my door. I tossed my purse into the passenger seat before squaring my shoulders and looking into my husband's eyes.

"Yeah," Kirk said. "And it's *bullshit*. Quarterman's already made his mind up about everything. As the headmaster, he should stay neutral. Finch is one of his students, too. *And* he's a *lifer*."

Lifer was the term given to kids who had been at Windsor since kindergarten—as opposed to those who joined in middle school or high school. I'd always been happy Finch had been among that group, if only for the sake of continuity, but I cringed at hearing it in this context. The implication was clear—Finch belonged at Windsor more than Lyla, and therefore was entitled to preferential treatment.

"Yes. But he has *no* defense. Zero," I said. "I think that was abundantly clear in there."

"Fine, Nina," Kirk said. "He has no defense. But he's confessed and he's apologized. And this just isn't suspension worthy. Not after years of perfect behavior. It was one stupid mistake."

"I think others will beg to differ," I said, wondering what he thought qualified as "suspension worthy." In my mind, this was worse than cheating on a test, or drinking on school property, or getting in a fistfight, all of which resulted in suspension. "And it's not up to us. It's up to Windsor."

"Well, I'm not going to let Finch's fate end up in the hands of a few leftist wing-nut academics."

I bit my lip, then lowered myself into the car. I could feel my husband's stare—and it felt like a dare to reply.

"I don't think you have a choice here," I finally said, glancing up at him.

It was a foreign concept to Kirk—that something would *actually* be out of his control—and although in the past I'd found this quality attractive, it now filled me with disdain bordering on disgust. I tried to pull my door shut, but Kirk held it open with his hand.

"Just do me a favor," he said.

I raised my eyebrows, waiting.

"Don't do anything. . . . Don't talk to anyone. Not even Melanie."

"Melanie already knows everything going on," I said, thinking of the half dozen phone conversations we'd had since Saturday night. I think part of her felt culpable and worried that there might be some fallout or punishment for *her* son. After all, Beau had hosted the party, and she and Todd had, perhaps unwittingly, supplied the booze.

"Yes, but she doesn't know about this conversation we just had, does she?"

"No," I said. "But I'm sure she'll call and ask."

"Okay. Let her ask. But just keep the details on the down low. . . . Let me handle this for now."

I almost asked what "handling this" entailed, but I felt pretty sure I already knew. Over the next twenty-four hours, I imagined that Kirk would call his lawyer buddies, lining up a defense should things not go his way sooner. He'd then place a call to Lyla's father, ask to meet with him "man to man." He would get the meeting— and then would find a way to convince this man to just "let it all go." That this result would be in "everyone's best interest."

I RETURNED ABOUT twenty minutes later to an unusually quiet house. On any given day, there were often people milling about our home and property. Landscapers and repairmen; pool boys and Pilates instructors; our occasional chef, Troy; and at the very least, Juana, our full-time housekeeper, who had been with us forever, even when we lived in our old house in Belmont and she only came once a week.

But that afternoon, nobody was there, and I had over an hour to kill before Finch got home from school. The rare solitude filled me with simultaneous relief and panic. I put my bag down in the kitchen and considered making myself lunch, but I had no appetite. So I went to my office, designed as the "servants' room" back when the house was built in the twenties. It was where I worked on my charities, answered emails, and did my online shopping.

I sat down at the built-in desk, gazing out the window onto the sun-drenched courtyard lined with boxwoods and blue hydrangeas. The view was beautiful, and it usually put me in a cheerful mood, especially this time of year. But now something about it pained me.

I lowered the roman shades and stared down at my desk, searching for a distraction. Still a paper-calendar girl, I flipped open my planner for at least the third time that day, though I already knew nothing was on my schedule this evening—almost as unusual as our empty house. I closed the leather book, then eyed a box of stationery, contemplating writing an overdue thank-you note and an even longer-overdue note of sympathy. I couldn't muster the energy for either, so I got up and began to pace aimlessly around the house. Every room was neat, pristine, clutter-free. The hardwood floors shone. Throw pillows were fluffed and perfectly arranged. Orchids were in full bloom on three coffee tables in three different rooms. I made a mental note to thank Juana—something I didn't do enough—for her work and attention to detail. Our home was nothing short of exquisite.

But as with the view from my office window, the beauty inside our home only unsettled me further. It suddenly felt like a farce, and as I passed through the butler's pantry, I had the urge to grab a piece of crystal from the lit shelves and smash it against the marble countertop, the way people did in the movies when they were really upset. In real life, though, I knew the satisfaction wouldn't approach the effort required to clean it up. Not to mention the possible risk of cutting myself. Then again, a trip to the emergency room might be a nice diversion, I thought, reaching up to touch a wine goblet.

"Don't be stupid," I said aloud, dropping my hand to my side. I turned and made my way down the hallway toward the master suite, which had been added to the house sometime in the nineties. I looked around, my eyes settling on a white-velvet chaise longue I'd had shipped from a Deco furniture store in Miami. It had been a splurge—too much to spend on one chair no matter what name it was given—but I'd told myself I would use it often, meditate or read there every morning. Unfortunately, that seldom seemed to happen. I was always too busy. But I walked over and sat on it now, thinking of Kirk, wondering about his character. How could he so easily gloss over what Finch had done to Lyla? Had he always been this way? I really didn't think so, but if he hadn't, when did he change? Why hadn't I noticed? What *else* was I missing?

I thought about how often my husband traveled and how seldom we were intimate these days. I had no real reason to think that he'd ever been unfaithful, and frankly he seemed to be too into his work to bother with an affair. But I still put the fidelity odds at only about eighty–twenty, then mentally lowered that to seventy–thirty, perhaps a by-product of having a best friend who practiced divorce law.

It had been a few days since Julie and I had communicated even by text, a long stretch for us, and I had to admit that I'd been avoiding her, at least on a subconscious level. I dreaded telling her what Finch had done. It wasn't that she was holier than thou. In some ways, though she had very high moral standards, she was actually the least judgmental person I knew. But ever since the seventh grade, she'd always given it to me straight. It had caused a few arguments over the years, as sometimes she hurt my feelings with her bluntness. But I cherished our filterless relationship and considered it the truest measure of a best friend, greater than pure affection. Who was the person you trusted enough to be your most transparent self with, in both good times and bad? For me, that person had always been Julie.

So, just as I'd called to tell her about Princeton, feeling confident that there would be no element of competitiveness or resentment in her reaction, I knew I could trust Julie with this. I found my phone in the kitchen, returned to my chair, and dialed her number.

Julie answered on a late ring, sounding breathless, as if she'd just run up a few flights of stairs—or more likely, down the hall of her small law firm.

"Hey. Can you talk?" I asked, part of me hoping she couldn't, having sudden second thoughts about sharing everything when I was already so drained.

"Yeah," she said. "I was just reviewing a PI report. It's a doozy."

"*Your* PI?" I asked

"Unfortunately, no. The other side," she said with a sigh. "I'm representing the wife."

"Do I know her?" I asked, though I knew confidentiality would prevent her from sharing anything specific.

"Doubt it. She's younger than we are. In her mid-thirties . . . Anyway, she thought it was an excellent idea to make out with her also-married boyfriend in the Walmart parking lot."

"Oh my God. Are the pictures . . . clear?" I asked, partly stalling, partly taking bizarre solace in the fact that my life wasn't the only one in turmoil.

"Yep," she said. "Great camera."

I took a deep breath and said, "Oh no. Well, speaking of scandalous photos . . . I have something to tell you."

"Uh-oh," she said. "What's up?"

"It's about Finch," I said, my stomach cramping and head pounding. "Are you sure you have time for this now? It's sort of a long story. . . ."

"Yeah. I have a few minutes," she said. "Hold on. Lemme close my door."

A few seconds later, she returned and said, "So what happened?"

I cleared my throat and told her the story, beginning with Kathie showing me the picture in the ladies' room and ending with the conversation I'd just had with Kirk in the Windsor parking lot. She interrupted a few times, but only to ask questions, in her fact-gathering, lawyer mode. When I finished, she said, "Okay. Hang up and send me the picture."

"Why?" I asked, thinking that I had been fairly explicit about the image already.

"I need to see it," she said. "To fully gauge the situation. Just send it, okay?"

The request, along with her tone of voice, was bossy and borderline abrasive, but also strangely comforting. Julie had always been the take-charge alpha dog in our friendship and was unusually good in a crisis.

So I did as I was told, hanging up, then staring at the image while I waited for her to receive it. It took her a sickeningly long time to call back, and I wondered if the photo hadn't gone through or whether she just needed that much time to process it. The phone finally rang.

"Okay. I saw it," she said when I answered.

"And?" I asked, bracing myself.

"And it's *really* bad, Nina."

"I know." My eyes welled up, though I wasn't sure whether I was more embarrassed or just plain sad.

Silence waited on the other end of the line—which was unusual for the two of us, at least a silence that felt awkward. She finally cleared her throat and said, "I'm surprised that Finch would do something like this. . . . He was always such a kind kid. . . ."

I heard the past tense in her statement—which brought more tears—as I thought about how much time the three of us shared when Finch was little. During those early years, I'd go back to Bristol at least once or twice a month, whenever Kirk had to travel for more than a day or two, and although we stayed at my parents' house, Finch always clamored to see Auntie Jules. On one visit, as Julie was really struggling with infertility, she told me that Finch gave her some peace. That even if she couldn't have children of her own, she'd always have her godson. That's how real and special their bond was.

Even after her twin daughters, Paige and Reece, were born when Finch was about five, we still got together often, including a week's vacation at the beach every summer. Finch was so sweet to the girls, spending hours patiently playing in the sand, building castles, digging holes, and letting them bury him when he would have rather been out in the surf.

I asked her now what she would do if something like this happened to the girls.

She hesitated, then said, "They're only in the seventh grade. So I can't imagine it . . . yet."

"Yes, you can," I said because one of Julie's many gifts was her imagination, a by-product of a highly evolved sense of empathy.

"Okay, you're right," she said with a sigh. "Well . . . I'd hang him by the balls."

Her response was a punch in my stomach, but I knew it was the truth, and I now felt a little scared thinking of legal ramifications beyond Windsor's walls. "Meaning what, exactly?" I said.

"I'd press charges," she said, with what seemed to be anger. Was she angry with me or with Finch? Or was she simply angry on a young woman's behalf?

"What charges would those be, exactly?" I said softly.

She cleared her throat, then said, "Well. There's a new law in Tennessee. A sexting bill passed last year . . . Any minor sending sexually suggestive photos could be labeled a felon or sex offender for involvement with child pornography—which means he'd be put on the Sex Offender Registry until age twenty-five. It also means that the minor would be required to report this on all job and college applications."

Now full-fledged crying, I couldn't speak.

"I'm sorry, Nina," she said.

"I know," I managed to reply, hoping that she couldn't tell just how upset I was.

"Of course . . . Adam might try to talk me out of pressing charges," she said, speaking of her husband—a laid-back, even-keeled firefighter who, incidentally, occasionally hung out with my high school ex-boyfriend Teddy, now a cop.

"Why's that?" I asked.

"I don't know. I just think he'd say we should let the school handle it. And for what it's worth? I don't think this will go to the courts, either. . . . For all the money you guys pay for school? I think this girl's father will probably trust them to handle it."

"Maybe," I say.

She sighed and said, "So has Finch apologized to her yet?"

"No. Not yet."

"Well, that needs to happen. . . ."

"I know. What else do you think we should do?"

"Well . . . let's see. . . . If one of my girls did something like this to one of their classmates? . . ." She mused aloud.

"They would *never*," I said, thinking that they had zero mean-girl tendencies.

"Yeah . . . but I guess you never *really* know," she said. It was a generous statement, and I could tell she was grasping at straws to comfort me. "Anyway . . . I don't know what we'd do, exactly. . . . But I *do* know that we wouldn't be trying to get them off the hook."

I stiffened. "We're not trying to get Finch off the hook, Julie."

"Really?" she said, sounding skeptical. "So what is Kirk going to do when he calls this girl's father?"

"Well, for one, apologize," I said, wishing I had left off that part of the story—or at least my own conjecture that Kirk had manipulative intentions. After all, he hadn't spelled anything out to me. Maybe *all* he had in mind was an apology.

"And for another?" she asked.

"I don't know," I said.

More silence.

"Well," Julie said. "I think this is a real fork in the road for Finch. . . . And I know Kirk is thinking in terms of Princeton. . . . But there is much more at stake here."

I was pretty sure I knew what she was getting at, but it still hurt to hear, and part of me was getting a little resentful, too. She really could be harsh, especially when it came to Kirk. "I'm sure it will work itself out," I said, my voice sounding strained.

If she noticed the tension, she pretended not to. "Well, I'm not so sure a thing like this just 'works itself out,'" she began. "And maybe I shouldn't say this, but—"

"Then don't," I blurted out. "Maybe some things are best kept to ourselves."

The exchange was unprecedented in our friendship, but then again, so was the feeling that she questioned the character of my only child. Her own *godson*. For some reason, that was easier to focus on than the fact that *I* was wondering about his character, too.

"Okay," she said, her voice softer but not at all remorseful.

I told her I had to go, then thanked her for her advice.

"You're welcome," she said. "Anytime."

chapter nine

TOM

On Monday evening, as I was cleaning up the dinner dishes, I got a call from a blocked number. Something told me I should answer it, and I listened to a man's voice I didn't recognize say, "Hello. Is this Thomas Volpe?"

"Yes. This is Tom," I said, stopping in my tracks.

"Hi, Tom," the man said. "This is Kirk Browning. Finch's father."

For a second, I couldn't speak.

"Hello?" he said. "Are you there?"

"Yeah. I'm here. What can I do for you?" I said, my fist clenched as I gripped the phone with my other hand.

His reply was slick and fast. "It's not what *you* can do for *me*. I want to do something for *you*. I want to try to repair what my son has done."

"Huh," I said. "I'm really not sure that's going to be possible."

"Yes. I realize that may be the case," he said. "But I was wondering if there's any way we could get together and talk?"

My instinct was to say no, there was nothing he could say to me—and I had less than nothing to say to him. But then I told myself there actually was a lot I wanted to tell this man. "Yeah. Okay," I said. "When?"

"Well, let's see. . . . I'm out of town at the moment . . . back on Wednesday morning. Does Wednesday night work? My house around six?"

"Um, no. That actually won't work for me. I'm with my daughter in the evenings," I said to make a point.

"Well, you tell me when," he replied—which was what he should have said in the first place.

"Wednesday at noon," I said, hoping it wasn't at *all* convenient for him. That he might even have to get on an earlier flight.

He hesitated, then said, "Sure. That works. I land at eleven. Can we say twelve-thirty just to be safe?"

"Fine," I said.

"Great. Can I give you my address?"

"Yeah. Just text it to me. And this time? Don't block your number."

LIVING IN A city like Nashville my whole life, I'd seen plenty of impressive homes, and I knew by the Brownings' Belle Meade address that their house was going to be very nice. But I was still blown away when I pulled down their long driveway, past the tall hedges, and got a load of that brick and stone English Tudor mansion in a downright fairy-tale setting. I'm a big fan of older homes, and I couldn't help but admire the architectural details of this one. The steeply pitched slate roof with cross-gables. The half-timbered exposed framing. The tall, narrow windows, stained and leaded. I got out of my car, closed the door, and walked toward the mammoth double front doors, made of mahogany, elaborately carved, and flanked by flickering lanterns. I shuddered to think what their gas bill must be, let alone their mortgage—then reminded myself that people like this probably didn't have mortgages.

I approached the front porch, trying to pinpoint exactly what I was feeling. I was still just as pissed as I'd been on the drive over, but now I was feeling something else, too. Was I intimidated? No. Was I jealous? Not at all. Did I begrudge them their fortune? I really didn't think so. My problem, I decided as I eyed the doorbell, was that it was just so *predictable* that the rich boy did the shitty thing to the poor girl, and I hated being part of that cliché. Frankly, I was also extra angered by his asshole father's staggering lack of self-awareness. Who but a total clueless *idiot* would ask a stranger to meet at his own home if it looked like *this,* especially if his jack-ass kid was in the wrong? Had he done any research on Lyla or me whatsoever? Did he have any idea that she was one of the few kids at Windsor on financial aid? It would have taken him about ten seconds on Google to discover that I was a carpenter (the kind he'd probably hire, then nickel-and-dime to death)—which meant either he hadn't bothered or he had looked me up and didn't give a shit what I'd be feeling. I wasn't sure which was worse, but I hated him more by the second.

With a heavy chip weighing down my shoulder, I pushed the doorbell, listening to the formal chime echo inside. At least thirty seconds passed, during which I reminded myself that all these people had on us was money. I had all the moral high ground, and the leverage that came with it.

Finally, the door opened, and there stood an older Latina woman, who told me to please come in, she'd get Mr. Browning. The whole scene was so *classic*—especially when "Mr. Browning" immediately materialized behind her. Clearly he could have gotten to his own door first, but he *wanted* his brown housekeeper to open it for him. *Look important at any and all costs* was, I'm sure, one of his rules to live by.

Then, without thanking her or introducing her, he sort of pushed past her and filled the doorway. I hated everything about

97

his appearance. His ruddy complexion—like he'd just been drinking on a golf course. His gelled hair, too dark to be his real color. His pink linen shirt, unbuttoned two buttons too low.

"Hi there, Tom," he said, reaching out to shake my hand, his booming frat-boy voice matching his foolishly firm grip. "Kirk Browning. Please come in."

I nodded, then forced myself to say hello as he stepped inside to let me in. I glanced around the foyer, surprised by the cool contemporary décor. A gigantic pale-blue abstract painting hung over a black lacquered chest. It wasn't my usual taste, but I had to admit it was pretty stunning.

"Thanks so much for coming," Kirk said, downright beaming. "Shall we go chat in my office?"

"That's fine," I said.

He nodded, leading me through a formal living room, down a wide corridor, and into a dark, wood-paneled office decorated with mounted deer and fowl—yet another radical design departure.

"Welcome to my man cave," he said with a chuckle.

I gave him a tight-lipped smile as he gestured toward a fully stocked bar cart.

"Too early in the day for scotch? It's five o'clock somewhere, right?"

"No, thanks," I said. "But you go right ahead."

He hesitated, as if seriously contemplating a solo drink, but decided against it. He then gestured toward a couple of armchairs floating in the middle of the room. I had the feeling they were freshly staged, and it gave me the creeps. "Please," he said. "Have a seat."

I chose the chair with a view toward the doorway, my back to the gas fireplace. Of course the pussy wasn't going to burn real logs, I thought, as he sat down, planting his feet perfectly parallel to each other. His pant legs came up enough to reveal bare ankles. No socks with fancy loafers—typical Belle Meade.

"So. Thanks for coming over, *Tom*," he said, exaggerating the pronunciation of my name with a low hum.

I nodded but said nothing, determined not to make this easy for him.

"I hope it's not interrupting your workday too much?"

I shrugged and said, "I'm flexible . . . self-employed."

"Ahh," he said. "And what is it that you do, Tom?"

"I'm a carpenter," I said.

"Oh. Wow. That's great," he said, his voice and expression oozing condescension. "They say the happiest people work with their hands. I wish I were more . . . handy." He looked down at his open palms, which were undoubtedly as soft as they were useless. "I have trouble changing lightbulbs!"

I resisted the urge to ask him how many people he had on staff to do that for him, then figured what the hell. "You must have a guy for that?" I asked.

He looked taken aback for a beat but quickly recovered. "Actually my wife, Nina, is good at that stuff. Believe it or not."

I raised my brow. "At changing lightbulbs?"

"Ha. No . . . I mean . . . all sorts of mini home projects. . . . She enjoys them. But yes, for the more complicated ones, we do have a handyman. Great guy. Larry," he said, as if all of us manual laborers knew one another.

I glanced around the room and said, "So. Where *is* your wife? Will she be joining us?"

He shook his head and said, "Unfortunately, she had a prior engagement."

"That *is* unfortunate," I deadpanned.

"Yes," he said, "but I thought it might actually be better if we could talk . . . you know . . . man to man."

"Right. Man to man," I echoed.

"So, Tom," he said, after taking a deep breath. "Let me begin by apologizing on behalf of my son. The photo he took of your daughter was absolutely inexcusable."

I squinted, pretending to be confused, cueing more babble.

"It was *terrible.* . . . And believe me, Finch understands that now."

"*Now?*" I asked. "So he didn't understand that *before?* When he posted it?"

"Well," Kirk said, holding up his hands, now palms out. "To be clear, he didn't actually *post* anything—"

"Oh, pardon me," I said, an expression I never used. "He didn't understand that it was wrong when he *sent the photo* to his buddies?"

There was no way he could answer this question in the negative, I thought, but sure enough, he did.

"No," he said. "Not at first. He wasn't thinking at *all.* You know teenage boys. . . . But now he gets it. Now he sees. Completely. And he's sorry. Very, *very* sorry."

"Has he told Lyla that?" I asked, feeling sure I knew the answer.

"Well. Not yet. He wants to . . . but I told him to wait until I talked to you. I wanted to apologize to you first."

I cleared my throat and chose my words carefully. "Well, *Kirk,*" I said. "I appreciate the apology. I do. But unfortunately, it doesn't undo what your son— I'm sorry, what's his name again?"

"Finch," he said, nodding, his chin nearly reaching his chest. "His name is Finch."

"Ah, yes, that's right. As in . . . *Atticus* Finch?" I asked.

"Yes, indeed!" He grinned. "*To Kill a Mockingbird* is my wife's favorite book."

"Huh. Mine, too. Imagine that," I said, uncrossing my arms before slapping my thigh in a sarcastic way.

"Wow. What a coincidence. I'll tell her," he said, smiling. "So. Where were we?"

"We were talking about what *your son* did to my daughter. *Lyla.*"

"Yes . . . and I can't tell you how sorry Finch is."

"Try," I said, forcing a fake smile. "*How* sorry?"

"Oh, very. He's very, *very* sorry. He's a wreck. He hasn't been able to eat or sleep—"

I interrupted with a brittle laugh, feeling myself start to lose my composure. "So . . . wait. Are you . . . Do you . . . Am I supposed to feel *sorry* for your son?"

"No, no. Not at all. I didn't mean *that,* Tom. I just meant that he understands that what he did was wrong. And he's extremely sorry. But he didn't mean the caption the way it sounded. He just meant it as a . . . joke."

"Does your son often make *racist* jokes?"

"Of course not," he said, finally starting to squirm. "Is your daughter even . . . Hispanic?"

"No."

His face lit up. "I knew it," he said, as if the case were now closed.

"Her mother's *Brazilian.*"

His smile faded into a look of confusion as I continued, "So technically, I think the word you're looking for is *Latina. Hispanic* is a demonym that only includes Spaniards and other speakers of the Spanish language. And as I'm sure you know, the language of Brazil is Portuguese." It was all information Lyla had fed me in recent months, research she had done to try to understand exactly who she was.

"Very interesting," he said, as I got the feeling he was either patronizing me or searching for a good angle for his kid. "So . . . Brazilians *aren't* a different race?"

"Brazilians can be any race, *Kirk*," I said slowly, like I was talking to an idiot. Which I was. "Just like Americans."

"Oh, sure. Right," he said. "That makes sense. So Lyla's white?"

"Mostly," I said, unwilling to dignify this man with a breakdown of her lineage. I wasn't even sure exactly what it was, other than that Beatriz's mother was Portuguese Brazilian and all white, while her father was something like a quarter black. Which I guess made Lyla one-sixteenth African-Brazilian.

"Mostly?" Kirk asked.

"Look. Bottom line . . . Although Lyla's mother did, at one point, have a green card, Lyla is one hundred percent American," I said.

"That's wonderful," he said. "Just wonderful."

"Which part?" I asked.

"All of it," he said. "That her mother came here. That Windsor has this kind of diversity—"

"I actually don't think it's all that diverse. . . . But it *is* a great school. I've been very impressed with the academics. And the headmaster," I said purposefully.

Kirk nodded. "Yes. Walt's very good at what he does. And I recognize that he's in a tough position now. With this incident . . . And I think for everyone's sake, he's hoping we handle it privately. . . ."

"Privately?" I asked, knowing exactly where this was going.

"Yes. Between the two families. I can assure you that Finch is being severely punished . . . and we would like to compensate you both for your . . . your time from work . . . and also any distress this may have caused you and your daughter."

I stared at him in disbelief as he walked over to his desk, opened a drawer, and pulled out a white business-size envelope. As he returned to hand it to me, I could see my name written on it, and I was overcome with a fight-or-flight feeling. Should I punch this guy in the face? Or should I take the money and run? At the very least, I wanted to know how much this joker thought it would take to buy us off. Maybe he had done his research after all and already *knew* I was a carpenter. Maybe he even assumed I was a *"Hispanic"* carpenter. Maybe he had multiple envelopes in his desk. Envelope number one for the minority laborer. Envelope number two for the blue-collar white guy. Envelope three for a fellow suit. *Fight or flight, flight or fight?* Wasn't it supposed to be an instinct, not a choice?

In any event, I decided to flee, standing to take the envelope from him. As I put it in my back pocket, I could tell it contained bills. A *lot* of bills.

A look of palpable relief crossed Kirk's face. "I'm really glad we could have this talk, Tom," he said. "I think it's been very, very *constructive.*"

"Yes," I said. "It really has."

"And if you'd just let Walt know that we settled this . . ." His voice trailed off as I guess even *he* wasn't brazen enough to actually spell it out: *I'm paying you off.*

In the ultimate head fake, I nodded, smiled, then allowed myself to be cheerfully shown to the door.

chapter ten

NINA

Kirk returned home from the airport only thirty minutes before his scheduled meeting with Lyla's father. As he unpacked his roller bag, moving back and forth between his closet and our bathroom, I tried to engage him in conversation. I asked him what he planned to say to Thomas Volpe—and if he was sure he didn't want me to join them. To my guilty relief, he said he was *quite* sure—then added that he'd rather not discuss the details.

"I don't want to sound too rehearsed," he said. "It needs to be natural."

I nodded, not quite buying it but once again relieved.

A few minutes later, I left the house in a low-key panic. As I tried to distract myself with mindless errands, I thought a lot about my husband, how what I'd once loved most about him was now what frustrated me to no end. He *had* to be right. He *had* to be in charge. But in our earlier years, I was occasionally the exception to the rule. I could persuade him when nobody else could. At the very least, we had once been a partnership. Equals.

I thought of an earlier childhood crisis, when Finch and another boy had dipped the ears of a neighbor's cocker spaniel puppy in blue paint. He'd denied it, despite overwhelming proof to the contrary, including the blue paint I'd found on the treads of his small Nike sneakers. Kirk and I had argued about how to handle it; he was in favor of brute force to extract a confession. But I'd convinced him to let me try my way first. The three of us sat at the kitchen table together as I told Finch we would always love him, no matter what, and how important it was to tell the truth.

"I did it, Mommy," Finch finally said, breaking down in tears. "I'm so sorry!"

I still remember the way Kirk looked at me, the way we later made love and he told me that he'd picked the most wonderful mother for his son.

It had been a long time since he'd looked at me like that.

ABOUT AN HOUR later, as I was still running errands, Kirk called, asking if I wanted to meet him for lunch.

"Oh, no. Was it that bad?" I said, thinking that Kirk never had time for lunch. At least not a lunch without a business purpose.

"No. It wasn't bad at all. It went great, actually," he said, his voice notably chipper.

"Really?" I said.

"Yeah. We had a good talk. I like him."

"And . . . did he like *you*?"

"Of course," Kirk said with a laugh. "What's not to like?"

I ignored his question and asked for more details.

"I'll tell you everything over lunch. Meet me at the club?" he said, referring to Belle Meade, the country club to which we belonged—and his family always had.

"Um, can we go somewhere else?" I said, remembering how I'd

felt about the club when I first started to go with Kirk and his family. It had made me uncomfortable—the fawning staff in their stiff white jackets, the formal rooms filled with Oriental rugs and antique furniture, and most of all, the lily-white membership. There were no black members at all until 2012, and almost all the staff were people of color, though to be fair and as Kirk had pointed out, plenty of African Americans had been approached to join but had simply declined. I couldn't say I blamed them.

Somewhere along the line, though, I had succumbed to the luxury, focusing less on the exclusivity and more on the beauty and serenity and utter convenience of our membership. It was a rare week that I didn't spend at least a few hours there, whether playing tennis, meeting Finch and Kirk at the casual grill for dinner, or having drinks with my friends on the veranda overlooking the golf course.

"Do you have something against the club now?" Kirk said, as if reading my mind.

"Nothing," I said. "I'm just not in the mood to talk to people. Given everything . . ."

"Okay," he said, acquiescing faster than I'd thought he would. "Want me to call Etch or Husk?"

The likelihood of running into someone I knew was pretty high at those restaurants, too, but I didn't want to be too difficult. Besides, I *loved* Husk. It was probably my favorite restaurant in the city. So I told Kirk I would meet him there.

"Great," he said. "See you soon."

Twenty minutes later, Kirk and I were seated at a cozy table on the art-lined lower level of the restaurant, set in a nineteenth-century home in Rutledge Hill. He *still* hadn't told me what happened, keeping me in total suspense, insisting that we have a glass of wine first. I was annoyed but hopeful, as we chatted with a waitress we'd had several times before, then put in our order for a burger (him) and shrimp and grits (me), as well as one glass of wine to split.

As soon as she departed, I said, "All right. Could you please tell me *now*, Kirk?"

He nodded, then took a deep breath. "So. He got to the house right after you left. . . . We went to my office and made a little small talk. . . . Then we got into everything. At first he was a little touchy, but then I just gave it to him straight. . . ."

"Meaning?"

"Meaning . . . I told him how sorry Finch is. How sorry we are, too."

"And what did he say?"

"Honestly, not too much. He was pretty quiet. But I think he agrees that we can handle this privately. . . ."

"He does?" I said, more than a little surprised.

"Yes."

"Meaning he doesn't want it to go before the Honor Council?" I asked.

"Correct," Kirk said as the waitress brought two rolls to the table. He began to butter one of them, looking smug.

"But . . . how? Why?" I said. "He just agreed with you?"

"Well. Let's just say I gave him a little . . . incentive. . . ."

I stared at him, my heart sinking. "What kind of incentive?"

"A financial one," he said with a shrug.

"*What?*" I said.

"What do you mean 'what'? I just gave him a little cash," he said, stone-faced. "No big deal."

"Oh my God. How much did you give him?" I asked.

He shrugged again, then mumbled, "Fifteen thousand dollars."

I shook my head and let out a whimper. "Please, please tell me you're kidding."

"Oh, c'mon, Nina," he said, his expression confirming that this was no joke. "You don't think our son's future is worth fifteen grand?"

"It's not the *amount*," I said. "If we're just discussing the *amount*, I'd question the lowball—"

"Fifteen thousand is a *lot* to the average person," he interjected, always a man of the people when it was convenient to his narrative. "And this guy's a *carpenter.*"

"That's not the point!" I shouted. I glanced around, reconfirming that we didn't know anyone seated in the galley area, but still lowered my voice. "The point is—you gave him *hush* money."

He rolled his eyes and gave me a condescending smirk. "This isn't a gangster movie, Nina. It's not *hush* money. I'm not asking him to be *quiet* about anything."

"Then what's the point?"

"Well, for one, it's a token of our apology. For another . . . it's an incentive."

"An incentive to do *what*?"

"An incentive to tell Walt he doesn't want this thing to move forward to the Honor Council."

"Did you actually *tell* him that?" I asked, my disapproval growing by the second.

"Didn't have to. It was understood," he said. "Look, Nina. The guy willfully and gladly took the cash."

"You gave him fifteen thousand in *cash*?"

"Yes. And again—he *took* it. It was a meeting of the minds, for sure. A contract."

I pressed my lips together, thinking. There was so much wrong with what he was telling me, I wasn't sure where to start. "What about Finch?" I said. "Are you going to tell him about this little contract?" I said.

"I wasn't planning on it," he replied. "I think it's better if we leave Finch out of this."

"Leave out the person who single-handedly caused all the harm?"

"We're leaving him out of the solution. Not the punishment. He *is* being punished, Nina. Remember?"

"Okay. But what if it gets out? What if Finch finds out his father did something shady?" I asked. "And his mother went along with it?"

He shook his head. "No way. This guy's not going to talk. . . . Think about it this way. . . . When you slide someone a fifty to get a table at a restaurant, do they make an announcement? No. They don't. Because it's shady on *both* sides."

"So you *do* admit you're being shady?"

He shrugged. "You want me to admit that? Sure. I'll admit that. It was a little shady. But I did it for a good cause. I did it for Finch. And it worked."

"How do you know it worked?" I said.

"Because he took the money, Nina. . . . And before that, he was giving me an immigration lecture on how Brazilians aren't Hispanic. And that his daughter is an American. Yada yada . . . He had an attitude. But then I handed him that cash and suddenly he was all cool, calm, and collected. So you tell me, Nina. Did it work?"

When I didn't reply, he answered his own question. "Yes. It *did*. And you can sit there and be self-righteous all you want, but deep down, you have to agree that it was worth it."

I stared back at him, my thoughts scattered and racing. A very small, guilty part of me was relieved that Lyla's father had been complicit. Besides, what choice did I have? I couldn't make him give us the money back.

"Well, putting that aside, I really think it's high time that Finch apologizes to Lyla. Face-to-face," I said as the waitress poured our glass of wine.

I paused as Kirk tasted it and okayed it, then resumed when she left. "And I would also like for the three of us to sit down again and talk a bit more in depth . . . about *everything*. He's been avoiding me for two days . . . for longer than that, really. . . . And I can't tell if he's sorry or pouting," I said, getting a little bit choked up. "I can't tell what's in his *heart* right now."

"He's sorry, Nina. And you know he has a good heart. . . . We'll get through this, I promise."

I started to say that I *thought* I knew Finch's heart—but Julie was right, the sweet kid I once knew could never have done this to a girl. To *anyone*. It just didn't make sense.

But there was something so reassuring and strong about the way Kirk was looking at me that I just couldn't bring myself to argue with him. Instead, at least for the moment, I put my faith in my husband, believing that he was right. That the three of us would get through this, somehow.

THAT NIGHT, I tried to talk to Finch. Kirk and I *both* did. But he insisted that he had to study for a test. Could we talk tomorrow? We relented, and then Kirk went to bed early, declaring himself exhausted. I tried to do the same, but I found myself lying in bed next to him, wide awake and more anxious than ever.

Around midnight, I got up and went to my office and pulled the

Windsor directory from a desk drawer. I flipped to the end of the alphabet and found the entry for Lyla and Thomas Volpe. No mother was listed, unlike most divorced families with dual entries, and the only explanation I could think of was that she had died. I hoped not recently; then again, I would have wanted Lyla to have had as many years with her mother as possible. Feeling increasingly melancholy, I scanned down to read their address. They lived on Avondale Drive, a street that didn't sound familiar, though I knew the 37206 zip code was in East Nashville, over the Cumberland River. I opened my laptop and typed it into Google Maps, seeing a street view of the small bungalow located in Lockeland Springs. From what I could tell of the blurry photo, the house sat up high on a narrow lot, stairs leading from the street to the front door. There was one small tree in the yard and a few bushes planted along the house. After studying the picture from every angle, I typed the address into Zillow. I saw that Thomas Volpe had purchased the home in 2004 for $179,000. I felt a stab of sheepishness approaching shame, thinking of our own house, its price tag just under $4 million. From there, I pulled up our online AmEx statement, cringing at what we'd spent over the last billing cycle. It was amazing how quickly things added up, a few hundred dollars at a time. This particular month, I was the most culpable of the three of us, but I did spot Finch's thousand-dollar charge at the Apple Store, a $200 charge at Imogene + Willie, and $150 at Pinewood Social, the night before Beau's party. I seemed to recall a conversation about him "needing" a new phone but couldn't remember if he'd asked me for permission or simply informed me of the purchase after the fact. I felt certain that he hadn't mentioned any shopping or dining otherwise. Not that we had any real rules around his spending.

In fact, money was something Kirk and I seldom discussed with our son. Five years ago, when the financial picture had changed, the analysis of what to spend became pretty simple in our family. The question wasn't "did we need it" or "could we afford it," but simply "did we want it." If the answer was yes, we typically got it. The result was that Finch didn't dwell on money—or think about it at *all*, really—and had no clue about budgeting or anything normal people, let alone those in actual *need*, went through. I told myself to stop going off on this mental tangent. What did money or material things have to do with any of this, anyway? Nothing. Character has nothing to do with finances.

And yet, I had the feeling Julie might say otherwise, especially if she knew about Kirk's bribe—which now seemed increasingly significant. What if Thomas actually needed the money? Did that change the analysis at all? Did it make Kirk's attempt to buy him off better or worse? I wasn't sure, so decided to look for more evidence, biting my lip, logging on to Facebook, and typing in "Thomas Volpe." Three of them came up, but none was local. I tried a more general Google search and once again found nothing that seemed to fit. I then searched for Lyla, finding her on Facebook and Instagram, though both accounts were private. All I could see were her profile pictures, two different shots from the same summer day. It was clearly the same girl from Finch's photograph, but in these pictures she looked so happy, standing on a dock in a ruffled, off-the-shoulder top and white shorts. She was a pretty girl with a slender figure and beautiful long hair. I thought about her mother again, wondering not only when, but *how* she had died. Then, looking back at the directory at Thomas Volpe's email address, I couldn't stand it another second. I took a deep breath and began typing.

Dear Thomas,

My name is Nina Browning. I'm Finch's mother. I know you met
my husband today, and he shared with me a bit about your conversation. I'm not sure how you are feeling, but I believe that
more needs to be said and done to make things right. . . . I was
wondering if you'd consider meeting me to talk? I really hope
you say yes. More important, I hope Lyla is doing okay, in spite
of the horrible thing my son did to her. I'm thinking of you both.

Sincerely,

Nina

I quickly proofread, then sent it before I could change my mind
or even tweak any of the wording. The swoosh sound filled my office, and for a second, I regretted making contact. For one, I knew
Kirk would view it as a strategic blunder and an even greater betrayal of him and Finch. For another, and from a strictly practical
standpoint, what was I going to say to this man if he agreed to
meet with me?

Just as I convinced myself it was a moot point because Thomas
likely wouldn't write back (after all, he *had* taken Kirk's cash), his
name popped onto my computer screen. My heart quickening with
a mix of relief and dread, I went to my in-box, opened the email,
and read: Tomorrow 3:30 pm @Bongo East? Tom.

That works, I typed, my hands shaking. See you then.

THE FOLLOWING MORNING was nothing short of torture as I
paced around the house, stared at the clock, and counted down the
minutes until my appointment with Tom. At eleven, I made myself
go to a meditation class with one of my most Zen instructors, but
it did no good whatsoever. A jangled mass of nerves, I came home,

showered, and blew out my hair. It came out a little too full and "done," so I put it in a ponytail, then loosened a few strands around my face. I did my makeup with a light touch, skipping eyeliner altogether, then went to my closet to pick out an outfit. The transitional spring weather is always tricky, especially when it comes to footwear. It was too warm for boots, too chilly for sandals. Pumps felt too dressy, and flats stripped me of confidence—which I very much needed. I finally selected a simple nude wedge and a navy-blue DVF wrap dress. I kept my jewelry simple with diamond studs and my wedding band, removing my showier engagement ring. I knew it was ridiculously superficial to focus so much on appearances at a time like this, editing such small details, but I also believe that first impressions matter, and I wanted to show him respect without being at all ostentatious.

Overcompensating for Nashville traffic and my own tendency to run late, I arrived at Five Points twenty minutes early, finding one of only three parking spots in front of the small stand-alone building housing the East End coffee shop. I'd never been inside before, but I'd passed it plenty of times and remembered Finch telling me that it was also known as Game Point. I could see why. On the back wall, simple wood-and-iron shelves were lined with more than a hundred board games, many of them vintage, all available for patrons to play. Nearby, an older couple played Battleship. They looked to be newly dating, very happy. At other tables sat many solo customers, most with laptops or reading material.

I got in a very short line, scanning a colorful chalkboard menu. I ordered a latte and a sweet-potato white-chocolate muffin that looked interesting but that I knew I probably wouldn't eat because my stomach was in knots. I paid, dropping a dollar bill into a tip jar that read: AFRAID OF CHANGE? LEAVE IT HERE!, then stood to the side, waiting for a tattooed male barista to make my drink. Glancing around, I took note of the exposed HVAC lining the industrial ceiling, the concrete floor painted evergreen, and the bright sunlight filtering through high glass-block windows. The place was so mellow, a vibe unlike the Starbucks and juice bars in my neighborhood. When my latte was ready, I took it from the counter, along with the muffin they'd microwaved and put on a plate, and found a table against the wall close to the game corner. I sat in the chair facing the door, where I sipped my coffee and waited.

At exactly three-thirty, a man of average height and build walked in and glanced around. He looked slightly too young to have a teenager, but as his eyes rested on me, I felt sure that it was Tom Volpe.

I did a half stand and mouthed his name. He was probably too far away to read my lips, but he clearly got the gist of my body language, because he nodded, lowered his head, and walked toward me. With brown hair a little on the longer side, a couple days of beard growth, and a strong jaw, he *looked* like a carpenter. A second later, he was standing at the edge of my table, looking right at me. I stood the whole way. "Tom?" I said.

"Yes," he said in a low, deep voice. He did not initiate a handshake, or smile, or do any of the typical things people do when they meet, yet there was nothing about him that seemed hostile. His demeanor was a small relief but almost more unsettling than anger. It gave me no starting point.

"Hi," I said, running my palms along the sides of my dress. "I'm Nina."

"Yes," he said. His gaze was empty.

"It's nice to meet you," I blurted out, instantly regretting it, as there was nothing *nice* about this moment—and we both knew it.

But he let me off the hook, announcing that he was going to get a coffee, then turned abruptly and headed toward the cash register. I waited a few seconds before sitting back down, then looked over my shoulder, covertly studying him further. He appeared fit and athletic, or at least naturally strong. He was wearing faded blue jeans, an untucked gray Henley, and rugged boots that were hard to put in a category. They weren't country or western, nor were they of the lug-sole "workman" variety. And they certainly weren't at all Euro or trendy, like the ones lining the shelves of Kirk's closet.

I watched him pay, drop his change into the tip jar, and collect his coffee before heading back my way. I lowered my head and took a few deep breaths, still uncertain of exactly what I was going to say.

A moment later he was sitting across from me. I watched him flip the lid off his coffee with his thumb, then wave the steam away from the cup. As he met my gaze, my mind went blank. Why wasn't I better prepared? No wonder Kirk never trusted me to take important meetings alone.

Tom spoke first, saving me, though I knew that wasn't his intention. "You look familiar," he said, squinting a little. "Have we met before?"

"I don't think so," I said. "Maybe just from Windsor?"

"No. It's not that," he said, shaking his head. "I feel like it's something else. . . . Longer ago."

I bit my lip, starting to sweat, and wishing I hadn't worn silk. "I don't know . . . I'm not very good with faces. Sometimes I think I have that disorder. . . ."

"Which disorder is that?" he said with a slight tilt of his head. "The one where you don't pay attention?"

I was pretty sure he'd just made a jab at me, implying that I was self-absorbed. But I was in no position to be defensive. So I simply said, "No. It's a real *thing*. Facial blindness, I think it's called. . . . I'm pretty sure I have a touch of that . . . but anyway."

"Yes. Anyway," he echoed, glancing down to put the lid back on his coffee. It took him a second to get it on, pressing it all around the perimeter, clearly in no rush whatsoever. He raised the cup to his lips and took a long sip before looking at me again. This time he didn't save me.

"So," I finally said. "I'm not sure where to begin."

"I'm sorry. Can't help you there," he said, with the first real trace of animosity.

"I know . . . I just . . . Well, as I said in the email, I don't think my husband handled things with you the right way. . . ."

Tom nodded, his light brown eyes somewhere between cool and loathing. "Oh, you mean his attempt to buy me off?"

My stomach dropped. "Yes," I said. "That. Among other things."

It fleetingly occurred to me that Tom could have already deposited or spent the money—and then what would I be saying about *him* as well? But no, he had used the word *attempt*.

Sure enough, he reached into his back pocket for his wallet, opened it, and pulled out a stack of crisp, new bills. He slid the pile of cash across the table. I looked down and saw Benjamin Franklin's familiar grimace, feeling queasy as I tried to formulate a sentence.

"For what it's worth, I can't believe he did this," I said, staring down at the money. "I mean I know that he did . . . give you this . . . but I had nothing to do with his decision. This isn't how I wanted to handle things."

"And how did *you* want to handle things?"

I told him I didn't know exactly.

117

He winced, then took another sip of coffee. "But you weren't in favor of *bribery?*" he asked.

"No," I said, completely flustered. "I had no idea he was going to give you . . . *this.*"

"Yep. Fifteen thousand dollars," Tom said, glancing at the stack again. "And it's all there."

I looked down at it, shaking my head.

"So? What was he bribing me to *do,* exactly?"

"I don't know," I said, meeting his gaze again.

He gave me an incredulous look that bordered on a smile. "You don't *know?*"

I swallowed and made myself say what I really thought. "I believe that he was trying to . . . *motivate* you to tell Walter Quarterman that you don't think Finch should go before the Windsor Honor Council."

"You mean *bribe* me."

"Yes."

"And what do you think?"

"What do you mean?" I stammered.

"Do *you* think Finch should go before the Honor Council?"

I nodded. "Yes. I do, actually."

"Why?" he fired back.

"Because what he did was wrong. *So* wrong. And I think he needs to face some consequences."

"Such as?" Tom pressed.

"Well, I don't know. . . . Whatever the school decides is right. . . ."

Tom let out a caustic laugh.

"What's funny?" I said, feeling a stab of indignation. Couldn't he see how hard I was trying? Couldn't he cut me a break? Just a small one?

"Nothing's funny . . . believe me," he said, his smile fading into another stony gaze.

We stared at each other for a few seconds before he cleared his throat and said, "I was just wondering, Nina . . . how much do you and your husband give to the school? Above and beyond tuition?"

"What do you mean?" I asked, although it was perfectly clear what he was getting at.

"I mean . . . do you have any *buildings* named after you on Windsor's campus?"

"No," I said, although we *did* have a conference room in the library named after us. And a fountain. "Honestly, I don't see how that is relevant. . . . Despite what Kirk tried to do—which is awful— Mr. Quarterman isn't like that—"

"Isn't like *what*?"

"He's a good person. He's not going to make a decision here based on what we've given to the school," I said.

"Okay, look," Tom said, leaning over his coffee, his face close enough to mine for me to make out the flecks of gold in his beard. "Say what you want. But I know how the world works. And so, apparently, does your husband." His voice was calm but his eyes were angry as he pushed the pile of bills toward me.

"Well. Obviously, my husband got it wrong this time," I said, my voice shaking a little. I gestured toward the money, then finally got rid of it, sliding the bills into my purse.

Tom refused to grant me the point and instead said, "Your son got into Princeton. Am I correct?"

"Yes," I said.

"Congratulations. You must be really proud."

"I *was*," I said. "But I'm not proud *now*. I'm ashamed of my son. And my husband. And I'm just so sorry—"

He stared at me, then said, "Look. Here's the way I see it. Your husband wanted to make this go away with money. And you're trying to do the same thing with words. With a nice apology. You recognize your husband's a bit of an asshole, so you're trying to clean up after him. And ditto for your son."

My cheeks on fire, I shook my head and said, "No. That's not what I'm doing. I'm not here trying to *clean* anything *up,* or make anything go away. I'm just here to tell you I'm sorry. Because I am."

"Okay. And?"

"And *what*?" I said.

"Does that make you feel better? Telling me that? Are you hoping that I'm going to tell you not to worry about it? No hard feelings. All's forgiven. And . . . and you're not like your husband and son?" His voice was stronger now, and he was talking with his hands. I noticed calluses on them, and a deep, long cut on the back of his left thumb. The scab looked new.

I shook my head and said an adamant no, though deep down, I knew I wasn't being entirely truthful. That was *absolutely* part of why I was here. I wanted him to know that I was a good person—at least *I* thought I was—and certainly not the type to offer bribes to get my way. "No. . . . I'm here to tell you that I think it *should* go forward to the Honor Council," I said softly. "I think you should make *sure* that it does."

He looked at me and shrugged. "Okay. Fine. Noted. Is that all?"

"No," I said. Because there was something else, too. Another reason I was there. I made myself say it at my own peril. "I'm also here to . . . ask about Lyla. . . . How is she?"

A look of surprise crossed his face as he sat back a bit in his chair. Several seconds passed before he replied. "She's fine," he said.

"What's she . . . like?" I said, preparing myself to be told off again. For him to tell me that was none of my business.

But instead he said, "She's a sweet kid . . . but tough."

I nodded, sensing I was about to be dismissed. "Well . . . will you please tell her that I'm so sorry?"

He ran his hand over his stubble, then leaned forward, staring into my eyes. "Why are *you* sorry, Nina? Do you think *you're* to blame for what your *son* did?"

I hesitated, thinking, and then replied, "Yes. I *do*, actually. At least in part."

"And why's that?" he pressed.

"Because," I said. "I'm his *mother*. I should have taught him better."

AFTER LEAVING THE East End and crossing back over the Woodland Street Bridge, I couldn't make myself go home. Instead, I wound my way through Lower Broadway—the heart of Nash Vegas—with all of its neon honky-tonks and juke joints that I hadn't been to since the last of my friends' bachelorettes. It was a shame we didn't come here more—I love live music at Robert's and Layla's and Tootsies. But it really isn't Kirk's thing, unless he's wasted—in which case, it isn't *my* thing.

I kept driving, all around downtown, eventually turning onto Sixth Avenue, slowing as I passed the Hermitage. The same valet who had opened the Uber door for me the night of the Hope Gala was out in front again, and I found it almost impossible to believe that it had been only five days since the incident. So much had changed since then—or at least so much had been acknowledged in my own heart.

My phone vibrated in my purse with an incoming call. I didn't check to see who it was as I drove around the Capitol, then up into Germantown. Realizing I was hungry—*famished*—I pulled into City House. It had been a long time since I'd eaten a meal alone in public, and it felt liberating to sit at the bar by myself. Not only did Kirk dictate where we went but he always picked our table, too, and often ended up ordering for us. "Why don't we split the beef tartare and a chopped salad, and then get the trout and the rib eye?" he'd suggest because those were his four favorites. Passivity wasn't the worst sin in the world, but I made a mental note to start making my own menu selections. Baby steps.

At that moment, I went with a margherita pizza and a Devil's Harvest that the bartender brought in a can. He started to pour it into a glass, but I stopped him and said I'd do it, thank you. My phone vibrated again. This time I checked it, finding missed calls and texts from both Kirk and Finch, asking me where I was, when I'd be coming home, if I wanted to join them at Sperry's for an early dinner. I could tell they'd been communicating with each other, as their texts were worded so similarly, and I wondered what that meant. Was Kirk manipulating me? Or were they both just appropriately worried and upset? I wasn't sure, but I wrote them both back on a group thread, saying that I'd forgotten I "had something" and they "should just go ahead without me."

After finishing my pint and eating more pizza than I think I'd ever had in one sitting, I paid the bill and got back in my car. I drove aimlessly, headed toward the West End, ending up in Centennial Park, where Kirk and I used to take Finch, beginning when he was only a baby in a stroller. I tried to pinpoint my favorite stage of his life—our lives together—deciding that our best years were during middle elementary. Third and fourth grades, ages eight and nine or so, when Finch was old enough to really articulate his opinions and have interesting conversations with me, but still young enough to hold my hand in public. The halfway point of childhood. God, I missed those days so much.

As I sat on the steps of the Parthenon, which housed the art museum where we used to stroll as a family, one memory rushed back to me. It was late fall, both of us wearing jackets, and I sat in a spot close to this one while Finch collected leaves pretending to make rutabaga and collard green stew. He'd learned the words from a children's song, the lyrics all coming back to me now: *Victor Vito and Freddie Vasco / Ate a burrito with Tabasco / They put it on their rice, they put it on their beans / on their rutabagas, and on their collard greens!* I thought of how much Finch had loved to sing and dance. How much he'd enjoyed music and art and cooking.

"Girly things," Kirk had called them, always worrying that I was making our son "too soft."

I told him that was ridiculous, but at some point, I caved to my husband's wishes, allowing Finch's free time to be filled with more mainstream boy activities. Sports and technology (Kirk's interests) replaced music and art (mine). I was fine with that—I just wanted our son to be true to himself—but with hindsight, I had the feeling that he was following in his father's footsteps. In *all* ways.

Maybe it was an oversimplification, as I know a person isn't the sum of his hobbies. But I couldn't help feeling that I had lost my son. Lost *both* of them. I longed to go back. Do things differently. Give Finch fewer material possessions and more of my time. I would have tried harder to keep talking to him, even when he no longer wanted me to.

I thought back to my own time line—the uptick of my philanthropic work and all the socializing in those same circles that began a few years ago. How that swirl of activity happened to coincide with both the sale of Kirk's company and the onset of Finch's teenage years. It was hard to say which had happened first, but I wasn't blameless. I thought about the hours I spent on the trivial things that had become so integral to my life. Meetings and parties and beauty appointments and workouts and tennis games and lunches and, yes, even some very worthwhile charity work. But to what end? Did any of that really matter now? What was more important than squeezing in a conversation with my son about respecting women and other cultures and races? I thought about Kirk and the hundred-dollar bills in my bag—how they pretty much summed up his approach to life, at least recently.

I thought about our marriage, wondering exactly when our priorities had shifted away from our relationship and toward other things. I thought about all our small, seemingly insignificant daily choices and their cumulative effect. How they may have impacted Finch, even subconsciously. He certainly didn't see his parents talking much these days, and when we did, it was often about money or other superficial things. Even Kirk's compliments to me were nearly always about my looks or purchases, not my ideas or good works or dreams (though I wasn't even sure what those were anymore). Had it always been that way with Kirk and me? Or was I just noticing it now that Finch was older and consuming so much less of my time?

I felt a deep, aching loneliness, coupled with a painful longing for a simpler time. I missed all the chores that once felt so tedious— driving my son to school and to all his other activities, cooking breakfast and dinner for him, nagging him to go to bed, and even my least favorite, helping him with his homework at the kitchen table.

All of that segued into thoughts of Tom and Lyla. Their single-father/daughter relationship. Tom's reaction to Kirk, then me. Lyla's feelings about everything that had happened to her. I wanted to talk to her—so intensely that it didn't quite make sense. Only it *did*—as if there was no way *not* to make a connection between the present and the past, her story and mine, ancient and buried though the memories were.

IT HAPPENED IN the fall of my first semester at Vanderbilt, while I was still finding my footing and adjusting to a much bigger, fancier pond. I had been more than ready to graduate from high school and escape the mundane day-to-day of Bristol, but I was still a little homesick. More than missing my parents or home, my heart ached for Teddy, my boyfriend of nearly two years who was three hours away in Birmingham, going to Samford University on a basketball scholarship. Teddy and I talked on the phone every night, and wrote long letters by hand, always pledging our love and undying commitment to each other. There was no doubt in my mind that he was the "one."

In the meantime, though, I forged a fledgling friend group, consisting of my roommate, Eliza, and another two girls on our hall—Blake and Ashley. Although the four of us were different in many ways, including geography (Eliza was from New York, Blake from L.A., and Ashley from Atlanta), the three of them all shared a certain wealthy worldliness, something I distinctly lacked. They'd all graduated from fancy private academies while I'd gone to a run-of-the-mill public high school. They'd traveled the world and visited many of the same spots, like Aspen and Nantucket and Paris. They'd even been to more exotic places, like Africa and Asia, while my family's idea of a special trip was the Grand Canyon or Disney World. They were all foodies (before that really became a thing) and they constantly bitched about the cafeteria food (which I actually thought was pretty good). They lived for the emerging restaurant scene in Nashville and didn't think twice about dropping their dads' credit cards to pay for entrées in the double digits, which I could never afford. I avoided those outings—or declared myself "not very hungry" before finding something from the appetizer portion of the menu. Their wardrobes were insanely good (though Eliza and Blake went for edgier pieces than Ashley's Laura Ashley look)—while my clothes were extremely basic; the Gap was my version of style. Although they weren't *trying* to be snobs, they just sort of naturally *were* that way, and I found myself struggling to keep up with their sophisticated frame of reference, vacillating between feeling clueless and feeling embarrassed.

Frankly, Teddy didn't help matters. One weekend he borrowed his buddy's truck and drove to Nashville, showing up out of the blue to surprise me with a bouquet of wildflowers he'd picked himself on the way. I was thrilled to see him, of course, and touched by the romantic gesture, but as the girls came around to meet him, I found myself feeling inexplicably embarrassed. In Bristol, Teddy was a big deal—not only extremely handsome but also a star athlete. As I looked at him through their eyes, he seemed a little too sweet, too simple, and very country. Even his thick drawl, which I'd always thought was so cute (he was actually born in Mississippi and had grown up there until age twelve), now seemed to border on redneck, along with his many backwoods expressions (things weren't broken, they were "tore slap up"; they weren't catty-cornered, they were "cattywonked"; and he was never "about to" do something, he was "fixin' to"). His hair and clothes and shoes all seemed a bit off, too—nothing I could put my finger on exactly but somehow noticeably different from the boys at Vanderbilt, at least the ones my friends gravitated toward. Of course, it wasn't enough to shake my confidence in our love—I wasn't that shallow. But it did make me think a little about what my life would be like with him, versus with someone else.

Aside from anything having to do with Teddy himself, I also had the feeling my friends thought it was sort of lame of me to have come to school with such a serious boyfriend. One night, for example, the three of them were flipping through my yearbook (I never should have brought that sucker to college—they had all left theirs at home) and saw that Teddy and I had been named "most likely to get married." It amused them to no end, which I couldn't quite understand.

"Omigod! Hysterical!" Blake said, cracking up and exchanging a telling look with Ashley. It wasn't the first time I had the feeling that they'd discussed me behind my back.

I grabbed my yearbook from them and snapped it shut.

"It doesn't mean we *will* get married," I said, feeling slightly guilty toward Teddy. "Just that we'd been together the longest or whatever."

"Hmm," Blake said.

Eliza asked, "Did I hear you guys fighting last night?"

"We weren't really fighting," I said, trying to remember the precise topics from our marathon phone conversation. We always started and ended well, but occasionally there was some petty insecurity and jealousy sprinkled in.

"Long distance never works," announced Blake, the self-proclaimed authority on dating of any kind.

"Don't say *that*," said Eliza, often somewhat protective of me, perhaps because I'd confided more in her. "It *might*."

"Are you at least going to *see* other people?" Ashley pressed.

"Or just cheat on him?" Blake said, laughing.

"No, and no," I said, aware of how naïve I sounded to them but not caring.

"But don't you want to experience sex with someone other than Teddy?" Blake asked as she lit a cigarette. "He might suck, for all you know. You need a basis for comparison."

I swallowed and forced myself to make the confession I'd been avoiding. "Umm. I actually haven't slept with Teddy yet," I said.

Eliza looked surprised, and the other two laughed and said some variation of "you gotta be kidding."

"No," I said. "But we've done everything else."

This addendum didn't impress them.

"What? Why?" Ashley asked, as if I were the subject of a fascinating sociological study.

"I don't know. . . . I just wanted . . . to wait," I said, thinking of Julie and the vow we'd made during our freshman year in high school to wait as long as we could, and at least until college. I suddenly felt an intense pang of longing for the person I never had to explain these sorts of things to.

"Wait for what? Marriage?" Blake said. "Is it a religious thing?"

"No," I quickly said, feeling increasingly uncomfortable. Although Teddy believed sex outside marriage was wrong, he was willing to sin if I was.

"Oh. I thought Samford was a big Bible school?" Blake said, her tone slightly critical, though I wasn't sure whether she was judging the Bible—or Samford as an academic institution.

"Yeah, it's a Christian school," I said. "But he's not a *saint* or anything."

"Well, I think it's great to wait," Ashley said. Of all the girls', our values felt the closest, perhaps because we were both from the South.

Eliza and Blake nodded, but I could tell they weren't buying it—and that they put sex in the same category as sushi. By eighteen, you should have tried both—and California rolls and hand jobs didn't cut it.

For the first time, it occurred to me that they might be right and that I was playing it too safe. After all, I was in college now. I needed to be a little bolder, broaden my horizons, start thinking for myself instead of relying so much on Teddy.

"Okay, girls," I said, eager to change the subject. "I'm ready for a drink."

In my head, I was ready for *more* than one. I was ready to get good and drunk for the first time. It was something else Teddy thought was wrong, and the few times I'd had a beer at a party, he'd disapproved. I once tried to talk him out of his stance, pointing out that people were constantly downing wine in the Bible.

"But it also says to obey the law and be filled with the Spirit," he said, then explained to me that he'd gotten drunk once with friends and didn't like the way it had made him feel. "I was filled with spirits and not *the* Spirit."

I wasn't sure what he meant exactly, and why you couldn't be filled with *both*. But I admired him for it. I still *did* admire him, but I decided that Teddy was more than three hours away, and my college experience didn't have to mirror his.

So I stood up, went back to our room, and made myself a cocktail from Eliza's makeshift minibar. She was out of mixers, so I poured Smirnoff into a plastic cup, then added a scoop of Crystal Light. Not even bothering with ice from the machine at the end of the hall, I began to chug. Almost instantly, I caught a strong buzz, feeling a rush of happiness and great affection for my friends and all things Vanderbilt. I then borrowed a short, tight halter dress from Eliza, and all the girls agreed that I looked hot. Their compliments about my figure, hair, and face were sincere, wistful, and frequent. I was also aware of all the male attention that greeted us everywhere we went, and I decided that being drunk at a party was way more fun than whining to Teddy on the phone from under the covers of the top bunk. Maybe my friends were right about long-distance relationships, I remember thinking, as I flirted and danced and continuously drank, haphazardly mixing beer and liquor. At the very least, maybe Teddy and I needed to start seeing other people.

At some point, I got into a long, flirty conversation with one of Ashley's friends from home. His name was Zach Rutherford, and he had a mop of blond hair and the cutest dimples. He was several inches shorter than I was and on the scrawny side—not my type even if I didn't have a boyfriend—so I didn't feel guilty talking to him, then dancing with him. When he started to get really friendly, though, I told him that I was going to head back to my dorm.

"I'll walk you home?" he offered.

"I have a boyfriend," I blurted out.

"Duly noted," Zach said, laughing. "I'm not trying to hit on you, Nina—I'm just offering to walk you back."

I hesitated, then did a sidebar with Ashley, who reassured me that Zach was a good guy, adding that he was a nationally ranked golfer and could have gone to any school in the country. "Everyone in Atlanta wanted to date him," she said, her implication clear, even before she winked and added, "You never know!"

I shook my head and said, "He's just walking me back."

By then though, I'd felt my first stab of guilty attraction and intrigue over Zach. But I really *did* need to get back, as by then I was wasted, and I told myself I really could use a male chaperone across campus.

So off we went. Only before we got to my dorm, Zach asked if we could do a quick detour to his. He needed to get something, he said. I agreed, because I was drunkenly enjoying the walk and his company (though at that point, I would have enjoyed just about anything). When we got to his dorm, I started to wait in the lobby lounge area, but he suggested I come to his room. I went along with it. A few minutes later, we were cozied up on his futon, sharing a beer and listening to R.E.M. croon "Nightswimming." When he tried to kiss me, I went along with that, too, pushing Teddy as far from my mind as I possibly could.

That's pretty much the last thing I *vividly* remember from the night, until I woke up in a strange bed, naked, next to a naked boy. At first, I couldn't even place that it was Zach—but then it all came back to me in a rush of horror.

"Where are we?" I said, staring up at the bottom rails of a bunk bed.

"In my room," he mumbled.

"What happened? Did we . . . ?" I asked, knowing we had because it hurt. A lot. In the faint fluorescent light from his closet, I could make out the blood, both on his sheets and streaked down the insides of my thighs.

"Yeah," he mumbled, still either out of it or half asleep.

"Oh my God," I said. "No. *Nooo!*"

"You wanted to," he said, just as a flash of it came back to me. The moment he entered me. The pain. My balled fists and tears. My telling him—shouting at him—*no, stop, no.* It was like a bad dream, but it was real. It had happened.

The room spinning, I managed to sit up, frantically searching for my clothes, finding Eliza's white dress, twisted up in his sheets, along with my underwear.

"You wanted to," he said again, his eyes only half open, his voice still slurring, as I looked around in the dark for my shoes. I couldn't find them, so I headed out the door, barefoot, as Zach remained motionless in his bed.

I ran back to my dorm, but I didn't cry until I got to my room and discovered with relief that Eliza was still out. I checked her dress for blood, relieved that there was none. I hung it up, then stripped out of my clothes, wrapped up in a towel, put on my flip-flops, and walked to the communal bathroom. I took the hottest and longest shower of my life, sobbing the whole time, then returned to my room, where I finally forced myself to play back the four messages on the answering machine.

They were all from Teddy, as I knew they would be, his voice getting increasingly worried and agitated, asking me to call him no matter how late I got back. Ending every message with "I love you."

I wanted to hear his voice more than anything in the world, but it was four in the morning, and I told myself he would be asleep and had an early class. I shouldn't wake him up. But deep down, I knew the real reason was that I couldn't bring myself to tell him what had happened any more than I could bring myself to lie to him. Instead I called Julie, waking her up in her Wake Forest dorm room, telling her everything.

Almost immediately, Julie used the word *rape*.

"It wasn't *rape*," I whispered, huddled under my covers. "I was kissing him. . . ."

"It *was* rape," Julie insisted, ahead of her time, or at least ahead of my 1995 views of what constituted date rape. "You need to go to the campus police. Or better yet, the Nashville police."

I told her that was crazy. Besides, I'd already washed away all the evidence. "Nobody would believe me."

"Yes. They will," she said. "You were a virgin."

I started to cry again. "I can't go to the police," I sobbed.

"Why not?"

Because, I told her, at the very least, I shared the blame. It was my mistake, too. My fault for leading him on. My cross to bear.

I also told her that the only fair punishment was for me to lose Teddy. I would break up with him in the morning—or after his classes and practice. I *had* to break up with him. It was kinder than telling him what had actually happened.

"But you'll be punishing *him,* too," she said. "Don't do that, Nina. You have to tell him. You have to talk to him. He'll agree with me—that you need to go to the police."

"No. I can't do that to him, Julie. It would ruin him. My drinking . . . the kissing . . . everything. He deserves better than me."

"But he loves *you.* He wants *you.*"

"Not if he knew this," I said.

"God teaches forgiveness," she said, grasping at straws, knowing the way Teddy thought—and that *I* knew that was the way Teddy thought.

"No," I cried. "Promise me, Julie. You won't tell him, either. You won't tell *anyone. Ever.*"

She made the promise, and she kept it, too. For all these years. Even between the two of us, we rarely spoke of it directly, although she made veiled references whenever a similar case arose in the media. Once, she even mentioned that what happened to me was part of why she was an advocate for women, her clientele almost exclusively female. She said she wished she had done more when she was younger.

I guess the bottom line was, I wish I had done more, too. Because I know that Zach Rutherford raped me. And although I truly believed that Finch hadn't done anything nearly that horrible to

Lyla, it was still terrible. Just like Zach, my son had taken advantage of an innocent girl who was in a vulnerable situation. He had exploited her. Used her. Treated her like trash.

In many ways, Finch was Zach, and I was Lyla. And I didn't want Finch to haunt her the way Zach had haunted me.

So I stood up, slinging my purse full of cash over my shoulder, and walked back to my car in the setting spring sun. I wasn't sure what I would do next. But it would be more than *nothing*, that was for sure.

chapter eleven

TOM

I've always considered myself lucky that I could mostly earn a living by doing what I love, but a bonus has been the sheer escape that comes with woodworking. What do they call it? Being in the zone or the flow? Whatever the case, I did my best to push everything out of my head that afternoon in my workshop. As I measured, marked, and cut shelves for a spruce bookcase, I felt myself start to relax for the first time in days, my mind going blissfully blank.

Unfortunately, the shelves were *too* basic—I could have made them blindfolded. So before long, I found my thoughts returning to Nina Browning. I had almost been looking forward to hating her as much as I hated her husband and kid, and I couldn't wait to throw that goddamn pile of money in her face. Yet for some odd reason, I couldn't quite muster anything stronger than a mild, theoretical dislike for her, which was frustrating and disorienting. The fact that I felt like I'd met her before didn't help matters. Unlike Nina, I felt like I was pretty good with faces. But the full truth was I was good with *certain* faces, the same way I could remember an exceptional piece of furniture. Nina had that sort of vivid, memorable look. Very pretty but not at all generic.

I glanced at the old-school clock mounted on the wall over my workbench and saw that it was nearly seven. Lyla had gotten a ride home from school with Grace, but I tried to make it a point to be home for dinner, even when I planned to return to my workshop or squeeze in a few late-night Uber trips. I texted her now and asked what she wanted to eat, knowing she'd say she didn't care. Even when she wasn't angry with me, she had trouble making decisions. A minute later the predictable reply came in. Don't care. Not hungry.

As I swept up and put away my tools, my mind returned to Nina. Her face. Her legs, which I'd caught a glimpse of when she stood up to say hello. There was no denying she was attractive, which pissed me off almost as much as the fact that I didn't hate her. I blew sawdust off my drill bit and told myself it didn't matter. She was an asshole. I knew her type. Only an asshole married a guy like that, and only an asshole would raise a son who would do what hers did, especially when he had everything in the world going for him. Privilege, popularity, Princeton. She'd said it herself—she was his *mother*.

Women are just better at faking it if and when they need to, and clearly Nina Browning was either a good actress or just plain crafty. A regular con artist. She knew to ask about Lyla, feigning a little maternal compassion. Her ploy had very nearly worked on me, until she overplayed her hand. There was no chance she wanted me to pursue the Honor Council charges against her son, especially given that he'd just been accepted to Princeton. Zilch. Why would she risk that for a girl she'd never met? She wouldn't, plain and simple. And to think I'd almost bought her reverse-psychology bullshit. I pictured her now, drinking a martini with her friends, feeling smug about how she'd manipulated another guy with her bullshit lines.

And that's when it hit me. Where I had seen her before. It was about four years ago, maybe more, as I tended to underestimate the passage of time these days. She'd come to the home of a client who had hired me to redo cabinetry in what she called her "keeping room." This woman, whose name I couldn't recall for the life of me, was about the same age and profile as Nina—meaning she, too, lived in a Belle Meade mansion, though not as grand as Nina's. I'd actually gotten the initial call from her contractor explaining that she was impossible to please, hadn't been happy with the work of a former carpenter, and wanted to start over from scratch. She didn't like his design, though she had signed off on the drawings, nor did she like the materials he'd used, though she'd also approved his choice of teak.

"I wouldn't blame you for not touching this one," the guy had said. "She's a real pain in the ass."

I very nearly heeded his warning, but I needed the money, as always, so I took the gig. When I went over to meet her, I actually tried to talk her out of the redo, explaining the flaws she perceived in the teak would likely disappear with a coat of paint and certainly two or three, and that, in my opinion, she'd be wasting her money. She was unconvinced and undeterred, or maybe she just *wanted* to waste money.

So I took the job, agreeing to use mahogany and a new, more detailed design with a lot of flourishes and scrollwork that she'd pulled from a design magazine and that I actually thought were a little too McMansion-y.

Suffice it to say—the contractor was right. It was a long three weeks with this woman, though not because she was hard to please. She was thrilled with my work. But she never left me alone, never shut up or shut down her monologue of complaints about her life, whether online ordering snafus (her house was like a

FedEx depot) or tennis team drama. Every day at five o'clock sharp, she'd open a bottle of wine, which was my cue to try to leave, and her cue to offer me "overtime" and a glass of my own. I explained more than once that I didn't drink on the job, at which point she'd assault me with peer pressure I hadn't experienced since junior high. "Oh, come on, don't be such a Goody Two-shoes," she'd say. "One little glass." A couple times I relented, taking a few sips just to shut her up while she polished off the rest of the bottle, often then delving into complaints about her husband. How he was never around, that he didn't listen to her, that he bitched about her spending habits.

And that's where Nina Browning came in, quite literally, show-ing up one evening for what looked to be a big night out. What's Her Name wasn't quite ready, so she handed her friend a glass of wine and told her she'd be back in a second. At least a half hour passed in which I continued to work and Nina typed away on her phone in the adjoining kitchen. Meanwhile, we each pretended the other wasn't just a few feet away. At one point, she got a call, and I had the feeling it was from her husband or someone she was very close to. Because she started speaking in a hushed voice, complain-ing about how What's Her Name was always late. When she hung up, she caught me looking at her, let out a little laugh, and said, "You didn't hear that."

I smiled and said something like "Oh, yeah, I *did*."

"She's a great friend, but *never* on time."

"Maybe if she talked a little less. . . ."

This made her laugh a real laugh, showing a lot of big white teeth and how pretty she was and, perhaps more noteworthy, how unlike her friend she seemed to be. More real, less insecure. She was interacting with me as an equal and not as the carpenter she could pay overtime to drink with her.

A few minutes later, What's Her Name sauntered into the kitchen and announced that I could keep working; she "trusted me in the house." She meant it as the highest of compliments, but of course it was actually an insulting sentiment—which Nina picked up on with a subtle eye roll. Then they were gone.

That was it, really. Not much of a meeting at all. But it was still a reference point that made me think it was possible that our conversation today had been sincere rather than a coffee-shop performance. Then again, they *both* could have been performances. I shut off the lights, locked up my workshop, and walked to my truck, telling myself none of this mattered. Whether she was a decent person was in some ways as wholly irrelevant as her looks. It didn't change what her son had done, and it wasn't going to change my decision. Yet as I drove home, I found myself wondering about her—who she *really* was as a person. For some inexplicable reason, I wanted—somehow *needed*—to know the truth about Nina Browning. Which is why I was more than a little intrigued when I received her email that night—and unable to resist the back and forth that followed.

Tom,

Thank you so much for meeting me with me today. Although it was difficult, I'm glad we had the chance to talk through things. I was wondering if you'd be open to getting together again, this time with Finch and Lyla? Obviously I won't press the issue if you're uncomfortable with the idea, but I think it might be good for both of them. Let me know your thoughts.

Best,
Nina

• • •

139

Thank you for following up and for the offer. Let me talk to Lyla and see how she feels. Oh. And I think I figured out where we met. Do you have a friend who lives in a brick house on Lynwood? Pretty sure I met you while working there a number of years ago. T.

. . .

Oh my goodness! Yes, I do! Melanie Lawson. I totally remember chatting with you now! (And this proves that I *am* bad with faces, because I remember everything else about our conversation :)

Nina

ps You did a beautiful job at her house. She still raves about you.
pps She's a Windsor parent, too. Did you know that?

. . .

No. I'm not really into the whole Windsor social scene.

. . .

I hear you. I love the school, but it is quite a scene at times. We've been there since Finch was in kindergarten so I'm used to it at this point. . . . Also, I'm not sure that this is at all relevant, but I feel like I should tell you that that's where the kids were the night in question (at Melanie's house). Her son had a party (without her permission). Small world. Or something?

. . .

I'll go with "or something." And nothing is really in question, is it?

. . .

Yes. Two poor expressions to use under these circumstances. I'm sorry. And I'm so sorry again for what Finch did. I know those

140

are just words, but they are heartfelt. I really want to try to make things right. I hope you believe that. And I hope Finch will have the chance to meet with Lyla and tell her all of this himself.

. . .

Thanks. I'll talk to Lyla and be in touch soon.

chapter twelve

NINA

There was no such thing as a kept secret in the Windsor community, and although I hoped the fire would be contained, I knew that it was only a matter of time before it raged. Based on my experience with other people's drama, I gave it a week.

I was pretty much dead-on because by the following morning—six days after Beau's party—my phone was blowing up with friends, and even some acquaintances, gingerly "checking in on" me. I suppose some were genuinely concerned over the development. But I think most were more in Kathie's camp, on some level, perhaps even subconsciously, reveling in the gossip and indifferent to the fact that they were so casually and cavalierly deepening the crisis not only for Finch (who arguably deserved what he was getting) but also for Lyla.

I crafted a pat reply ("Thank you for your concern and kind words") and vowed to avoid my usual stomping grounds—all the places where I inevitably ran into people I knew. Starbucks and Fix Juice, the Green Hills mall and Whole Foods, my spin and yoga studios, and of course the club.

The only person I continued to discuss it with was Melanie, who was so fiercely partisan that I think I could shoot someone on Belle Meade Boulevard and she'd say I must have had a good reason. She sent me screenshot after screenshot from people opining on the matter, often with rumors they'd heard through the grapevine: Lyla was *completely* naked; Finch had put something in her drink; the two had engaged in sexual activity. The story was constantly being embellished.

Every time, Melanie came fiercely to Finch's defense, setting the record straight, typing replies in all caps with a bounty of exclamation points. Even when it came to the true parts of the story, she rationalized and insisted that this was "a good kid who had made a mistake."

On one level, I truly appreciated her loyalty, particularly when she was correcting falsehoods. On another, deeper level, her indignation made me incrementally more ashamed. After all, Finch *was* guilty. Maybe not guilty of all the accusations swirling around the rumor mill, but guilty nonetheless. It was a fact that seemed to be lost on her, just as it was on Kirk.

On Friday evening, she showed up at my house, distraught and in disarray—at least by Melanie's high grooming standards.

"What happened?" I said, opening the door.

"Didn't you get my texts? I told you I was on my way over. . . ."

"No. I haven't looked at my phone for a bit," I said, having put it away so I would stop checking to see if Tom had written me back. It had not been twenty-four hours since I'd asked to meet with Lyla, but I was starting to obsess over his decision. I led Melanie into the kitchen now.

"Sit down," I said. "Tell me what's going on."

She sighed and tossed her monogrammed Goyard tote at her feet before taking a perch on a kitchen stool. "That bitch Kathie—" She stopped, looked around and said, "Is anyone home?"

"Kirk's not. He was home for twenty-four hours—but left again. Finch is here—but up in his room," I said. "So fire away."

143

She pressed one hand to her temple as the other played with the folds of her tennis skirt. "That *bitch* Kathie is now telling people that *Beau* hooked up with Lyla. After Finch took the picture."

"Um . . . *did* he?" I asked at my own peril. Melanie and I had *never* had an argument, but she could be oversensitive and thin-skinned, especially when it related to Beau or her daughter, Violet, who had more diva tendencies than any child I'd ever known who wasn't on a sitcom.

"Oh, God, *no,*" she said, her spray-tanned leg bouncing on the barstool.

"What's she basing that on, then?" I said. "Just Lyla being on Beau's bed in the photograph?"

"I have *literally* no clue! But I bet Lucinda is behind it. She's a total *C-U-next-Tuesday*. I detest that child. . . . She's been posting articles on Facebook about sexual assault and misogyny." Melanie reached down and pulled her phone out of her bag, then began to read in a high, prissy voice, presumably imitating Lucinda. "'Forty-four percent of reported sexual assaults take place before a victim is eighteen. One in three girls is sexually abused prior to leaving high school. . . . And yet secondary schools are irresponsibly reluctant to act on this information . . . resulting in the current frequency of college sexual assaults.'"

I felt a stab of grief, thinking about both Lyla and my own experience at Vanderbilt. "I know Lucinda is as obnoxious as her mother. . . . But unfortunately, she's *right*. If it were coming from someone else—"

"It would *still* be obnoxious!" Melanie said. "Keep your opinions off social media!"

I actually disagreed with her—and thought that activism of this kind is one of the only decent upshots of social media. Otherwise, it's just a regular brag or snooze fest—a way to either show off your vacation or bore everyone with your Brussels sprouts. I almost said something along those lines, but Melanie was on a roll.

"I mean, Finch and Beau are good kids! From good families!" she said once again, removing an elastic band from her hair, shaking it out, then putting it up in a fresher ponytail. "And Lyla is *so* not their type."

"She *is* very pretty, though," I said, mostly just musing aloud.

"Have you seen her in person?"

I shook my head and said, "No. But I saw some other photos of her."

"Is she *mulatto*? . . . Beau said she is. Is that true?"

"Mulatto? I haven't heard that in years," I said, wondering if it was still politically correct and feeling pretty certain that it was not.

She shrugged. "Whatever the term is. Mixed? Biracial? I can't keep it straight. Is she?"

"She's half Brazilian," I said.

"Huh," she said. "So her mom must be foreign. Because I heard her dad's white. I *also* heard her mother's in jail for drugs and prostitution. No wonder Lyla's so promiscuous."

"Who said she was promiscuous?" I asked, thinking that Melanie was trying to have it both ways. Lyla didn't do anything that night with our boys, yet she was also promiscuous? Which one was it?

"Did you not see her outfit?" Melanie tugged on her tank as she made a cross-eyed, tongue-lolling face.

"Come on, Mel. You know better than that," I said, tensing. "An outfit doesn't make someone *promiscuous*. That's almost like saying 'She wore a short skirt, so she had it coming.' "

Melanie stared at me for a beat then said, "Okay. What's going on? Why are you so Team Lyla? I don't get it."

"I'm not," I said. "I just have the feeling she's a nice girl who got caught up in something she didn't ask for."

"And why do you think that?"

"Because. I had coffee with Lyla's father," I blurted out, as my mind exploded with a flowchart of possible repercussions that came from Melanie knowing this. She was well intentioned in our friendship but had an absolute inability to keep much of anything to herself.

"You *did*?" she said, probably already mapping out who she would tell the second she left my house. "*When?*"

"Yesterday," I said, making a split-second decision not to make it more irresistible by telling her to keep it a secret. "It was no big deal, really. . . . It just felt like the right thing to do."

She nodded. "So? What was he like?"

"You've actually met him," I said. "His name is Tom Volpe. Ring a bell?"

She gave me a blank stare, shook her head, then said, "Wait. That *does* sound familiar. How do I know that name?" She repeated *Volpe* under her breath a couple times, frowning as if trying to place him.

"He did your butler's pantry," I said. "And your keeping room shelves."

Her face suddenly lit up. "Oh yeah! *That* Tom! Right. He was *hot*. You know—in a scruffy, blue-collar way. . . ."

The characterization slightly annoyed me, though I couldn't pinpoint why, especially given that it was a pretty accurate description. In any case, I just nodded and said, "Yeah. I guess."

"Wait. *His* daughter is *Lyla*?"

I nodded.

"That's surprising," she said.

"Why?" I asked.

"I don't know. Because he's a carpenter, I guess? There aren't a lot of carpenters' kids at Windsor. . . . She *must* be on financial aid."

"Maybe. Who knows," I said, resisting the temptation to add *and who cares*. Instead I said, "But if she came in the ninth grade, then she also must be pretty smart. Or supertalented in some area."

Everyone knew that admissions standards became more stringent in high school, whereas the criteria for five- and six-year-olds were considerably broader and had much more to do with who your parents were. Nobody said it, but it seemed pretty clear that if two applicants were completely equal but for the ability to make a big donation, the big donation won. To Kirk, there was nothing troubling about that. It was just life.

"Or maybe she got in because of the mulatto thing," Melanie said. "You know how Walter is about *diversity*."

I shrugged, feeling intensely uncomfortable. To deflect, I pointed at a bottle of pinot noir that I'd opened with dinner and said, "Would you like a glass?"

"Maybe just a teensy one. I'm trying to cut down on sugar. . . . I'm *so* fat. Ugh . . ." She leaned forward so that she could get a pinch of skin covering her washboard stomach as I poured a glass and handed it to her.

She took a sip, then said, "So? Details. Did he *ask* to meet with you or what?"

"No. I asked to meet with him," I said, refilling my glass, too.

"*Why?* To talk him out of pressing charges?"

"No," I said. "To apologize to him."

"Oh yeah, of course. I just thought there might be something else," she said, bouncing her foot again and looking wounded. It was an expression she wore often. In some ways, I loved this vulnerability about her, even when it felt misplaced. It was unlike so many of the other housewives of Belle Meade, who wore perma-masks of bliss. From those types, the answer to the simple and actually not very curious question "How are you doing?" was always a gushing litany of how wonderfully full and satisfying their lives were. *Busy, busy, busy! Happy, happy, happy! All good! Busy, happy, and good!* I had one friend who would actually answer with a chipper *Better than terrific!* Her marriage, her kids, her holidays, her summer—were all, *always,* better than terrific.

Even the breezy *I can't complain!* grated on me. First of all, *sure* you *can* complain, and you *do,* and you *will.* You'll complain about your kid's teachers and coaches, your neighbors and your neighbors' pets, your fellow committee members on whatever charity or school function you're working on (whether it's because they're not doing their fair share or because they're being too bossy and trying to take the whole thing over); you'll complain when people don't reply fast enough to your correspondence or when they hit reply all, giving you needless information that swamps your oh-so-important in-boxes; you'll complain over your house-keepers and nannies and gardeners and anyone at all who comes into your home to do any kind of work for you. You'll complain over everything and nothing *unless* it is any kind of reflection on you, your kids, your marriage, or your life. And if, God forbid, you or your children make a misstep, you blame everyone else and insist that you're the victim from a "good family." I knew the drill.

"Can I just say?" Melanie began now. "It hurts my feelings a little bit that you didn't tell me. Especially since Beau's involved."

"But I just *told* you."

"I mean, sooner. Right away. Before you even met with him."

"I guess I forgot to mention it," I fibbed. "I'm sorry, Mel."

Her frown lines grew as deep as her Botox would allow. "Did he mention Beau? Or the party itself? Is he mad about that?"

"No," I said. "I'm pretty sure that's the least of his concerns right now."

Melanie nodded, then took a deep breath. "Listen. I admire you, Nina. So much. You're such a good person—and your heart's in the right place. . . . I admire the fact that you're trying to make this right. But . . . I really think you're being too hard on yourself. And Finch."

I nodded, torn. Her steadfast loyalty certainly *felt* better than Julie's tough love. Yet I was also frustrated by her inability—or at least refusal—to see what was at stake. I guess my friends couldn't win. I knew that's what Kirk would say if he could read my mind now. He hated when I got this way, at least when my feelings threatened his agenda. *You're impossible to please,* he'd tell me. *Move on and stop obsessing.*

Of course, he obsessed over plenty of things, too. But in his mind, those things were different. They were obsession-worthy because they were about the big financial picture—or another quantifiable issue. It was almost as if anything related to relationships or emotions was trivial to him. A disagreement with my mother? *She'll get over it.* A friend getting on my nerves? *Stop hanging out with her.* A feeling that I wasn't doing enough in the world or guilt about all we had? *We give more than enough money away to charity.* And now: our own son's character? *He's a good kid who made one little mistake. Move on, let it go.*

"Are you even listening to me?" I heard Melanie say.

"Sorry. I spaced out there for a second," I said.

"I was just asking about Polly and Finch?"

"What about them?"

"How's Finch doing? With the breakup?" she said, lowering her voice.

"They broke up? I hadn't heard," I said, feeling a stab of maternal guilt for being the last to know.

"Yeah. Honestly, though, I think Finch could do *so* much better than Polly. I've said that from the beginning. Everyone thinks so," Melanie said.

Marveling that Polly's inferiority to Finch could *still* be Melanie's conclusion given recent events, I said, "I don't know, Mel. I bet *she* broke up with *him*. . . . I'd break up with a boy for doing what he did to another girl. It was *so* mean."

"Please stop torturing yourself, honey. Kids make mistakes. Especially boys. Remember that psychiatrist who told us that the frontal lobe of a boy's brain isn't developed until, like, age twenty-five? . . . They use bad judgment without a fully developed frontal lobe."

I shrugged, then reiterated the point I'd made to Kirk. To me, this wasn't about judgment so much as *morals*.

"C'mon, Nina! You need to be an advocate for your own child!"

"What about Lyla? Shouldn't we be advocates for *all* children?"

"Let *Tom* worry about Lyla. Let *him* be her advocate. You need to be Finch's. You should always side with your kid. *Always*."

"Without regard to his actions?" I asked. "No matter *what*?"

"No. Matter. What," she said, crossing her arms.

"What if Beau *killed* someone?" I said, testing the theory.

"Well, then, we'd hire the very best defense lawyers. O. J. Simpson–type lawyers. And if we lost, I would visit him in jail every single day until I died." She took a deep breath. "Beau will always be my flesh and blood. I couldn't stop loving him. Ever."

"Of course. I get that," I said, feeling a wave of defensiveness. I mean, I, too, would love Finch no matter what. I could even see where she was coming from with respect to hiring the best attorneys and being hopeful that he might get a lighter sentence. After all, that *is* our legal system—which I *do* believe in.

But I also knew in my heart that I wouldn't *cover* for my son if he committed a terrible crime. *Any* crime. I wouldn't *lie* for him. I wouldn't obstruct *justice* for him. I would stand by him, but I would also want him to confess and truly repent and bear responsibility for his actions. I would want him to *earn* and deserve his forgiveness.

I tried to summarize the distinction to Melanie, but she wasn't having it, digging deeper with her next statement. "Well, I would do anything it took to protect Beau from pain. *Anything.*"

Our eyes locked as the truth slowly sank in—the fact that I just didn't feel the same. I thought of a sermon I'd once heard at Teddy's church, a long time ago. Pastor Sundermeier had said something along the lines of "Justice isn't only about what a person *deserves,* but also about what a person *needs.*" It was a crucial piece of the puzzle that Melanie and Kirk seemed to be missing.

"Well, for what it's worth, Kirk agrees with you," I said.

She nodded, looking vindicated. "Of *course* he does. He has *excellent* instincts when it comes to these things."

I thought about the fifteen thousand dollars, knowing that although Melanie probably would have approved of his ploy, she likely would also have scoffed at the amount, as she never minded overpaying, one of her mantras being *Just throw money at the problem.*

"Not always," I said. "Sometimes he's a little too . . . *results* driven. He always gets what he wants."

"Yeah," she said with a little laugh. "That's sort of why you married him, isn't it?"

She was referring to our "story"—the one Kirk loved to tell. How he had pursued me throughout our sophomore year at Vanderbilt, asking me out a half dozen times before I finally said yes. Of course he believed I was merely playing hard to get, which had raised my stock in his eyes. And I never told him the truth— that I'd been too scarred by the traumatic events of my freshman year to even consider dating anyone for a long time.

Looking back, though, maybe Melanie had a point. I *did* admire my husband's tenacity, and it probably *did* have something to do with why we ended up together. If I'm being honest, I have to admit I also liked how much my friends liked him. How well he fit in with everyone. He took my mind off bad things. He made me feel safe. Like nothing bad would happen to me on his watch.

"I guess so," I murmured as Melanie and I drank wine and I contemplated my *own* intentions.

Why did I so badly want to meet with Lyla, and talk to Tom again? Was it really just about Finch learning from his mistakes and my doing the right thing? Or was I seeking some sort of absolution—maybe even vindication for my younger self? I wasn't sure, but I suddenly and desperately wanted to be alone.

"Oh, my goodness," I said, forcing a fake yawn. "I'm *so* tired."

"Yeah. Me, too," she said. "I should go . . ."

I quickly stood, knowing how often *I should go* resulted in an additional hour of conversation.

"Hang in there, honey," she said, giving me a big hug. "Get some rest. And leave this to Kirk. Trust me, it will all be over soon."

As soon as Melanie walked out the door, I couldn't get to my phone fast enough. Amid the usual mass mail, two emails jumped out at me. The first was from Walter Quarterman, the second from Tom Volpe. My heart raced as I opened Walter's first and read the short message informing Kirk and me that Finch's "closed hearing" before the Honor Council was scheduled for this coming Tuesday at 9:00 A.M. He apologized for the delay but explained that two faculty members on the council had been away at a conference. He added that we were welcome to come to school that day but would not be permitted in the room during the questioning.

"Okay," I said aloud to myself, relieved to see the date finalized. Four more days.

I took a deep breath, then opened the second email.

From: Thomas Volpe
To: Nina Browning
Subject: Hello

Hi Nina, I think you're right. It is a good idea for the four of us to sit down together. Does this weekend work? Tomorrow around 11? You are welcome to come to our house. I'd prefer that to yours. Our address is in the directory.

Feeling intensely anxious, but also grateful and hopeful, I composed a reply:

From: Nina Browning
To: Thomas Volpe
Subject: Thank you

Tom, I greatly appreciate your decision. Tomorrow morning absolutely works. We will see you at your place at 11 A.M. Thank you again so much.

I hit send just as Kirk's name lit up on my phone. I answered as he barked into my ear. "That asshole took the cash and is still letting this go to trial! So much for a gentleman's agreement."

"A *gentleman's* agreement?" I said, so aghast by this ridiculous spin that I further rationalized not telling him that Tom had returned the money. I knew two wrongs didn't make a right, but he didn't deserve the truth. He *deserved* to feel screwed.

"A settlement. Yes."

"It wasn't a gentleman's agreement. Or a settlement. It was a *bribe*. You tried to pay him off to keep quiet. And it *backfired*," I said.

"Try not to sound so happy about it," he said.

"I'm not *happy* about this," I said. "I'm not happy about *anything* right now."

"Well," Kirk said. "That makes two of us."

A FEW MINUTES later, I went to Finch's room. His door was closed. I stared at it for a few seconds, thinking of how much things had changed, both quickly and gradually. When he was a little boy, his door stayed open and he often ended up in our bed. By the time he reached late elementary school, he would occasionally close it, but I felt free to open it without knocking. When he was in middle school, I did a quick knock before walking in. Once he was in early high school, I awaited his permission following the knock. And in the last year or two, all bedroom chats had become nonexistent. I barely entered his room at all, as Juana did his laundry and put away all his clean clothes.

I knocked now, then opened the door to find Finch on his bed. He was on his laptop and wearing headphones. He looked up at me blankly.

"Hi," I said.

"Hi," he replied.

"Can you take those off?"

"There's no sound," he said.

"Take them off anyway."

He did, with no attitude.

"How're things going?" I asked, my voice sounding stilted.

"Fine."

"Good," I said. "And how's Polly?"

"She's fine, I guess."

"You guess?" I took a step inside his room. "You don't know?"

"Not really," he said, expressionless. "We broke up."

"I'm sorry. Can I . . . ask why?"

He sighed. "I don't really want to talk about it, if that's okay?"

I bit my lip and nodded. "Well, I also wanted to tell you that your father and I heard from Mr. Quarterman. Your Honor Council hearing is scheduled for next Tuesday."

"Yeah, I know," he said. "I got an email, too."

"Oh," I said. "Have you talked to Lyla?"

"No."

"Why not?"

"Dad told me not to."

"He did?" I said. "When did he tell you that?"

"Last week. After our meeting with Mr. Q."

"Well," I said briskly. "I'm overriding that. We're going to see her tomorrow morning. You and I. Her dad will be there, too. It will be the four of us."

I braced myself for resistance, but he only nodded and said okay.

"And in the meantime, I want you to think about Lyla. *Her* feelings. This is about *her* right now."

"I know, Mom," he said, looking a little like his younger, earnest self.

"*Do* you?" I asked.

"Yeah."

"So you understand that this meeting with Lyla is not a strategy for *you*. It's an apology to *her*."

He nodded again. "Yeah, Mom. I get it," he said, holding my gaze.

Maybe he was humoring me or trying to avoid a lecture, but his expression really seemed sincere. It wasn't quite a relief—I was still worried about his character—but it was a very small consolation and maybe even a source of hope.

"Are you sure you don't want to talk about Polly? Or anything else going on in your life?" I gently pressed, feeling certain I knew what the answer would be.

"Yeah, Mom," he said. "I'm sure."

chapter thirteen

LYLA

On Friday night, right when I thought things couldn't get any worse, Dad came into my room and dropped another bomb on me. A *stealth* bomb.

"Get some sleep," he said, standing in the doorway in a Titans T-shirt and sweatpants. "We have a meeting in the morning."

"What kind of meeting?" I said, feeling suspicious because we never had appointments and stuff on the weekends. Dad knows that I love to sleep in on Saturdays, and it really is my only day to do so because he often guilt-trips me into going to mass with Nonna (who is sort of obsessed with being Catholic) on Sunday mornings.

"Finch Browning and his mother are coming over," he said all nonchalantly, like I wasn't going to notice.

I waited for the punch line, but there wasn't one. "What? *Why?*" I demanded.

"To talk," he said, taking another step into my room and glancing down at a laundry basket filled with clean clothes that he'd put there and asked me to fold the night before. Usually he does that for me—or at least refolds everything after I do a shit job (Dad is totally OCD about the weirdest things)—but I could tell he was trying to be stricter all of a sudden. As if his folding my laundry for me had been a contributing factor in my decision to drink at a party.

"Talk about *what*?" I said, horrified.

"What do you *think*, Lyla?" he said.

"I don't know, Dad," I said as sarcastically as I could. "That's why I asked you—since you obviously set this up."

"I would imagine—and this is just a wild guess—that we're going to talk about what Finch did to you," he said super-calmly and just as sarcastically.

I'm not sure exactly what I pictured going down tomorrow, but he might as well have just suggested that the four of us sit naked around a table playing Monopoly. Like, I really couldn't think of anything more painfully awkward than rehashing what Finch *did to me*.

"Wow. So you really *are* trying to completely ruin my life?" I said. It actually felt like an understatement. I held my breath because I wasn't fooled. I knew that at any moment, he could erupt. These days my dad went from zero to a hundred in no time at all. Actually, there was never a zero anymore. He was always pretty amped up and ready to explode.

"Not at all," he said. "I'm trying to be a good father. That's all."

"Yeah. Well. Good fathers don't usually try to destroy their daughters' lives."

I'd finally pushed his button, so he made a huffing sound, then threw up his hands like a pissed-off cartoon dad, and left the room mumbling, "You must have me confused with your *other* parent."

I almost chased after him to tell him to stop playing the martyr. I mean, yeah, I get that Mom completely sucked in the parenting department. But Mom's over-the-top sucking shouldn't give Dad extra credit for doing the same basic job that everyone else's parents were doing. I honestly couldn't believe I'd never thought to make the point before and couldn't wait to lay it on him, but I couldn't make myself get up. So I just lay in bed low-key crying until Dad came back to my room—which I knew he would. He'd never stated aloud the don't-go-to-bed-mad rule, but he more or less followed it. He'd always at least come back to say a civil good night. I heard Nonna once say that it was because he had "a weak stomach for conflict," but I think it actually might have something to do with the way Mom left us.

Neither one of them had ever been entirely clear about what had happened when she jetted off in the middle of the night, but I got the gist that they'd had a big fight over me. It was something about Mom drinking too much and almost letting me drown at a pool party. (Though Mom insisted that I knew how to swim from a few lessons at the Y, Dad maintains that I'd only learned how to turn my face to the side to blow bubbles.) Anyway, Dad was furious at her "negligence"—and she was pissed off at his "judgmentalness"— if that's even a word. She was so pissed off, in fact, that she *left*. For good.

"Your father made it clear that he thought you would both be better off without me. And I suppose he was right," Mom told me one of the times she came back. She was a master at painting herself as the victim even when talking to *me*, her abandoned daughter.

I almost pointed out that he wasn't *beating* her. Like, being judgmental just isn't *that* drastic. At least not drastic enough to choose abandonment, and obviously she had another choice besides completely throwing in the towel. She could have proven Dad wrong and tried to show him that she could be a responsible, good mother. Instead, she kind of proved his case for him.

As far as Dad goes, I think he can't help blaming himself just a little for the way things went down. And maybe he even thinks that if the two of them had had the don't-go-to-bed-mad rule, he could have convinced her to go to rehab or tried to figure their messed-up shit out. I doubt it, and I bet Dad doubts it, too. But I still wonder sometimes, and I bet he does, too.

In any case, when Dad came back in my room, I was glad, even though I was still really pissed. Before he could say anything, or throw another pity party for himself, I went off. "Look, Dad. I'm totally grateful to you for being a good father and everything, but this whole deal is really *killing* me."

"Killing you?" he said, doing the calm routine again.

"It's just an expression, Dad."

He nodded.

"Yes. I mean, honestly, the last thing I'd want to do in the *world* is sit down with the Brownings. Like, I'd rather walk through fire. Or pull my toenails out."

"It's not my idea of a good time, either," Dad said.

"Then why are we doing it? Whose idea was it, anyway?" I asked.

"Nina's," he replied. "Mrs. Browning's."

I stared back at him, processing the information, as well as her name. *Nina.* It was so classy and elegant, totally fitting the memory I had of her from senior night at the last home basketball game, which was the only time I had ever seen her. Finch was one of four seniors on the team, so he'd walked out to midcourt before the game with both his parents. I don't remember anything about his dad, other than that he was tall like Finch, but I remember thinking his mother was *so* pretty and stylish. She was petite, with shoulder-length honey-blond hair, and her outfit was *soo* good: dark denim, knee-high boots, and an ivory cape with a fringe of pom-poms.

"She called you?" I asked. I couldn't help being a little intrigued by their exchange.

"She emailed me," Dad said. He glanced down at the laundry basket again, then walked over to the edge of my bed.

"When?" I said. This business of him keeping secrets was another thing that had changed between us, although to be fair, that worked both ways. There was plenty of stuff I hid from him, too. And not just the drinking.

He finally sat down, and put his hand on my foot, squeezing it through my fuzzy sock. I instinctively pulled my knees up, hugging them to my chest.

He looked hurt or offended, maybe both, as he said, "A few days ago." He paused. "Then we met for coffee."

"Well, that's super weird," I said, in part because it just *was*, and in part because my dad never meets *anyone* for coffee.

"What's so weird about it?" he said, with an odd look on his face—because he totally knew it was weird, too.

"Besides, like, *everything*?" I said.

He shrugged. "Okay. Maybe a little. But we had a pretty decent talk."

"Great," I said, rolling my eyes. "I'm so happy for you."

"Don't be a smart-ass, Lyla."

"I'm not. I *am* glad you had a good talk and all. But can't that be a wrapski?" I said, using one of my dad's expressions.

"No. It can't be a wrapski," Dad said.

"Why not?"

"Because this boy owes you an apology, Lyla. It's important. It's important we all sit down together and talk about this. Nina and I agree on that."

"Okay. But why do we have to meet *here*?"

"What's wrong with meeting here?" he said, sounding *so* defensive. "Are you ashamed of where you live?"

"No," I said—which was sort of a lie. Ever since I started at

161

Windsor in the ninth grade, and realized how much money people around me had, I actually *was* a little embarrassed about our neighborhood and house. Of course I was even more embarrassed for feeling this way. "It's just awkward," I said again, trying to spare Dad's feelings.

"Not more 'awkward' than that photo!" Dad said, getting all agitated and huffy again. "That photo, Lyla, is pretty damn awkward."

I looked down, hit by a fresh wave of shame. More than all the drama at school, it killed me that Dad had seen me like that—passed out drunk with my boob hanging out of my dress—and whatever else he saw when I got home that night that I don't fully remember. He might have already guessed that I drank occasionally, but I'm pretty sure he didn't think I got shit-faced or had sex. Of course the photo wasn't confirmation of the latter, but it certainly was a strong clue that I wasn't the perfect angel he thought me to be.

"*Daaaad.* Why can't you try to have a little empathy here? If not for Finch, then for me?" I said, using a big hot-button word at Windsor. Mr. Q often touched on *empathy* during assemblies, and the concept trickled down into a lot of class discussions.

"Whoa, whoa," Dad said. "I'm sorry, what? I'm supposed to have empathy for *Finch* in this situation?"

"Yeah. You actually *are*. For everyone. It's called forgiveness, Dad. Ever heard of it?"

"Forgiveness is *earned*, Lyla. He's done nothing—"

"Well, isn't that why he's coming over?" I shouted over him. "I mean, what's the point of all of this talking with Nina . . . and . . . and coming over to apologize if you've already made up your mind about him?"

Dad shook his head, looking dumbfounded, then said, "I just

don't understand why you're not more pissed off by what this kid did to you. I really don't."

He paused, clearly expecting me to respond. But I had no response—at least not one I wanted to share with him.

"Finch is the one who should be worried about tomorrow," Dad continued. "Not you. But I bet he's not. Because he's an asshole."

"He's really *not,* Dad," I said, then started to cry again, more out of frustration than anything else. There was no way I was going to be able to explain to my father that kids take photos like that all the time. Of themselves, of each other. I mean, it wasn't like Finch had *posted* it. It wasn't his fault that it had spread like it did. Now, the caption was a different story, maybe. But even that had a context. He'd been playing Uno and screwing around and I think he was just trying to be funny. I'm not saying it *was* funny, but I think there's a difference between trying to be a dick and simply making a stupid, bad joke, especially when you're drunk. At least that's what I'd been telling myself. It was what I wanted to believe. *Needed* to believe.

Dad slid closer to me and put his arms awkwardly around my shoulders, kissing the top of my head. Part of me wanted to push him away, but I really needed a hug. "I'm so sorry, Lyla. I'm just trying to do the best I can," he said, but this time he didn't sound like a martyr—just a dad who really *was* trying.

"I know," I said, sniffling.

"And if it helps, I do think Finch's mother seems like a decent person. I think her heart's in the right place."

"You do?" I said, my voice muffled against his chest.

Dad backed up and looked at me, his brow all furrowed and sad. "Yeah . . . She's worried about you."

"She is?" I said, reaching past him for the wad of tissues on my nightstand.

"Yeah," he said. "So I *am* giving her—and by extension, her son—a chance tomorrow. Doesn't that part make you happy?"

"I guess so," I said, blowing my nose. "I just want this to be over."

"I know, kiddo," he said, nodding emphatically like we were in perfect agreement, when we both knew that my version of it being over was very different from his.

We sat in silence for a few seconds, and I could tell he wanted to say something else but didn't quite know how to say it. So I finally just said, "Anything else, Dad?"

"Actually, yeah," he said. "I did want to say one other thing. About your mother . . ."

"What about her?" I said.

"Nothing really . . ." he said, sounding uneasy. "Just that I don't think it's a terrible idea for you to visit her this summer. You're old enough now, and I trust that you'll make good decisions. She *is* your mother."

"Thanks, Dad," I said. "I think I'll do that. I miss her."

A look of hurt flickered across his face, and I realized, too late, that maybe I'd said the wrong thing. Then again, it was the truth. I *did* miss my mother. Maybe not even *my* mother but the idea of having one around. Especially at times like this, when a father's idea of empathy just wasn't enough.

THE NEXT MORNING, I got up early to shower and wash my hair. With thick, curly hair, I had to let it completely air-dry to look halfway decent, which gave me plenty of time to agonize over what to wear. All my stuff seemed either too "going out," too churchy, or too everyday. Of course I called Grace for advice, even though we'd already talked the night before for over an hour, breaking down the whole situation. In general, she was sort of on the fence about everything—not nearly as pissed off at Finch as Dad was, but definitely still upset.

As far as my wardrobe went, she simply said, "Don't try too hard. Go casual."

I agreed, as we talked through my options and settled on white jeans, tight and ripped at the knees, with a blue silk tank I'd found at a vintage shop. After she wished me luck for about the fourth time, I hung up and put on very light makeup. I wouldn't have worn any at all—that's how much Dad hates it—but I banked on him being too distracted by his frantic cleaning to really notice the subtle application. Our house is always freakishly neat, but that morning he really went to town, his OCD kicking in as he vacuumed and swept and Windexed every surface. At one point, he announced that he had to run an errand and returned with a bag of assorted pastries from Sweet 16th, which he proceeded to arrange on a dinner plate before transferring them to a platter he used when grilling out.

"The plate was better," I said, glancing up from my latest issue of *InStyle*, pretending to be calm.

He nodded, looking a little busted, then put them back on the plate, walking it over to the coffee table. He put it down, along with a short stack of napkins he spread accordion-style. I took it as a hopeful sign that he would keep his word about having an open mind. At the very least, I knew he didn't hate Mrs. Browning, as Dad never goes to any kind of effort when he hates someone.

At exactly eleven, the doorbell rang. Dad took a deep breath and walked slowly over to the front door as I stayed put on the sofa and ran my fingers through my hair, breaking up the crunch of the mousse. My stomach was in knots. Now out of my view, I heard Dad open the door and say hello. He then introduced himself to Finch and invited them in. I took a few deep breaths as they all came into sight, walking in single file, Mrs. Browning first, followed by Finch, then Dad. It was sort of surreal, the way it feels when you see a teacher at the grocery store or in another context besides school.

"Please. Have a seat," Dad said, pointing to the sofa next to me and one of the two chairs. He looked as nervous as I felt, but less pissed off than I expected.

Mrs. Browning sat on the sofa beside me, and Finch took the chair diagonally across from her, as both said hello. I kept my eyes on her, too nervous to look at Finch. She was even more beautiful and glamorous up close than she'd been from the bleachers in the gym, although her outfit was casual. She was wearing a crisp white blouse, the sleeves rolled in wide cuffs, skinny jeans, and gold flats. Her jewelry was cool and layered—delicate pieces mixed with chunkier ones, gold mixed with silver, or more likely platinum. Everything about her was chic but seemed effortless. As if she just woke up looking this put together.

"Lyla, this is Mrs. Browning," Dad said. "And you know Finch."

"Yes. Hi. Hello," I said, without making eye contact with either of them.

"Would you like a croissant?" Dad said, looking at Mrs. Browning, then Finch. It was the first time I'd ever heard him say the word, and it sounded weird. Too French or something.

Finch eyed the plate like he wanted one but shook his head and said no thank you. Mrs. Browning declined as well, rendering the pastries pure, awkward decoration.

"Can I get you something to drink?" Dad said, which he probably should have offered *first*. "A coffee? Water?"

"I have one, thanks," Mrs. Browning said, pulling a bottle of Evian out of her tote.

"Finch? Something to drink?" Dad said.

"I'm fine, thank you," Finch replied.

Meanwhile I just sat there, wanting to die, as Mrs. Browning announced that Finch had something to say to me.

I nodded, staring at a wide gold bangle sliding up and down on her arm as she pushed her glossy blond hair behind her ear.

"Yes," I heard Finch say. He then said my name, and I looked directly at him for the first time.

"I'm really sorry for what I did," he said. "I was drinking—not that that's an excuse. It was stupid and immature and a really awful thing to do. I'm really sorry."

"It's okay," I mumbled, but Dad interjected in a loud voice that it actually *wasn't* okay.

"*Dad,*" I said under my breath. "Stop."

"No," Finch said. "He's right. It's not okay."

"It's not," Mrs. Browning chimed in. "And for what it's worth, Finch wasn't raised like that."

"Like what?" Dad said, though he managed to sound more curious than confrontational.

"To be ignorant. Or mean. Or insensitive," Mrs. Browning said, her voice shaking a little as if she might cry. Something about her didn't strike me as a crier, though, and Dad's expression *tough cookie* crossed my mind.

Finch and I made eye contact for one second before he turned to Dad and said, "Mr. Volpe, do you think I could talk to Lyla alone for a moment?"

Dad looked speechless for a beat, then said my name in a question as if asking for my permission. I nodded, keeping my eyes lowered.

"Okay," Dad said. "Nina and I can step outside for a minute. . . ." His voice trailed off as they both stood. She followed him to the kitchen, then out the side door to the backyard.

When I heard the door close, I raised my chin and looked at Finch. He gazed back at me with those sick blue eyes. When he blinked, I could see the curl of his blond lashes. It made my chest ache, even before he said my name, as a low and whispery question.

"What?" I said softly, my face on fire.

Finch took a deep breath, then said, "I've been debating this . . . but I really think I need to tell you exactly what happened that night. . . ."

"Okay," I said, eyeing the back door and feeling sick to my stomach. I couldn't see Dad or Mrs. Browning but pictured them sitting together at the picnic table.

"So, you know how we were playing Uno?" he said.

"Yes," I said.

"Well, Polly and I got into an argument at one point. Did you notice?"

I shrugged, even though I had.

"Well, we did. . . . And it was over you."

"*Me?*" I said, shocked.

"Yeah. *You.*"

"Why?" I asked.

"She was jealous. You looked so hot in that black dress. . . . She saw me looking at you . . . accused me of flirting . . . and she got pissed."

"Oh," I said, a mix of emotions washing over me. Confusion that Polly would ever be jealous of *me,* worry that I had caused an argument, but mostly just a strange, warm tingling at hearing him call me *hot.* In the past, a few boys had said as much in the comments of my Instagram posts, but no one had ever said it so plainly to my face.

"Anyway," he said. "One thing led to another. . . ." His voice trailed off. "Are you following?"

I shook my head, confused by his *one thing led to another*. Was he talking about his fight with Polly? Or about me? I fleetingly wondered if something had happened between us. Something physical. But there was no way. I would have remembered *that*. I remembered every look Finch had ever given me.

"Listen, Lyla," Finch said, leaning toward me, saying my name breathlessly. "I wasn't the one who took that photo of you. I wasn't the one who wrote that caption. And I wasn't the one who sent it to my friends." He bit his lower lip, then ran his hand through his wavy blond hair. "Do you follow me?"

"What? No. Not really," I said, my mind and heart both in a dead sprint. Suddenly, a realization washed over me. "Wait. Was it Polly? . . . Did she have your phone?"

He slowly but distinctly nodded. "Yes. She took it because she thought you and I were talking . . . texting."

"Why would she think that?"

"Because of the way we were looking at each other."

"But we weren't texting, were we?" I said, remembering that my dad had gone through my messages. Maybe he had erased a thread? Was that possible?

He shook his head. "No. I mean, I *wanted* to. . . . If I had had your number, I might've . . . but no, it was just eye contact. . . . But Polly could tell. Women's intuition or whatever."

I nodded. Because of course I could tell, too.

"So I got buzzed and kind of lost track of my phone. . . ."

"And she used it to take that photo of me?" I asked, wanting to make absolutely certain I was hearing him right.

"Yes," Finch said. "That's *exactly* what happened."

"Wow," I said under my breath, mostly to myself. "What a . . . *bitch*."

"I know. . . . I mean—she's not usually that kind of a person. She's *really* not. . . . She's just going through some things."

I looked at him, feeling skeptical. What issues could Polly possibly have? She was rich and beautiful—the female equivalent of Finch. Plus she was *dating* him. She *had* him. So what if he flirted a little with me? That meant nothing compared to their long-standing relationship. Or *did* it?

"Anyway. We broke up over it," he finished.

"You did?" I said, my voice cracking. "Because of me?"

"No. Because of what she *did* to you."

My head spinning, I said, "Does your mom know? That Polly did it?"

He shook his head and said, "No."

"Does *anyone*?"

"No," he said again.

"Why not? Why haven't you told anyone the truth?"

Finch sighed and shook his head. "I don't know. . . . It's hard to explain, and I just can't get into everything. . . . But . . . let's just say Polly has a lot of issues."

"Like *what*?" I said.

Finch sighed and said, "I can't really say."

I stared at him, suddenly remembering rumors I'd heard earlier in the school year about an eating disorder and cutting. A very small, ugly part of me had sort of hoped they were true, if only to believe that nobody's life was that perfect. But a bigger part of me assumed that the rumors were lies, born from the same jealousy I felt when I scrolled through her glittery, glamorous Instagram. Now I believed them—and I couldn't help feeling sorry for her. More because she'd lost Finch than anything else. I told myself to get over that. She'd made her own bed. She didn't deserve my sympathy.

"You have to tell the truth," I said. "At your hearing. You have to tell them that you didn't do this. That *she* did."

He shook his head, adamant. "No, Lyla. I just can't do that to her. . . . Beyond her . . . issues . . . she's been in trouble before. This would be her second offense. . . . She'd definitely get thrown out. I don't want that on my conscience."

I glanced toward the backyard again, wondering how much time we had before Dad and Nina returned. "You can't take the blame for this," I said.

"Yes, I can," he said. "Please respect my decision."

"But you could get suspended or expelled. You could lose *Princeton*."

"I know," Finch said. "But I don't think that will happen."

"What *do* you think will happen?"

He sighed, shrugged, and said, "Well, hopefully, I go through this honor process, and take the blame for the picture. . . . But somehow I don't lose Princeton. And . . . Polly gets help. . . . And you don't hate me. . . ." His voice was soft and sweet—the way boys almost never sound except in the movies with slow, romantic songs playing in the background.

"I don't hate you," I said, my heart skipping random beats.

"Really?"

"Really," I said.

"Okay. So . . . given that you don't hate me . . ." He hesitated, dropping his eyes. "I was wondering . . . if you might like to hang out sometime?"

Light-headed, I tried to process what he was asking. Surely it was only a theoretical question. "You and me?" I said.

"Yeah. You and me," he said.

"When?" I said.

"I don't know . . . soon? Are you free tonight?"

"I'm not sure my dad would be cool with that," I said. A huge, *huge* understatement. "Besides, aren't you grounded?" I asked, having heard the rumors of his harsh punishment. That he wasn't allowed to leave his house for the rest of the spring and summer.

"Yeah. But given the circumstances, I'm betting my parents might make an exception here," he said, just as the side door opened and my dad and his mom reappeared.

"Was that enough time?" Mrs. Browning asked, peering over at us.

"Yes," Finch and I answered in unison.

She looked hesitant, but returned to her original seat on the sofa, as my dad stood nearby and offered coffee again.

This time, Mrs. Browning said, "Sure. I'd love one, thank you."

"Cream or sugar?"

"No, thank you. Black's fine," she replied.

Dad nodded and walked toward the kitchen, while the three of us just sort of sat there. I caught Mrs. Browning giving me a once-over, and then smiling at me.

"I love your top," she said.

"Thank you," I said, pleased. "I got it at a vintage shop."

"Oh? Which one?"

"Star Struck. On Gallatin. Do you know it?"

"Of course," she said.

"It's a little pricey. But sometimes you can find deals."

Mrs. Browning smiled and said, "Yes. Shopping can be a very strategic enterprise. Sometimes I think it's the hunt I like more than the actual purchase."

"Yeah. I know what you mean," I said. Then I added, "I really like your shoes."

She did a little Dorothy there's-no-place-like-home heel tap and thanked me as Dad returned with her coffee, handing her the mug.

It fleetingly occurred to me that Mrs. Browning was being *too* nice—and I felt a dash of suspicion. What if she and Finch had come here with the goal to win me over? A "good cop, bad cop" thing, though this was *two* good cops. I told myself that I was being crazy as Mrs. Browning looked at Finch and said, "So? Did you two . . . talk?"

"Yes," he said, nodding.

"And?"

"And . . . it was good, Mom," he said, his voice loud and clear.

Mrs. Browning looked at me, as I dumbly echoed Finch. "Yeah. It was good," I said.

Dad frowned. "Good *how?*"

"Good . . . in that . . . he's very sorry for what happened," I stammered.

"Yes. And I'd love the chance to talk with Lyla a little more," Finch added. "If that's okay with you, Mr. Volpe?" His voice rose along with his eyebrows.

"Now?" Dad asked.

"No," Finch said. "Not now. But maybe another time . . . Lyla and I could get together and talk?"

I held my breath, watching Dad process the request. "Are you trying to ask my daughter *out?*"

"Well . . . actually . . . yes, sir," Finch said.

"On a *date?*" Dad said, his voice getting louder and his face redder.

"*Dad,*" I said, mortified that he was trying to label it. "He didn't say a *date.*"

But Finch rose boldly to the challenge. "Yes, sir. On a date. I want to get to know her better. And I want her to know me. I'm just asking for the chance to prove that I'm really not a bad person. Although I know I've done nothing to deserve that chance."

I cleared my throat and made myself speak up. "Yes, you have," I said, my heart racing. "You coming here today means a lot to my dad and me. *Right,* Dad?" I said, prompting him, wondering if he was going to be a total hypocrite and recant everything he'd said about giving Finch a chance.

It took him another few seconds to finally answer. "I guess," Dad grumbled, shifting his gaze from me to Nina, then back to Finch. "But you know this changes absolutely nothing about your hearing next week?"

"Of course. Yes, sir," Finch said. "Besides. Even if I wanted to get out of it, my mom would never let me. . . ." He smiled.

Dad didn't smile back.

"But I don't," Finch added. "Want to get out of anything. I know I have to face my punishment."

Dad nodded, his jaw relaxing a little. "Okay," he said.

"So I have your permission to ask Lyla out?" Finch asked. "At some point?"

Dad rolled his eyes, then took a deep breath. "I can't stop you from asking her out," he said. "But I'd be *very* surprised if she said yes."

chapter fourteen

NINA

"How do you feel?" I asked Finch on the way home from the Volpes' house. We were in my car, but he was driving.

"I feel great," he said. "*Really* great. I'm so glad we did that."

I felt a wave of relief as I said to my son, "Doesn't it feel good to do the right thing?" The question was a little heavy-handed, but I couldn't help myself.

"Yeah," he said, glancing over at me. "It really does. . . . And Lyla? She's a *cool* girl. . . ."

He bit his lip, smiled, and slowly shook his head, the way he did when watching an amazing play in a football or basketball game. It was in stark contrast to Kirk—who always got up and clapped and yelled at the television.

"Yeah. She is," I said, thinking that there was something about Lyla that seemed lacking in other girls I knew through Finch, Polly in particular. A certain genuine quality. Polly was always perfectly polite, saying all the right things to me, making eye contact and fluid small talk. Yet there was something about her that seemed almost *too* polite, scripted even.

"Mr. Volpe was nice, too," Finch said.

I nodded, thinking of our conversation on the back porch. We'd talked about Finch and Lyla, wondering how it was going inside.

But we'd also discussed kids today in more general terms. How they hid behind their phones, saying things that they'd never say directly to someone's face—whether mean or sexual or just plain bold. We pitied them, and pitied ourselves as their parents. Tom never let Finch off the hook for what he'd done to Lyla, but he'd definitely softened since the coffee shop.

Finch slowed at a yellow light, then came to a full stop. His foot on the brake, he looked at me, big-eyed. "So, Mom. I think I am going to ask Lyla out at some point. . . . You heard Mr. Volpe say I could, right?"

"Yes," I said, still surprised Tom had left the door open on that possibility. "But you also heard him say she probably wouldn't go. . . ."

He nodded, now staring up at the light, waiting for it to change. "Yeah. Well. Maybe I'll just call her. I really want to talk to her some more," he said as the light turned to green.

I understood the feeling—I wanted to keep talking to Tom, too. Conversation felt healing, and we all needed that.

"In any case, I think you should wait until after your hearing," I said, part of me worried about how it would look: Finch manipulating the situation. On the one hand, I was tired of worrying about appearances, sick of making decisions based on what others might think. But on the other, this just wasn't a good idea.

"Yeah," Finch said. "I got it."

"Also, just so you know, I'm going to tell Dad about our meeting and your apology," I said. "As soon as he gets home . . ."

"Okay," he said with a shrug.

"Your father and I have had some differences lately, but we need to be a united front. Especially when it comes to you."

Finch glanced at me knowingly, then nodded, as if he, too, had noticed the sea change in our home and marriage—which seemed to have begun when Kirk sold his business.

I thought about that time now. At first, the three of us were thrilled—*giddy*. But things quickly turned tense, even ugly, during the winding-down period, which included parting ways with his top executive, Chuck Wilder. Chuck had no real piece of the business, as Kirk had put up all the capital and had one hundred percent ownership, but Chuck put in a lot of sweat equity over the years, giving up more lucrative jobs because he believed so much in Kirk's vision. I think he'd also had an expectation of being included in the massive payout, and in my view, it wasn't an unwarranted one.

But Kirk flatly refused, even after Chuck's wife, Donna, showed up on our doorstep, confiding that she was extremely worried about her husband's "mental state."

"It's not personal," Kirk had said. "It's just business."

"But it *is* personal," Donna had said. "Y'all are *friends*."

"I know we're friends, Donna. But I have to separate that from my business decisions," Kirk had replied calmly and coldly.

I remember feeling shocked, but also *not*. It was in keeping with Kirk's attitudes toward tips. He was perfectly capable of leaving a paltry amount, and in extreme cases nothing, if he deemed the service bad. And effort didn't count; ineptitude was ineptitude. In any event, Donna, just like a waitress or two along the way, ended up in tears. Kirk was unyielding.

In the hours and days that followed, I had searched for signs of remorse, but Kirk's only reaction was indignation. How dare Chuck put Donna up to this shameless attempt at manipulation? He'd paid Chuck a great salary for years and owed him nothing further.

"But we made so much money," I remember saying. "Why can't we just throw him a bone? A hundred thousand dollars or something?"

"Hell, *no*. Why would I do that? That's not the way things work. It was *my* capital."

His use of the word *my* instead of *our* made me uneasy, as I'd noticed that the more money Kirk made, the more likely he was to call it *his*. But I also remember telling myself that it really didn't matter. Because he always had the best interests of Finch and me at heart.

I compared our current situation to that one, and at first blush, they felt similar. Our family was *still* first.

But as Finch stopped at another traffic light, I thought of a rather significant difference. With Chuck, Kirk had operated under a completely rational set of rules. Fair was fair. Rules were rules. But those same reasoned principles went out the window when they conflicted with *Kirk's* best interest. Suddenly things weren't so clear-cut; his black-and-white world had turned gray. In Kirk's mind, Finch was a "good kid" who had saved up enough points to be given some leeway. He had essentially earned one free pass—or more precisely, a *fifteen-thousand-dollar* pass.

"So what time is Dad coming home?" Finch asked now, clearly thinking about Kirk, too.

"Sometime this afternoon," I said, pulling my phone out of my purse to check the flight information, just as a text came in from him that read: Hey, do we have anything on the calendar tonight?

No. Why? I wrote back.

Thinking about staying another night. Getting a migraine and just want to lie down. Will take an early flight tomorrow.

Okay. Feel better, I wrote back, relieved that I could put off our conversation about Tom and the money a little longer. I gave Finch the update on his father's return, and he just nodded.

"Does Dad know you and Polly broke up?" I asked.

"I dunno," he said. "I don't think I mentioned it."

"Have you talked to her?

"Not much. . . . She's *nuts*, Mom."

I felt myself tense up, having long noticed that this was something men (and boys, obviously) did after any breakup. Dub their exes "crazy." Discredit them, make it seem as if the men were lucky to have gotten out of the relationship. In fact, Julie had once told me it was the most common narrative in the aftermath of a divorce—the justification men used for their own misconduct. A form of misogyny.

"Don't say that, Finch," I said.

"Sorry, Mom. But there's a lot of stuff you don't know. . . . She really can be a bitch—"

"Finch!" I said. "Don't *ever* call girls names like that. It's so incredibly demeaning." I wanted to add, *Have you learned nothing from all of this?*—but I stopped myself. It was the most we'd talked in such a long time, and I didn't want it to end on a sour note.

"Sorry, Mom," he said again as he turned onto our street. "I just lost a lot of respect for her recently. Ya know?"

"Yeah," I said, nodding. "I know how that can be."

A SHORT TIME after we arrived home, Finch found me in my office.

"Hey, Mom? What do you think of me going out tonight? There's a pop-up show at Twelfth and Porter," he said. "Luke Bryan's playing. I know I'm grounded—but after that conversation with Lyla and all the drama with Polly, I could really use a night out. Please, Mom?"

179

I hesitated. My gut told me to say no, but my heart wanted to say yes. We really had made so much progress today. "I don't know, Finch," I said, still thinking.

"Can I at least email Bob Tate?" he pressed, referring to Kirk's ticket broker, who could not only produce last-minute tickets to any show or sporting event, but also swing VIP passes or any other perk Kirk wanted. "See if he can get tickets?"

"How much do you think they'll cost?" I asked, feeling determined to make him more aware of money.

"I don't know," Finch said, glancing down at his phone, typing something. "Maybe a couple hundred apiece since the venue's small. . . ."

"A couple hundred *apiece*?" I said, shocked—not so much by the price itself but by Finch's nonchalance.

I made myself say no, then compromised. "You can go out, but find a way to have some cheaper fun."

"Fine, Mom," he said, looking disappointed.

For one second, I felt bad. It was so much more fun to make Finch happy, and my general overall philosophy was: if you can say yes, why not say yes? Of course that was Kirk's philosophy, too, which had led us down the path of virtually always saying yes to our son, no matter the cost. After all, Kirk would point out, wasn't it arbitrary to pick a random amount of money as a cutoff? If we could easily afford an eighty-thousand-dollar car for Finch, why get him a forty-thousand-dollar car he'd love so much less?

Now I wanted to go back to that conversation about Finch's car—and so many other things. I wanted to list all the reasons *why not* for Kirk. *He shouldn't take these things for granted. . . . He needs to earn it. . . . If the bar is already that high, where will he go from here? . . .* And most of all: *There is a difference between privilege and entitlement.* It was a concept that seemed as lost on Finch as it did on his father. What made Finch, as an eighteen-year-old kid, think he could reach out to his dad's ticket broker? That money was no object, although he'd never earned a dime on his own?

I watched Finch type something else on his phone, then look back up at me. "I need to go get a haircut. . . . If that's okay with you," he said with a trace of an attitude.

"Watch your tone," I said, although I knew my admonition probably fell under the category of "too little too late."

"Sure thing, Mom," he said, sliding his phone into his back pocket as he walked out the door.

MORE THAN THREE hours later, Finch returned to the house with the same shaggy hair he'd left with.

"I thought you said you were getting a haircut," I said, annoyed—with both the state of his hair and the fact that he hadn't done what he'd said he was going to do.

"The place was packed," Finch said, referring to the Belle Meade Barber Shop—where he always went to get his hair cut. "I waited forever . . . and then finally left."

"You waited for three hours?" I said, thinking that while the place could be busy, it was never *that* busy.

"I had other errands to run. . . . And then I hit some balls at the club. With Beau."

"Okay," I said.

"And guess what? . . . He actually has tickets to Luke Bryan tonight. And he offered me one of them."

"Oh, really?" I said, wondering if Melanie had anything to do with this, or if Beau and Finch had just finagled it on their own. It crossed my mind, not for the first time, that Beau hadn't been grounded for the party he threw. He was *never* punished.

"Yeah. So? Can I go?"

Something inside me told me to *still* say no—that the whole thing seemed a little fishy. But I'd explicitly told him that the price of the tickets was my issue, and now that was resolved.

"Please, Mom?" Finch said, putting one arm around me. "Just this one night?"

I sighed, then relented. "Okay," I said. "But your punishment resumes tomorrow."

"Got it," Finch said, grinning and already texting.

I cleared my throat as loudly as I could, cueing him to look up at me. "Anything else you might want to say to me?" I asked, attempting light-heartedness, but also making a final point about the importance of basic gratitude.

"Oh, yeah," he said. "Thanks, Mom. Seriously, I really, *really* appreciate it."

I nodded, then stepped forward to initiate a hug. It felt a little awkward, as it had been a while since we shared any real physical affection. "You're welcome, honey," I said. "I love you so much."

"I love you, too, Mom."

As he began to pull away, I held on to him for an extra few seconds, whispering, "Please be good tonight. No more trouble."

"No more trouble, Mom," he said. "I promise."

chapter fifteen

TOM

I've never been to therapy—not because I don't believe in it but because I can't afford it (although I guess it would be more accurate to say that I would rather do *other* things with my limited disposable income).

A few years back, however, I did start spending time with a retired shrink. Her name is Bonnie, and she's an older widowed lady with just the right amount of eccentricity, who had hired me to build a tree house for her grandkids. A couple weeks into the project, when I discovered that her fanciful Swiss Family Robinson design exceeded her budget, she suggested we trade services. At first I agreed to the deal only to be nice—so that I didn't leave a half-finished tree house in her yard—but I quickly grew to really enjoy our time together.

I liked her open-ended questions, especially because I could work while I talked (which seemed a lot less intense than sitting on a couch saying all the same things). Anyway, we started with Beatriz and Lyla, quickly touching on all my single-father woes. That eventually led her to the subject of women and why I wasn't dating and then my entire romantic past. She asked about my first time— how, where, and to whom I'd lost my virginity.

I gave her the full scoop, telling her all about the summer I turned fifteen, when my buddy John landed us jobs at Belle Meade Country Club. John lived on my street and grew up basically like I did (i.e., not exposed to golf). But somehow he developed a love for the game. I was pretty indifferent myself, but it was an easy, decent-paying gig. All John and I had to do was pick up balls from the range, clean the carts and clubs after use, and work with the caddies to get the members' bags ready to play. Incidentally, all the caddies at Belle Meade were black. We heard the reason was because members didn't want their daughters falling in love with them. Rather than worrying about the obvious racist implications of this, John and I took it as an insult to *us,* i.e., why weren't members worried about their daughters falling in love with us white bag room boys?

Cue Delaney.

At sixteen, Delaney was an older woman—a *rich* older woman—who drove a cherry-red BMW convertible, a birthday gift from her father. As if that wasn't impressive enough, Delaney had a reputation for being somewhat advanced. (We called it something a little different at the time.) We saw the way she sauntered around the pool in the tiniest string bikinis, undoing her top while she sunbathed facedown, exposing ample side boob (which we heard had also been a gift from Daddy). She loved to flirt and did not discriminate, shining her bright sexual light on everyone— married men, black caddies, and lowly bag room boys.

John and I both developed a crush on Delaney, viewing her more as a potential sexual conquest than as a girl we thought we could actually date. At some point, we placed a far-fetched bet— twenty-five bucks for every base one of us got to with her. Over the course of the summer, we managed to work our way into Delaney's social circle through another bag room boy who knew some members, and the bet no longer seemed so unrealistic. Then, one evening in early August, in addition to getting a blow job from Delaney in the backseat of her convertible, I earned myself seventy-five dollars from John. A true windfall. Unfortunately, word got out about our escapade—and I was fired. Delaney tried to intervene on my behalf, but her father quickly squelched her campaign for justice. He also told her she could never see me again, which only fueled our interest in each other, as those things have a tendency to do.

We ended up going all the way a few nights later, which should have earned me another twenty-five dollars from John, but I didn't charge him. It just didn't seem right to get paid for your first time, especially with a girl as hot as Delaney.

"Did it cross your mind that this was a sexist, demeaning bet?" Bonnie asked as she sipped her tea.

"Yeah," I said, sanding away. "I think it did. A little. But it wasn't her first time. Besides, I got the feeling she was using me, too."

"So you *were* using her?"

"At first. When I made the bet, yeah."

"But then?"

"But then I started to like her. A little."

"And how was she using *you*?" Bonnie drilled away. "Also for sex?"

"I like to think so," I said with a smirk.

Bonnie smiled back and shook her head.

"I'm kidding. Delaney could have slept with anyone. . . . I just made her feel like even more of a rebel."

"How so?"

"You know 'how so.' Sleeping with a bag boy—a status that was beneath her. She got off on bucking the system, whether in the form of her swimwear or her choice of screws."

"Did she tell you that?"

"Not in so many words. But she talked about that shit a lot. Money and social class. She even used that word a lot. *Classy.*" I rolled my eyes, feeling the inferiority all over again.

"So you didn't feel like . . . star-crossed lovers?"

"No. I felt like a pawn," I said. "Then, one night, she *really* went too far."

"Uh-oh. What did she do?" Bonnie asked.

"She used the expression *salt of the earth* to describe my mother."

Always getting it, Bonnie winced, then groaned.

"Yeah. I kinda lost my shit. I told her it was a condescending expression," I said, envisioning Delaney sitting on the cement floor of my basement, sipping from a can of Budweiser, calmly insisting that the term was a compliment—synonymous with *sweet and wholesome.*

I told Bonnie how I had asked Delaney what about my mother came across as sweet or wholesome when all she had done was say, *Hello. Nice to meet you. Would you like a drink? We have Diet Pepsi and OJ.*

Bonnie laughed a hearty, openmouthed laugh. "And her reply?"

"She got defensive. She didn't like *getting* called out. She liked *doing* the calling out. . . . But I pressed her. I asked if she'd ever call a doctor or lawyer 'salt of the earth'? Or if there were any country club members who she would describe as 'salt of the earth'? . . . She said no, because they all 'sucked.' I remember thinking that they couldn't *all* suck, any more than *all* single mothers were 'salt of the earth.' But I dropped the subject. I figured it didn't matter enough to argue about it."

"Why didn't it matter enough?"

"Because *she* didn't matter enough," I said with a shrug. "I was over it. Her. Right then and there."

"So you broke up that night?"

"Yup," I said, not admitting that we'd actually had sex a few other times before I decided, once and for all, that I didn't want to be the guy she slummed with.

It didn't take Bonnie long to give me her full hypothesis. She didn't use the words *chip on your shoulder,* but more or less that's what she said. Basically, she concluded that I'd felt used by Delaney, my self-esteem damaged by both her and the whole Belle Meade Country Club experience. Somewhere deep within myself, she believed, *I* believed that I didn't measure up—and afterward sought out people and situations where I'd feel less vulnerable to rejection. The irony, of course, was that I ended up with Beatriz, who ultimately left me, too, hence reinforcing my fears and sense of isolation. Bonnie's words, not mine.

Her theory made good sense, but for the fact that I didn't spend a lot of time dwelling on the past. Nor did I think much about my present lack of friendships. In fact, the only time I really thought about my social life at all was when Lyla pointed it out, sometimes in the form of concern ("You should go out more, Dad") and sometimes in the form of an accusation when I would tell her she couldn't do something ("You want me to be like you and have no friends?").

But then all this happened with Finch, and suddenly I *did* feel a little lonely. Lost. It kept striking me as pretty pathetic that I had nobody to discuss the situation with.

Which is how I remembered that I actually *did* have someone to talk to. So I drove over to Bonnie's.

"You think it's weird how few friends I have?" I asked her pretty much out of the gate, as we stood in her kitchen and she fired up her stove to make us tea. Tea was the starting point of all of our visits.

"Weird? No. I wouldn't use that word. You're an introvert. Not everyone needs a *posse*," Bonnie said, stressing the word *posse*. She loved to sprinkle in what she considered to be current slang— although she was usually about a decade off.

"But I had a posse as a kid. Before Beatriz," I said.

Bonnie nodded. "Yes. I remember you mentioning that. One of the fellows was the guy who got you the golf course job?"

"Yes. John. Also Steve and Gerard," I said, giving her a run-down on our foursome, how we had grown up together, roaming around the woods near our neighborhood as boys, then coming of age with a backdrop of beer, pot, and heavy metal music. When I think back to high school, I think of that group of guys, plus John's longtime girlfriend, Karen, as cool as any dude, sitting around and just shooting the shit, talking about everything and nothing. Our favorite topic was how much we hated Nashville, at least our part of town—and how much we wanted to get the hell out of there and have lives different than those of the grown-ups grinding it out in low-paying jobs around us. With the most book smarts and drive among us, only John actually succeeded in doing that. He went to Miami of Ohio for undergrad, Northwestern for business school, then landed on Wall Street, trading bonds, smoking expensive cigars, and wearing his hair all slicked back like Michael Douglas playing Gordon Gekko. Meanwhile, I went to junior college for three semesters before running out of money and going into carpentry, and Steve and Gerard went into their respective family trades, becoming an insurance salesman and an electrician. The only real twist in the story is that when John and Karen broke up, she ended up dating Steve, then breaking up with Steve to marry Gerard. It was a wonder we'd survived those breaches of the man code at all.

"So who do you now consider your closest friend?" Bonnie

asked as her kettle began to whistle, then screech. She grabbed the handle with an oven mitt, moving it to a back burner, instantly silencing it.

I smiled and said, "Other than the lady who stiffed me for the tree house?"

Bonnie laughed and said, "Yes. Other than that old bat."

I shrugged, explaining that the four of us, sans Karen, still tried to meet up when John came back to town to visit his folks every other Thanksgiving or so, but the dynamic felt a little forced.

"So are you lonely? Or is this about something else?" Bonnie said.

I looked at her, thinking that she was kind of brilliant. "Something else," I said. "But I might need something stronger than tea."

Bonnie smiled, turned off the stove, and poured us both a glass of clear liquor, neat.

"What's this?" I said, swirling it in my glass.

"Gin," she said. "It's all I have."

I nodded, then took the glass and followed her to her back porch, where we sat on wicker chairs and gazed up in the tree at my handiwork. As we sipped, I told her the whole story. Everything. Ending with Nina and Finch's visit, and Finch asking for my permission to ask Lyla out.

Bonnie whistled and shook her head. "What did you tell him? Wait. Let me guess. Over your dead body?"

"Not exactly, actually."

"*Really?*"

"Yes, really. Why so surprised? I thought you believed in forgiveness?" I said. "Letting go of bitterness and all that stuff?"

"*I* do," she said. "But *you* don't."

"Good point," I said. "But I'm trying to set a better example. I'd rather Lyla be like *you* than *me*."

Bonnie smiled.

"So. I'm hoping she says no on her own. That she accepts his apology but still wants nothing to do with him. I am hoping this has taught her a few things about self-respect."

Bonnie nodded, then squinted up at the sky. The late afternoon sun highlighted all her lines and wrinkles, making her look older than I thought of her as. Then again, she probably was in her early seventies by now, which somehow seemed so much older than one's late sixties. At forty-seven, I thought about how fast I would get there, too. I was almost *fifty*, for fuck's sake. How had that happened?

"What if she says yes? What if she ends up really *liking* him?" she asked tentatively, reaching down to stroke one of her two black cats, who was just moseying by.

"I guess I'd cross that bridge," I said. "With your help."

"Do you think he likes her? Or is he . . . ?" She struggled to find the right slang.

"Playing her?"

Bonnie nodded. "Yeah. That."

"I can't tell," I said. "Maybe both? . . . I know I'm biased, but Lyla really is a special girl."

Bonnie squinted harder, deep in thought. "Well. What could it really hurt if they did go out?"

"She could get her heart broken," I said.

"God forbid she take that risk," she quipped, clearly making a separate point.

"It's not the same thing," I said, knowing she was about to get on her soapbox about my personal life. "I don't have *time* for that stuff—"

"Nonsense," she said. "People make time for what matters to them."

"Not interested," I said. "I've seen what's out there. No, thanks."

"If only Nina were single, huh," she said breezily, almost under her breath.

"What's that supposed to mean?" I said, though I knew *exactly* what it meant.

"I think *you* like *her*."

"I do like her," I said, playing it cool.

"*Like* her, like her."

I rolled my eyes, trying to remember exactly what I'd just said about Nina. That she was attractive? That she was much nicer than her husband? That she'd been kind to Lyla? Certainly none of that indicated I had *feelings* for her.

"Don't be an ass," I said, feeling a little guilty about calling an older lady an ass. But I knew Bonnie could handle it, maybe even liked it.

"You're denying it?" she said.

"Hell, *yeah,* I'm denying it. . . . For one, she's married."

"So?" Bonnie said. "When has that ever stopped anyone?"

"Cynic," I said, thinking that I had never touched a married woman.

"Well?"

"Well . . . for another, she's the mother of this jerk kid."

"The same jerk kid who you gave permission to ask your daughter out?"

"I told you. I want Lyla to come to her own conclusions. . . . And maybe, if she and Finch become friends, she could spend a little time with Nina. That would be good for her, no?"

Bonnie nodded, a hint of a smirk on her face.

"What?" I said.

"Nothing."

"Tell me."

"You don't feel anything for this woman? Not even a teensy-tiny crush?"

"That's the wrong word for it entirely."

"What's the right word?" she said. "What's that look you keep getting on your face when you talk about her? Intrigue?"

"That's too strong, too. . . . At most? . . . Maybe I'm a little curious."

"About?"

I shrugged. "I don't know. I just kind of want to know her deal . . . like how she ended up with that douchebag of a husband."

Bonnie rubbed her fingers together in the universal sign of money and raised one eyebrow.

"Yeah. Maybe," I said. "But I get the feeling it's not that simple. . . . She just doesn't strike me as a gold digger. . . . Something else is going on there. It's almost as if she's . . . I don't know . . ."

"Do you think there is *abuse*?" Bonnie said.

"No. Nothing that sinister. That's not my read, anyway . . . but something doesn't add up," I said. "She's clearly not in sync with the guy. . . . Like, I don't think she's told him we've met. At all. She seems trapped. At the very least, unhappy. Really unhappy."

Bonnie nodded, then said, "What if she ends up having a romantic interest in you?"

"Not possible," I said as quickly and adamantly as I could, even while I wondered what it might be like to kiss Nina.

WHEN I GOT home a few hours later, I noticed that Lyla had changed clothes and was now wearing a sundress that I hadn't seen before.

"That's pretty," I said, pointing at it. "Are you going out?"

"Yeah," she said. "I'm going to the Luke Bryan concert. If that's okay?"

"With who?" I said.

"Grace," she said.

"Where's the show?"

"Twelfth and Porter."

I nodded. "How are you getting there?"

"Grace is picking me up. We're getting ready at her house."

"Why not get ready here?"

"She has a bigger bathroom."

"Okay. But remember. Your curfew is eleven."

"I know, Dad," she said with a loud sigh.

I looked at her a long beat, then said, "All right, Lyla. Have fun. . . . Just please don't let me down."

LATER THAT NIGHT, after Lyla was picked up by Grace, and I did a few things around the house, I decided I'd drive a little to distract myself from my feeling of doom and gloom. So I did about four uneventful trips, including a back-and-forth from the airport, all with solo passengers and no conversation, exactly how I like it.

A little before ten, I got pinged for a pickup at 404 Kitchen, a nice restaurant in the Gulch. The drop-off was for No. 308, a bar on Gallatin Avenue. I knew from experience with those locations that I was probably getting one of two rides—either a couple on a date or a girls' night out. If the latter, they'd likely be single women or divorcées (married women typically got together on weekdays, not weekends). Either way, they'd be drunk, or well on their way, which I guess was the whole point of Uber.

Sure enough, when I pulled up to the restaurant, I saw a pair of middle-aged women who looked like they were having a big time. As they both slid ungracefully into my car, their intoxication was confirmed by all the usual hallmarks—most notably, loud, shallow, repetitive commentary. I quickly gathered that the alpha, bitchier of the two was married; the other, who happened to be prettier but perhaps a bit dimmer, was either single or divorced. To be clear, I gathered all that not because I was interested in anything they had to say but simply because it was impossible to tune them out. At the moment, they were focusing on some guy they'd just run into outside the restaurant.

"You know who that was, right?" Married said.

"No. Who?"

"The CEO of Hedberg. He's worth a bloody fortune. And his wife just passed away. Cancer," she said as if announcing tomorrow's weather forecast.

Single sighed and said, "That's *soo* sad."

"Yes. Which means he's going to need *lots* of comfort." Married let out a snort.

"Jackie! That's awful," Single said, but she did not sound appalled, as the two turned their attention to their phones, namely the selfies they'd just taken outside the restaurant.

Here we go, I thought. The debate about which photos to delete and which to post.

Sure enough, a very familiar and painful script ensued:

Delete!

Why don't you like that one? It's adorable of you!

No, my arms look so fat! Delete it now!

I can crop that.

Only if you crop my pale face, too.

I have the best app for that!

And on and on, until Married concluded, and the apparently more photogenic Single reluctantly agreed, that none were "postworthy." At which point they promptly began a hair and makeup session followed by another photo shoot complete with a discussion about their respective "good sides." A second later, I was blinded by a flash.

"Whoa," I said under my breath.

"Aw, I'm *sorry*," Single said, reaching up to tap my shoulder. "Are we bothering your driving?"

"I'm fine," I said, aware that these kinds of women were the most likely to slap you with a one-star rating.

"He's probably enjoying the show," Married said, as if I couldn't hear her. Against my better judgment, I glanced in the rearview mirror in time to see her cleavage bulging out of her bra, as excessive as the perfume one or both of them had doused themselves with.

"Sir, do you often have hot women taking selfies in the back of your car?" Single asked proudly.

Here we go, I thought again, preparing myself for full-on engagement. Because typically, it was all or nothing. They either ignored me completely or wanted to delve into a deep conversation about my life, which was really just a way to segue back to theirs.

"Not as often as I'd like," I said, on autopilot.

The two laughed, and Married reached up and put her hand on my arm. "Wait. I didn't catch your name?"

"Tom," I said.

She repeated my name, turning it into a singsongy two syllables, then said, "You're *very* strong. Do you get those muscles from driving Uber?"

"Jackie," Single said under her breath. "Obviously he works out. . . . Right, Tom?"

"Not really," I said as Married commenced massaging my shoulder and neck.

"Jackie," Single said. "Let him *drive*."

"But he's so cute. *You* should be talking to him. . . . Tom? Are you single?"

I said yes, aware that I was now moving into Uber pawn territory.

"Divorced or never married? What's your story? Do you have a story?" Married pressed.

"Everyone has a story," Single said. "Right, Tom?"

"Nope," I said. "No story here."

"Oh my *God*!" Single gasped. For a second, I thought maybe she somehow knew who I was. Perhaps I'd worked on her house or made her some custom piece of furniture. But then I saw in the rearview mirror that she was staring down at her phone. "Speaking of married, guess who just texted me?"

"Who?"

"Kirk Browning. Be still, my heart."

I gripped my steering wheel more tightly. I had overheard plenty of incriminating conversations from the backseat of my car and in some cases, had had things directly confessed to me. But nothing like this. Nothing that felt *pertinent* to me. I told myself it wasn't. Not really.

"Ugh. Is that still going on?" Married asked.

"Nothing's going on. We're *friends,*" Single said. "He just wants to talk."

"Yeah, *right,*" Married said.

"He's going through a lot right now," Single said. "All this stuff with Finch and the Mexican girl. . . . Have you heard?"

I bit my lip so hard I could taste blood. Now it *was* pertinent to me.

"Of course I heard. Saw the photo, too. I feel so sorry for Kirk."

"Why?" Single said, and for one second, I thought she was

196

going to redeem herself with a bold defense of Lyla. Instead, she said, "Because his son's in trouble? Or because he's married to such a *bitch*?"

A jolt of hate passed through my body as Married laughed and said, "She really *is*. And so full of herself. It's like—hey, honey, it's not *your* money."

"No shit. I heard she grew up in a *trailer park*."

"Really?" Married asked.

"Yeah. Pretty sure."

"But isn't she Jewish?"

"She *is*?" Single gasped. "Well, that's a combo you don't see every day. Trailer park Jew."

They laughed together. Then Single said, "So what do you think will happen?"

"With Nina? Or Finch? Because I bet they both get axed. . . . I hear the headmaster over there's a huge liberal."

As I white-knuckled the steering wheel, I felt another tap on my shoulder. "Aren't you glad you don't have to deal with this Belle Meade drama?" Single asked.

I unclenched my jaw and said, "Oh. You'd be surprised. . . ."

"Oh, dear. Were you listening to us?" she said, so full of herself.

I told myself to play dumb, but I just couldn't.

"Yes," I said, then continued in a loud, clear voice. "And for what it's worth? I agree. I don't think Finch will get away with what he did to that girl. Who, by the way, isn't Mexican. Although that's kinda beside the point."

Silence filled the backseat.

"So you *know* the girl?" Married finally asked, suddenly sounding sober.

"Yeah," I said, pausing for a satisfying beat just as I pulled up to their destination, put my car in park, and stared at them over my shoulder. "She's my *daughter*. So yeah, I know her pretty damn well."

THE SECOND THEY were out of my car, I called Nina, ready to give her my enraged report. But in the few seconds it took for her to answer the phone, I calmed down just enough to change my mind. As pissed off as I was at what I'd just heard (for both Lyla's sake and Nina's), getting involved in someone else's marriage was never a good idea. Things were already hard enough.

"Hello?" she said. "Tom?"

"Yes. Hi," I said, wondering how it was possible to feel both rattled and relieved to hear someone's voice.

"Is everything okay?" she asked me.

"Yeah," I said. "Everything's fine. I just wanted to say thanks for today . . . for coming over . . . with Finch," I said. Because I had to come up with something. But I also meant it.

"Of course," she said. "Thank *you*. It was really amazing of you to give him that chance. . . ."

"You're welcome. Listen. I didn't realize it was so late. . . . I'm sorry about that. I hope I didn't wake you? Or your husband?" I said, tensing up just thinking about that guy and so wishing I could meet him in a dark alley.

"No. It's fine. You didn't. Kirk's actually out of town. . . . He travels a lot. . . . And I was just sitting here . . . reading a little . . ."

"That sounds nice," I said, and although a quiet Saturday night reading *did* sound nice in theory, she sounded more lonely than anything else.

"What about you?" she asked. "What did you do tonight?"

"Oh, I just worked some."

"On someone's house? Or were you making furniture?"

"Neither. I drive for Uber on the side. Easy money. Flexible gig. And I've always liked driving. It relaxes me," I said. Although they were all true statements, I didn't like the insecure feeling I had in my chest as I said them.

"I know what you mean," she said. "I like driving, too, sometimes."

My heart started to race, as I carefully crafted my next statement. "Yeah. So funny thing . . . I actually drove a couple of women I think you might know."

"Oh, really? Who?"

"One was named Jackie."

"Jackie Allen?"

"Yeah. I think that was it," I said, trying to remember her last name from the ride request. "Tall blonde. Big hair. Big . . . breasts."

"Yep. That's her," she said with a laugh.

"But the other woman . . . I didn't catch her name. Generic looking. Strong Southern accent. Oh. And she might be divorced?"

Nina sighed. "Unfortunately, that doesn't narrow it down very much these days."

"Yeah. I guess not."

"So wait . . . how did you put together that I know Jackie?"

"Well, that's actually a funny story . . . not ha-ha funny . . . shitty funny," I babbled.

She said nothing, waiting.

"Well. Finch and Lyla came up . . . the incident . . ."

"Oh, *no*," she said.

"Yeah."

"What did they say?" she asked.

"You probably don't want to know," I said, wondering if she would press me, sort of hoping she would.

"People are so gossipy," she said with a sigh.

"Yeah," I said, trying to think of something else to say—or at least a way to get gracefully off the phone.

But then she said my name as a question, all whispery.

I caught my breath. "Yes, Nina?"

She hesitated, then said, "Nothing . . . I'm just glad you called tonight."

"You are?" I said.

"Yes. Very. Thank you."

"You're welcome," I said.

Then, with a huge knot in my chest, I made myself tell her goodbye.

chapter sixteen

LYLA

"Wow. That was ah-ma-zing!" I said over the ringing in my ears as the four of us left the show and walked the few blocks toward Finch's car. I'd been to concerts before, sitting in seats my dad referred to as the "nosebleeds" while I watched all of the action on the jumbotron—and even that had thrilled me. But the experience tonight had been totally different. For one, there were only about three hundred people in the entire audience. For another, we were so close to Luke that I could see individual hairs in his beard and the stitching on his jeans and the sweat on his cheeks. It was, without a doubt, the best night of my life so far, and that had as much to do with Finch as with Luke Bryan. No star could have melted me as much as Finch did when he put his arm around me during "To the Moon and Back." It wasn't done in a coupley way, more like a friend hug, the same way I occasionally had slung my arm around Grace's shoulders. But still, the contact and closeness killed me. "*Totally* amazing," I said again, almost in a state of disbelief.

"Yeah. It was a cool vibe," Finch said, his voice all chill and mellow.

"So cool," Grace said, her ponytail swishing back and forth as she and Beau walked in front of us. "And he's *so* hot."

"Why, thank you!" Beau said.

She laughed and gave him a little shove. "Not you, dummy," she said. "*Luke.*"

"Hey now," Beau said, putting his hands over his heart. "Dummy? Aren't we on a date here?"

"No, we aren't on a *date*," Grace said, continuing their flirty banter, which had been going since about midway through the show. "You didn't even invite me. Lyla did."

Technically, she was correct. When Finch had called about the tickets that afternoon, he'd said there were four, and that I was free to bring a friend. I'd made the mistake of telling Grace this part of the conversation, to which she'd replied that the whole thing seemed kind of sketchy. "Like, why wouldn't Beau want to pick his own date?" she had asked.

"I don't know," I'd floundered. "Maybe he likes you."

"Highly doubtful," Grace had said, but I could tell she didn't hate the idea. "And why isn't Finch taking Polly?"

"They broke up."

"When?" she'd asked, sounding suspicious. "Why haven't I heard anything about that?"

"Like a day ago," I'd said, making a split-second decision not to tell her the full story. I didn't want to lie to Grace, but I also wanted to keep my promise to Finch. At least for now. I told myself I could always tell her everything *after* the show. Depending on how things went. "I think maybe he's just trying to be *nice*. To, like . . . make up for things," I said, the words coming out awkwardly.

"Okay. I guess I'll go with you," she'd said, some part of her probably intrigued by the idea of going out with the two most popular senior boys. "But don't get your hopes up."

"Oh, God, no. It's not like that. . . ." I'd said, even though I hoped beyond hope that it was *exactly* like that.

"So what're you tryin' to say?" Beau said to Grace now. "I'm not gonna get it in?"

It wasn't the *first* outrageous thing he'd said tonight, but it was definitely the *most*. Grace groaned, then laughed and hip-checked him, a tough feat given that she came up to only his rib cage. "Not with *me*, you're not."

"Whoa! You're pretty strong for an imp," Beau said, pretending to trip on the curb.

"What the fuck's an *imp*?" Finch said, as he walked along beside me while reading something on his phone.

"It's, like, a little woodland creature. Like a gnome or some shit." Beau laughed, then nudged Grace and said, "What do you weigh, anyway? A buck o' five soaking wet?"

"I have no idea. I don't go around weighing myself with *no clothes on*," Grace said, her voice turning all high and coy, like she *wanted* him to picture her naked.

As we neared Finch's car, parked in a surface lot a few blocks up on Grundy next to the World Gym, he said, "Lyla calls shotgun."

"Good deal," Beau said as he opened the door for Grace, and Finch did the same for me. "I get to sit with my date."

"I'm not your date." Grace giggled, climbing into the car.

"We'll see about that," Beau said, getting in beside her, then sliding into the middle seat.

"Move *over*," she said, laughing and pushing him away.

"I'm good here, thanks," he said, putting his arm around her.

She shoved him again, unsuccessfully. As Beau and Grace continued their antics, Finch walked around to get in the car, then slowly fastened his seatbelt, started the engine, and put the car in reverse. His foot on the brake, he glanced over at me, then looked into the rearview mirror. "So what next?" he said to all of us. "Y'all wanna grab a bite? The Flipside or Double Dogs?"

"Oh my God, *yass*. The Flipside," Grace said, as I saw out of the corner of my eye that she and Beau were now getting handsy.

"Lyla?" Finch said.

I hesitated, checking my phone. It was ten after ten. "Yeah. I guess we could," I said, waffling, trying to do the calculation of time and distance, both of which I pretty consistently misjudged. "I just need to be back by eleven." I'd referenced having a "lame cur-few" a couple times already, but it was the first time I'd come out and announced exactly what it was.

"E-*lev*-en?" Beau yelled, fumbling around behind my seat for a black backpack I'd noticed on the way over.

"Yeah. I know. It sucks," I mumbled, thinking that it didn't help matters that I lived on the other side of town from everyone else. "Lemme ask my dad if I can just be back to *Grace's* by eleven."

"Or you can sleep over?" Grace said.

I shook my head, feeling sure he'd say no to a sleepover, espe-cially given the last time I'd been at her house. So I composed a text making a smaller request: Concert just got out. Starving, can we go get something to eat real fast? Can be to Grace's by 11, then home a little after?? I threw in a few praying emojis for good measure, then watched his ellipses start to scroll. *Slooooww* typing was my dad's trademark, and it didn't seem to matter how short his replies were—they always took forever.

Sure enough, his delayed response was still brief and to the point. No. Be HOME by 11. Dad.

"Ugh," I said, reading it aloud in the voice I often used to imi-tate my father—part nerd, part drill sergeant.

Finch laughed. "He signs his texts 'Dad'?"

"Yeah," I said with a chuckle.

"That's hilarious. Okay . . . I'll take you back to Grace's," Finch said, pulling up his Luke Bryan songs on his phone.

As we turned out of the parking lot and onto Grundy Street, I felt myself start to relax, my concert high returning. Clearly Finch wasn't judging my curfew or really worried about anything, including Beau, who was now clicking his JUUL, the same orange one I'd seen him use at his party. A few seconds later, the car filled with a cloud of vapor as Finch unrolled the two back windows about halfway. Over my shoulder, I watched Grace take a hit, murmuring that it tasted good.

"You think that's good . . . you should taste something else," Beau said.

"Eww! Gross!" Grace laughed as she passed the vape back to him.

"Anyone up there?" Beau said, reaching into the front seat, offering it to us.

I glanced at it, tempted. But I played it safe and shook my head. "No, thanks," I said casually. "Not tonight."

"Bro?" Beau said, now angling it toward Finch.

"I'm good," Finch said, looking distracted as he read something on his phone. "Can't you see I'm driving precious cargo here?" He gave me a little smile but then turned back to his phone, texting with one hand.

As I glanced out the window, Grace suddenly piped up from the backseat. "Well, if she's precious *cargo,* then you should probably stop texting and driving."

Her voice sounded harsh, and it made me glance over at Finch. Looking busted, he immediately dropped his phone to the seat, then tucked it under his left thigh. A weird vibe settled over the car before I cleared my throat and said, "She was just kidding."

"No. I'm not," Grace said. I glanced into the backseat and gave her a panicked look, but she continued, all preachy and pissy. "Texting and driving kills more people than drunk driving."

"God. Grace. *Chill*," I said under my breath as I looked at Finch to gauge his reaction.

"Nah. She's right," he said, giving me a little wink and one of his awesome smiles. "Bad habit. I'm *really* sorry, girls."

"*Precious* cargo?" Grace said about fifteen minutes later, after we'd been dropped off at her house and were alone in her driveway. She opened her mouth and made a gagging sound.

I knew she was quoting Finch, but I had no clue what her point was, and why she'd gone from carefree party girl to complete buzzkill in a span of three miles and ten minutes, totally ending the night on a bad note.

"What's with the one-eighty?" I said. As we walked toward her car, I typed a quick text to Finch, thanking him again for the tickets.

"Well. Let's just say I'm good at reading texts over people's shoulders."

"What's that supposed to mean?" I said, stopping to stare her down. "I'm not trying to hide anything." I held up my phone, showing her what I'd just written. "I just thanked him for the tickets. Since you kinda forgot to."

"I'm not talking about *your* phone. I'm talking about *Finch's*. I saw him texting *Polly*," she said. "In the car. He was holding the screen away from you, but I could see it all."

My heart sank as I asked her what, exactly, she saw.

"Well. I saw Polly's name. I saw an 'ILY.' I saw a kissy emoji. And I saw the word *lame*."

"*Lame?*" I said.

"Yeah. *Lame.*"

"What was he calling lame?" I couldn't resist asking, just as it occurred to me that it might be a *who*, not a *what*.

"I don't know. Does it matter? You fill in the blank. *Lame* concert. *Lame* date. *Lame* night. *Lame* effort to pretend to break up with someone and like someone else so that she'll get you off the hook next week."

"Okay. First of all," I said. "He could have been calling a lot of things 'lame' that had nothing to do with us. . . . Second of all, they *did* break up."

"Doubtful," Grace said, adjusting the strap of her Miu Miu cross-body bag. "Highly doubtful."

"Oh my God, Grace. Because he texted her? What do you want him to do? *Block* her?" I said. I'd never been in a serious relationship, but I saw how breakups worked. In most cases, it seemed that couples didn't just go cold turkey. They often kept talking or fighting or begging or getting temporarily back together only to re-break up, in some combination.

"I didn't say he had to *block* her. But typically after you break up, you don't tell that person that you *love* them. And you don't throw shade at the girl you asked out on a date. I mean, *shit*, Lyla. He used the word *lame*."

"Well. Maybe he feels sorry for her. . . . Maybe he's worried about her. . . . Maybe he still loves her on some level. . . ."

"Yeah. And maybe he and Beau just set your ass up. With Luke Bryan tickets."

"*God*, Grace. It was a *fun* night. A really fun night."

"Yeah. And I bet Finch is *still* having fun. I bet he's on his way to see her right now. I bet she doesn't even know he went out with you tonight. Or maybe she does, actually. Maybe she's in on the whole plan."

"Okay, look," I said, glancing down at my phone. "It's ten-forty. I gotta get home. Are you okay to drive?"

"Yeah. I took, like, one hit," she said. "I'm totally fine."

"I didn't mean *that*. I mean . . . your foul *mood*. Why are you so pissed at *me*?"

"I'm not pissed at *you*. I'm pissed at *them*," she said, our shoulders now squared toward each other as we stood behind the new white Jeep her parents had just given her for no reason at all.

"*Them?* So now you're mad at Beau, too? Because you seemed pretty into him all night."

"I'm not *into* him," she said, making no moves to get in her car. "Besides. That was *before* I saw the text calling us 'lame.' "

"He called *us* lame? Or you just saw the *word* 'lame'?" I said.

She didn't answer, just kept staring at me.

"Look, Grace. This curfew thing isn't just a loose suggestion. My dad *means* it. You want me to just call him to get me? He's probably out driving anyway. . . ." I usually avoided mentioning my dad's side job, even to Grace. But at that moment, I really didn't give a shit about appearances of any kind.

"No. I'll take you," she said, finally getting in her car.

As I got in beside her, I inhaled the new car smell and felt a wave of resentment. Although I never held Grace's money or nice things against her, they all irritated me now. Along with her shitty, cynical attitude. Maybe she, with her music industry dad, could take a night like this for granted. There were plenty more sweet concerts with front-row seats in her future. But she wasn't going to rain on my Luke Bryan parade. At the very least, I wanted tonight to be a good memory.

We drove in silence for a few minutes, before she cleared her throat and said, "I'm sorry, Lyla. I just don't want you to get hurt. *More* hurt."

"I know," I said. "But it really *is* more complicated than you realize."

"How?" she said, shrugging while she kept her hands on the steering wheel.

"It just is," I said.

"How?" she said again.

I swallowed, feeling myself cave to her stronger personality and my need for her approval. Without Grace, I really had nothing at Windsor—and we both knew it. "If I tell you something, do you promise not to tell anyone?" I asked, knowing that it never worked that way, and maybe hoping that it wouldn't. That she might tell Mr. Q or a guidance counselor or another close friend. That the truth might come out.

"Of *course*," she said.

"Okay. So. Here's the thing." I paused, taking a few deep breaths. "*Finch* didn't take that photo of me. And he didn't caption it. And he didn't send it to anyone."

She looked at me, her eyebrows raised, then returned her eyes to the road. "Who did?"

"*Polly*," I said. "From *his* phone."

I expected a complete transformation—or at least a softening—but instead she slapped the steering wheel and started to laugh. "Oh my *God*! He told you that?"

"Yes."

"And you actually *believe* him?"

"Yes. I do, actually," I said, delving into the rest of the details. How he wasn't trying to get out of trouble; he just wanted me to know the truth. That he was willing to take the blame for Polly because he was genuinely worried about her stability.

"*Wow*, Lyla. I thought *you*, of all people, would have more street smarts than this," she said, shaking her head.

"Why would I have street smarts?" I said, my face burning. "Because I grew up on the wrong side of the river with a single dad who makes furniture and drives Uber?"

"What the heck does *that* mean?" Grace snapped back.

"Never mind," I said because I knew I might be overreacting. Maybe I was reading too much into the expression. Maybe Grace simply meant that I usually had good instincts about people. Maybe it had nothing to do with any of that other stuff—and those were just *my* paranoid, insecure issues. "Can we just drop it?"

"Yeah. Sure. We can drop it," Grace said, going all passive-aggressive on me as she cruised along in her pretty white Jeep. "No problem*o*."

BUT SHE *DIDN'T* drop it. Instead, about twenty minutes after I got home, when I'd already been doubting myself, and doubting Finch, and generally feeling like shit, Grace sent me three photographs of Finch's car parked in the driveway of a big brick house, along with a text that said: Look who went straight to Polly's.

My heart sank. After all, it was one thing to text his ex, it was *another* to go over to her house the second he dropped us off. I still wasn't convinced that Polly hadn't taken the photo of me, but I decided that it really didn't matter. Either way, it seemed pretty clear that they were working as a team, and that Grace was right. The Luke Bryan tickets were a bribe of some sort. A last-ditch effort to win me over.

I scrolled back through my text thread with Finch, starting around one o'clock, when he'd first asked me what kind of music I liked.

A little bit of everything, I'd written back, trying so hard to be cool. I kept reading, cringing at myself, wishing that, at the very least, I'd played a little harder to get.

Finch: Top 5 fave artists?

Me: That's too hard!!! So many!

Finch: K. Just 5 ur listening to lately?

Me: Walker Hayes, Bruno Mars, Jana Kramer, Jason Aldean, and Kirby Rose (new artist, but love her).

Finch: Cool . . . So mostly country?

Me: Yeah.

Finch: What about Luke Bryan?

Me: Love him.

Finch: He's playing tonight. Wanna try to go?

Me: Seriously?

Finch: Yeah. Why not? Let me see if I can get tix.

Me: OMG. That would be amazing! ☺

Finch: Got four tix. Wanna go with Beau and one of your friends?

Me: Yes! I'll ask Grace!

Me: Grace is IN!

Finch: Awesome. Did you mention Polly?

Me: I told her y'all broke up.

Finch: But the rest of the stuff?

Me: No.

Finch: Thx. Don't want the drama. Have enough already!

I scanned the rest of the thread, which was a discussion of logistics about the concert, followed by my final text, which I'd sent from Grace's driveway, thanking him. He had yet to reply to that one, of course. Picturing him with Polly, maybe hooking up, or maybe just laughing at me, I told myself I had to do *something*. At the very least, I had to let him know that I wasn't as stupid as he thought. My mind raced with all the things I could say to call him out, but I played it a little safe, settling on a snarky Having fun?

I stared at my screen, waiting. Seconds turned to minutes. Just as I was about to give up and take a shower, my phone rang. It was him. My hands shaking, I answered with a snippy hello.

"Hi," he said, sounding oblivious.

"Where are you?" I asked as I sat down on my bedroom floor.

"In my car," he said. "On the way home."

"On the way home from where?" I said, hugging my knees with my left arm as my hair formed a protective curtain around me.

"I just dropped Beau off. We ended up going to The Flipside," he said, lying so easily I got a chill. "Why do you ask?"

"*Why?* You tell *me* why," I said. "Why are you lying to me?"

"Why do you think I'm lying?"

"Because you *are*," I said, trying to channel Grace. *Any* strong girl. Or at least someone who didn't care enough to get hurt like this. I thought of my mother—how nothing really fazed her, at least not that she'd ever shared with me.

"What are you even *talking* about?" Finch said.

"I *know* where you were tonight. After you dropped me and Grace off. I'm not *stupid*."

I braced myself for more lying—since that's what liars do. But instead he folded immediately. "Okay, Lyla. You're right. I'm sorry. I wasn't with Beau. And I didn't go to The Flipside. I was with Polly."

"You're an ass," I said, welling up. "A *total* ass."

He said nothing, though I could tell he was still on the phone.

Seconds passed before he sighed and said, "Okay. Can I please just explain?"

"No," I said, telling myself to hang up on him but knowing I wouldn't. Instead, I just sat there, waiting and listening, a sick part of me hoping, once again.

"Polly knows about you," Finch said.

"What about me?" I said.

"She knows I went to the concert with you. She knows I like you. *And* . . . " Finch said, pausing dramatically as the hope expanded in my chest so quickly that I felt as if my heart would explode. "She knows I'm going to tell the truth about what she did to you."

chapter seventeen

NINA

R ight after Finch left for the concert, I poured myself a glass of wine. It crossed my mind that I was doing this too often and that drinking alone was a sign of a "problem"—much like the one I sometimes accused Kirk of having. But I rationalized that wine was simply the nighttime version of coffee—more of a ritual than anything else—especially if you had only a glass or two.

At some point, I called Kirk, partly because I was feeling lonely. But also because I was feeling guilty for keeping secrets from my husband. No matter what mistakes he'd made, I wanted to be honest. He didn't pick up, though. So I left a message, telling him that I hoped he was feeling better.

A few minutes later, he called me back. Only he hadn't—at least not *purposefully*. He'd simply made an inadvertent pocket dial. I called out his name a few times, but when that didn't work (it never does), I listened, more out of boredom than any real curiosity or concern. Even after I heard a woman's voice, I told myself not to jump to paranoid conclusions. Yes, he'd said he had a migraine and was going to bed. But that didn't necessarily make this nefarious. Hell, she could be a female concierge, helping him get his headache meds from a nearby pharmacy. My service industry explanation calmed me for a few seconds, but then their interaction continued, an easy, back-and-forth rhythm suggesting a certain familiarity. Mostly, it was Kirk talking and the woman laughing. It reminded me that my husband could be really funny and charming, and I felt a pang for a dynamic that had seemed to slip away as gradually as Finch's open-bedroom-door policy. I couldn't remember the last time Kirk had had this much to say to *me,* let alone the last time he'd actually made me laugh. I strained to make out their words, but everything was too muffled. Even the volume was coming in and out, as if they were in motion, in a car or walking somewhere.

Then, suddenly, their voices got clearer and louder, and I heard the woman say "Honey" followed by my husband's unmistakable "Oh *shit.*" Then he *hung up* on me. I sat there, stunned, yet still struggling to give him the benefit of the doubt. Maybe I'd misheard her *honey.* Maybe he'd said *oh shit* about something else. He could have made a wrong turn. Or stepped in a wad of gum. Or realized he'd left his credit card at a store where he'd bought me a sweet token of a gift. It could be anything, really. People said *oh shit* all the time in the normal course of things. And some people just used terms of affection like *honey.* It wasn't as if I'd just heard him having sex with a woman—or professing his love to her. It wasn't as if I had irrefutable visual evidence. Maybe he hadn't hung up on me at all. Maybe he'd just lost the connection at that instant.

This was an exercise I'd engaged in before, especially in recent years, one on which I actually prided myself, believing that it said as much about my self-confidence as about my faith in my husband. But I didn't feel very proud or confident in that agonizing moment, as I sipped my wine, waiting for my husband to call me back.

When after several minutes my phone still didn't ring, I told myself to be proactive and try him again. It went to voicemail. I left a message, then texted another. And another.

I began to freak out—at least *my* version of freaking out, which was really just sitting very still, staring into space, and imagining Kirk kissing a younger, more beautiful woman. I told myself that her age or beauty was irrelevant. Unfaithful was unfaithful. Maybe someone my age or older who had real substance and life experience and significant accomplishments might actually hurt *worse*.

Finally, he called. I took a deep breath and said hello.

"Hey, what's up?" he asked, so innocently that it made him sound even *more* guilty.

"Nothing," I said. "Where are you?"

"What do you mean?" he asked through a yawn that sounded fake, or at least exaggerated.

"I mean, *where* are you?"

"I'm in Dallas."

"*Where* in Dallas?"

"My room."

"Which hotel?"

"The Mansion on Turtle Creek," he said. "Where I always stay."

"Who are you with?"

"Nobody."

"Who were you with an hour ago? When you pocket-dialed me?"

"I pocket-dialed you?" he said.

"Yeah, you did, Kirk."

"Well . . . let's see . . . an hour ago? . . . I was with Gerald Lee. . . ."

"I heard a *woman's* voice, Kirk."

"You didn't let me finish."

"So, finish."

"I was with Gerald—*and* his fiancée. Did I tell you he got engaged?"

"No," I said, thinking that it had been years since I'd even heard him *mention* Gerald, making his old college friend a very convenient alibi. "You sure didn't."

"Yeah. So anyway, we had a quick bite. . . ."

"I thought you had a migraine?"

"I did. Still do. But I had to eat. And now I'm headed to bed." His voice was suddenly both hushed and hurried.

"I'm so sorry you're not feeling well," I said as insincerely as I could.

"It's okay. I'll be fine," he said. "Everything okay there?"

"Sure," I said, pausing, listening to the conspicuous silence in his background. I pictured him huddled in a marble hotel bathroom, someone waiting for him in the next room. Maybe she was even beside him in bed, craning to hear my every word so they could analyze it together.

"Okay. Well. I'll see you tomorrow?" he said.

"Yeah," I said, then made myself say the last three words I wanted to say to him: *I love you.* It didn't feel like the truth at that second, more like a test, as I waited to see what he'd say in return.

"You, too," he simply said back, failing with flying colors.

A FEW SECONDS later, my phone rang again. I expected it to be Kirk, attempting to apologize for his abruptness, fix things, talk to me. But it was Tom. Surprised, I answered hello. He said hello back, sounding tentative as he went on to thank me for coming

217

over this morning. I told him of course, then thanked him for *allowing* us to come. After an awkward pause, he told me a disturbing story about him overhearing a conversation between two women I apparently knew. Something about Lyla and Finch and the incident. But it was a comfort to hear from him—and a welcome interruption in an intense period of panic and loneliness.

Bolstered by the brief exchange, I went to Kirk's office, determination replacing sadness. I sat in his desk chair, swiveling to the left and right, staring at the neat piles of papers, his pewter pencil cup filled with only black Pilot rollerball pens. I opened his drawers, one at a time. Three down the left, three down the right, and one long, skinny one in the middle. I don't know what I was looking for, but I methodically combed through everything. I found nothing suspicious but ascribed the lack of evidence to his fastidiousness, not his innocence. I turned on his laptop. I didn't expect to find anything there either, as he knew that I knew his password. But I still scrutinized his email in-box, just in case, scanning rows of names and boring subject lines.

Just as I was about to give up, I saw an email dated today from Bob Tate, Kirk's ticket broker. I clicked and read the thread—a complicated back-and-forth among Bob, Kirk, and Finch—and pieced together a very different story than the one Finch had given me earlier. In a nutshell, Finch wanted four tickets to the show (not two), for the express purpose of making amends with Lyla Volpe (he didn't think she'd go if it were just the two of them). Kirk summarized the request to Bob, who came through in grand style, explaining that the price was steep because they were limited admission and last minute. Kirk said no problem, and he'd settle up in cash when back in town.

Son of a bitch, I said aloud, the magnitude of their betrayal sinking in. My son and husband had, essentially, conspired against me. It occurred to me that I had done the same thing this morning. I had brought my son to the Volpe home unbeknownst to my husband. I had encouraged Finch to lie to his father, at least by omission. But I believed in my heart that there was a vital difference. I had been trying to do what was right—and show my son how important that was; Kirk was, as always, simply trying to manipulate others in his quest to get his way.

There was really no way around it. My husband, whom I'd once thought of as charming and take-charge, was simply a user and a liar. And the worst part of it all was that he was teaching our son to be those very things.

I'd always pictured marriages severing more dramatically, with an explosive fight or irrefutable proof (stronger than a pocket dial) of an affair. But in that quiet moment in Kirk's office waiting for our son to return from a concert with a girl he had mistreated and maybe even manipulated, I felt in my bones that my marriage was over.

I wanted a divorce. I was done. *So* done.

I WOKE UP the next morning to a disjointed dream about Tom and suddenly remembered his call the night before. It almost seemed like a dream, too, coming, as it had, during so much turmoil. I found my phone on my nightstand and started a text to Tom, confessing that I'd had something of a rough night, and apologizing if I'd acted a bit off. I reread my words, then deleted them, the statement sounding a little inappropriate.

Inappropriate.

I repeated the word in my head, realizing how much I despised it. It was a favorite of Kathie and all her Bible buddies, the catchall for any behavior they wished to judge. *Her dress was inappropriate for a wedding. . . . That book selection was inappropriate for teenagers. . . . The conversation they were having in front of children was inappropriate. . . . Her political post was inappropriate. . . . A text to a single, attractive father asking about a drunken conversation? So. Very. Inappropriate.*

Screw being appropriate, I thought, as I dialed Tom's number, hoping he would answer. He did, almost immediately.

"Hi. It's Nina," I said, my palms turning clammy.

"Hi," he said.

"Did I wake you?" I asked.

"No," he said. "I've been up for a while."

"Oh," I said.

"Are you all right?" he asked.

"Yeah. I was just thinking about our call last night . . . and your Uber ride."

"I should have kept my mouth shut with those women, but . . ."

"But you didn't," I said, feeling a surge of respect for him.

"Correct," he said with a hint of a laugh.

"What did you say to them, exactly?"

"Just the facts. That I was her father. And that she wasn't Mexican." He started to say something else, but then stopped.

"What?"

"Nothing."

"You were going to say something."

"Yeah," he said. "I was."

"What was it? Please tell me."

"It was about your husband."

"What about him?" I asked, both dreading his response and praying that he'd give me more evidence. Say something bad about the man I wanted to leave.

"I probably shouldn't get into that. It's really none of my business," Tom said. "And it could complicate our . . . situation."

"Our situation?" I repeated, wondering if he meant our two kids and the hearing on Tuesday—or the unlikely connection we seemed to be forging.

"You know . . . everything else that's going on," he replied vaguely.

"Yeah," I said, my head pounding from the swirling subtext.

We sat in silence for another few seconds before he cleared his throat and said, "Look. Those women were drunk. *Really* drunk. Who knows if anything they said was true. . . . And I could have heard them wrong. . . . I was driving."

I closed my eyes. "Lemme guess. They were talking about Kirk cheating on me?" I said.

"Yes," he said softly but swiftly. "They were. I'm sorry."

"It's fine. You're not telling me anything I don't already know," I said. It was an overstatement—I didn't know anything for *sure*—but I didn't want Tom to feel guilty.

I could hear him draw a deep breath, then say my name on a weary exhale. It sounded like a plea.

"Yes?" I said in response.

"I don't know you very well," he said slowly, as if very carefully choosing his words. "But you deserve better than this."

"I know," I managed to reply. "Thank you, Tom."

Right after we said goodbye and hung up, I realized that I'd forgotten to mention Lyla and Finch and my strong suspicion that they had gone out the night before. I told myself I needed to call him back. But I couldn't make myself do it. I was just too disappointed in Finch. In my life.

Instead I called my best friend and told her I needed to see her. That I was having a crisis. She asked no questions, simply saying she'd be home all day, waiting for me.

I then went to check on Finch. I'd heard him come in the night before, around midnight. I went upstairs now, lightly knocking on his door. When he didn't answer, I opened it. He was sound asleep and lightly snoring, the covers tucked up under his chin. I walked over to his bedside and put my hand on his shoulder, shaking him gently, then harder, until his eyes opened and his mouth closed.

"Yeah, Mom?" he said, squinting groggily up at me.

"Hi. I just wanted to let you know I'm headed home. To Bristol. I'll be back sometime tomorrow. But Dad will be here in a few hours."

"Is everything okay? With Nana and Gramps?" he asked.

"Yes," I said, comforted that he'd shown himself capable of concern. "I just feel like I need to go home."

"Okay," he said, blinking.

"Do you want to come with me?" I asked, knowing he would not. His lack of interest in his grandparents these days made me sad, but right now it was obviously low on the list of things to be sad about.

"I have a lot of homework. . . ." he replied, his eyelids fluttering and closing again.

I stared at his face for a few seconds before reaching out to lightly shake his arm.

"Yeah, Mom?" he said, his eyes still closed.

"How was the concert?" I asked.

"Fine," he said. "Fun."

"Good . . . I'm glad. . . . It was so nice that Beau could get those tickets," I said.

"Uh-huh."

"And it was just the two of you? Or did you go with other people?"

"Just the two of us."

"Okay . . . well. Remember your father's coming home today," I said, feeling sick on so many levels. It was the way divorced people talked. *Your father* rather than *Dad*.

"Yeah. You already said that, Mom."

"Does he know you went to the concert?" I asked, giving him one *final* chance.

"Nope," he said, finally opening his eyes so he could lie right to my face. "I haven't talked to him."

Strike three, I thought, walking out of his room.

I ARRIVED IN downtown Bristol shortly after two o'clock, going first to Julie's house, a small cottage that she and Adam had lived in forever. As I got out of my car, I spotted her on one of two rocking chairs on the wraparound front porch they'd recently painted. I'd selected the color for her—Benjamin Moore Tranquil Blue.

"Hey there," I called out with a little wave. "I *love* your porch. It looks so pretty!"

She waved back at me, still rocking in her chair. "Thanks to you!"

I climbed the porch stairs as she stood and held out her arms, then pulled me into a long, tight hug. It was comforting, as was the familiar scent she'd been wearing since high school—Chanel No. 5, which she'd once joked was the only Chanel she'd ever own.

"Have you lost weight? You feel tiny," I asked, backing up to look at her. Other than brisk walks and swims at the Y, Julie never worked out, and she was built like a delicate bird. Sort of the opposite of her personality. "Tinier than *usual,* I should say."

"I don't think so," she said, pulling at the waistband of her khaki shorts and glancing down to check the space between the fabric and her stomach. "I don't have a scale, so I'm not really sure."

"You don't have a *scale?*" I said, thinking I weighed myself at *least* twice a day, mostly out of mindless habit but also due to general vigilance. My being thin was so important to Kirk—and so it had become that way to me, too.

"Nope. Not since I caught the girls weighing themselves," she said as we each took a rocking chair. "I didn't think much about it until Reece declared herself the winner because she was a pound lighter than Paige." She shook her head as she snapped her fingers, making a crisp sound. "I nipped that in the bud."

"God, you're so good about that stuff," I said, wondering if it was ever tough for Paige, who had inherited more of Adam's stocky build; Reece looked just like her mother. I was ashamed of having the thought and saw it as another sign that I'd been focusing on the wrong things. I felt sure it wasn't something Julie had ever worried about. Her lack of shallowness, coupled with feelings of self-acceptance, transferred to everyone close to her, most of all her daughters. "It's a good thing I had a boy. I'd have screwed up a girl even worse. . . ."

"No, you wouldn't have," she said but conspicuously did not deny that I'd screwed up Finch. I told myself this wasn't the time to get defensive. I needed to have a thick skin. After all, if I'd wanted someone to help me take the easy way out, I would have called Melanie.

"Anyway," I said.

"Yes. Anyway . . . would you like some lunch? I made some chicken salad."

"No, thanks," I said. "I'm not really hungry right now."

"Something to drink? Coffee? Sweet tea? A glass of rosé?"

Although I actually could have used some caffeine, I didn't want to interrupt the moment. I wanted us to stay exactly where we were, for as long as possible. "No, thanks," I said. "Where are Adam and the girls?"

"They're running errands. . . . I gave them a very *long* list."

I smiled and thanked her, knowing she'd done this for my sake, probably changing her own plans for the day, too.

"Of course. No problem," she said. "So tell me, what's going on? I assume this is about Finch?"

"Yes and no," I said, then caught her up on everything. Our visit to Tom and Lyla. Finch's apology. The tickets to see Luke Bryan. Finch's lies. Kirk's lies. All of them.

"Bastard," Julie said under her breath. "I knew it."

As she started to get all worked up, I raised my hand and stopped her. "Yeah. But honestly, that's the least of it," I said. "It's more . . . the kind of husband and father he is. The person he's become. It's everything. . . . I think the affair is just a symptom of it all. . . . And I just can't do it anymore."

"Meaning?" she said softly.

"Meaning . . . I think I want a divorce," I said.

Julie didn't miss a beat. It was almost as if she'd been waiting for this. "Okay," she said. "Let's back up. Did you find something? Texts or receipts?"

"No. Just the pocket dial—and what Tom told me he over-heard," I said. "I know it's circumstantial, but it's just a feeling I have. A very *strong* gut feeling."

"And there's a lot to that," she said. "But I still think you need a PI. I know a guy in Nashville. He's incredible."

I shook my head. "I don't need proof. I know what he's doing."

"Yes, but we still should have it. Tennessee's a fault-based state."

"Which means?"

"Which means adultery is a factor in alimony. It's also leverage. Kirk cares so much about how things *look* to people."

"No, he doesn't," I said, shaking my head.

"Well, he cares about how things look to *some* people. That's why he does his philanthropy bullshit."

"Maybe," I said. "But those people give him a pass no matter what . . . because of his money. They love him *for* his money."

"I know," she said. "It's *disgusting*."

We rocked in silence for several seconds, both of us looking out over her front lawn, which consisted of a small square patch of grass, a beautiful magnolia, and a row of white hydrangea bushes planted along the front of the porch. The landscape was so simple it reminded me of a child's drawing, right down to the yellow butterfly fluttering on a flower near us. I could tell Julie was watching it, too, both of us tracing its flight, in and out of the dappled sunlight.

"So you'll be my lawyer?" I said.

Julie sighed. "I don't know, Nina—"

"What do you mean you don't *know*? You're my best friend *and* you're a Tennessee divorce lawyer." I let out a dry laugh.

"I know. And I'm happy to take your case," she said, as I noted her telling use of the word *happy* in this context. "And I certainly can handle it. But you may want to consider some bigger hitters."

"Bigger hitters?" I said. "C'mon, Jules. Nobody hits harder than you."

"True," she said, smiling back at me. "But you know what I mean. There are lawyers who specialize in high-net-worth and celebrity clients. . . ."

I shook my head and said, "No. I want *you*."

"Okay, then. You have me. *Always*."

I nodded and said, "So what's next?"

"We get the PI . . . and you gather all the information you can. Any financial information, bank statements, investments, a list of all your assets. . . . We'll eventually subpoena records. But get everything you can for now. Once we get our ducks in a row, we will file a complaint. That's followed by a mandatory sixty-day cooling-off period. From there, we do discovery. . . ."

My stomach lurched. "So you think this will go to trial?"

"Maybe. Probably."

"But don't a lot of people settle? Or do mediation?"

"Yes," she said. "But honestly, I don't see mediation working with Kirk. Do you? He doesn't know the word *compromise*."

"Yeah . . . He's going to be so *shocked*."

"Oh, will the poor thing feel betrayed?" she said, her voice dripping with disdain.

"You really hate him, don't you?"

She stared at me for a beat, as if trying to restrain herself—for the sake not of her new client but of her old friend. Yet she couldn't help herself.

"Yeah," she said. "I *hate* him, Nina."

"Since when?" I asked, thinking back to when Kirk had sold his company, feeling sure she would cite that as a turning point.

"Um. Since the night I met him. When he cheated in putt-putt."

Looking up at the sky, at least as much of it as I could see from the porch, I rewound to the first time I'd brought Kirk to my hometown from Vandy. I actually had a photograph from that night, which was unusual, because it was pre–camera phones. In it, Kirk, Julie, Adam, and I were all standing in the run-down parking lot of the Putt-Putt Fun Center on Bluff City Highway. The three of us from Bristol were wearing sneakers and T-shirts, but Kirk had on a polo shirt, khakis, and driving moccasins—which at the time I just thought of as loafers with funny rubber things on the bottom.

"What did he do, exactly?" I said, picturing him nudging the ball with his foot—or taking an extra turn. The joking, impatient ways a lot of people cheated in minigolf.

"He was keeping the scorecard, of *course,*" she said. "And Adam kept busting him shaving off his own strokes. *Blatant* cheating."

"Wow . . . What else?" I said.

"What do you mean 'what else'? Other than the *cheating*?" She raised her eyebrows. "Isn't that sort of like saying 'other than his shitty character'?"

"I meant what else do you remember," I said, feeling the tiniest bit defensive. Not of Kirk per se. But of the whole notion that his actions that night automatically translated to irredeemable character flaws. "Other than the minutiae around minigolf?"

"Minigolf," she said with stone seriousness, "is a metaphor for life."

I smiled and said, "Oh, really?"

"Yes. I mean, think about it. . . . Do you take it seriously? Too seriously? Do you enjoy it? Do you keep careful score? Do you get upset when you lose? Do you cheat? And if you do cheat, how do you react when you're busted? Are you sheepish? Sorry? Do you do it again?"

I held up my palms and said, "Okay, okay . . . All I'm saying is—I think cheating on your wife is a little worse than cheating at putt-putt. . . . And I don't think Kirk was *that* bad back then," I said. "After all, I fell in love with him, right?"

"*Did* you?" she asked, looking more than a little skeptical.

"Uh . . . yeah. I *married* him, Julie," I said, hearing how lame my comeback sounded given everything that was happening in our lives.

She heard it, too, raising her eyebrows as I continued.

"I don't regret our *whole* marriage. That would be akin to regretting Finch. . . . I just regret . . . the past few years. Since Kirk sold his business. I think that's when he changed," I said, stopping short of mentioning money directly.

Julie nodded and said, "Yeah. Well, he definitely got worse after that. More arrogant, more entitled . . . What's the saying? *Money makes you more of what you already are?*"

"Yeah." I nodded. "Something like that."

Julie looked thoughtful for a beat, as if trying to figure something out, then said, "You know, in the past decade, I don't think I've ever been around Kirk for longer than thirty minutes in which he didn't excuse himself to go 'make a call.' " She imitated his deep voice, then muttered, "Self-important prick."

I winced at her words, knowing she was right, thinking of how he couldn't bear to be separated from his phone. In fact, the only time I'd seen him without it for any length of time was at the Masters every year, where cellphones were absolutely forbidden—no matter how wealthy or powerful you were. It was one of the few rules he actually respected—perhaps unsurprisingly, given the elitist context.

"Like, nobody's *that* important. Herman Frankel doesn't do that, and he's a freaking brain surgeon," Julie continued, referring to the valedictorian of our class, with whom Julie was still friends.

"He never mentions his work unless other people bring it up. And he won't even make plans to go out if he's on call because he doesn't want to have to insult people by stepping away from the table."

She was on a roll now. Part of me was embarrassed for my husband—and myself for putting up with his behavior for so long—but I also felt oddly comforted by her rant. It was almost like therapy or validation.

"He's *such* an insufferable snob," she continued. "I mean, Nina, forget what he can *afford*. Because I get that—if you can pay for nice hotels and first class, fine, get your nice hotels and first class. I'd do it, too, if I could. . . . I don't begrudge Kirk all the perks that come with wealth and success. But he thinks of himself as a higher class of *person*. Like he, along with his rich, white, male friends, is truly *better than* the rest of us."

"I know," I murmured, thinking of all the offhanded disparaging remarks he'd made about average, hardworking Americans, the kinds of people you might see at a professional sporting event or an amusement park or the zoo. The *public,* he called them, and that was the nicer of the terms. I'd also heard him use *riffraff, dregs, proles,* and *plebs.* He usually pretended to be joking, but the sentiment was real. That was how he felt. If something was accessible or populated by "those people," he wanted no part of it.

Even *Disney World,* I thought, reminding Julie how much I had wanted to take Finch when he was little, and how Kirk had refused to go until he learned about the VIP tour guides that movie stars used. How you could access everything from the backs of the rides. Circumvent all lines. Avoid the commoners. Yet he still managed to squeeze in remarks about all the "fat people with their turkey legs who were riding in scooters because they were too lazy to walk." And the worst part was that he would sometimes make such comments within earshot of Finch. I shushed him, of course, or came right out and told him that wasn't nice, but I still worried that some of those ideas would rub off on our son.

Julie listened, her lips pursed, then chimed in with more. "And he only pays attention to people who have a lot of money. Otherwise he sees right through you, doesn't give you the time of day. Do you know he has never, once, asked me about my work? And I'm an *attorney*. So forget Adam's job. It's as if fighting fires is . . . is . . . I don't know." She threw up her hands, at a rare loss for words.

"Is equivalent to being in *jail*?" I said.

"Exactly," she said. "Although that might depend on what *kind* of jail. In his eyes, a white-collar criminal in a cushy federal prison probably has more status than a firefighter."

I nodded, thinking of how Kirk *still* defended Bob Heller, a neighbor of ours who had been sent to prison for running an elaborate Ponzi scheme. And it wasn't because Kirk believed in mercy, redemption, or forgiveness—*that* would have been admirable—but because he insisted his friend was a "good guy" who got a "raw deal" and "hadn't ripped anyone off *that* much."

"So Adam hates Kirk, too?" I said, wondering how much they'd discussed us.

Julie shrugged. "I wouldn't say *hate*. Adam doesn't *care* enough to hate him. And honestly, I wouldn't either except for the fact that he's married to my best friend. I hate him for *you*. And for Finch."

And there it was. The point of no return. My realization that if I didn't divorce Kirk for me, I had to do it for my son. Staying in the marriage any longer was giving tacit approval to everything Kirk had done. Finch needed to know that there were repercussions to his father's entitled mindset and selfish behavior. I had to make him see that there was another way to be.

Tears stung my eyes, and I tried to blink them back, telling myself I had to be strong. But I couldn't. I expected Julie to glance away, as most people do when you start to cry, no matter how close they are to you.

But Julie didn't look away. Instead she fiercely held my gaze and my hand, telling me it was time—high *fucking* time—and that Kirk wouldn't be ignoring her anymore.

chapter eighteen

LYLA

I thought kissing Finch was a distinct possibility when he invited me over, especially after he made it a point to say that his parents wouldn't be home. But I didn't think we'd do anything more than that.

Backing up, I should say that I'm not a virgin, but I'm also not a slut. I've only had sex with one guy. His name was—still *is*—Caleb King. We vaguely knew each other from middle school, where he'd been a grade ahead of me. But then he went on to Stratford, the public high school near us, and I went to Windsor the following year. So he never really crossed my mind again until last spring, when we ran into each other at the Gulch, shopping at Urban Outfitters. I didn't notice him at first (I get really focused when I'm shopping), but then he tapped me on the shoulder and said, "Hey, didn't you go to Dalewood?"

I put down the T-shirt I'd been considering and said, "Yeah. Hi. It's Caleb, right?"

"Yeah. That's right," he said, smiling at me. "And you're . . . Layla?"

I smiled back at him. "Close. Lyla."

He asked me where I went to school, and after we covered those basics and a few others, he told me I had beautiful eyes. A few minutes of flirting later, he asked if I wanted to hang sometime. I was more flattered than psyched by the idea, but I still said yes, then gave him my number before he left the store.

It was all good until Grace, who had been standing impatiently nearby, started dissing Caleb, saying he was annoying and came on too strong. Maybe he had been a little aggressive, but I somehow got the feeling that she had a bigger problem with the fact that Caleb was (still is) black. It surprised me because I'd never thought of Grace as being at all racist, and she certainly had never said anything negative about our friend Hattie (who is white) dating Logan (who is black). I'd once even heard her say something about how cute their babies would be. So I gave her the benefit of the doubt. Until she threw out the word *ghetto,* that is.

"Ghetto?" I said. "Caleb lives in my neighborhood."

"I don't mean *where* he lives," she said, ignoring the actual definition of the word. "I mean . . . his whole *look.*"

"What about his look?" I said, then reminded her that we were all shopping in the same clothing store.

"He was wearing a gold *chain.*"

"I think some guys can pull off a chain," I said, even though I didn't love jewelry on guys, either.

"Maybe. If you're, like, Brad Pitt or Robert Pattinson."

"You mean *white*?" I asked, which was as close as I came to calling her out.

I waited for her to get defensive, but either my question was too subtle for her or she just didn't mind the implication, because she sloughed the comment off with a shrug. "Okay. Maybe the chain's okay, but *nobody* can pull off those *saggy* jeans," she said, making her way to the cash register with about seven items, none of which were on sale.

"His jeans weren't *sagging*," I said, empty-handed and super-annoyed. "They were just . . . loose-fitting."

"What's the diff?"

"The *diff* . . . *is* . . . his jeans weren't falling down," I said, think-ing that I *distinctly* remembered watching Caleb walk away from us. "I know for a fact his boxers weren't showing. At all."

Grace shrugged. "Still. I just think you could do better. *Way* better," she said, then went on this whole tirade about how I needed to aim high in life, and wasn't that why I was at Windsor in the first place?

I knew she just wanted the best for me, and maybe there really was something legit about Caleb that she didn't like but couldn't put her finger on. But I still felt like she was being really rude to him and condescending to me, and I couldn't help feeling offended. It wasn't the first time she'd made me feel like her little pet project, the poor girl she had taken under her wing—not just because she liked me, but because she felt I needed *help. Her* help, as a rich white girl from the heart of Belle Meade. I almost told her that my dad hadn't sent me to Windsor to change up my dating pool. I was there for an education. Period. But I figured it wasn't worth dis-secting all of that. I was grateful to have Grace, and I didn't want to jeopardize our friendship by playing the race card or making a big deal out of something so little. Nobody was perfect, after all.

Still, when Caleb and I started hanging out that summer, I didn't really fill Grace in on many specifics, just played it off as us being friends. (I might not have told her anything at all, but I wanted the satisfaction of informing her that the pendant Caleb wore on a chain around his neck had belonged to his grandmother before she died.) Incidentally, I also kept Caleb a secret from my dad, knowing he'd freak out about *any* guy, especially an older one, and figuring there was no point in worrying him. So I'd wait until he left for work, or pretend to have a babysitting gig, then ride my bike the two miles over to Caleb's house. (His mother worked, too, but unlike with my dad, there was never a possibility of her returning home during the day since she had a nine-to-five receptionist job.)

Anyway, Caleb and I had fun hanging out together, and he turned out to be more nerdy (in a quirky, good way) than ghetto (which he wasn't at *all*). We spent a lot of time watching funny YouTube videos and playing board games. And of course we hooked up a lot, too, sex seeming more inevitable with every passing day until I finally told him I wanted to do it.

It certainly wasn't the most romantic thing I'd ever pictured, as there was never any mention of love or even *dating*. But it still felt right *enough,* all the important boxes being checked. For one, I trusted Caleb in terms of STDs and stuff (he'd been with two girls before me, but both had been virgins). Second, I trusted him not to blab my business (although our friends didn't overlap, anyway). And third, I'd just turned sixteen—which felt like the right age to lose my virginity (fifteen had seemed too young). My final concern was the biggest: getting pregnant. Caleb said he could use condoms, although he didn't like them because he couldn't feel as much. I wasn't too concerned about maximizing his pleasure, but I'd heard plenty of stories about condoms tearing—so I decided to get on the pill. I then called the only person I could think of who would be able to help me but who also wouldn't judge: my mother.

A few days later, she surprised me by sailing into town on a twenty-four-hour birth control mission, taking me to an appointment she'd scheduled herself at Planned Parenthood. I was very grateful, as I knew how expensive her airline ticket from L.A. was (she mentioned it at *least* three times). At the same time, it was a little bit strange that she chose this, over all the other things in my life, to be proactive about. She was downright giddy about what she called my "rite of passage," yet oddly never once asked anything about Caleb. It was as if he was totally *beside* the point. Maybe she was just that sexually liberated. Or maybe she was simply trying to make up for a lot of lost years and missed benchmarks. Or maybe she liked the idea of getting one over on Dad (that thought made me feel guilty).

Regardless, I told myself it wasn't about my mother or my father. It was about *my* decision to have sex—and what mattered was that I was handling that decision responsibly. So after my being on the pill for the requisite seven days, Caleb and I had sex on his twin bed in the middle of the day. It hurt—a *lot*—and the whole bleeding thing was totally embarrassing and disgusting. But Caleb was really cool and nice about everything. He was very patient and went really slow and kept reassuring me that there was nothing gross about blood, adding that his mother wouldn't see the sheets because he did his own laundry. So even though I wound up thinking the whole sex thing was pretty overhyped, I still considered my first time a success in that I felt no regret and was glad I'd picked Caleb.

Over the next month, we ended up having sex eleven more times—and toward the end, I actually thought I might be falling for him. But then we went back to school, and we both got really busy, and we talked less and less until Caleb started straight ghosting me. I was a little hurt, but it was more my pride than my heart, especially when I discovered through standard social-media stalking that he had gotten a legit girlfriend. I got over it pretty fast, though, my crush on Finch kicking into high gear.

And now, as I got in Finch's car the morning after the concert, my feelings were becoming *really* intense. Like *way* more than I'd

ever felt for Caleb, even after we'd had sex a dozen times. If anything, I think our fight last night had made me feel *more* for Finch.

"Hi," I said, a little out of breath from frantically trying to get
ready and out the door before my dad came back from wherever
he'd gone. "We meet again."

It was a lame thing to say, but Finch smiled and said, "Yep. We
meet again."

I glanced up the street, then behind us in the opposite direction.

"You okay?" Finch said.

"Yeah. Just go," I said with a nervous laugh, motioning for him
to drive. "I told my dad I was studying with Grace."

"Got it," Finch said, pulling away from the curb. I did a quick
scan of his outfit—a pair of gray Windsor sweats, a T-shirt with a
sailboat logo of some sort, and Adidas slides. As sharp as he'd
looked last night, I decided he looked sexier dressed down like
this.

He caught me looking at him and shot me the cutest smile.
"What are you thinking?" he said.

"Nothing," I said, smiling back at him. Because I really *wasn't*
thinking much of anything. I was too busy *feeling* things. All of
them good.

As we drove toward his side of town, he turned on the radio,
then shuffled through his playlist, asking what I wanted to listen to.

"Luke," I said—because it felt like our music. Our songs.

He nodded and then played "Drunk on You," singing along
here and there. His voice kind of sucked, but for some reason, it
only made me like him more.

There was never much traffic in Nashville on Sundays, especially during church hours, so within a few more songs, we were
pulling into Finch's driveway. His house was amazing, even bigger
and more beautiful than Grace's or Beau's—which was saying a

lot. I wasn't really surprised, as I already knew he was loaded, but I was still sort of blown away—and a little intimidated, too.

We got out of his car and walked up to his front porch, where Finch unlocked the door and motioned for me to go in first. The alarm started to go off, and he turned and quickly punched a keypad, silencing it.

"So," he said, closing the door. "What do you want to do?"

I shrugged, looking around his extremely fancy foyer. "Whatever you want . . . Where are your parents again?" I asked, even though he hadn't told me.

"My mom's in Bristol," Finch said. "Her hometown."

"She's from *Bristol*?" I said, having imagined that she was from somewhere more chic, like New York or California.

"Yeah. She grew up poor," he said super-matter-of-factly.

"Oh," I said, wondering what constituted "poor" in his mind and whether I qualified. I told myself it didn't matter—and that I should stop overthinking things. "And your dad? Where's he?"

"He's coming back from Texas today . . . but his flight doesn't land for a few hours."

"Oh. Cool," I said, as Finch turned and led me down a hallway and into a gorgeous white kitchen. "Can I get you a drink?"

At first I thought he meant alcohol, but then he clarified and said, "Tea? Juice? I think we have orange and grapefruit. . . . Water?"

I said water would be good.

"Sparkling or still?" he said, a question I'd only ever heard posed at a really nice restaurant Nonna had taken me to once.

"Um. Either. Still, I guess," I said, as I noticed the gigantic slab of marble on the kitchen island, veins running through it like the lines in one of my dad's oversize paper road atlases.

Finch opened the door of an enormous stainless-steel refrigerator and grabbed two bottles of SmartWater. He handed me one, then paused to unscrew his and take a sip. I did the same, and we swallowed in unison, then smiled at each other.

"Let's go to the basement," Finch said.

I said okay, suddenly picturing Caleb's unfinished basement, with its concrete floors and cinder-block walls, and odor of cat litter, mildew, and Clorox. I knew Finch's would be nothing like that, but as we went downstairs and he turned on the lights, I almost laughed out loud at the contrast. It was like a freaking hotel casino—with a fully stocked bar, a pool table, several old-school videogames and pinball machines, and a huge leather sectional along with a bunch of stand-alone recliners all positioned around a mammoth TV that looked more like a movie screen.

"Welcome to my man cave," he said.

"Wow," I said, too impressed to play it cool. "This is *incredible*."

He said thanks, flashing me a modest smile, then walked over to the sofa and sat down, patting the cushion next to him. I followed him and took a seat, leaving only a few inches between our legs.

"You have a favorite movie?" he asked, grabbing one of three remotes from the coffee table in front of us. He flipped on the TV, then pulled up a menu of movies.

"Not really," I said, my mind going blank because I wasn't thinking about movies.

"Just pick something. Anything," he said, scrolling too quickly for me to read the titles.

I threw out *Mean Girls*—because it was the first thing that popped into my head—and within a few seconds, we were watching the opening credits of a movie I'd virtually memorized, I'd seen it so many times.

Finch put his feet up on the table, then grabbed another remote, hitting a button that turned off all the lights at once, trans-forming the room into a private theater. A beat later, he slid down a few inches, closing the gap between our legs. Then he took my hand, his entire forearm resting in my lap. It was so comfortable and natural, yet my heart still pounded in my chest, racing even harder as he caressed my thumb with his.

For a long time, we stayed like that, my hand in his, watching and laughing. It felt intimate and *amazing,* but not *sexual,* and I began to wonder if maybe he *wasn't* going to kiss me after all. Then, in the middle of the four-way-call scene—one of my favor-ites—he hit the pause button and said, "These bitches remind me of Polly and her friends."

I started to laugh but then glanced at his face and saw that his expression was stone serious, maybe even a little pissed.

"Yeah," I said. "Me, too."

I waited for him to unpause the movie but was glad when he didn't. Instead, he let go of my hand, then reached down for his bottle of water. As he took a sip, I knew what was coming, so I took a sip of mine, too, preparing myself for his next move. It came smoothly, in the form of a quarter turn of his body toward mine, his arm extending behind me, draping along the back of the sofa.

"Hi," he whispered, as I angled myself toward him, too.

"Hi," I said back, feeling completely light-headed.

He held my gaze for another few seconds, then closed his eyes, our faces coming together until it was finally happening. Finch was kissing me. And I was kissing him back. It sounds so cheesy to call it a dream come true, but that's what it was—something I had imagined so many times alone as I was falling asleep in my bed.

Only this was better. Because he kept kissing me, more and more passionately, until we were lying down beside each other, our faces illuminated only by the light of the frozen screen. I glanced over at it, and he took that as a hint to reach for the remote and turn it off altogether.

He kissed me again, now in complete darkness, then rolled onto his back and pulled me on top of him, running his hands under my shirt from my shoulders down my back. They were big and strong, soft and warm. At first, I was too overwhelmed to react, but then I moved my hips in motion with his, sliding one hand down the back of his sweatpants, touching the top of his ass, as far as I could reach. He had such a good body.

We stayed in the PG-13 zone for several minutes, before things escalated again and he reached up under my bra, unfastening the front closure after a couple tries. He cupped my breasts with his palms and told me how perfect they were.

The compliment made me feel bold, and I sat up and took my shirt all the way off, then rolled back on top of him, straddling him as he worked on the button fly of my jeans. It was taking too long, so I finished the job while he took off his own shirt, then sweats. Only his boxers and my red Victoria's Secret thong were between us. I was glad I'd worn it, just in case.

Now on top of me, he reached down and touched me through the silk, whispering how good I felt, how wet I was. Then he slid his middle finger around the edges of my thong, dipping it inside me, just a little bit.

I arched my back, raising my hips up to his hand, both because it felt good and because it seemed like the sexy thing to do, and I desperately wanted to be sexy for him. I fleetingly thought of Polly, how much hotter she was than me, but I reminded myself that he wasn't this hard for her or moaning her name right now.

"I want you, Lyla," he added. "I want you *so* bad."

"I want you, too," I said.

"Have you ... before?" Finch whispered, kissing my ear, his breath giving me goosebumps everywhere.

I hesitated, then tried to answer by reaching down and taking hold of him with my hand. My strategy seemed to work for a second, as he made a little groaning sound. But a second later, he seemed to remember his question. "So you're *not* a virgin?" he pressed.

"No," I finally said, because I didn't want to lie—and because I thought he might stop if he thought I was a virgin. And I didn't want him to stop.

chapter nineteen

NINA

I left Julie's and drove the three miles to my parents' house around suppertime (I only called it "supper" when I was back in Bristol; otherwise it was "dinner," no matter how casual or early). As I pulled into our cul-de-sac, then parked behind my dad's white Cadillac in the carport, I vowed to keep things light, both because I was too drained for more deep conversation and because I didn't want to prematurely worry them. But the second I walked into the house from the garage, my mom started firing questions at me.

"Is everything okay?" she said before the door was even closed.

"Everything's fine," I said.

"Why the last-minute visit?" she asked, standing in the direct path of the kitchen.

I took a deep breath and said, "Because I wanted to see you. And Julie. I had a lovely afternoon with her." It probably wasn't the most accurate characterization of our day, but it wasn't a lie either.

Clearly Mom wasn't buying it, though, because she literally started wringing her hands—something I'd never seen anyone actually do. "What are Finch and Kirk doing today?" she asked, frowning.

"Kirk's coming back from a business trip. He was in Dallas," I said, hearing that woman saying *honey* again.

"And Finch?" Mom said.

"He had to study . . . exams coming up."

I set my purse down on the small wooden pew that had been in the back hallway adjoining the laundry room, powder room, and kitchen for as long as I could remember. It was where my brother and I used to stow our book bags and rain boots and sporting equipment. I felt a pang of nostalgia, a feeling I associated with my mother—one of her defining traits. She was generally a happy person but had a tendency to live in the past, making frequent references to "when you kids were little."

I played on that theme and said, "Can't a girl visit her parents without an inquisition?"

"A girl *can*," Mom said as I navigated my way around her. "But *this* one usually doesn't."

It was a fair point—my trips back to Bristol had become few and far between in recent years, usually only for my parents' birthdays or a major holiday. And sometimes not even then. Occasionally, I'd squeeze a guilt-induced weekday into the mix, but our weekends were just too crammed with social plans. "Well. Times are a-changing," I said, thinking aloud.

"Oh?" Mom said, raising her eyebrows, her radar *really* going off now. "And why's that?"

"Well, you know. With Finch going off to college," I said, wondering if it would still be Princeton, "I'll have more time."

It was what I always said to my parents. What I always told *myself* as the months and years had flown by. As soon as we get out of this stage or that stage. Out of middle school, once Finch can drive, once he gets into college. And yet somehow, life had only gotten busier, *more* complicated.

"Hey, whatever works for you," Mom said. "We're just glad to see you."

"Yes. We're thrilled to see you, sweetie," Dad said, walking into the kitchen from the front hallway, giving me a big hug. He was wearing one of his fishing shirts, even though he didn't fish, using all the assorted loops and pockets for reading glasses or writing instruments. Tonight, he was showcasing not *one* but *two* mechanical pencils.

"You, too, Dad," I said, as I inhaled his famous Sloppy Joes simmering on the stove. I spotted a fresh pack of Wonder hamburger buns, the primary-color dots on its package conjuring childhood, and next to it, a tinfoil-lined baking sheet covered with thawing frozen French fries. I noticed they were *sweet potato,* my mom's idea of gourmet.

Dad opened a bottle of merlot sitting amid piles of unopened mail and other clutter. The wine was a new thing—they didn't really drink when I was growing up—but the clutter was a fixture. I honestly didn't know how they ever found anything.

"Would you like a glass of wine?" Dad said.

"No, thanks," I said, pacing mindlessly over to the edge of the kitchen, looking into the family room, comforted by the sight of so many familiar knickknacks, along with stacks of magazines and newspapers and paperback books. Though their tastes differed, my parents were both big readers—and the presence of books in every room (to actually *read,* rather than simply display) was one of the things I really missed about my childhood home.

"So what's going on with you?" I asked as cheerfully as I could, prompting Mom to launch into a detailed, long-winded update of all their neighbors and friends. *The Joneses just got back from a European riverboat cruise—six countries in ten days! . . . Mary Ellen had a hip replacement the same week John had a kidney stone—imagine that bad luck. . . . The middle Clay girl got engaged to her longtime boyfriend. . . . The Floyds had to put Sassa-*

fras down. . . . Oh, and guess who I ran into at the grocery store this afternoon and might join us for dinner?

I mentally flagged her final run-on question as I glanced into the dining room and saw that the table was set for four.

"Oh, God, Mom. Who did you invite to dinner?" I said, my mind ticking through all the possibilities of people I did *not* want to see.

"Oh. He's not coming for *sure,*" she said. "But—"

"*Who,* Mom?"

"Teddy," she said with a little shrug.

"As in—my ex-*boyfriend*?" I said, knowing there was *no* other Teddy in our world.

"Yes!" she said. "*That* Teddy."

I stared at her, doing my best not to show my annoyance and offset all the goodwill I'd created by coming home. "And *why,* exactly, did you invite Teddy over?"

"I told you. I ran into him at Food City."

"And?" I said. "That just naturally segued into a dinner invitation?"

"More or less," she said, not seeming the slightest bit sheepish—which was the most ridiculous part. At the very least she could have *pretended* to be apologetic.

"Can you explain that for me?" I said, exchanging a glance with my dad.

"Sure. So I saw him in the frozen vegetable aisle," Mom said. "And I mentioned you were coming home. . . . Then he said he hadn't seen you in years. I said he should stop by and say hello if he was free. . . . He said he was—and that he might just do that."

"That doesn't look like a *might,*" I said, gesturing toward the set table. "That looks like a *definite.*"

"Well, I hope so," Mom said. "For his sake. He's lonely, Nina."

"He told you that?" I asked, feeling very certain that he had *not*. Except for a pathetic type, which Teddy had never been, it wasn't the kind of thing a grown man would offer up to an ex-girlfriend's mother in the aisle of a grocery store.

"Well, not *specifically*. But I could just tell he is," she said, then went into further detail about how she had heard, through the grapevine, that Kara, his ex-wife, had remarried and moved to Charlotte with her new husband. "Apparently he got some big job. Teddy's brokenhearted. He misses the boys so much."

I had actually heard some of this through Julie, who had represented Teddy in a very straightforward divorce agreement, which included an amicable, flexible custody agreement and a clean division of minimal assets (or, as the case might be, debt). Their split had surprised me, if only because I'd heard that Kara was as Christian as Teddy, although I obviously knew religious couples divorced, too. I hadn't pressed Julie for further details, knowing how closely she guarded the confidentiality of her clients. At least that was the excuse I made to myself, so I didn't have to think about other reasons that the subject of Teddy made me uncomfortable.

"How often does he get to see his boys?" I said, feeling grateful that Finch was the age he was. Then again, maybe things would have been different for him if I had made the decision to leave Kirk sooner.

"Not often. It's a really long drive. It's just so sad."

I murmured something noncommittal as my mother continued with further unsourced rumors about Teddy's ex-wife's current husband. She finished with a long sigh and "Anyway. There's nothing quite as sad as a single man's grocery cart."

I exchanged another look with my dad, this one of the smirking variety as Dad asked, "Nothing, Judy? Really? Not war? . . . Cancer? . . . Death?"

"You know what I mean," Mom said. "All those sad TV dinners and that lonely six-pack of Corona . . . I just *had* to invite him."

I cut her some slack as I really did appreciate my mom's compassion for the down-and-out—whether for a chained-up hound on an ASPCA commercial or a bachelor in a grocery store. She was proactive about her compassion, too. A giver, albeit a *meddling* giver. I knew this was just another example of those qualities—and that she wasn't trying to put me in an awkward situation. I told myself it really wasn't that awkward anyway. It wasn't as if we'd *just* broken up or either of us held a candle for the other. At least *I* didn't. And I assumed Teddy didn't, either; otherwise he probably would have *declined* her invitation. "I'm sure he'll be fine," I said. "It never takes a man long to remarry."

"Yeah. Someone will scoop him up soon," Mom continued. "He's so nice-looking."

"Maybe he's already been scooped up," I said, thinking dinner at our house didn't preclude a relationship. After all, I was *married*—and it hadn't stopped my mother.

"No," Mom said, adamant. "He's definitely single. . . . *Hey!* I have an idea! Maybe you could set him up with one of your rich, divorced Nashville friends?"

There were multiple things that disturbed me about this suggestion (though I was surprised it had taken her more than ten minutes to use the word *rich*). "Um, Dad. Can you help me out here?"

"Judy," Dad said, shaking his head and chuckling. "That's a little bizarre, don't you think? To assign Nina as matchmaker for *Teddy*?"

"Why is it bizarre?" Mom said as I wondered if she was pretending to be obtuse—or actually was. It was often a close call.

"Well . . . *because* . . . that's like me setting up Patty," Dad said, referring to his college sweetheart, who got way too much airtime. Not from Dad but from Mom, who clung to her jealous grudge after all these years. No matter that she had actually been the one to steal Dad from Patty. No matter that Dad had no contact with Patty whatsoever (*Mom* had friended her on Facebook). It made no sense—and was therefore a great source of amusement for Dad and me.

"It's not the same thing at *all*," Mom said.

"Oh? Why isn't it?" Dad said.

"Yeah, Mom," I chimed in. "Why isn't it?"

"Because," Mom said, trying to suppress a mischievous grin. "Patty is a hag."

Dad shook his head as I burst into laughter. "Oh my God, Mom. A *hag*? You're *terrible*."

"I speak the truth," Mom said. "She *is* a hag, and you both know it."

"Well, put out another place setting!" I said in the voice of a game-show host, complete with Bob Barker–like gestures. "Because guess what? I *invited* that *hag* to *dinner*!"

"Now why would you go and do that?" Mom said, helping me set up my joke further.

"Because I felt sorry for her haggedyness. Her cart was so sad. Filled with Entenmann's coffee cake and prune juice."

Dad laughed as Mom pretended to be mad—all part of her anti-Patty schtick.

"So . . . what time 'might' Teddy arrive?" I said, glancing at the clock on the microwave.

"Six o'clock," she said proudly. "So any minute!"

"Ugh. I'll be right back," I muttered then retreated to the back hall to get my purse. I ducked into the powder room to brush my hair and touch up my makeup. It wasn't that I specifically wanted to look good for *Teddy;* it was something I'd do for *any* guest, particularly someone I hadn't seen in several years. A simple matter of pride.

The doorbell rang as I was returning to the kitchen.

"You should get it," Mom said.

"Why should *I* get it? You're the one who invited him."

"Nina," my mom said, her voice rising in a warning. "Be nice."

I sighed, then went to the door, trying to remember the last time I'd seen Teddy, deciding it would be our first topic of conversation. An icebreaker, if you will.

"Hi, Teddy," I said, swinging open the screen door and smiling at a middle-aged stranger who, but for those ice-blue eyes, bore little resemblance to the boy I used to date. Don't get me wrong—it's not that he looked *bad*. He was still in decent shape—or at least hadn't gained much weight—perhaps a function of being tall and having an active profession as a police officer. His hairline had receded more than I'd expected, but with a strong jaw and a nice-shaped head, he could pull it off. If anything, I thought he looked a little better *now*, having finally shed his aw-shucks boyishness.

"Hi, Nina," he said, looking and sounding uneasy. "I'm sorry about this. Your mom wouldn't take no for an answer."

I laughed and rolled my eyes, saying, "Believe me, I *know*." Then, worrying that my statement might have come off as rude, I leaned in and gave him a quick hug. "It's really good to see you again," I said.

"You, too," Teddy said, giving me a big smile, which instantly transformed him back to his old teenage self. Too sweet for me, I thought, thinking of all the Boy Scout clichés that had defined his character because they were things he actually *did*. How whenever he found a spider in the house, he'd catch it in a container, setting it free outside. How he had shoveled snow for the old lady on his street without charging her—or even taking credit for it. How he never cussed, using ridiculous substitute words like *dagnabbit* and *jackwagon*. How he prayed before every meal, including breakfast and lunch, but did it quickly and discreetly so as not to make anyone uncomfortable. He was sort of the opposite of Kathie, come to think of it. Pure of heart without any showiness.

"So, it's been a while," I said, as I led him into the kitchen.

"Sure has," he replied, then exchanged robust hellos with Dad, the two of them shaking hands with a simultaneous back clap.

"Good to see you, buddy," Dad said as my mother descended upon Teddy, giving him an embrace that looked more like the kind you'd give a relative who'd just returned from Afghanistan than like the way you'd greet your daughter's ancient-history ex-boyfriend.

"It's been since our ten-year, right?" I said, milking the topic, remembering that I'd missed our twentieth reunion for Melanie's fortieth-birthday trip to St. Barths, a source of slight contention with Julie, who had wanted me to press Mel for a date change. It was one of the rare times I disagreed with Julie, insisting to her that benchmark birthdays of close friends trumped school reunions.

Teddy shook his head. "No. I've seen you since then. . . . Remember? At Cootie Brown's a few years back?"

"That's right," I said, remembering the brief encounter we'd had at one of the most popular barbecue restaurants in town. I think I'd been back to see Julie's girls' ballet recital. Regardless, Teddy had been with his wife and sons, and they'd all seemed happy. I remembered feeling vaguely embarrassed for him. I think it must have had something to do with his still living in Bristol, still going to Cootie Brown's. For some reason, I made an exception for

Julie, as I knew her worldview was constantly evolving and that no part of her mindset ever felt provincial.

"When was that, anyway?" I asked, trying to distract Teddy from my mother's awkward, trancelike beaming. "Four or five years ago, right?"

"Six, actually," he quickly replied, then hesitated and added, "It was right after my brother had his first kid."

"How are they doing?" I asked.

"Good. Great. They had another baby. A girl."

"That's great," I said as Mom, slipping on her oven mitts to check her fries, chimed in with "I saw photos of her on Facebook. Quite the head of red hair! Which side does she get that from, anyway?"

"Dad's side," Teddy said. "His mother—my grandma—had red hair."

Mom closed the oven but kept her mitts on, pointing at Teddy with one. It looked like a foam hand from a sporting event. "You know what? I bet the two of you would have had redheads," she said, then glanced at me. "It runs on my side, too, you know. . . ."

"*Wow*, Mom," I said under my breath as Teddy's ears and cheeks turned a bright pink. I'd forgotten how easily he blushed.

"Well, he *was* almost my *son*-in-law," she announced, making it even worse.

Dad chuckled and said, "Sorry, Teddy. I'm sure you recall that my wife lacks a filter."

"Yes, sir. I actually *do* remember that about my *almost* mother-in-law," Teddy replied with a wink.

None of us had expected this joke—at least *I* hadn't—and I laughed out loud, feeling myself relax. Teddy seemed to loosen up, too, going on to ask about my brother.

"What's Max up to these days?" he said.

"He's still living in New York," Mom said. "Still single."

Teddy nodded and smiled.

"Can I get you a drink, Teddy?" I said, opening the fridge to find a six-pack of Corona, clearly purchased *after* my mom took note of his cart contents. Quite the thoughtful touch.

"Sure," he said. "If you're having one."

I hadn't planned on it but took two bottles out, putting them on the counter as I washed my hands and then took a lime from our always-stocked fruit bowl. (Mom tried to make up for her lackluster cooking with a bounty of fresh produce.)

As I listened to her grill Teddy about all the latest crimes in town, I sliced the lime into wedges, picked the two best, and tucked them into the tops of the bottles.

"Cheers," I said, holding up my beer as I handed him the other.

Teddy smiled back at me, tapping the neck of his bottle against mine, and said, "To reunions."

"And Sunday supper," I added, as we both plunged the limes into our beers and took long sips.

Mom sighed a loud, wistful sigh and said to Dad, as if we couldn't hear, "Those *two* . . . they were always so cute together."

SUPPER TURNED OUT to be stress-free, even pleasant, the topics flowing easily from Bristol happenings to larger current events, including politics, one of Dad's favorite subjects. Everyone stayed calm and unusually neutral, as I realized that I had no clue about Teddy's political leanings. On paper, I would have guessed he was a Republican, but I couldn't recall a single conversation I'd ever had with him about politics.

Then, right at the end of the meal we all simultaneously ran out of topics, creating an awkward silence and a frightening vacuum for my mother to fill.

"So," she began, rising to the occasion. "How is Kirk? You haven't mentioned him at *all*."

On the surface, it was a fine question, but I could tell by her expression that it was loaded and at least partially merlot-induced.

"He's fine," I said, then imprudently added, "I guess."

She seized on my hesitation. "You *guess*?" she said.

"He's been in Dallas," I said.

"Doing what?"

"Just . . . business-type stuff," I said, sounding either cagey or dim-witted.

"Hmmm. He sure does travel a lot lately," Mom said, as I caught Dad shooting her a look. I think Teddy must have noticed it, too, because he conspicuously glanced away.

"Right. Well. Maybe you're onto something there, Mom," I said, throwing her a curveball.

She looked a little stunned—or maybe just confused. "What does that mean?"

I hesitated, thinking of all the ways I could change the subject, then made a spur-of-the-moment decision that I was finished with small talk and surface conversation and diversions and lies of any kind, no matter how small. At least for right now, as I sat at my parents' dining room table, with a kind man who had once loved me, and who still prayed to God before supper.

"It *means*," I finally said, gathering strength I didn't know I had, "I am filing for divorce."

chapter twenty

LYLA

So it *actually* happened. I had *sex* with *Finch*. He would forever be the second person on my list. The *act* itself lasted only a couple of minutes, but that was okay. I think I actually preferred it on the quicker side—at least for our first time. For one, there was absolutely no mistaking how turned on he was. For another, it got us to my favorite part faster—which was just lying there together in the dark, feeling his chest rise and fall against mine.

"*Wow,* that was good," he finally said, running his fingers through my hair.

"Yeah," I murmured, more thrilled with every passing second.

"I'm sorry it was so . . . quick," he said—which I thought was really sweet of him.

"No. It was *great,*" I said. "It was perfect."

"Your *body* is perfect," he said, kissing the top of my head.

The compliment melted me, but before I could thank him, we heard the basement door open and a woman's voice.

"Finch?" she said, as light spilled down the steps, illuminating our bodies, reminding me of just how naked we were.

We both jumped, then froze. Finch put one finger to his lips, instructing me not to make a sound. I responded with a telepathic blink, praying that the door would close. After an agonizing few seconds, it did, darkness hiding us once again.

"Hurry. Get dressed," Finch whispered, as we both bolted upright, frantically searching for our clothes. One of his elbows jabbed me in the side, and I could feel fluid running out of me, down my leg, but those were the least of my concerns.

"I can't see!" I said when I realized I was about to put on his shirt instead of mine.

"Hold on," Finch said, producing his phone from somewhere, then panning the lit screen around the sofa area as we gathered our things and dressed in about twenty seconds.

"I thought you said she went to Bristol," I said, feeling grateful that Finch hadn't lasted any longer than he had.

"Um, yeeeah, Lyla. That wasn't my *mom*," Finch said.

"It *wasn't*?"

"No."

"Who was it?" I asked, although I suddenly knew, placing her voice.

"Polly," he confirmed, now scrolling through his text messages.

"Is she still here?" I asked.

"How should I know?" he said, sounding a little harsh.

I couldn't tell if he was annoyed at me for asking a stupid question or simply pissed at Polly and the situation, but I said I was sorry, just in case.

"It's not *your* fault. It's *her* fault. She's a *psycho* coming over here like this. And why are *we* hiding? This is *my* house." Then he stood up and said, "Come on. Let's go."

"Okay," I said, only because it seemed to be the answer he wanted. Then I stood up and trailed behind him as he charged up the stairs. But as he turned the corner, I stopped, just in time to hear her shriek.

"Oh my God, Finch!" she said. "You scared the *shit* out of me! What are you doing?"

"What am *I* doing?" Finch yelled back at her. "*You're* the one who broke into my house!"

"I didn't *break* in. The door was unlocked. . . ."

"That doesn't mean you can just barge in."

"I saw your car."

"So?"

"I thought maybe something was wrong. You wouldn't return my calls or texts," she said, her voice sounding whiny and desperate. "I thought maybe you'd gotten carbon monoxide poisoning or something."

I rolled my eyes, thinking, *Yeah right.*

"Don't be ridiculous," he said.

"Why wouldn't you answer your phone? Or text me back?"

"Because," he said. "I'm busy."

"Doing *what*?" she demanded.

"Watching a movie."

"A *movie*?" she said, as I could hear in her voice the accusation that was about to come. "Are you alone? Is there someone downstairs with you? Is Lyla here?"

It was horrifying to hear my name, yet also somehow validating, especially as I processed the jealousy in her voice. Polly was jealous of *me.*

And then it got more surreal. Because then Finch said, "Yep. She sure is. Hey, Lyla?" He belted out my name. "Come on up! Polly wants to say hello."

It was my cue to frantically retreat, but Polly was too quick for me, whipping around the corner and staring right into my eyes.

Later, I would process that my first and most immediate thought was that she'd done a shitty contouring job, her makeup way too dark for her complexion, likely in an attempt to cover up her freckles, which I'd heard she hated. But my second and more dominant thought was, Oh shit, she's going to cry.

Sure enough, she burst into hysterical tears, returning to the kitchen, where she and Finch began to scream at each other.

"First the concert and now this?" she shouted. "How could you do this to me?"

"We're broken up, Polly," he said, words that filled me with relief. Not that I'd doubted his story, but it was still good to hear confirmation. They *were* broken up; I hadn't just slept with another girl's boyfriend.

"I want you back."

"No."

"Please, Finch. Just talk to me."

"No. You need to leave, Polly. Now."

"But I love you," she sobbed. "And I know you love me, too."

"No," he said, his voice ice cold. "I don't, Polly. Now get *out*."

At that point, I started to feel a little bit sorry for her—which sucked because I wanted to just hate her. I told myself not to be fooled. To remember what she had done to me. Then, as if refreshing my memory, I heard her voice turn from pitiful to cruel as she screamed, *You can't possibly actually like that pathetic slut?* And if that weren't bad enough, she added some really colorful stuff about how I'd probably give him an STD and try to get pregnant on purpose so I could get some of his money.

I forced myself to stop listening at that point, focusing only on my breathing, fighting back tears, convincing myself how absolutely ludicrous her charges were. I'd *never* had an STD, and the *last* thing in the world I wanted was to get pregnant. I didn't like

Finch for his money—I didn't want his money at *all*. She had me all wrong. She knew *nothing* about me. And I had no reason to feel bad about myself.

So why then, I wondered, long after Finch had gotten rid of her and then driven me home, profusely apologizing all the way, did I feel so ashamed? Like maybe she was right, and I actually *was* a little bit of a slut?

chapter twenty-one

NINA

A fter a cursory kitchen cleanup (Mom always insists we leave the dishes for later), I excuse myself to check my phone. There is a text from Kirk that came in while we were eating, saying simply: I'm home. Finch says you're in Bristol? I don't answer it. I then check my voicemail, finding a lone message from Melanie. Her tone is frantic and dramatic, as she gives me a convoluted report about hearing from Kathie, who heard from her daughter, who heard from someone else, that there had been some sort of "Lyla-Polly showdown" at our house this afternoon. *"Lovely,"* I say aloud, contemplating what to do.

Instead of calling Melanie back, or trying to reach Finch to get to the bottom of things, I realize my only concern is for Lyla. So at the risk of being a tattletale, I text Tom: I'm not sure if you're aware, but I have good reason to believe our kids have been spending time together. . . . I believe they went to a concert last night, and I understand from Melanie (and the usual rumor mill) that Lyla was at our house today. I'm in Bristol at my parents' and don't believe Kirk was home, either. Although we do not have a rule against girls being over when we're not home (we should!), I did not give Finch permission to invite Lyla over, and something tells me you did not grant yours, either. I also heard that there was a situation with Finch's ex-girlfriend, Polly, coming over and confronting Lyla. Details unclear and very possibly blown out of proportion, but given everything, I felt it was the right thing to share this information with you. I'll be home tomorrow, but feel free to call me tonight. I'm sorry. Again.

I wait a moment, hoping for a response, relieved when I get it: She did not have my permission. Thank you for letting me know. I'll talk to her and be in touch.

Feeling sick, but deciding there is nothing more I can do for now (and that there is certainly no point in trying to enlist Kirk's assistance), I put my phone back in my purse. Then I join Teddy and my parents, who have retired to our back porch. Mom is serving her signature Pepperidge Farm mint Milano cookies with glasses of crème de menthe. I can see Teddy has declined the sweet nightcap and is sticking with his Corona.

As I take the only free seat, on the sofa next to Teddy, I have the distinct feeling they have been discussing me.

"What did I miss?" I say.

"Oh, nothing, really," Dad says. "Is everything okay at home?"

We all hear that it's a rather ridiculous question—so I smile and say, "No worse than usual!"

"Are you sure you don't want to talk about it?" Mom says.

After dropping my bomb and accepting their condolences, I'd insisted that I would be fine and that it was all for the best. I'd even tossed in the glib but often true statement *It is what it is.*

"Yes, I'm sure. Not tonight," I say, desperate for an emotional escape. "Why don't you just tell us some stories?"

You never have to ask my mother twice.

She launches into a long, rambling story about my brother and me trying to get "lost" in the woods on a family vacation so we could be like Bobby and Cindy Brady. She then finishes by saying, "That was back when Nina was willing to go camping. These days her idea of roughing it is a Comfort Inn or Hilton Garden." She laughs, then looks at me and adds, "Though come to think of it, I bet you wouldn't do those, either!"

"Stop it," I say, feeling defensive. "I've stayed at my share of Comfort Inns and Hilton Gardens."

"In the last few years?" she says.

"Abso*lutely*," I say, pleased that it's actually the truth, although I don't offer that it only happens when Finch plays basketball in remote rural locations and I literally have no other choice. Nor do I confess that I've been known to pack my own pillow and linens.

"Well, you definitely haven't gone *camping* in the last twenty years," Mom says, as it occurs to me that she may be nostalgic not only for the "good ol' days" but also for the old *me*. "Other than *glamping*!" she adds, shaking her head with something approaching glee.

"*Glamping?* As in 'glamorous camping'?" Teddy asks, clearly as amused as Mom.

"Bingo!" Mom says as the two laugh. Even Dad smiles.

"That's a real thing?" Teddy asks me.

Mom answers for me, "Yes! In Montana. Right, Nina?"

"Right," I mumble, grateful that she doesn't also remember our glamping excursions in Big Sur and Tanzania.

"And, Teddy, you should see these 'tents,'" Mom says, making big air quotes. "Plumbing, heat . . . even heated floors! Fanciest tents you've ever seen!"

I can't tell if she's calling me out or bragging—but she has the same look on her face she gets whenever she asks me how much I paid for something. *I know this is none of my business,* she always starts. *But how much did* this *set you back?*

"Subject change, please, *Mom*," I say, abrasiveness creeping into my voice.

Mom's smile quickly fades as she gives me a sincere under-her-breath apology, knowing she went a little too far.

"No, *I'm* sorry," I say, regretting being so sensitive and dampening the jovial moment. I really need to lighten up. After all, it's not a big *secret* that my life has changed—and that that change has a lot to do with money. "It's just a little embarrassing. . . ."

"You shouldn't be embarrassed," Mom says. "I think it's *wonderful* that you've had so many neat experiences."

"Me, too," Teddy says, nodding.

"Me three," Dad chimes in.

"Yeah. I've been lucky. In *some* ways," I say. It's a reference to Kirk, and I can tell that at least Mom picks up on it.

"Yes. Nobody has the 'perfect life,' " she says.

"True," Teddy agrees. "There are pros and cons to everything. Every life."

I nod.

"I mean, I hate that my boys aren't with me full-time since the divorce," Teddy says. "It stinks that they live in Charlotte. *But* . . ." He pauses, as I wonder where he's going. What the *pros* to this situation could possibly be. "They're in this fancy private school getting a really good education. An opportunity they wouldn't have had here. Not to knock Vance and Tennessee," he says, referring to the local middle and high schools that we attended and where Julie's kids go now. "But Charlotte Country Day is way better. I could never have afforded a school like that. But their stepfather can. And he is happily paying for every dime. It's a silver lining, for sure. You can always find one if you look hard enough."

"I really hope so," I say.

Suddenly my mom announces that it's past their bedtime, but that "you kids" should keep catching up. Teddy looks as if he's going to announce his own departure, so I quickly intervene. "One more beer?"

I'm not sure whether I actually want him to stay—or just want to avoid a divorce talk with Mom, but I am happy when he says, "Sure. One more."

As my parents and Teddy stand to hug goodbye, I go to the fridge and grab a Corona. While I'm putting in the lime, my parents walk into the kitchen behind me.

"You okay, sweetie?" Mom says, as she initiates a hug.

"Yes. I promise," I say, hugging her back. "We can talk all about it in the morning."

"Okay. Or come get me if you can't sleep," Mom says, the way she did when I was little. "Are you staying here or with Julie?"

"Here," I say. "I just have to get my bag out of the car."

"I'll get it," Dad says.

"Thank you," I say, feeling a wave of love for my father. For *both* of them.

"Anything else you need?" Mom asks.

I shake my head. "No, thanks. . . . I'm just really glad I'm here."

"We are, too," Dad says.

As I nod, collect Teddy's beer, and head back toward the porch, I can feel Mom watching me. "Have fun," she says a little too eagerly. "You *never* know what could—"

"Don't say it, Mom," I cut her off, glancing over my shoulder.

But she says it anyway, a goofy grin on her face. "Well, it *could* happen. . . . You and Teddy, after all these years."

"I FORGOT HOW awesome your parents are," Teddy says when I get back to the porch, this time sitting across from him.

"Yeah. My mom's a little nuts, though," I say. No matter how much you don't like your son-in-law, and I suspect that it may be a great deal in her case, normal people just don't say something like that on the same evening their daughter tells them she's getting a divorce. Then again, my mom clearly isn't normal. For better or worse.

"She cracks me up," Teddy says, chuckling to himself. "Always has. No filter. And I just love how she calls you out."

"Oh, really?" I say, smiling back at him. "And why do you love *that*?"

"Because. She puts you in your place."

"Yeah. But there's a lot of hyperbole with her, too."

"Really?" Teddy raises his eyebrows, then takes a sip of beer. "So you don't actually *glamp*?" I can tell he's suppressing a smile.

"Oh, stop it," I say, as it occurs to me that he's probably a little more clever than I've given him credit for.

"You know I'm teasing you," he says.

"Yeah. But you think I'm a snob," I say.

"Think?" Teddy grins. *"Shoot.* I *know* you are."

I say his name in a whiny voice, the sound of it putting me right back in high school.

"Let's put it this way," Teddy says, as I hold my breath. "You definitely like the finer things in life." He speaks slowly, as if choosing his words diplomatically, but I still hear a euphemism for materialism.

I must look embarrassed because he adds, "Hey—I get it. I'd drive an Aston Martin if I could."

I smile, comforted by this admission.

"And anyway . . . I know you're a good person, Nina," he says.

I'm not sure whether this statement is true, but I believe in this moment that *Teddy* thinks it is, and hearing it heals my heart a little. More important, it gives me hope for the son I've raised.

"Thank you, Teddy," I say.

He nods as we stare at each other for a few seconds. Then he says, "I'm really sorry about your marriage. . . . Divorce is hard. . . . It's a little bit like death . . . or . . . a house burning down to the ground."

I give him a sad smile, digesting the analogy. "Yeah. I haven't really processed it yet, but I know it will be difficult."

"And just to warn you? It'll probably get a lot harder before it gets easier. . . . At least that's the way it was for me. But it helps to know you're doing the right thing."

"That's just it," I say. "I mean . . . it's complicated. Yet also *not*."

"I know. People always want to boil divorce down to one thing. A one-line explanation. 'He cheated.' 'She's an alcoholic.' 'He gambles.' 'She spends too much.' It's usually not that simple. But you still just know it's right. . . ."

I can't tell whether he's asking me what happened, or just thinking aloud. "Yeah," I say. "Our issues have been gradual—and cumulative. There's probably not a tagline. But if I had to come up with one—I'd say we just don't share the same values anymore. Maybe we never did. . . ."

Teddy nods. "Yeah. Well, you'll figure it out. You're the smartest girl I've ever met."

"Oh, c'mon. We both know Julie's way smarter," I say, still feeling flattered. I also realize how much I've been craving compliments about things other than my looks—all I ever get from Kirk.

"Julie's up there," Teddy says. "But she married a man who puts a uniform on every day and stayed in Bristol. She can't be *that* smart, right?" He smiles and sips his beer.

"What's *that* supposed to mean?" I say, wondering whether he's being self-deprecating or revealing his own insecurities.

"I'm kidding," Teddy says, taking another sip.

"Well, look," I say, just in case. "You're right. Julie married a fireman and stayed in Bristol. I married a rich guy and live in Belle Meade. And *who's* happier?"

Teddy shrugs, as if it's a close contest.

"'*Not I,* said the little red hen,' " I say, one of my mother's expressions.

Teddy frowns, looking deep in thought.

"What are you thinking?" I ask him.

"Honestly?"

"Yeah. Of course. Tell me."

He lowers his eyes. "I was just thinking about you breaking up with me."

"I didn't break up *with* you," I say, knowing that's *exactly* what I did. "We just . . . broke up."

Teddy meets my gaze, then, not bothering to dispute a basic fact, says, "On some level, you didn't think I was good enough for you. You wanted *more*. It's okay. You can admit it."

"That's not true," I answer quickly and emphatically.

"Then what was it?" he says. "Was it Kirk? Had you already met him?"

"No," I say. "I promise. That wasn't it."

"Then why? Not that it matters at this point . . ."

My stomach in knots, I'm at a loss for what to tell him other than the truth. In a million years I would never have imagined sitting on my parents' porch with Teddy, twenty-some years later, telling him how I was raped. But that's exactly what I do. I report the facts, like a journalist, trying to get through the story without breaking down.

"So you see? I didn't think *you* weren't good enough for *me*," I finish, feeling eighteen again—Finch's age. A brokenhearted eighteen. "I felt *I* wasn't good enough for *you*."

"Oh my *God,* Nina," Teddy whispers, his eyes filling with tears. "I had no idea."

"Yeah. That was the point," I say. "I didn't want you to know."

"You should've told me. I would have been there for you."

"I know," I say, wishing I could go back in time. Wishing I could do so *many* things differently.

chapter twenty-two

LYLA

I forgot to close my blinds before bed last night, and the first thing I see when I wake up is Dad outside my window, crouched on our front porch with the garden hose, a big brush, and a bucket. The sleeves of his sweatshirt are pushed up, and his intense scrubbing motion reminds me of watching him saw or sand in his workshop. With a sickening hunch of what's happening, I get out of bed and go over to the window. That's when I see the neon orange letters sprayed onto the front porch. *SLU* is all that remains, but I know what letter is missing, and what the word once was.

I feel as if I'm going to throw up—literally—so I run to my bathroom, flip open the lid of the toilet, and wait. Nothing happens, fear and dread replacing my nausea. I walk back out to the hall, avoiding my reflection in the mirror, then open the front door, feeling the chill of the spring morning.

Dad, who is still on his hands and knees, glances up at me and says, "Go back in the house." His voice is calm, but I know from experience not to be fooled. We are in the eye of a really bad storm.

I tell myself that I need to follow his instructions, but I just stand there. I just stand there, staring. Most of the *U* is now gone, leaving only the *SL*. There are so many things I could be thinking right now, but I find myself feeling extreme gratitude that the paint is washable when it could have been permanent. Somehow I know that Dad isn't seeing that bright side.

"I said *go back in the house*!" Dad raises his voice this time but does not look up at me.

I back away a few steps, retreating inside, then run to my bedroom to get my phone. I have no new messages, nothing that came in since I last checked, sometime in the middle of the night. I quickly dial Finch.

"Good morning," he says, sounding day-after-sex chipper.

"No, it's *not,*" I say, watching Dad from the window again. He is standing now, spraying the area with the hose, the nozzle on the most concentrated setting. Orange-tinted sudsy water runs down the steps and onto the edges of our lawn.

"What's wrong?" Finch asks.

"Somebody spray-painted our porch," I say.

"Huh?" he says.

"Like, with graffiti. Someone vandalized our property. Our porch."

"Oh, *shhit,*" Finch says. "What'd they write?"

It takes me a second to answer. "*Slut,*" I make myself say, feeling a wave of shame. "My dad's out there cleaning it off right now. He's *so* pissed."

"God. That sucks. I feel *terrible.*"

"It's not *your* fault," I mumble, my face burning. "I bet it was Polly."

"I'm *sure* it was. . . . Do y'all have cameras?"

"No," I say, thinking of the Brownings' security alarm—and all the nice things inside their house that need to be protected.

"Maybe your neighbors do?"

"Pretty sure they don't," I say, feeling a twinge of annoyance. I get that he's just trying to be helpful—but he has to know that nobody has security cameras in my neighborhood.

"I'll call Polly," he says. "I'll get the truth out of her."

"No," I say, knowing it won't do any good—she'll just deny it, and it might even make things worse for me. "Please don't do that."

"Okay," he says, but he still sounds really pissed.

"Finch?" I say nervously. "Can I ask you something?"

"Sure," he says.

"Did you . . . *tell* anyone?" I ask, my voice shaking a little. "What we *did*?"

"Hell, *no*," Finch says.

I believe him but want more reassurance. "Not even Beau?"

"No. *Nobody*," he says. "I don't kiss and tell, Lyla."

"Okay," I say, wishing, for one second, that it were only a question of *kissing*. Polly would still think what she was going to think, but I'd sure feel better about looking my dad in the eye. I also can't help but think of how much easier it is to be a boy than to be a girl. Nobody is gonna write the word *slut* on Finch's porch, that's for damn sure.

"Did you take a picture?" Finch asks. "Of your porch?"

"Um, no. Why would I do that?"

"For evidence. You need to show Mr. Q."

"No, Finch. There's no way I'm telling Mr. Q. I don't want this spread all over school. It's bad enough that everyone's gonna know I went over to your house yesterday."

"So?" Finch says. "You have every right to come over to my house and hang out. We're *friends*."

My heart sinks as I blurt out, "Is that all we are?" I hate that I'm asking the question, but I can't help myself.

"You know what I mean. . . . I mean . . . it's more than that, obviously. I'm totally *into* you," Finch says, his voice turning soft. "And I love what we did yesterday."

I smile, feeling warmth spread across my body, my regret immediately dissolving.

"I want to do it again," he whispers.

Dizzy, I whisper back, "Me, too."

DAD DOESN'T SPEAK to me on the way to school, and I can't tell if he's more mad or upset. I decide that it's too risky to initiate conversation of any kind—so I keep my mouth shut for the entire torturous ride. When we arrive, he parks in a visitor spot rather than pulling into the circular driveway for drop-off, and I panic.

"What are you *doing*?" I ask him, though it's perfectly clear.

"I'm going in. To talk to Quarterman."

My mind races for a reasonable objection, as I lamely point out that he has paint all over his clothes and hands.

"So?" Dad says.

I think of the movie *Jackie*. How Mrs. Kennedy kept her blood-splattered pink suit on because she wanted everyone to see what had been done to her husband. Not that *I'm* comparing the assassination of a president to our vandalized porch, but I can tell Dad, on some level, is *glad* that he's covered in paint. After all, he could have easily changed his clothes before we got in the car.

"Dad. Please let me handle this," I begin to plead, but he shakes his head, as if to tell me there's nothing I can say that will change his mind. Then he adds, "Is there anything you want to tell me before I go inside?"

I shake my head.

"So you don't know who did this?"

I shake my head again. "I don't, Dad."

"Do you have a clue? An . . . *inkling*?"

"Not really."

"Not *really*?" he says.

"I mean . . . it could be anyone. It could be totally *random*."

My last statement is ludicrous, but Dad nods, maybe wanting to believe that this could be true. That it *was* random vandalism—that nobody actually thinks his daughter is a slut.

"Okay. So hopefully this has *nothing* to do with the concert on Saturday night? Or you going over to Finch's yesterday?" Dad says sarcastically.

I look at him, shocked and ashamed, as he shakes his head sadly, then gets out of the car.

chapter twenty-three

TOM

I'm far from composed, but somehow I manage to keep my shit together for the first few minutes in Quarterman's office. Even as I show him the photo of the word *SLUT* sprayed across our porch, I keep my voice low, just as I did in the car with Lyla. Somehow, it helps that Quarterman is visibly outraged.

"I am *so* sorry, Tom. This is terrible. Just terrible," he says, shaking his head. "Do you have any idea who did this?"

"No," I say.

"Does Lyla know anything?"

"She says she doesn't."

"Do you believe her?"

I let out a big sigh and shake my head. "No. Actually, I don't. But I can't figure out whether she's covering for someone—or whether she's just scared."

"Of repercussions?" Quarterman asks.

"Yeah . . . This whole situation . . . with Finch . . . It's gotten so out of hand. . . ."

Quarterman furrows his brow, peering over at me. "How so? What's going on now?"

I exhale, then say, "I don't even know where to begin. . . ."

275

"Just share whatever you'd like to share," he says. "I promise you, Tom. I'm on your side here. I just want to help you and Lyla."

For some odd reason, and despite the knowledge that he has to also be concerned about his other students, as well as the reputation of his school, I *do* trust him. Or maybe it's just sheer desperation. But I start talking. I tell him about my meeting with Kirk, Nina and Finch's visit Saturday morning—and Finch's apology while I was out of the room. I tell him about the concert—and that Lyla went over to the Brownings' yesterday, without permission or supervision. I read aloud Nina's text message about Polly.

"Have you spoken with Nina?" he asks when I finish. "Since those texts?"

"No," I say, shaking my head. "Not yet . . . But crazily enough, I feel like she's an ally here. To Lyla."

"Yes," Quarterman says, nodding. "I think she's really trying to do the right thing."

Before I can respond, we hear a knock on the door.

"Yes?" Quarterman calls out.

We both stare at the door, waiting, as it opens a crack.

"Yes?" Quarterman says again, now sounding annoyed. "May I help you?"

The door opens farther, and there stands Finch.

"Excuse me, son," Quarterman says in a stern voice. "We're in a meeting here."

"I'm sorry," Finch says, but he doesn't budge, other than to open the door a little more and throw out some bait. "But I just had some information about . . . what happened last night."

Quarterman stands and waves Finch over to his desk. "In that case, come in. Have a seat."

I tell myself to remain calm, as Finch sits in the chair beside me.

"Who did it?" I say, my voice rising. "Who spray-painted our porch?"

Finch takes a deep breath, finally showing his nerves—or at the very least, some pretty solid acting skills. "Polly did it," he says, speaking rapidly. "Or one of her friends. If she didn't do it herself, she knows who did. She was involved for sure."

"Son, this is a pretty big accusation to make," Quarterman says. "Do you have *any* sort of proof?"

"Not concrete *proof*," Finch says. "But yesterday . . . Polly called Lyla . . . that word."

"You mean a *slut*?" I force myself to say, my heart pounding in my ears.

Finch holds my gaze, then slowly nods. "Yes, sir. That's the word she used."

Something inside me snaps, and I lean toward him, seething. "Do you think *you're* at all responsible here?"

Finch shakes his head and says, "No, sir. I didn't do anything to your porch."

"Well, don't you think *your* photo of my daughter contributed to *this*?"

Finch returns my angry glare with a blank stare. Any goodwill built up from his visit Saturday morning goes out the window, and I have to fight a strong urge to lunge at him.

"I don't understand what you mean—" he begins.

"What Mr. Volpe is saying," Quarterman translates for me, "is that *your* photo—the one *you* took of Lyla—has perhaps put all of this in motion."

Finch blinks, then boldly shakes his head and says, "No, sir. With all due respect, I do not agree with that statement."

This time, I *do* leap out of my seat, taking some satisfaction at the look of fear on his face.

"Mr. Volpe! Wait! Please listen!" he shouts, holding his palms up. "I didn't take that photo of Lyla! And I didn't write the caption. And I didn't send it to *anyone*!"

"What?" Quarterman and I shout in unison.

"I *swear*!" Finch continues. "Ask Lyla. She knows it's the truth!"

"Well, you either lied then, or you're lying now. Which is it?" Quarterman asks.

"I was lying *then,* sir. And I'm very sorry for that. But I'm telling you the truth *now*. I didn't take the photo of Lyla."

"*Well?*" I yell at him. "Who took it, then?"

"Polly took it," he says, glancing at Quarterman, then back at me. "I was covering for her. . . . But after what she said to Lyla? And what she wrote on your porch? She doesn't deserve my help."

He shakes his head, then stares me down so boldly that I am positive only one of two scenarios can be true. Finch is either completely innocent or a total sociopath. He's either more like his mother or exactly like his father. I have no clue which one it is, but I *will* find out.

chapter twenty-four

NINA

I wake up a little after 4:00 A.M. in my childhood bedroom, knowing that I won't be able to fall back asleep. I'm just too anxious, my mind spinning with thoughts of the past, the future, and the miserable moment of limbo that I'm in. Part of me regrets my candor last night. First in telling everyone about my plans to file for divorce—because no matter what he's done, Kirk deserves the respect of hearing my decision before others. But also in telling Teddy about what happened to me in college. I know what they say about the truth setting you free, but really, what was the point in worrying and upsetting everyone?

Worse than regret about my past decisions, I dread what's to come. I dread seeing Kirk, and I dread confronting Finch about the concert and the incident at our home. But I know I must, and that there is no point in stalling any further. So I get up, quickly make the bed, brush my teeth, and get dressed. I throw my pajamas and toiletries back into my overnight bag and tiptoe downstairs, expecting to leave a goodbye note and slip out the door. But my mother is sitting in her bathrobe at the counter, playing solitaire on her laptop.

"You're leaving?" she says, glancing up at me before clicking on her next move. "So early?"

"Yeah. I have a lot of stuff I need to do today."

She nods, then asks if she can make me a cup of coffee for the road.

"That would be great, Mom," I say. "Thank you."

She stands, walks over to the stove, and turns on the kettle. I smile to myself, realizing that she means *instant* coffee. Sure enough, she pulls out a jar of Folgers, along with powdered creamer and packets of Splenda and Equal.

"Black's fine," I say, thinking I might dump it out once I'm on the road and wait until I pass a Starbucks, or at least a Chick-fil-A. Then again, maybe my mom's instant coffee is *exactly* what I need right now.

We both lean against the counter, waiting for the water to boil, looking straight at each other. "I'm so sorry about you and Kirk," she finally says.

"I know, Mom," I say. "I'm sorry, too."

"I know this is none of my business, and you don't have to tell me if you don't want to," she begins—which is sort of an unprecedented disclaimer for my mom. "But . . . do you think there's someone else?"

I shrug and say, "Honestly, Mom? I'm not really sure. Probably so . . . But that's not really why I'm leaving. . . . I could get over an affair, I think, if that were the only issue."

"You *could*?" she says.

"Yeah. I think so. Good people make mistakes," I say, hoping this statement applies to Finch. "But . . . I'm afraid that Kirk *isn't* a good person anymore."

Mom nods, not even making a cursory attempt to come to the defense of her son-in-law.

"Did you *ever* like him?" I ask, thinking of Julie's putt-putt memories.

"Of course I did," she says a little too automatically.

"Really?" I say. "You can tell me the truth . . . please."

Mom sighs, then says, "Well, in the beginning? I was unsure. I liked him, but I thought he was a little snobby, and that you two didn't really . . . fit together. . . . But I could tell you felt he was what you needed. . . ."

"I did," I say, nodding, amazed that my mother saw this so clearly—even before I did. Yet I also feel wistful for how things could have turned out. How we could have evolved together in a different direction.

"And I did love how he took care of you. He was a gentleman. But somewhere along the line that changed," she says. "*He* changed. He seems a bit . . . *selfish* now."

"I know," I say, thinking that was an understatement. "When do you think that happened? When he sold his company?"

"I think so, yes," she says. "He just got a little big for his britches. And I also think he started to take you for granted. . . . There's a certain . . . lack of respect that disturbs your father and me."

I nod, knowing she's right, cringing at the example Kirk has been setting for Finch—and the fact that I've allowed it to go on for so long. I say as much to my mom, and then add a hopeful, "Better late than never?"

"Definitely," Mom says, scooping a generous tablespoon of coffee crystals into a University of Tennessee travel mug that I can trace back to the eighties. "I think Teddy would agree with that statement, too." She looks up at me hopefully.

"*Mom,*" I say, shaking my head.

"What?" she says with wide-eyed innocence. "I'm just *saying.*"

ABOUT TEN MILES outside of Nashville, I get a call from Walter Quarterman. "There's been a development," he says. "Can you please come in?"

"What sort of development?" I say, my heart sinking, wondering if it has anything to do with Melanie's voicemail.

"I'd rather not discuss it over the phone," Walter says.

"Okay," I say, then ask if he's talked to Kirk.

"No. I called you first," he says.

"Thank you," I say, then tell him that I'll be there just as soon as I can.

TWENTY MINUTES AND several traffic violations later, I park in front of Windsor and run into the school.

"I have a meeting with Mr. Quarterman," I tell Sharon at the front desk. "He's expecting me."

She nods and tries to hand me that damn sign-in clipboard, but I blow her off, muttering that I'm already late and dashing down the hallway.

When I arrive at Walter's office, I knock, then walk in to a small crowd of people. Walter is behind his desk, and in front of him, in a semicircle of chairs, sit Finch, Tom, Polly, and Polly's parents.

My stomach drops as Walter stands to greet me, then points to the only remaining free chair, which happens to be right next to my son. As I sit, I acknowledge Tom, Polly, and her parents with a nod, glancing at Finch last. Everyone looks relatively composed except Polly.

"Will Kirk be joining us?" Walter asks.

"No, he won't be," I say. "Can you tell me what's going on?"

Walter nods. "Yes. As I told you on the phone, Nina, there's been a development . . . and unfortunately, we have two very different versions of the story."

Polly lets out a sob, covering her face with her hands, as her father puts his arm around her and softly shushes her.

"Can someone please . . . cut to the chase?" I say.

"Sure thing," Tom snaps, his voice cold and livid. "Someone wrote *slut* on our porch."

"Oh my God," I say. "I'm so sorry."

Tom ignores this and simply says, "Finch says *Polly* did it."

Out of the corner of my eye, I can see Finch nodding, while Polly wails in protest. "It wasn't me! I swear!"

Her father tries to soothe her again, as Tom continues, "Whether or not the artwork is, in fact, Polly's, she did call Lyla a slut yesterday. At *your* house. Polly admits this much is true. Which is really lovely."

"She's very sorry for using that word," Polly's dad says. "But she had *nothing* to do with your porch being vandalized. She was home all night with us."

Walter attempts to cut in, but Tom talks right over him. "Now Finch is *also* saying that he didn't actually take the infamous photo of Lyla. That actually, *Polly* took it, and he's been covering for her all this time."

"That's not true!" Polly yells, her face covered with tears and snot. "It's a total lie!"

"You're the one lying," Finch says, perfectly calmly.

Walter sighs and says, "Well, hopefully tomorrow's proceedings will bring some clarity."

"Clarity?" Tom shouts. "The only clarity I see is that my daughter is getting victimized left and right and somebody here is lying. Maybe *both* of them are. Maybe this whole thing is an elaborate plot to make sure *no* one gets blamed."

"I can assure you, Mr. Volpe. That's not what is happening here," Polly's dad says. "My daughter has admitted to calling your daughter a terrible name, but—"

"But *what*?" Tom fires back. "But 'no big deal'?"

"Tom, please. I know it's hard, but *please* try to calm down," Walter says.

"Don't you *dare* tell me to calm down! This is a circus. A *total* circus!" Tom stands suddenly, nearly knocking over his chair, before storming to the door. "Someone get my daughter outta class! *Now!*"

Walter looks completely rattled as he grabs his phone, dials an extension, and says, "Can you please have Lyla Volpe report to the front entrance? . . . Yes. Right away, please."

Meanwhile, Tom is out the door, slamming it behind him.

I jump, my heart racing, as I make eye contact with Finch. He stares back at me, with his hand over his heart. "I swear, Mom," he whispers. "I didn't do it."

chapter twenty-five

TOM

I don't know if I've waited three seconds or three minutes, but when Lyla doesn't immediately materialize in the lobby, I start pounding on the ledge of the check-in desk, yelling at that smug receptionist, and demanding that I get my daughter *now*. I even make a move down the hall in the general direction of the high school classrooms.

"Mr. Volpe, you can't go down there!" The receptionist stands up in a panic, as if I were an armed intruder.

Sure enough, her voice trembles as she adds that she is going to have to push a button for the police if I take another step.

I stop, turn, and walk back over to her. "Please don't pretend you don't know what's going on around here. Because I'm pretty sure you know *everything* that's going on around here!"

I pound my hand on her ledge one more time for good measure, just as Lyla rounds the corner and rushes toward me, looking mortified.

"Dad? *What* are you *doing*?" she says as I catch the receptionist staring nosily at us over her reading glasses.

"C'mon. We're leaving. *Right now*."

"I can't *leave*, Dad!" she says, glancing around, looking desperate. "I'm in the middle of a science quiz! And I don't even have my stuff."

"Now!" I yell.

She starts to protest again, but I turn around and walk out the front door. I am nervous about what I'll do if she doesn't follow me. I feel pretty sure that it would involve that woman's panic button. Fortunately, we don't have to find out, because a few seconds later I hear Lyla's footsteps on the pavement behind me.

I only walk faster, my strides getting longer. By the time Lyla climbs in the car beside me, she is completely unhinged, crying so hard that she is starting to hyperventilate. Part of me wants to put my arms around her and calm her down. But my anger, along with my desire to get the fuck out of Belle Meade, outweighs any sense of compassion.

So I start driving, passing countless motherfuckers in Range Rovers and BMWs and Mercedes. What in the *world* was I thinking sending my daughter to this neighborhood every day with these soulless, money-worshipping, lying sons of bitches? Why didn't I learn my lesson when I was a bag boy at the Belle Meade Country Club? When I slept with Delaney and realized that she was using me as her pawn—a sick way to make a point to her daddy and her bullshit high society? Well, Lyla has become a pawn, too, and I'm not going to allow it any longer. Effective today, my child will not be attending that godforsaken school. No education is worth all of this. I mean, what's the endgame? An elitist education gets you what, exactly? An elitist group of friends and a jackass husband like Kirk Browning? Fuck *that*. I'd rather Lyla grow up and live paycheck to paycheck like I do than turn out anything like these people. I'd rather she be lonely and *alone* than lonely with *them*.

Us versus them.

It is the drumbeat in my head as I drive. The entrance to 440 looks jammed, so I keep going through town, hitting stoplight after stoplight, Lyla's tears never letting up. Every few minutes, I think of Quarterman and Nina, and know that I am brushing with too broad a stroke. Then again, they are right in the mix, playing the goddamn game. I mean, how could Quarterman run a school like Windsor if he weren't drinking the Kool-Aid on all the bullshit? And I really like Nina—I can't help myself—but her son is shady. Maybe he didn't take the picture or write on our porch, but he definitely lied at some point—and at Lyla's expense.

"Dad, slow *down*!" Lyla screams as I nearly slam into the back of a black Lexus. I hit my brakes just in time, my heart pounding, my hands sweaty on the steering wheel.

"Sorry," I say under my breath, telling myself to get a grip. To get help. Then I think of Bonnie and make a left where I should make a right.

"Where are you going?" Lyla stops crying just long enough to ask me.

"To see a friend," I say.

"What *friend*?" she asks.

The question is telling. She thinks I have none.

Without answering, I keep driving, weaving my way through historic Belmont, until I get to Bonnie's quaint, old foursquare. Her ancient Volvo station wagon, covered with bumper stickers, is sitting in her driveway at a virtual diagonal. If it were any other day, her parking effort would have made me smile.

"Dad, whose house is this?" Lyla says. She is still upset, but her curiosity has dampened her hysteria.

"I told you. My friend's house," I say, parking behind the Volvo. "Her name is Bonnie. I sometimes talk to her about things. About you . . . Come on and meet her."

We both step out of the car and close our doors as Lyla trails behind me to the front door.

"Are you ... *dating* her?" she asks, wiping her nose on her sleeve.

At that second, Bonnie appears through the glass door panes, wearing enormous glasses and a weird shawl that looks more like a blanket. Her gray hair is wilder than usual. I catch a fleeting look of disappointment in Lyla's eyes.

"Well, hello there, Tommy boy," Bonnie says, as she opens the door.

"Morning, Bonnie," I say. "Sorry for the surprise visit."

"Well, it's a *nice* surprise, Tommy. A *very* nice surprise," she says, looking past me. "And you must be Lyla?" Her expression becomes even warmer.

"Yes, ma'am," Lyla says, forcing the mandatory tight-lipped smile that comes with an introduction to an adult.

"How positively wonderful to meet you. I'm Bonnie," she says, one hand appearing from the depths of the shawl. She shakes Lyla's hand, then pulls her into a half hug. "Come in, sweetie."

As Lyla takes a step into the house, and I follow, we are bombarded by the smell of baking, though I can't identify the exact scent. Maybe cinnamon? By now, I can see that Lyla is intrigued, not only with the concept of me having a friend but with Bonnie *herself*. For once, it feels like I made a decision that my daughter and I can agree is the right one.

Bonnie leads us onto her back sunporch, which is drenched in morning light and decorated with jewel-toned upholsteries. I take an emerald chair, and Lyla chooses the sapphire-blue one across from me.

"May I make you a cup of mint tea?" Bonnie asks in her musical voice, which almost sounds Irish. "It's delicious."

We both nod and watch her walk back toward the kitchen. Neither of us speaks for several minutes. We just sit there and wait until Bonnie returns with a small wooden tray. On it are three steaming teacups on mismatched saucers, along with pink Happy Birthday napkins. The tray also holds a miniature pitcher of milk and a bowl filled with sugar cubes that remind me of Lyla's tea set when she was little. Lyla and I each take a cup before Bonnie places the tray on a wicker chest doubling as a coffee table. She then sits on the red chair beside Lyla's, sharing her view of the backyard. She points out the window, up into the trees. My back is to the window, but I know what they're looking at.

"Do you see that marvelous tree house?" Bonnie asks Lyla.

She nods, looking transfixed.

"Know who built it?" Bonnie says, slowly stirring two lumps of sugar into her cup. She makes that tinkling spoon-on-china sound that is hypnotic.

"My dad?" Lyla guesses.

Bonnie smiles, nods, and taps her spoon on the edge of the cup before placing it back on the tray. "Yes. *Your* dad . . . I'm biased but I have to say—it's the best tree house in all of Tennessee. Maybe *anywhere*."

As Lyla smiles back at her, my heart floods.

"So tell me," Bonnie says, furrowing her brow and putting on her shrink face. "Why aren't you at school?"

Lyla puts her cup down on her saucer, then says, "Ask my dad that question. He's the one who made me leave in the middle of a science quiz." She glares at me.

"Does this have anything to do with the photo? Taken of you at the party?" Bonnie asks, looking directly at Lyla. I give her bonus points for being so straightforward.

Lyla nods, then quickly and adamantly insists that Finch's ex-girlfriend took that photo—and that he is innocent. *Completely* innocent. Without addressing her claims, I fill in a few important blanks—namely Lyla's visit to Finch yesterday, and our vandalized porch. Lyla says Polly did that, too, then finishes with an account of this morning's episode in the school lobby, calling it "humiliating" and accusing me of "always" making things so much worse than they have to be.

"So Finch is innocent, and I'm the bad guy?" I say, Bonnie's soothing effect starting to wear off.

"Dad! I was in the middle of a *test*!"

"You said it was a quiz."

"Same difference!"

Bonnie gives her a compassionate nod, then says, "Okay. So, Lyla? How would you have preferred your dad handle this situation today?"

Lyla sighs, then gives a long-winded, rambling answer, covering everything from the orange paint on my clothing to the way I was shouting in the lobby. "Like, couldn't he have just *called* my headmaster and not made a huge scene? Covered in *paint*?"

Bonnie looks at me. "Do you understand how she feels?"

"Sure. I guess," I say. "And she's right that I shouldn't have lost my temper . . . but I had to do *something*. And sometimes it feels as if Lyla is more concerned with little details . . . and *appearances* . . . than the bigger picture. . . . For example, I really don't think it matters that I have a little paint on my clothes."

Bonnie gives me a hint of a smile, then looks at Lyla again. "Do you know what he's trying to say?"

Lyla shrugs, then grants Bonnie the same answer I gave her. "I guess," she says.

Bonnie clears her throat and continues, "And don't you think he's trying to do the best he can to help you?"

"Yes, but this actually *isn't* helping me," Lyla says. "At *all*. He has no clue what it's like to be me . . . and this is *my* school he's barging into. *My* world."

"Not for long, it isn't," I say under my breath.

Lyla makes a loud huffing sound, points at me, and says to Bonnie, "See? See! He wants me to leave my school over this! Tell him that's ridiculous. And *soo* unfair! This isn't *Windsor's* fault."

"Okay. But do you understand *why* your father feels some animosity toward Windsor? After all, *someone* from the school took that photograph of you. And *no one* has yet been punished for it. All these days later," Bonnie says, articulating the reasons for my anger and frustration so beautifully and succinctly that I want to high-five or hug her.

"Yeah. Okay. I get that," Lyla says. "And I appreciate that he's a really good father and stuff. . . . But . . . he's always so *angry* at everyone. . . . It's like he thinks the whole world is against us or something. And they're not. They're just . . . *not*."

The truth of her statement hits me hard, and I feel them both staring at me as I catch my breath.

"Tom?" Bonnie says softly.

"Yeah?" I ask, my head spinning.

"Does Lyla have a point here?"

I slowly nod. "Yeah. She does."

Holding my gaze, Lyla says, "I mean, Dad, some people in Belle Meade *do* suck. Some people are huge snobs and look down on us. But a lot of them aren't like that at *all*. Some of them are just like *us,* only with more money . . . and if money and appearances and stuff like that don't matter, then they shouldn't matter either way." She looks so earnest and emboldened.

I nod again, hearing her and feeling the truth of her words on a level deeper than I thought possible.

"I just want you to trust me sometimes," she continues. "To make my own judgments about people . . . which might not be the same as yours. Whether that's Grace . . . or Finch . . . or anyone else. And *yeah*, I'm going to make mistakes . . . but now it's time to trust me. If I mess up, I mess up. But I want—and *need*—your faith in me."

"Okay," I say, nodding and blinking back unexpected tears. "I'll try."

"And, Lyla?" Bonnie says. "You'll try, too? To cut him some slack? And understand how hard it must be to raise you on his own?"

"Yes," Lyla says, first looking at Bonnie, then shifting her gaze to me. "I'll try, too. I promise, Dad."

Her answer pushes me closer to the edge of crying, though I manage to keep it together by taking a sip of tea.

"Well," Bonnie says. "This is a *really* good start."

"Yeah," I say.

"Yeah," Lyla echoes.

"Now," Bonnie says briskly. "What do you say we take a little tour of the world's finest tree house?"

chapter twenty-six

NINA

After Tom's grand exit, Walter dismisses Finch for the rest of the day, instructing him to return to school in the morning for his scheduled hearing. I don't speak to him until we get outside, telling him to go straight home. That I'll meet him there.

Finch nods, then turns toward the student lot while I walk straight ahead to my car. I get in, put on my seatbelt, and take a few deep breaths. Before I start the ignition, I make myself call Kirk, knowing that I can't drive and talk at the same time. Not to him. Not about this.

"Hey!" he says with what I can tell is forced cheer. "Where've you been?"

"I thought Finch told you?" I say. "I went to Bristol."

"Yeah, he told me. . . . What gives?"

"What *gives*?" I say.

"I mean, why did you go home?" he asks, as I see Finch's Mercedes appear in my rearview mirror. He drives past me, then up to the front gate, and makes a right turn toward home.

"To see my parents. And Julie," I say.

"Okay. Well, why didn't you call me?" he asks.

"I was just really busy. . . . I needed to get away. . . . Kirk, we have to talk."

293

"All right," he says. "How about dinner tonight? Just the two of us?"

"No. Now. I actually need you to come home right now. Finch and I are on our way. Walter just asked him to leave school for the day."

"*What?* Why? What's going on?" he says.

I finally have his full attention—and not some patronizing portion of it. "I'll see you at home, Kirk. I'm not doing this over the phone."

SOMEHOW KIRK BEATS me home from his office. *Dammit,* I say under my breath. I pull into my usual spot in front, then run inside before they have time to get their stories straight. Clearly, they are doing exactly *that* when I walk into Kirk's office. In midsentence, Finch suddenly stops talking, as they both stare up at me.

"Did I interrupt something?" I say, feeling as sick as I did when I read the email exchange with Bob Tate.

"No," Kirk says. "Of course not." He walks toward me, as if to hug me, and says, "Nice to see you, too."

I take a step back and say, "Kirk, I need you to tell me the truth. For *once.*"

He blinks, chuckles, then says, "What are you talking about *now?*"

"*You* tell *me,*" I say, then turn my gaze to Finch. "Or our son can tell me."

"Mom—" Finch begins to say. "I *told* you the truth."

"No, Finch," I say as loudly as I can without actually yelling. "You did *not.*"

Finch glances furtively at Kirk, who paces back over toward the fireplace and leans on the paneled wall.

"Kirk," I say. "Do you have anything you want to tell me? Maybe something about those concert tickets?"

"Honey, *please*—" Kirk says. Because of course he'll never just confess. Not unless he knows for a fact that he's been busted; maybe not even then. "What are you talking about?"

"I'm talking about Bob Tate . . . and the *four* tickets to see Luke Bryan that *Beau* allegedly paid for?"

Kirk and Finch exchange a fleeting look that causes something inside me to snap. "Stop lying to me! Both of you!" I yell, fighting back tears of desperation and anger. I stare at Kirk, then Finch, then back at Kirk. Only one of them looks the slightest bit contrite, and it isn't the man I married.

"I'm sorry, Mom," Finch says, running his hands through his hair. "I just wanted to—"

"What *you* wanted," I say. "See? That's just it. It's always about what *you* and your *father want.*"

Finch closes his mouth, then bites his lip. "I'm sorry," he says again, this time in a whisper.

I cut my eyes to Kirk and say, "How could you do this? To him? To me? To our family?"

"Do *what*?" he has the audacity to ask me. "Let him go to a concert with a girl he likes?"

I swallow and shake my head. "No. How can you teach him to be this kind of person?"

"*Mom,*" Finch interjects with a note of desperation that makes him seem a good three years younger than he is. It gives me a pang in my chest that physically hurts.

I raise my brow, waiting.

"I promise you, Mom," he continues to plead. "I *swear* to you. I'm not lying about the picture and Polly. I didn't take the picture. *She* did."

"So let me get this straight," I say, staring at my son. "You were lying the night of the party, and on the Monday after the party in

Mr. Quarterman's office, and the day of the concert when you said Beau got the tickets. But . . . you aren't lying now?"

Finch nods and says, "Yeah, Mom. That's correct."

"So what changed?" I say, desperately wanting to believe him.

"Well, I've been doing a lot of thinking. . . . And . . . and, Mom, I was trying to do the right thing all along," he stammers. "I only wanted those tickets so I could show Lyla how I feel about her. And Dad knew that. That's why he let me go."

Out of the corner of my eye, I can see Kirk nodding, his son having just made a solid closing argument. I feel both of them staring at me, awaiting my reply.

"Well," I say. "Do you know that your father tried to bribe Mr. Volpe?"

"Nina," Kirk says. "That's enough."

I shake my head. "No, Kirk! He should know this," I say, looking at Finch again. "Did you know your father gave Tom Volpe fifteen thousand *dollars* so that he'd make this Honor Council hearing go away?"

Finch hesitates, just long enough to give himself away. He already knows. He was in on that, too.

"Never mind," I say, amazed that my disgust could still be growing. "Although, while we're on the topic, Kirk . . . Tom gave back your money."

"That guy's a loser," Kirk replies under his breath.

"No, Kirk. Tom Volpe is far from a loser. He's a good person. And a great father raising a wonderful young woman, who, for some reason, really likes our son!"

"For *some* reason?" Kirk says. "Wow, Nina. That's *real* nice."

I take a deep breath. "Can we speak privately for a moment?" I ask Kirk.

He nods, then follows me to our bedroom, surprising me with the first thing out of his mouth. "Look, Nina. I'm really sorry—"

"What are you sorry for, Kirk? The bribe? The lies about the concert? Or being unfaithful to me?"

"Unfaithful?!" Kirk says, way overacting with the most shocked, indignant look I've ever seen from him. "Why would you say that? What's gotten into you lately? You're not acting like yourself at *all*."

"I know," I say. "I haven't been acting like myself for several years now. Not since I let you turn me into some Belle Meade trophy wife."

"Trophy wife?" he scoffs. "We've been together since college. What are you *talking* about?"

"You know what I'm talking about, Kirk. I'm an accessory. That's how you see me. Our whole life is so . . . phony and fake. I'm done with it."

"Done with what, exactly?" he shouts back at me. "Our beautiful homes? Our trips? Our lifestyle?"

"Yes. All of the above. But mostly? I'm done with *you,* Kirk. With your fucked-up priorities. Your lies. Your ego and bullshit. The example you've set for our son—"

"Our son? You mean how he's a really good kid who just got accepted to Princeton? That kind of example?"

"Oh, *God.* Enough of the *good kid* routine. *Please,* Kirk. Good kids don't scheme against their mothers. Good kids don't lie right in the faces of their headmasters."

"He did that to cover for Polly. It was . . . chivalrous."

"I don't think so, Kirk," I say, my doubts finally crystallizing. "I'm not saying Finch took the picture. But there is more to the story than he's telling us. At least more than he's telling *me*. And . . .

and I just can't be on board with this dynamic any longer. . . . I want a divorce."

As Kirk stares at me, mouth agape, it occurs to me that there is actually one thing he could say to change my heart, at least a little. He could tell me that I'm right—or at least that he's sorry. *Genuinely*, this time.

Instead, he looks right through me and says, "I think you're making a really big mistake. But if this is what you truly want . . . then I won't try to stop you."

I shake my head and feel tears start to pour down my face. "You know what, Kirk? Teddy . . . at age *nineteen*, protested more than this when I broke up with him in college."

Kirk rolls his eyes and says, "Well. I'm sure you could still get him back if you wanted to."

"Maybe," I say. "Because he *really* loved me. . . . But I don't want Teddy back. I just want *myself* back. And *my* son . . . if it's not too late."

Twenty-five minutes later, I've crossed the river, and am driving through the bungalow-lined streets of what used to be Nashville's streetcar suburb. I didn't memorize the Volpes' address from our last visit, but I remember how to get there—down Ordway and a left on Avondale. When I arrive, I pull past their house and park on the other side of the street. As I'm about to get out of the car, Melanie calls me. Before I can think better of it, I answer.

"Finally!" she says, sounding frantic but relieved. "What the heck is going on?"

"What do you mean?" I say, wondering what exactly she's referring to, and how much she knows.

"I mean with Polly? I heard that she was the one who took the photo, after all! And then she called Lyla a slut! And vandalized her porch!"

"Where did you hear that?" I ask, marveling once again at how quickly gossip spreads.

"Beau. He just texted from school. Said he heard y'all just had a meeting with Walter? And that Polly and her parents and Tom Volpe were there, too?"

I tell her she is correct.

"Beau also told me that Walter's questioning kids today. Bringing them in one by one. It sounds like he's on a *rampage*. A total witch hunt. I'm panicked that he's going to suspend more of them for drinking."

"Maybe," I say. "Or maybe he's just trying to get to the bottom of what happened. It's coming down to a he said, she said."

"Yeah. But it's clear Polly had a motive. *Jealousy,* pure and simple."

"I don't know, Mel," I say, as I survey the scene of the crime—at least one of the crimes. The Volpes' house is set on a rather steep hill, two flights of concrete steps leading up from the street to the front porch, a small grassy landing in between. There is no cover whatsoever, and it would take nerves of steel to climb all those steps and vandalize an exposed porch so close to the street. "I just can't see Polly doing this."

Melanie sighs, clearly annoyed. "The picture or the porch?"

"Either. I wasn't at the party. And I wasn't home last night," I say. "I was in Bristol with my parents."

"But wasn't Kirk home?" she asks. "Wouldn't he know if Finch left your house?"

"You would *think*. But maybe Finch sneaked out. Or maybe

Kirk just . . . looked the other way. He's not exactly reliable these days," I say.

I then ask her if she knew that the boys went to the Luke Bryan concert with Lyla and her friend.

She hesitates, then says yes, she did. "I'm sorry I didn't tell you. But Kirk told me not to mention it . . . because you'd say no . . . and I thought it was a sweet gesture. I'm sorry."

I almost tell her that I can't believe she lied to me, but I actually *can*. I'm suddenly as done with her as I am with Kirk, thinking that Julie would never in a million years conspire with anyone against me. And certainly not with Kirk.

"Nina?" Melanie asks, as I see Tom and Lyla pull up to the curb on the other side of the street. "Are you still there?"

"Yeah," I say, watching as father and daughter get out of their car and walk up to the front door, neither of them noticing me.

"Honey. We're just trying to save you from yourself. . . . Please don't take this the wrong way," she continues, which is almost always a precursor to an insult, "but you're so . . . *irrational* these days. I mean why would Finch vandalize her property when he's already going to the Honor Council?"

"I don't know. To frame Polly?" I say, desperately hoping that that's not the case.

Melanie continues to tell me how unstable I sound, how worried she is about me, how nothing is more important than "our boys."

I can't hear another word of it. I tell her that I have to go. And that, for the record, I can think of a few things that are just as important—maybe more.

"Like what?"

"Like honesty and truth and *character*?" I say.

"Oh my *God*, Nina," she says. "It's like you think you're better than all of us."

"Better than who?" I say, really wanting to know.

"Your husband. And all of your *friends*. At least I *thought* we were your friends."

"Yeah," I say. "I really thought so, too."

chapter twenty-seven

LYLA

A few minutes after we get home from visiting Dad's friend Bonnie (who I never even knew *existed* before today), Mrs. Browning shows up at our house. Dad's back in his bedroom, so I answer the door, feeling reassured to know that he actually has friends.

"Hi, Lyla," she says, looking and sounding frazzled. She's wearing almost no makeup and workout clothes, her hair in a messy ponytail.

"Hi, Mrs. Browning," I say. "Would you like to come in?"

"Yes, please. I'd really like to talk to you and your dad," she says, just as he appears in the hallway behind me.

I brace myself for a tense exchange, but Bonnie's calming effect seems to have lingered because he just says hello and asks her to come in. Then we all walk into the living room. The two of them sit on the sofa, and I take Dad's chair.

Mrs. Browning speaks first, staring down at her hands. "I'm so sorry about everything that's happening." She looks up at my dad, then turns her gaze to me.

"It's okay," I say, betting that Dad will correct me, and announce that it's *not* okay.

But he doesn't, saying only "Thank you, Nina."

"Yeah," I say. "Thanks."

Mrs. Browning takes a deep breath, then says, "May I ask *you* something, Lyla?"

I nod, staring back at her.

"Who do *you* think took that photo of you? Finch? Or Polly?"

I hesitate, not because I have any doubts whatsoever, but because I know she or my dad will probably ask for my reasons next, and it's really hard to put everything into words.

"Go ahead, Lyla. Tell her what you think," Dad says.

"I think Polly took it," I blurt out. "And I think she wrote that word on our porch, too. . . . I think she's done everything out of jealousy . . . because she knew she was losing Finch. And now she's lost him. For good."

My cheeks burn as I say the last part, picturing what Finch and I did in his basement, and knowing Polly has very good reason to be jealous. I don't dare look over at Dad, for fear that he'll be able to figure that last part out.

"But weren't they still dating on the night of the party?" Mrs. Browning asks, looking so worried and confused. "When the photo was taken?"

"Technically, I guess," I say with a shrug, acknowledging to myself that maybe Finch's version of the story doesn't completely add up. But then I remember the way he looked at me when I was standing in Beau's kitchen. And it all makes sense again.

Dad and Mrs. Browning wait for me to say more, but when I don't, they look at each other instead. It's almost as if they're having a conversation with their eyes. Not the kind that Finch and I have had—more of a we're-in-this-bullshit-together type gaze. I take the opportunity to stand and slip out of the room, feeling immense relief when neither of them tries to stop me.

A few seconds later, I'm alone again. I close my door, find my phone, and climb into my bed. All I want to do is talk to Finch. I feel certain that he has a positive update, too, and that we are only hours away from his name being cleared. One step closer to being together—if we aren't already.

But I quickly discover that Finch has not called or even texted. Instead I see a text from Polly. My heart sinks. The last thing I want to do is read her attacks. But you can't just ignore a message from your enemy. So I open it and read.

> Dear Lyla, I am so sorry that I called you a slut. It was a really ugly thing to say, and I actually don't think that about you. I've just been really upset and confused about so much. But I did NOT take that picture of you. It was Finch and Beau. And I have proof. I also have something else really big to tell you. Will you please call me? Please, Lyla. I'm desperate and scared and begging you. From the bottom of my broken heart, Polly

I finish reading, telling myself that she's full of shit. Just trying to cover her ass and pin everything back on Finch because that's how bitter and jealous she is. The very definition of a hater. I tell myself to delete the text and erase every word from my memory.

But I can't and don't. Because deep down, I'm feeling pretty scared, too.

THE AFTERNOON CRAWLS by as I read Polly's text over and over and over, believing her a bit more each time. What makes me feel so much worse is that Finch doesn't call or text. I end up falling asleep, with my ringer on high just in case.

Around six o'clock, I awaken to another text message from Polly. This one is a photo. I brace myself as I click on it, waiting for it to download, somehow knowing that it's going to be bad.

But it turns out to be much, *much* worse than anything I could have imagined. Because it's another photo of me on Beau's bed. A close-up of my face with a semi-hard penis resting on the bridge of my nose, pointing toward my mouth, almost touching my lips. At first I think it must be Photoshopped in—it's just so shocking and horrible and *disgusting*. But after staring at it a few seconds, I can tell that it's not. It's real. A real penis touching my face. I can't say for sure who it belongs to, but I think I may recognize it, along with the hand holding it.

My heart shatters as another ellipses appears, followed by a plea. Please, please call me.

This time, I do.

Polly answers, saying only *hi*. But in that one syllable, I can tell she's been crying, probably for a long time.

"Where did you get that?" I say, too shocked to cry myself. "Did Finch send you that?"

"No. It's actually a photo I took off his phone. They don't know I have it," she says, her words slurring together a little.

"*They?*" I ask, even though I already have a pretty good guess who his wingman is.

"Finch and Beau. I found so many photos of them with girls," she says. "Including me."

"*You?*" I say, floored.

"Yeah. And videos of me and him, too," she mumbles. "Sex videos he told me he deleted. But they're all there. On his phone . . ."

"Oh my God, Polly!" I say, completely freaking out. "You have to tell on him. We both do!"

"No," she says. "I can't. My parents would *kill* me."

"But we can't let him get away with this!" I say. "We can't!"

"It's too late."

"What do you mean it's *too late*?" I shout. "The Honor Council meets tomorrow. It's not too late at all!"

"I can't. . . . I'd rather be in trouble for what they're saying I did than have my parents see all of this."

"No!" I say. "You didn't do anything wrong! You just had sex with a boy you liked."

"You don't know my parents," she says, her voice sounding oddly distant. "I can't deal with this anymore. I can't . . . I just want to disappear . . . *forever*."

"No, wait! Polly!" I yell into the phone, but she's already hung up.

My mind races, wondering what to do, just as I hear my dad call me for dinner. I suddenly want to see him—if only not to be alone—and practically run to the table.

"Voilà. Linguine and clams," he says when I get there. "Just pretend they're not from a can. And the broccoli's not from a bag!"

I manage to force a smile. But of course he sees how fake it is and says, "Are things really that bad?"

"Yeah, Dad," I say, feeling shaky. "Kinda. Yes."

"Talk to me," he says through the steam still rising from our plates of pasta.

I *want* to tell him. I really do. I even take a deep breath and *try* to tell him. But I just can't. Not about this. I get one of my intense pangs of wishing Mom were around. Well, maybe not Mom *herself*. But a normal mother.

"Lyla? What's going on?"

I shake my head, then tell him the truth. That I love him and he's a great father, but this just isn't the kind of thing I want to talk with him about. "I'm sorry, Dad."

I expect him to get frustrated, maybe even angry, but instead he reaches into his back pocket and pulls out a Post-it note. He slides it across the table and says, "Here."

I look down and see Nina Browning's full name printed in small, pretty script. Under it is her phone number. "She gave me this today—to give to you."

"Why?" I say, picking it up, surprised to realize that there is nothing I'd rather be holding at this second than Mrs. Browning's phone number.

Dad shrugs and says, "I guess because she's worried about you. And she likes you. She said you could call her. Anytime."

"Wow," I say. "That's so nice."

Dad nods and says, "Yes. She *is* nice." Then he picks up his fork and suggests we eat.

"Dad? Can I please be excused?" I ask.

He looks surprised, and maybe a little disappointed, but simply says, "Yes. Go ahead. You can eat later."

A MINUTE LATER, I'm back in my bedroom, the note still in my hand. I dial her number. "Mrs. Browning?" I say when she answers on the first ring.

"Yes. Is this Lyla?"

"Yes. My dad just gave me your number. . . . Are you busy?"

"No," she says. "I was just finishing coffee. I'm at Bongo. The one near you."

Feeling overcome with relief that she's so nearby, I ask her if she'll come get me. I tell her that I need to talk to someone about Polly. That it's kind of an emergency. That I'm worried she may try to hurt herself.

Her voice is calm and reassuring as she tells me she's going to hang up and call Polly's parents—and she'll head over to see me after that.

"Are you sure?" I say, feeling guilty. "I know it's getting late."

"I'm sure, Lyla," she says. "I'll be right there."

chapter twenty-eight

NINA

After leaving Tom and Lyla's house earlier this afternoon, I do not go home. I can't. Instead, I drive around again. Only this time, it's not quite as aimless. As filled with despair as I am, I have a vague purpose now, along with hope. I am looking for somewhere to live after I move out, trying to imagine the beginning of a new, different life. I decide East Nashville really might be the answer. Not the *only* answer—I can actually picture moving back to Bristol for a while. Or maybe I'll get an apartment in Princeton—or wherever Finch winds up going to college. But if I *do* stay in Nashville, I want to be on *this* side of the river, with people less like Kirk and Melanie, and more like Tom and Lyla. All I know for sure is that Finch is now my only real priority, and wherever I physically end up, I will do everything I possibly can to help him become a good man. The person I know he can be.

As afternoon becomes evening, I wind up at the same coffee shop in Five Points where Tom and I first met. Our table is taken, but I sit at the one next to it, laying out the real estate brochures and newspapers that I've picked up over the day. I then pull a pen from my purse and start circling listings while I sip a decaf latte. I allow myself to dream a little about all the possibilities of a new life that could lie ahead for Finch and me.

Then, just as I'm gathering up my things with thoughts of going home, my phone rings with a number I don't recognize. At first I think it might be a realtor calling me back, as I've contacted a few already. But when I answer it, I hear a girl's voice saying, "Mrs. Browning?"

"Yes," I say. "Is this Lyla?"

"Yes. My dad just gave me your number. . . . Are you busy?"

"No," I say. "I was just finishing coffee. I'm at Bongo. The one near you."

"Oh, wow," she says, then blurts out, "Could you come get me?"

"Now?" I say.

"Only if you can. . . . I'm just worried, and it's kind of hard to talk to my dad about this," she babbles, then uses the word *emergency*. Of all things, she says she's worried about Polly. That she may do something to hurt herself.

"Why do you say that?" I ask, heading toward my car. "What happened?"

"She's just really, really upset about some things," Lyla says.

I tell myself that teenage girls are prone to melodrama, and yet, I can't help but think of some of the calls I've answered for Nashville's suicide helpline, as well as the girl from Windsor who took her life. The very reason Kirk and I went to the gala the night of Beau's party. "Honey, let me try to call the Smiths," I say. "Then I'll head over to see you. Okay?"

"Are you sure?" Lyla says. "I know it's getting late."

"I'm sure, Lyla," I say. "I'll be right there."

In a low-grade panic, I hang up and log on to the Windsor directory, finding the Smiths' home and cell numbers. I don't expect them to answer—and they don't—but I leave multiple messages asking them to please call me. I add that it's urgent and about

Polly. Then I start my car and drive back to Avondale for the second time today.

When I arrive five minutes later, I see Lyla standing by the street, her white high-top sneakers, light jeans, and a silver bomber jacket all glowing in my headlights. There's no way that I could miss her, but she still waves frantically at my car, then runs up to my window.

"Hi," she says, out of breath. "Did you call Polly's parents?"

"Yeah. I tried them, but no one answered."

"She's not answering her phone, either," Lyla says.

"Okay," I say, trying to stay calm. "I think I'll drive over there and knock on the door. Just to be sure."

Lyla nods, then asks if she can come with me.

For reasons I can't pinpoint in the adrenaline-filled moment, I feel relieved by the offer. Her mere *presence*. "Okay," I say. "Is it all right with your dad?"

"Yes. I told him you were coming over. But I'll text him," she says, then runs around my car and gets in. The second her door is closed and her seatbelt fastened, she pulls her phone from her jacket pocket.

As I do a quick three-point turn, then make a right on Ordway, I ask Lyla to tell me more about her conversation with Polly.

I feel her looking at me as she hesitates, then says, "She told me that she has proof it wasn't her who took that picture of me. And that there are other pictures, too. Of other girls."

"What kind of pictures?" I say.

"You know . . . embarrassing . . . sexual-type pictures she doesn't feel like she can tell Mr. Q or her parents about."

As things start to come into horrifying focus, I clench the steering wheel to keep my hands from shaking. "Lyla?" I say. "Did Finch take these pictures?"

311

"Yes. Along with Beau, apparently," Lyla says softly. "I might not have believed her . . . but Polly sent me one of them tonight. It was of me. And Finch. When I was passed out. And it was . . . really bad."

"*Oh my God,*" I hear myself say, my heart shattering.

As I press down on the gas pedal, I am bombarded with images of Finch. The perfect newborn baby sleeping in my arms. The spirited five-year-old, making rutabaga stew on the steps of the Parthenon. The ten-year-old at the beach, building sand castles with Julie's girls, only half his age.

I just can't *believe* it. What's happening now. The person my son has both slowly and suddenly become.

And yet I do. Because sometimes you just can't see the things that are the closest to you.

BY THE TIME we pull into Polly's driveway, my focus has returned to her, and what we need to do in the moment. All the lights are on and two cars are in the driveway. I take it as a hopeful sign, although I can still think of a bad scenario, too.

"What should we do?" I say, as if Lyla's the adult and I'm the child.

"I dunno. Go ring their doorbell?" Lyla says, just as a figure passes by one of the front windows. "Is that her?"

"I can't tell. . . . It might be her mom," I say.

"We should probably just go find out," she says.

"Yeah," I say, but I feel paralyzed with fear.

Lyla, on the other hand, swings open her door and gets out of the car. I stare at her, marching toward the house, amazed by her bravery. I make myself follow, reaching her as she's ringing the doorbell, noticing how much her stoic profile resembles her father's.

A few seconds later, we can hear someone coming to the door. I hold my breath, then stare into Mr. Smith's eyes. His first name suddenly escapes me.

"Hello, Nina," he says, looking first startled and confused, then angry but calm. "What brings you here so late?"

As I open my mouth to reply, he shifts his gaze to Lyla and says, "And *you* are . . . ?"

"Lyla Volpe. The girl from the photograph," she says, talking quickly and utterly matter-of-factly. "But we're not here for that, Mr. Smith. We're here because you and Mrs. Smith weren't answering your phones . . . and neither was Polly. And I'm . . . *we're* . . . really worried about her."

He furrows his brow and says, "Worried how?"

"Um . . . Well . . . Polly called me earlier today. And she sounded really upset. . . ."

"She *is* upset," he says, shooting me a harsh look.

"Is she here?" Lyla presses onward.

"Yes. She's in her room," he says, now looking full-fledged pissed. "But she has nothing more to say about this."

Meanwhile, Polly's mother appears over his shoulder. "Yes. None of us do," she says.

"I know," I say. "And I'm so sorry for overstepping . . . but could you just . . . check on her? Lyla's worried that Polly may be in trouble. . . ."

"Just what are you suggesting?" Mrs. Smith says, her voice ice cold, pushing past her husband.

"I'm suggesting that your daughter may be trying to hurt herself," I say, my voice finally conveying my sense of panic.

I watch as their expressions drastically change, both of them spinning away from us and flying up the spiral staircase. Mr. Smith takes the steps two and three at a time, his wife not far behind. I feel frozen again but manage to turn and look at Lyla, her expression mirroring the way I feel. One second later, we hear horrible shrieking. First them calling Polly's name, then frantic shouts for us to call 911. Lyla finds her phone first, her fingers dialing those three dreaded digits.

"I'm calling to report an emergency," she says, her voice shaky but slow and clear. "I think someone has tried to kill herself. . . . Yes, just now . . . a girl . . . seventeen. . . . The address? . . . Hold on. . . ." She looks at me, wide-eyed with fear.

I blank for the second time in minutes, unable to conjure even the street name. What is *wrong* with me, I think, as Lyla heads right up the stairs, shouting, "I need your address! I'm on with 911!"

I hear more hysterical screaming. Then nothing. A second later, Lyla reappears at the top of the staircase, wildly motioning at me. "Mrs. Browning! You need to move your car! An ambulance is coming!"

In a state of shock, I do as I'm told, running to my car, then back to the foyer, where I pace and pray. For both Polly *and* Lyla.

chapter twenty-nine

LYLA

It is totally *impossible* to process. Both where I am and what I am watching unfold, second by second. Only a few hours ago, Polly was my mortal enemy, and now I am standing in the corner of her enormous bedroom, the walls painted a muted gray-lavender, witnessing the most intensely personal, gut-wrenching moment of her life. A moment that could possibly end in her death.

Her parents are here, too, of course, both of them hysterical, and no less so since the arrival of two paramedics—a badass all-female team doing what I've seen so many times on *Grey's Anatomy* and countless other shows and movies. Checking Polly's vitals. Moving her from her canopy bed (the same one I've admired in the Restoration Hardware Teen catalog) onto a stretcher. Cutting her black sweatshirt right down the front with a huge pair of scissors. Ripping open packages of vials and other supplies. Inserting a tube down Polly's throat. All the while, they talk to each other in a foreign medical language, while trying to keep Mr. and Mrs. Smith at bay.

At one point, when Polly convulses and her mom *really* starts to freak out, one paramedic looks up at me and shouts for my help. "Get her back," she says.

"Mrs. Smith. Let them work!" I say, rushing forward to hold her arm for a moment. Before I retreat again, I get an unwanted closer look at Polly. Her body is completely limp, her skin pale. Yet, thank God, she still looks more asleep than dead. Then again, I've never seen a dead person. I pray that Polly won't be my first. She just *can't* die.

I look away from her, returning my gaze to the empty bottles of Ambien and Maker's Mark that her dad was holding when I first ran into the room and that are now on the floor next to the bed. Her *mom's* pills and her *dad's* booze—details gleaned when the paramedics first arrived and asked their questions. *How many pills were left? How much whiskey was still in the bottle?*

At least a dozen, Mrs. Smith said.

Half a bottle, Mr. Smith said.

I wonder now whether the combination was purposeful. Polly's one-two punch to her parents, whom she felt she couldn't talk to in a crisis. Or maybe, actually, her relationship with them was more like mine with my dad. Maybe Polly loved her parents so much that she would rather die than see shame on their faces.

If only she could see how much worse *this* is. How much more painful, even if she winds up being okay.

I can't help thinking of my dad on the night he picked me up at Grace's. How much it must have hurt him to see me the way I was. I vow that no matter what, I won't ever do something like this to him. That I will take better care of myself. Make better decisions. Be more like him and less like my mother. It's the least I can do.

Suddenly Mrs. Browning is in the room beside me, holding my hand. I notice that her back is to Polly—that she doesn't look at her once, not until the stretcher is being carried out of the room and down the stairs and to the ambulance. Mrs. Browning and I follow, then stand on the porch, still holding hands, watching as Polly's parents climb into the back with the stretcher and one of the paramedics, while the other one runs around to get in the front and drive. We stand there, frozen in place, watching as the ambulance races away in a blur of red lights and wailing sirens.

After everything is silent once more, I turn and close the Smiths' front door. We then walk to Mrs. Browning's car and get in, both of us staring out the windshield.

"Do you think she's going to be okay?" I say to Mrs. Browning but mostly to myself.

She shakes her head, then wipes away tears. "I don't know, sweetie. But if she is? It will only be because of you."

"And *you*," I say. "Thank you for helping me."

Mrs. Browning looks into my eyes. "You're welcome. . . . And I promise you, Lyla, I'm going to *keep* helping you."

"Thank you," I say, my mind returning to the photograph Polly sent me, just as Mrs. Browning brings it up, too.

"Lyla. You have to come forward about the pictures Finch took. You know that, right?"

I stare at her.

"You *have* to . . . for Polly . . . for yourself. For all the girls who have ever had something like this happen to them." She pauses, glances away, and then looks back into my eyes. "To *us*."

"*Us?*" I say. She can mean only one thing. But I ask for her confirmation anyway. "Are you one of those girls, Mrs. Browning?"

She doesn't answer me. She just pulls away from the curb, driving in the direction of my house. At some point, though, she begins to talk, telling me a story of when she was a freshman at Vanderbilt. It is a horrible story about a boy raping her. She tells me that she didn't report it because she was ashamed and blamed herself. She tells me everything that happened afterward, too. How she broke up with her boyfriend the very next day. How she told only one person—her best friend—but made her promise to keep the secret forever. How she eventually moved on from the heartbreak, meeting, dating, and then marrying Finch's father. How she desperately wanted to make her life seem and look and *be* perfect. She talks to me about the dreams that she both *had* and *still* has. Dreams I share. She talks about love. And she talks about truth. She talks a *lot* about truth.

She doesn't finish until we get to my street, and I don't speak until her car is in park again. The first thing I say is for *her* sake, to try to ease *her* pain.

"Finch isn't *that* bad, Mrs. Browning," I say.

She looks unconvinced—and so sad.

"I mean . . . what happened to me isn't anything like what happened to you."

"Maybe not," she says, tearing up again. "But, Lyla, Finch is plenty bad *enough*."

I don't know what to say to this, because I know she's right. So I just tell her again how much I appreciate her help tonight. How grateful I am for *her*.

"Oh, sweetie," she says, leaning over to hug me. "You're the one who did everything. . . . I'm so proud of you. . . ."

"Thank you," I say, then ask her again if she thinks Polly's going to be okay.

"I do," she says this time. "And Lyla?"

"Yes?" I look at her, waiting.

"I also think you may have saved more than one life tonight."

chapter thirty

NINA

When I get home, I hear Finch and Kirk talking and watching television in the family room, sickeningly oblivious to the fact that Polly is fighting for her life. I go straight down the hall to my bedroom and start packing. I grab a small duffel bag, and I put in only essentials: jeans, T-shirts, pajamas, socks, underwear, and toiletries. I then remove my wedding ring, along with all the pieces of jewelry that Kirk has given me, laying them on his nightstand.

I tell myself to remember this moment later, if and when we are fighting over money. I tell myself that although I will try to get what is fair, I actually don't *want* anything from him anymore.

I glance around the room, thinking back to when we bought this house, how excited I was when we moved in—even happier as I slowly decorated it with furnishings, rugs, and art. The memories make me feel sheepish and shallow, borderline *nauseated*, until something else dawns on me. I realize I never wanted it to be about accumulating beautiful *things* or presenting a mere façade of a good life. It was always about creating a *home*. Something beautiful and real on the inside, too. Something meaningful for the core of our family.

But it all seems like a lie now. And even the parts that weren't always a lie now feel tainted. *Ruined.*

Just as I'm turning to go, I hear footsteps. I know it's Finch before his face appears in the doorway. I feel sure that his father has put him up to it; there's no way he'd come back here unless instructed.

Sure enough, he glances at my bag and says, "Mom? What're you doing? Dad says you're *leaving* us?"

I stare back at him, my heart breaking, as I say, "I'm leaving your father . . . and this house. . . . But I'm not leaving *you*, Finch. I would never leave *you*."

"Please don't go, Mom," he says, his voice nearly as deep as Kirk's. "Don't leave Dad. Don't do this to him. To *me*."

I want to scream at him. I want to shake him and tell him that his actions may have killed a girl. Instead, I walk over to him and take his face in my hands and kiss his forehead, inhaling his sweet, boyish scent. It is the same as it has always been, despite so many other changes.

"Don't do this to me," he says again.

"Oh, Finch. I'm not doing anything *to* you. I'm doing this *for* you."

"Polly's lying, Mom," he says.

But unlike all the other times he's told me this, his statement now rings hollow. It's as if he's no longer even *trying* to be convincing. It occurs to me that maybe Lyla already spoke to him about the photos. Maybe he knows that we somehow have proof.

Regardless, I shake my head and say, "No. She is *not*. *You* are."

His lower lip quivers. I wait for more, but there is nothing else.

"Finch. Please confess," I plead. "Please do the right thing. Princeton doesn't matter. *People* matter. . . . And it's never too late to say you're sorry."

He nods ever so slightly. I have no idea if I've actually reached him on some level, or if he is just giving me what I want.

Regardless, it's not a battle I can fight tonight. I'll start again tomorrow, and will fight as hard and long as it takes. "I'll see you in the morning," I say. "I'll be at school for your hearing."

"Okay, Mom," he says.

I lean in closer, kiss his cheek, and whisper, "You'll always be my baby, Finch. And no matter what, I will *always* love you."

He inhales as if he's about to reply. But he can't, because he's now crying. We both are. So I just whisper good night. Then I walk past him and right out the front door of what was once our family home.

WHEN I GET downtown to the Omni Hotel, I discover, from a young girl at the front desk, that my credit card has been declined. She is embarrassed for me—and I want to reassure her that a declined credit card is nothing in the scheme of life. I hand her another, although I suspect what will happen even before that card is also declined.

It is all so absurd—so classically Kirk—that I find myself laughing. This is why Julie told me to have my ducks in a row. Because she knew he was capable of this petty bullshit. I consider stepping aside to call her, but then remember that I still have fifteen thousand dollars in my purse. So I check in using some of those bills, then take the elevator to the eighteenth floor. I use the plastic key to unlock my door and walk into the room, looking out over the city where I've lived my entire adult life.

I feel as alone and devastated as I've ever been, including that horrible night at Vanderbilt.

But in some other ways, I've never felt stronger or more certain of my path. I take a shower, then put on my pajamas and get in bed. My curtains are still open, and as I stare out at the lights of Nashville, my phone rings.

It's Tom.

Feeling tremendous relief, I answer, saying hello.

Without saying hello back, he simply tells me that Polly's going to be okay. "She's staying at the hospital overnight, but she's stable."

"Oh, thank *God*," I say. "How do you know?"

"Lyla tracked down her parents."

Of course she did, I think, amazed by her once again. "Can I talk to her? Is she still awake?"

"No. She just fell asleep," Tom says. "Pretty rough day."

"I know," I say, thinking back to standing with my mother in my parents' kitchen early this morning. How that now seems like a lifetime ago.

"Want to hear the craziest part?" he asks.

"Sure," I say, adjusting my head on the pillow, listening.

"So right after you and Lyla left . . . guess who just happened to . . . show up?"

"Who?"

"Lyla's mother." Tom lets out a wry laugh. "She just sailed into town for a surprise visit."

I laugh back, in spite of everything. "She sounds as awful as Kirk."

"Worse," he says. "At least Kirk stuck around."

I swallow, as it occurs to me that maybe I'm no better than his ex, checking out when the going gets tough. But I tell myself I'm not giving up—I'm just taking a stand. There is a difference. I then return my focus to Lyla and say, "I just want you to know . . . how truly incredible your daughter was tonight. So, *so* brave."

"Yes. She's pretty great," he says. "And so are *you*, Nina. . . . Lyla told me everything. About Finch. About the photos. And about how much you're supporting her."

I start to well up as I tell him how sorry I am.

"I know you are," he says. "But for what it's worth? . . . I think there's still hope for Finch."

Tears stream down my face as I ask him why he thinks this. I wait for his response, telling myself I will trust my friend—along with whatever answer he gives me.

"Because . . ." Tom finally says, his voice soft in my ear. "Because *you're* his mother."

LYLA

Since graduating from high school nearly a decade ago, I rarely return to Nashville. Dad usually comes to visit me instead. I'm not really sure why, but I think it has more to do with how hectic my life has been—first at college, then at law school, now in the Manhattan District Attorney's Office—than with any lack of fondness for my hometown. I can also say with complete confidence that it has *nothing* to do with Finch Browning or the events of my sophomore year. That is ancient history.

Of course Finch still crosses my mind now and then—flashbacks to his basement, and Polly's attempted suicide, and especially the day Mr. Q called Dad and me into his office and broke the news that Finch had gotten off. *Completely*. With tears in his eyes, Mr. Q told us that the Honor Council, composed of eight students and eight faculty members, had concluded there "wasn't enough proof." It was outrageous, of course. What proof did they need beyond a photo of Finch's *dick* on my face? But I guess they weren't willing to go down the penis-forensics road after Finch introduced his Photoshop defense.

Maybe if Polly's parents had let her return to Windsor, or send me the rest of the photos, things would have turned out differently. Then again, maybe not. Maybe the cards were *that* stacked in

Finch's favor (or, as Dad believed, Mr. Browning really pulled off the Belle Meade bribery scheme of the century).

For several months, Dad and I contemplated bringing real legal action—or at least writing a letter to Princeton. But ultimately, I just wanted to move on, and with Bonnie's help, I was somehow able to convince Dad that Finch's fate really had very little to do with me. Karma would sort him out. Or *not*, as the case may be. Either way, I had my own life to live.

Along those lines, I also persuaded Dad to let me stay at Windsor. It was the right decision for so many reasons. For one, I was genuinely happy there. Grace and I remained close friends (I was recently a bridesmaid in her wedding), while branching out and extending our duo to include a few other strong, like-minded girls. For another, I became superfocused academically, finishing second in our class and getting into Stanford. Dad says I deserve the credit for that—not Windsor—but the education I got, along with a glowing recommendation from my headmaster, certainly didn't hurt. Besides, it was good training for real life. A reminder that no matter where you are, you can find a silver lining—along with good people like Mr. Q and Nina.

I actually still keep in touch with Mr. Q, who is now retired, our email-based friendship mostly consisting of an exchange of *New Yorker* cartoons and articles about the dire state of the world. We both remain hopeful, though, and I think some of that hopefulness I learned from him during those dark days at Windsor.

Against the odds, Dad and I stayed close to Nina, too. After her divorce was finalized, she and Dad even started a boutique design business together—he did his carpentry thing and she decorated and helped Dad be more commercial. The coolest part of their gig was their custom tree houses, like the one in Bonnie's backyard.

Most of their clients were pretty well off, and included a few celebrities, but my favorite project was a gift to the children staying at an abused women's shelter in Nina's hometown of Bristol. It wasn't the fanciest, but I knew from the photographs I'd seen that it had brought the most joy.

Their work—and especially that joy—was good therapy for both of them during their empty-nest days. I know Dad missed me a lot, and Nina probably missed Finch even more, because he barely spoke to his mother during his years at Princeton. I'm not sure if it was punishment for siding with me, or for leaving his father—but things got worse before they got better.

According to Dad, Nina never gave up on him, though, and sent him long, handwritten letters every week, until at some point he returned to her. Dad pretends to have a cynical view of the shift, saying out of Nina's earshot that it probably had more to do with some sort of financial scandal Mr. Browning got caught in rather than any real change of heart. But I can tell Dad wants to believe something different. That like me, he might have faith that it was as simple—and powerful—as a mother's love.

I'm thinking about all of this now as my Uber turns onto Avondale and I see Dad standing on the front porch at the exact spot where that terrible word was once written. He waves, watching me get out of the car and climb the steps.

"I can't believe you wouldn't let me pick you up at the airport." He shakes his head, muttering something about my hardheadedness, then gives me a long, tight hug. "Thank you for coming," he says. "I know how busy you are."

"Of course," I say. "I wouldn't miss this for anything."

"It's really not that big of a deal," Dad says, downplaying the design award he and Nina are receiving this evening. "But it's going to mean a lot to Nina. And remember—*your* being here is a surprise."

"I know, Dad," I say, smiling. "You've only told me a hundred times."

"Well . . . I just want tonight to be perfect."

"You're so sweet to her," I say.

"She deserves it. She's the best," Dad replies.

It is wild praise coming from him, and I find myself wondering, as I often have over the years, if there's something romantic between them. They swear up and down that they're just friends—*best* friends—and in some ways, I think that's even sweeter.

"So . . . is he coming?" I say, referring to Finch, knowing that Dad invited him, too.

"No," Dad says, shaking his head. "Work conflict. Although to be fair, he does live in London now."

"*London?*" I say, annoyed that Finch managed to land himself in the only city in the world better than New York.

"Yeah. He took some job . . . something financial."

"Well. Whatever," I say, with a shrug. I'm disappointed for Nina but relieved for myself. "We're going to have a wonderful time regardless."

A FEW HOURS later, Dad and I are walking into the lobby of the Frist Center. He's wearing his only nice suit and a light blue tie I feel sure Nina picked out for him.

"Okay. She's up in the Turner Courtyard," he says, flustered as he reads a text message. "Where the event is being held . . . Do you know how to get—"

"Yes, Dad," I say. "I know."

"I better go before she walks down here and sees you."

"Go. Go," I say. "I can fend for myself."

Dad kisses my cheek and thanks me, his unease seeming to shift into excitement. Maybe even pride. After all, it's *his* award, too, and he's come a long way since his solo carpentry and Uber days.

As he turns to go, I head to the bar to get a glass of champagne, thinking that it's nice to be back in Nashville. I really should visit more often.

And that's when I see him, rushing into the lobby. With glasses and short hair and a little extra weight, he looks so different. Older. Somehow changed. But as he gets closer, I can tell that he's still unmistakably Finch, and remind myself that people seldom *really* change.

My instinct is to duck away and avoid him, but I make myself walk directly toward him, looking right into his eyes.

"Hello, Lyla," he says, breathless, with flushed cheeks. He nearly hugs me but then stops, likely thinking better of it.

"So you made it after all?" I say.

"Yeah," he says, giving me a half smile. "My boss might fire me. . . . But I made it."

I smile back, though I don't fully mean it.

"Did you get my letter?" he asks.

I nod and say yes. "Thank you," I add, though I'm not really thanking him for his letter, but for being here tonight in Tennessee, wearing a crumpled overcoat that smells like an airplane. For showing up for his mother.

He nods, looking sad but determined. "Well . . . we better go up. . . . Your dad said eight o'clock, right?"

"Yes," I say, glancing at my watch and seeing that it's a couple minutes past. I finish my champagne, put the glass on a highboy table, then follow Finch up the steps into the ballroom.

The lights are low, but as I scan the room, I see Bonnie and a few of my dad's old contractor buddies. The others I don't recognize.

There is a woman at the podium, talking about Dad and Nina and the work they're doing for abused women's shelters across the state. *Plural.* I thought there was only the one in Bristol.

"Wow," I say to myself, though Finch must hear me, because out of the corner of my eye I can see him nodding.

"Yes," he murmurs in agreement.

A second later, Dad and Nina walk onto the stage together as everyone applauds. She is wearing an Audrey Hepburn–style pale blue dress that matches Dad's tie and, come to think of it, the lettering on their business cards. His hand is on her back as he walks behind her, guiding her. My father has always been a gentleman in his own way, but I've never seen him like this before. He looks so confident, sparkling. They *both* sparkle.

Dad takes the microphone first, thanking everyone. But then he steps back and Nina does the talking. She speaks about their journey together, how they both were looking for a way to follow their passion and also help others. There is a slide show of women and children, smiling, laughing, playing in tree houses and tranquil communal living spaces. She talks about how materialism can lead us astray, but that we all need beauty in our lives. And a sanctuary. A home and people who will always have our backs.

She finishes, thanking everyone again. As the crowd applauds, I feel my eyes welling up and risk a glance to my left. I'm surprised to see tears streaming down Finch's face.

Still watching Nina, he whispers, "I'm sorry. I'm just *so* sorry. . . ."

Then he tilts his chin down and looks right into my eyes, and in that instant, for the first time, I forgive him. Or maybe I don't.

I'm not sure how I'll feel later, after the emotion of the evening has worn off.

I can sense that he wants to say more to me, but this is not the time. So before he can speak, I say, "They are amazing . . . aren't they?"

"Yes, they are," he says, as we both gaze back up at Nina and my dad. His hand is on her back again, protective, so proud.

"She *saved* me," I say, putting it into words for the first time.

"I know," he says again, his tears still flowing.

Maybe he's thinking about his younger self—and what Nina saved me *from* all those years ago. But maybe, I hope, he's simply thinking about his mother—and how she somehow managed to save *him,* too.

ACKNOWLEDGMENTS

While writing a novel is mostly a solitary endeavor, I have many individuals to thank for their generous contributions to this book.

I am indebted to my editor, Jennifer Hershey, for her guidance and brilliance from start to finish (especially the finish!). If you enjoy this story, it is in no small part due to her extraordinary talent.

Thank you to Mary Ann Elgin and Sarah Giffin, my mother and sister, for their chapter-by-chapter insight and endless moral support. I love our threesome, born in the seventies and still going strong.

I am thankful for Nancy LeCroy Mohler, my best friend, first reader, and most loyal copy editor. She knows these characters as well as I do, and there isn't a paragraph in this book (or any of my nine books, for that matter) that she and I haven't discussed together. I am very lucky to have her.

Many thanks to Bryan Lamb for providing so much Nashville flavor and manly insights ("You would never bribe someone with a check; it's gotta be cash" and "You don't have to specify 'flat-screen' TV; we know Finch doesn't have a Magnavox."). The Belle Meade Single Barrel Bourbon helped, too.

I am so grateful to my amazing assistant Kate Hardie Patterson; my longtime publicist Stephen Lee; and to all my friends and family who provided specific input or otherwise helped me through the birth of this book, especially: Steve Fallon, Allyson Wenig Jacoutot, Julie Wilson Portera, Laryn Ivy Gardner, Jennifer New, Harlan Coben, Martha Arias, Jeff MacFarland, Jim Konrad, Fred Assaf, Ralph Sampson, Lori Baker, Mara Davis, Ellie Fallon, Sloane Alford, Mike Pentecost, Courtney Jenrath, Lisa Elgin Ponder, Mollie Smith, Lea Journo, and Bill Giffin.

On the professional side, I thank my incomparable agent, Theresa Park, as well as Emily Sweet, Andrea Mai, Abby Koons, Mollie Smith, and everyone at Park Literary.

And to my team at Penguin Random House, including Gina Centrello, Kara Welsh, Kim Hovey, Scott Shannon, Matt Schwartz, Theresa Zoro, Susan Corcoran, Jennifer Garza, Isabella Biedenharn, Emma Thomasch, Sally Marvin, Sanyu Dillon, Debbie Aroff, Colleen Nuccio, Melissa Milsten, Denise Cronin, Toby Ernst, Paolo Pepe, Loren Noveck, Victoria Wong, Erin Kane, Cynthia Lasky, Allyson Pearl, and the entire PRH sales force: Thank you for your expertise, passion for books, and commitment to bring my stories to so many wonderful readers.

And finally, I am eternally grateful to my husband, Buddy Blaha. I couldn't have picked a finer father for my children. Edward, George, and Harriet: May you grow up to have your dad's grit, heart, and rock solid character. I love you all so much.

ABOUT THE AUTHOR

EMILY GIFFIN is the author of eight internationally best-selling novels: *Something Borrowed, Something Blue, Baby Proof, Love the One You're With, Heart of the Matter, Where We Belong, The One & Only,* and *First Comes Love*. A graduate of Wake Forest University and the University of Virginia School of Law, she lives in Atlanta with her husband and three children.

emilygiffin.com
Facebook.com/EmilyGiffinFans
Twitter: @emilygiffin
Instagram: @emilygiffinauthor

ABOUT THE TYPE

This book was set in Sabon, a typeface designed by the well-known German typographer Jan Tschichold (1902–74). Sabon's design is based upon the original letter forms of sixteenth-century French type designer Claude Garamond and was created specifically to be used for three sources: foundry type for hand composition, Linotype, and Monotype. Tschichold named his typeface for the famous Frankfurt typefounder Jacques Sabon (c. 1520–80).

The following *All We Ever Wanted*
bonus material is exclusive content
for this Target edition:

Go behind the scenes with Emily Giffin
on the writing of *All We Ever Wanted*
in the following Q & A . . .

And then reflect on your experience
of the novel with questions for discussion.

Dear Target Guest:

As a thank-you to one of my favorite retailers for their continual amazing support of my books and of reading generally, I offer this inside look at some of the inspirations for my latest release, *All We Ever Wanted*.

Much of the beauty of humankind lies in the differences we celebrate, but in the most essential and fundamental ways, I believe we are more alike than we are different. Most of us are good people at heart. We love our friends and families. We nurture our most valuable relationships. We strive to act morally and create happiness in our lives.

And yet sometimes, our most diligent, well-intentioned efforts turn into an unrealistic quest for perfection—or at least the *illusion* of perfection. Amplified by the pressures of social media, we construct our lives (and Instagram feeds) to look a certain way, while sometimes losing sight of what really matters. At various junctures over the years, as I went to law school, practiced in the litigation department of a large New York firm, and then transitioned to a full-time writing career, I have caught myself focusing too much on approval, appearances, or achievement for the sake of achievement—rather than being true to myself and following my heart. I believe that many of us fall prey to such pitfalls and that we must all work vigilantly to focus on living authentic lives of purpose.

For me, having children has raised the stakes exponentially. My twin sons, Edward and George, are now fourteen, and my daughter, Harriet, is ten, and as I navigate my way through parenthood,

I often think of Jackie Kennedy's famous quote: "If you bungle raising your children, I don't think whatever else you do well matters very much." This means many things to me, but above all, it means teaching my children by my own example and showing them that it is more important to be both kind and true to themselves (and their causes) than it is to achieve popularity with their peers or quantifiable success. They should do their best, but it is the effort and what is in their heart that matter—not the actual grades on their report cards or wins and losses on the playing fields. In a competitive world, this focus isn't always easy, and the temptation to make the journey smooth and painless for our children is considerable. I remember one incident in particular, in which one of my children made a mistake and I had to decide whether to "fix" things for him (and make both of us *look* better) or require him to take responsibility and face the consequences of his actions. I chose the more difficult path. I've made plenty of mistakes in life (and many as a parent), but the decision I made that day is one that I am most proud of.

All We Ever Wanted was in part inspired by similar parenting dilemmas and choices: the struggles of achieving a balance between wanting to protect my children from any pain and give them every advantage, while also recognizing the dangers of paving the way too much for them.

My husband and I have worked hard to give our children some advantages we didn't grow up with. They live in an affluent part of Atlanta, are getting an exceptional education at a wonderful private school, and have had the opportunity to travel fairly extensively. But at times I wonder, is the privilege they enjoy a net positive or negative thing? How do I prevent privilege from becoming entitlement? Does a little hardship build more character? How do I, in a society that cares so much about image and the success of the individual, teach my children to be compassionate and outward-looking? To prioritize integrity over materialism?

We are all works in progress. And we are all seeking love, happiness, and truth in a competitive, judgmental world. This story is about Nina, Tom, and Lyla's complicated search for that fulfillment. I hope you connect with these characters, and that their journey helps you, at least in some small measure, as you navigate your own choices and lives.

With warmest wishes and many thanks again!

Emily Giffin

A Conversation with Emily Giffin

What inspired this novel?

That's always a difficult question to answer, as my books usually
have several seeds of inspiration. For *All We Ever Wanted*, I knew
I wanted to explore the themes of privilege and entitlement, especially how these relate to parenthood. More broadly, I wanted to
write about parental hopes and fears, especially during the teen
years. I have twin sons who are now fourteen years old, as well as
a ten-year-old daughter, and I've begun to observe so much about
the choices we make—both in my own household and in the wider
community—and how sometimes even well-intentioned decisions
can impact children in a negative way. To put it a different way,
when does privilege become entitlement?

**You wrote from three different points of view, including a man's.
Was this your first time writing from a male perspective? How was
that?**

Yes. *All We Ever Wanted* marks the first time I've written from
the male point of view, though there have been important (and
I hope well-developed!) male characters in all of my previous
eight novels. It was a lot of fun being in Tom's head, and in some
ways, I felt that I got to know him better than my female charac-

ters as I wrote this book. I think we would be close friends in real life.

What is your writing process like? Do you outline ahead of time?

My books are character-driven, so my writing process always begins with them. And while I generally have a vague sense of beginning, middle, and end at the outset of each novel, only when I've written the initial chapters and get a feel for who my characters are—as well as the relationships between them—does the plot really begin to develop. In essence, I allow my characters to drive the story, as opposed to the story driving them. It may not be as efficient as outlining a book beforehand, but I enjoy the more organic approach and the surprises along the way.

Do you feel that you have evolved as a writer? How is this novel different from your previous books?

I like to think that I have! I write about relationships, as I always have and always will, but I think my evolution as a writer parallels my own personal growth and change. After all, I'm no longer the single, twenty-something, childless woman who sat down to write *Something Borrowed* in her London flat. Now, as a married mother of three kids living in Atlanta, my priorities have much more to do with their lives than my own. My themes and plots have evolved in a similar fashion, with a sharper focus on the dynamics of family, parenthood, and their attendant complexities. And while I've touched on parenting in previous books, this is the first time I've specifically constructed a story around the relationship between adults and their children.

You began the novel in 2016, before the #metoo movement swept the nation. Do you feel that you anticipated something as you sat down to write?

I did not see the #metoo movement coming, but I definitely wanted to tell a story that focused on women learning to take control of their lives and, more pointedly, fighting back against having our voices and our concerns minimized. In other words, I am certainly aware of the sexism, and sometimes outright misogyny, in our society, and I think some of these concerns shaped the story, as well as Nina and Lyla's story arcs.

You are active on social media. How does your relationship with your readers affect your books, if at all?

I love interacting with my readers on social media. That has changed so much since I first started to write—then I really only interacted with readers during book tours. And while I love hearing their feedback and commentary, I do make a conscious effort to keep those voices outside of my head whenever I am writing a new book. One of the best pieces of writing advice I've ever read was in Stephen King's *On Writing,* in which he talks about writing with the "door closed," i.e., making sure to write without regard for what others might want you to be writing. In other words, my characters try to live authentic lives—but aren't always going to win a popularity contest!

Much of this novel has to do with a character trying to balance her own values with her loyalty to her family. Can you talk about that a bit?

You know, Jon Stewart has a great quote about this: "If you don't stick to your values when they're being tested, they're not values. They're hobbies." And that's one of the things I really wanted to highlight with this book: What happens when our values are tested in the most extreme ways? And how do we best support the people closest to us—by protecting them at all costs, or by trying to set the example for what's right? Ultimately, I think what Nina discovers through the story is that these things—loyalty to her family and adherence to her values—are not in opposition even if it sometimes feels that way. That, for her, having the courage to do what she knows in her heart is right, even if it means that her son will have to suffer in the immediate aftermath, is the truest expression of love.

Questions and Topics for Discussion

1. How do you feel about the parents in the book? Which of them can you relate to the most?

2. Nina tries her best to steer Finch on the right path, as does Kirk. However, they have very different ideas about what the "right path" is. Do you think either of them could have done anything differently to prevent Finch's mistakes?

3. Tom is furious about the transgression against his daughter and believes she deserves justice. How do Tom's responsibilities as a parent come into conflict with the ethics of respecting Lyla's wishes?

4. As the book progresses, Nina finds herself siding with Tom's values rather than her husband's. Do you feel that Nina is betraying her family by aligning with Tom? Is she betraying herself if she does not stick to her beliefs? Whom does she owe her loyalty to more?

5. What responsibility does Nina have to ensure her son learns the right lessons, even if the consequences hurt him (such as having his acceptance to Princeton revoked)?

6. What role do money and economic standing play in how events unfold? How might the story have differed if Tom had been wealthy, and Nina and Kirk much less so?

7. At one point in the story, Tom rails against the entire moneyed, privileged community at Windsor. Do you feel that it's fair, on any level, to equate money and privilege with a certain kind of entitled behavior?

8. What do you think of Finch? Are his actions redeemable? Do you think people can change?